# Whiskey Peddler

# Whiskey Peddler

## Johnny Healy, North Frontier Trader

William R. Hunt

Mountain Press Publishing Company

Missoula, Montana

**Library of Congress Cataloging-in-Publication Data**

Hunt, William R.
    Whiskey peddler : Johnny Healy, north frontier trader / William R.
Hunt.
       p.        cm.
    Includes bibliographical references and index.
    ISBN 0-87842-284-6 : $12.00
    1. Healy, Johnny, 1840-1908. 2. Pioneers—Northwest, Pacific—
Biography.    3. Peddlers and peddling—Northwest , Pacific—
Biography.    4. Gold miners—Northwest , Pacific—Biography.
5. Soldiers—Northwest , Pacific—Biography.  I. Title.
CT275.H48595H65   1992
979.5'041'092—dc20
[B]                                                92-39478
                                                    CIP

MOUNTAIN PRESS PUBLISHING COMPANY
P. O. Box 2399
Missoula, Montana 59806 • (406) 728-1900

*To Tom, a man of learning*

# Also by William R. Hunt...

*Dictionary of Rogues*  (New York: Philosophical Society, 1970)

*North of 53: The Wild Days of the Alaska-Yukon Mining Frontier 1870-1914*  (New York: Macmillan Publishing Co., 1974)

*Arctic Passage: The Turbulent History of the Land and People of the Bering Sea, 1697-1975*  (New York: Charles Scribner's Sons, 1975)

*Alaska: A Bicentennial History*  (New York: W. W. Norton, 1976)

*To Stand at the Pole: The Dr. Cook-Admiral Peary Controversy* (New York: Stein & Day, 1982)

*Stef: Biography of Explorer Vilhjalmur Stefansson*  (Vancouver: University of British Columbia Press, 1986)

*Distant Justice: Policing the Alaskan Frontier*  (Norman: University of Oklahoma Press, 1987)

*Body Love: The Amazing Career of Bernarr Macfadden*  (Bowling Green: Bowling Green University Popular Press, 1989)

*Front Page Detective: William J. Burns and the Detective Profession 1880-1930* (Bowling Green: Bowling Green University Popular Press, 1990)

*Golden Places: The History of Alaska-Yukon Mining*  (Anchorage: National Park Service, 1990)

*Mountain Wilderness: History of Wrangell-St.Elias National Park* (Anchorage: National Park Service, 1991)

*Passage to the North*  (Harrisburg, PA: Stackpole Books, 1992)

*Roadside History of Alaska*  (Missoula: Mountain Press Publishing Co., forthcoming)

# Contents

# Preface

On a rainy day in Seattle some years ago I located the Healy family burial plot in Lakeview Cemetery. Johnny Healy's modest stone—overshadowed by the monuments he raised to his first wife, his son, and his granddaughter while he was still rich—tells a story. I regretted that no one thought to add a few words to Johnny's stone suggesting his place in the frontier history of several states. "Here Lies a Featured Character in a Jack London Novel" would catch the eye, or "Here Lies a Whiskey Peddler Who Became a Merchant Prince."

Well, never mind. Johnny Healy could have looked after his own epitaph had he cared about it. His reflections on his career are recorded elsewhere in some detail and make interesting reading for those who would understand the pioneers.

"The days of the watchful campfire are passed," Johnny noted in 1905. He considered those earlier, dangerous days on the prairie the best ones of his diverse life, recalling in his later years: "My life among the buffalo hunters is the most exciting and instructive. I often sigh for the rib-roast, the boiled boss-rib, the roasted shoulder-blade, the boiled depuyer and the back fat . . . and the hot brains of an antelope, raw liver and kidney satisfied when a man dared no fire."

Ironically, the old man longed most for the period he had worked so vigorously to destroy. Did Johnny know in his wanton buffalo-killing and Indian-corruption days that painful nostalgia lurked in the years ahead? Probably not. And the life he knew on the plains would have ended even if he hadn't shared in the fleeting profits.

Yet, buffalo and Indians fell before his guns; more Indians died abusing the liquor he sold. He did what he needed to protect his scalp and keep his stomach full. He was a trader, not a missionary. He helped extend his civilization to the frontier—to several frontiers—and he was damned proud of it!

# Acknowledgements

Staff of the Montana Historical Society was invariably helpful over the several years of my research, as were the librarians of Dartmouth College's Baker Library. Dartmouth acquired its significant Edwin Tappan Adney collection when it bought Vilhjalmur Stefansson's library. I received additional assistance from the Northwest Collection and other branches of the Suzzalo Library of the University of Washington, the University of Alaska Anchorage Library, and the wonderful people at the Resources Library in Anchorage.

John F. O'Connell of County Cork provided material of the Healy family history, and Virginia Burlingame advised me in locating of some important sources of information. Terrence Cole, Hugh Dempsey, Claus Naske, Frank Norris, and William Lang read my work, as did Robert Spude, who also provided photographs and important information on Healy and the early communities of Lynn Canal.

*John J. Healy, 1893.* —Montana Historical Society

# 1

# The Way West

*O, Ireland must we leave you,*
*Driven by a tyrant hand,*
*Must we seek a mother's blessing*
*In a strange and distant land?*
                    —Irish Folk Song

"You have seen me at my worst and at the same time at my best," wrote the old man to his young and eager would-be biographer on November 1, 1905. Edwin Tappan Adney understood what John J. Healy meant by this remark. When Adney first encountered him, Healy was a commercial king of the fabulously rich Klondike—the field director of a fleet of ocean ships, river steamboats, numerous stores, and hundreds of valuable mining claims. Yet, Healy was under fire from other company directors and the public, making it also his worst time.

Adney renewed contact with Healy after first meeting him in New York in 1904 because he wanted to write Johnny's biography. Healy stood alone in American history, Adney believed. Johnny's life combined adventures on the frontier in several places with a meteoric rise to prominence as a merchant and promoter. Added to that distinction, Adney's subject had claims to literary fame, serving as the model for a leading character in a Jack London novel.

Artist and author Adney, born in Ohio in 1868, devoted himself to painting wilderness scenes and mastering Indian handicrafts. His first publications detailed instructions on building the sort of birch-bark canoe New Brunswick Indians were still using in the 1880s. *Harper's Weekly* commissioned Adney to go to the Klondike in 1897 to sketch and report on gold-rush scenes. His book, *The Klondike Stampede of 1897-1898*, one of the best of the many narratives describing those exciting days, was published in 1900. Adney later went to Nome to observe the gold rush there for *Colliers*.

From 1904 to 1906 Adney and Healy corresponded extensively. Healy fascinated Adney, who felt sure his book about the adventuresome pioneer would win acclaim for presenting a truthful, significant account of western history. He was aware of Healy's biases but had no quarrel with them; he recognized from Johnny's Indian-fighting and buffalo-killing days that the frontier trader belonged to a different time and place. But before long Adney's biographical project faltered, giving way to commercial matters. Healy drew Adney into his tangled business and promotional affairs, which interested Johnny more than historical pursuits.

Years later, in the 1930s, Adney again started work on Healy's biography. Again he failed to finish. Despite his inability to complete the project, Adney made a significant contribution in preserving Healy's letters, in which Johnny freely expressed his views of the Northwest frontier during the 1860s to 1880s and also discussed Alaska's history prior to the gold rush. Through these letters we know who Healy admired and who he despised, which changes he appreciated and which he deplored.

# Ireland and Brooklyn

Healy rarely talked about his youth in Ireland and Brooklyn. As a practiced raconteur he found few incidents in his early days of much interest. He saw himself as just another Irish immigrant, though one who exhibited unusual grit. As with most other Irishmen, Johnny blamed the English for the terrible famine that had dimmed his youth, and he shared the customary Irish antagonism toward the English.

John Jerome Healy saw his first light in Cork, Ireland, in 1840—a bad year for his countrymen. Economic conditions worsened for the Irish over the following years, and the Healy family, once reasonably prosperous, suffered heavily in the years of Johnny's youth.

For the Irish these were the famine years—"the hard times"—a devastating period that raised questions throughout Europe about England's responsibility to Ireland. Travelers from the continent who visited Ireland during these years described the wretchedness of the poor and wondered why the English showed so little vigor in their relief efforts. It must have embarrassed the English to hear of the disgusting conditions from a Frenchman. Frances Beaumont, earlier a traveling companion of Alexis De Tocqueville, the perceptive American visitor, described what he saw:

> I have seen the Indian in his forests and the negro in his irons, and I believed in pitying their plight, that I saw the lowest ebb of human misery; but I did not then know the degree of poverty to be found in Ireland. Like the Indian, the Irishman is poor and naked; but he lives in the midst of a society which enjoys luxury and honours wealth. . . . Today the Irishman enjoys neither the freedom of a savage nor the bread of servitude.[1]

The Healys of Cork probably shared few of the French traveler's reflections. What did they know about "the Indian in his forest?" America barely made an impression on young Irish lads of Johnny's time until they became aware of its place as a refuge for starving compatriots.

But the Healys and all their neighbors in Donoughmore Parish knew the terror of famine intimately. An entry made by a priest in the parish register for December 1847 recorded the local disaster:

> This was the Famine year. There died of famine and fever from November 1846 to September 1847 over fourteen hundred of the people and one priest, Rev. Dan Horgan, requiescat in pace. Numbers remained unburied for a fortnight, many were buried in ditches near their houses, many without coffins, tho there were four men employed to bury the dead and make graves and sometimes four carpenters to make coffins. This year also we were visited by the cholera—five only died of it in the parish.[2]

3

Of the Healys in Cork during this time we only know that they suffered along with others.

In earlier times the Healys had been the leading family in Donoughmore, a region west of Cork. They held land since the seventh century a.d. and had defended it against the Danes and other enemies of the Lord of Muskerry—the local baron—for centuries. The Healys' last campaign for the Lord of Muskerry was in 1641-42 in resistance to the English. After Oliver Cromwell's forces established their superiority in 1652, the English confiscated the Healy lands. Some Healys converted to the Church of England and prospered, but Johnny's ancestors remained loyal Roman Catholics and were prohibited from owning land. Some of the Catholic Healys emigrated to France and became soldiers; others struggled along in Ireland as farm tenants. After the English relaxed some of the restrictions on Catholics in the nineteenth century, Tim and Maurice Healy became political leaders in the long struggle against the nefarious system of landlordism.

John Healy, Johnny's grandfather, was a miller who had six sons: Thomas, John, Maurice, Joseph, William, and Matthew. Thomas, Johnny's father, and his youngest brother, Matthew, carried on the family's mill at Ballinadee and shared a government contract during the famine years. Among the short-lived, penny-pinching relief efforts funded by the English government was a subsidy to some local millers to make biscuits for starving people, and the Healys provided grain. When the government's relief subsidy ended in 1848, Maurice and his family immigrated to Australia, and Thomas took his family to New York. In emigrating, the Healy brothers made the decision thousands of Irish made during those awful times. In both cases, the families fared better in the new lands.

The Healys who remained in Ireland eventually took part in the "Troubles" of the fight for independence in the 1920s; the English executed young William Healy, Johnny's cousin, at the Cork County jail in 1923 for his part in Civil War resistance. Johnny never returned to visit Donoughmore. The old parish never recovered from the famine. In 1840 its population was 9,000; a century and a half later it stood at only 1,200.

The Thomas Healy family disembarked at Ellis Island in the mid-1850s, most likely in 1853, when Johnny was thirteen. Johnny was Thomas's eldest son; he had four brothers—Thomas, Maurice, Anselm, and Joseph—and one sister, Mary. Once ashore in New York the Healys moved only as far as Brooklyn, which became their home. Presumably the boy found work there, since he never mentioned going to school in America. But his education in Ireland, however limited, apparently empowered Johnny to speak and write effectively. And he gained a thirst for knowledge and an enjoyment of reading that lasted throughout his life.

We don't know what jobs Johnny may have held in Brooklyn. Perhaps he mucked out livery stables and honed his appreciation of fine horses. He heard much about the West—a marvelous place where men were men and spaces were wide. But how could he get west? The idea of getting out of New York grew on him.

# A Soldier's Life

Johnny's realized his aspirations when the United States Army opened its enlistment books to raise an army for the Utah campaign against the Mormons. The military needed troops to garrison Salt Lake City in the Kingdom of the Saints and impose American law upon the Mormons. Some Americans felt Brigham Young and his followers openly defied the Constitution. The Mormons' polygamous activities especially upset much of the public; others enjoyed telling ribald jokes about the practice.

Johnny felt little antagonism toward Mormons or anyone else—he just wished to put New York behind him and commence an adventurous life. In March of 1857 or 1858 he joined hundreds of other New Yorkers who enlisted for two-year hitches. The fairly husky, dark-haired, blue-gray-eyed eighteen-year-old stood five-feet five-inches tall.[3]

The Army moved the green recruits from New York and elsewhere in the East to far-distant Fort Leavenworth on the Missouri River for training. Veterans of the Fifth Infantry, which had been fighting Indians in the Florida Everglades, also received orders to go there and were unhappy about it, thinking they deserved a respite. The stifling heat of Kansas in summer added to their plummeting morale and affected that of other units. Spirits among Johnny's unit, the Second Dragoons, had not yet sunk so low, but desertions and loses from scurvy slowed their training.

During this long, hot summer "Bleeding Kansas" was undergoing riots over the slavery question. Seven companies under Lt. Col. Philip St. George Cooke helped keep order through the summer, while other detachments, including Johnny's, pushed on toward Utah to control the Mormons. Private Healy had little to say in later years about his military duties beyond observing that former soldiers such as himself played a role in the gold discoveries of the Northwest. But apparently the young trooper liked his new life better than his former one in Brooklyn, even though the initial training and trek westward must have been uncomfortable.

The march to Utah was tedious. Each day the troops rose at sunrise and had two hours to eat breakfast and prepare to march. All day the infantry trudged along in the heat and dust on foot while the much envied dragoons rode. By early afternoon, after covering fifteen to twenty miles, they reached a predesignated camping place that had water and forage for the animals. They followed the same route as the overland pioneers: west from Leavenworth to the Big Blue River, then north along it to the Little Blue, and northwest along that river to the wide and shallow Platte—the grand highway to the Rocky Mountains.

By August they reached Fort Kearney, a dull post on the plain that lacked amenities, prolonging the boredom and discomfort of the marching soldiers. At least the men got some rest at Kearney; then they set off to the fork of the Platte and along its southern arm. The countryside turned to rolling hills and the great Rocky Mountains appeared in the distance. It's easy to imagine how Johnny's first sight of the great mountain range stirred him. He was coming into a country far different from any he had known—a grand, far-reaching country that could make old Ireland and Brooklyn look bland in comparison.

At Fort Laramie the troops got another rest and a little ceremony as Col. Albert Sidney Johnston took formal command of the forces on September 11. After marching seven hundred miles the men thought the commander revealed few secrets when he spoke of "the toil, privations, and hardships incident to frontier service."[4]

Probably, as Johnny looked over the country and heard about the green Northwest at the end of the Oregon Trail, he resolved that someday he would see the Pacific Ocean. But for now a less pleasant situation occupied him. The weather had turned cold, making water and forage hard to come by. And Mormon horsemen constantly hovered in the distance to keep tabs on the soldiers. As the march continued, the Mormons became more active. They stalled, sent back, and even destroyed Army supply trains, stampeding stock animals on several occasions. Yet no shooting broke out. Though the soldiers had no enemy to grapple with, strong Mormon resistance stopped them dead in their tracks; the threat of starvation in the teeth of winter halted their advance.

Colonel Johnston made a winter camp called Camp Scott near old Fort Bridger, which the Mormons had burned to deny the army shelter. The winter passed slowly, but it provided inspiration for Johnny Healy. Jim Bridger, the famed old mountain man, visited Camp Scott; everyone there knew of his adventures as a trapper, Indian fighter, and trader who defied Young's efforts to restrict him. Bridger became the young soldier's idol, though Johnny probably had little chance to talk to him. Johnny decided that when he got out of the Army he would follow in the footsteps of Bridger and live the free, wonderful life in the wilderness. Johnny's relaxed military duties during the winter allowed him plenty of time to develop the horseman, marksman, and woodsman skills he would need as a man of the mountains and plains.

Before winter's end Brigham Young and the territorial governor, Alfred Cumming, came to terms and averted war. Colonel Johnson, unsatisfied that Young's capitulation to federal authority was complete, insisted upon marching his army into Salt Lake City. Ignorant to the larger political manipulations, the soldiers delighted in leaving the unpleasant encampment at Camp Scott. As they marched forth they sang gleefully:

> The Mormons knew that Uncle Sam
> Had troops upon the route,
> And Brigham prayed the Holy Lamb
> Would help to clean them out.
> The distance then, one thousand miles,
> Me in the face did stare,
> For Brigham swore no damned gentiles
> Again should winter there.

In June 1858 the Mormons acceded to the authority of the federal government, and President Buchanan issued a pardon for Young and other leaders. Tensions continued to run high while Healy and his comrades remained in Utah to assert federal authority.

# The Frontiersman

Johnny Healy received his discharge from the Army in August 1860 and began taking up the more adventurous life of a frontiersman. New residents flowed into Utah in the wake of the Army's presence, but Johnny did not want to settle down among the saints. He wanted excitement, so he decided to head for the Northwest and joined a party of forty emigrants at the Portneuf Bridge on the Snake River.

Herman Beebe, sixty-five years old, "full of grit," and exceedingly profane, was one of the leaders of the Oregon-bound pioneers. To Healy's surprise the emigrants showed little appreciation for the Indian warriors they might encounter. Beebe and others considered themselves the match of any braves, although having women and children along worried them. Healy, who knew that the Snake Indians had disposed of larger and tougher emigrant trains than this one, was wary on the march.[5]

Soon after Healy joined the emigrants he encountered a threatening situation when, acting as advance scout, he stumbled into an Indian camp at Salmon Falls. Unable to immediately judge whether the Indians were hostile, and with his worn-out horse incapable of flight,

7

Johnny boldly rode straight into the center of the camp. The Indians gathered around, held his horse, and asked questions. Johnny was frightened, but he bluffed the Indians, claiming the approaching wagon train had a soldier escort. The Indians, unimpressed, briefly discussed his fate before deciding to kill him. As one warrior prepared to shoot him, Healy tensed for a shootout, intending to take some victims with him. Just then another of the emigrant party, a man famed for his interminable and loud hymn singing, approached the Indian camp, as usual, praising the Lord with full voice. This distraction nudged the Indians to resist their violence and visit the wagon train, and they allowed Healy and his companion to lead the way.

At the train the Indians performed in a familiar manner—half threatening, half begging for food. Old Beebe was weak at negotiating, or even tolerating, the demands of Indians. Riled up, cursing passionately at the Indians' manner, he ordered them away. Meanwhile the hymn singer, who loved wrestling almost as much as singing, had thrown down several braves in friendly combat, and a high-spirited young emigrant woman had flung a pan of hot grease at a warrior who filched food. Healy, who already considered himself an expert in dealing with Indians, was aghast at his party's deportment and wondered how long peace would last.

Beebe would not accept advice from a young fellow like Healy. His and the other men's contempt for the Indians rested in their ignorance of the perils they faced. Healy recalled the incident in 1878 when writing his series of columns for the *Fort Benton Record*: "What!" exclaimed Beebe at Johnny's suggestion to use caution in dealing with the Indians, "Do you mean to tell me that those half-starved monkeys would dare attack a white man?" The old man even offered to take his bull whip into the Indian camp and run off the whole bunch.

The train moved on, but Indians harassed the emigrants on several occasions. Johnny successfully dealt with the threat by putting up an aggressive front whenever Indians appeared. His companions lost something of their arrogance and deferred to the younger man's judgment for their defense. When they reached The Dalles on the Columbia River Healy felt much relieved. The Army post at The Dalles offered protection, and the westward route from that point held no threat of Indian aggression. At The Dalles Healy learned why his train escaped an all-out attack. The Indians were busy instead wreaking havoc with a larger train that followed some distance behind Beebe's; they killed many of the emigrants after blocking communication between the two trains.

This Oregon Trail experience tested Healy's mettle. For the first time he had to show leadership in perilous circumstances. He found his

8

encounters with Indians enlightening. Dealing with Indians involved more than fighting skills and firepower—at times a man had to bluff, threaten, and negotiate. Johnny considered it essential to know the Indian mind and ways. Jim Bridger, Johnny's hero, had survived because he understood the Indians. And Johnny believed that he had learned a lot about them, too.

Johnny went on alone from The Dalles to Portland, where he spent the winter of 1860-61. News of the imminent Civil War did not bear on his plans. The great cry raised in the West was of new gold discoveries. Some men argued that the Northwest would prove richer than California, if enough men could be brought into the country for prospecting. This glittering talk sounded good to Johnny and to his friend, John Kennedy, whom he had met on the Oregon Trail. The young Irishmen figured they had as good a chance to find gold as anyone. They were tough, energetic, and footloose—good qualities for prospectors.

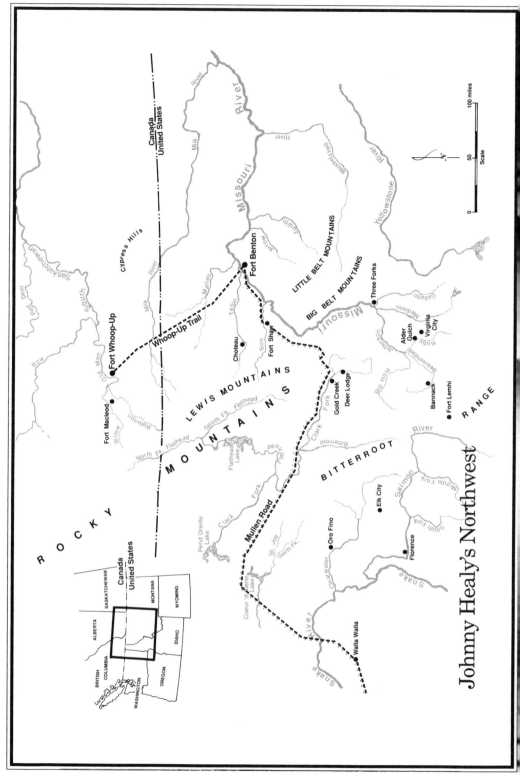

Johnny Healy's Northwest

Trudi Peek

# 2

# Idaho Gold

*A man is an ass who reports*
*on any property through*
*magnifying glasses.*
— Johnny Healy

In spring 1861 Johnny Healy, John Kennedy, and several others set off to find gold. They voyaged on a sidewheeler upriver from Portland to the cascades of the Columbia, then took horse-drawn cars around the rapids. Writing some seventeen years later in his "Frontier Sketches" column for the *Fort Benton Record*, Johnny recalled the famous stretch of turbulent water: "The falls are not perpendicular, but consist of two steep rapids, about seven miles in length, between which there is a whirling eddy of comparatively smooth water. The lower rapid, though very swift and dangerous, is frequently navigated by canoes, but the most fearless Indian dare not trust himself upon the upper falls, which rushes over the ragged rocks with tremendous force."[6]

Above The Dalles the prospectors bought pack animals and riding horses. Johnny found the 180-mile stretch between The Dalles and Walla Walla familiar, since he had traveled it the previous year on his way west with the emigrant train. Some of the prospectors had just learned how to ride horses and knew nothing about handling pack animals. "The struggles with obstinate pack saddles and bucking cayuses would have made a mule laugh," Johnny noted in his column. "It was not until after passing John Day's river that the horses and their masters seemed to have come to a proper understanding of the situation, as up to this point the trail was marked with gold-pans, picks, shovels, and provisions of all kinds, which had been left behind by the frisky broncos owing to the unskillful manner in which their packs had been tied on."

At Walla Walla the gold excitement intensified as everyone discussed reports and rumors from the goldfields. Healy and Kennedy teamed with four other men from Portland, and they all headed for the diggings. They crossed the Snake River on a ferry, ascended the Clearwater, then crossed the Potlatch River, and finally reached the center of activity at Oro Fino.

The prospectors found the mountain trail leading farther east to Pierce City tough, especially as the weather got warm and the snow turned into mush and mud. They met one large party that had abandoned its horses because of the hard going; the men were carrying everything they owned on their backs. Johnny and his companions tried a less drastic alternative—traveling at night after the ground froze hard enough to prevent bogging down in the mud. Eventually they reached the top of Rummer's Hill and looked down on Pierce City. On the hill and below it a thousand men lived in tents. Johnny and the others moved in and started prospecting. Their high spirits permitted time for both work and play, the latter usually in the form of sending greenhorns hotfooting off on some false lead to an alleged treasure. Johnny called the miners the jolliest crowd he'd ever known.

South of Pierce City Johnny and his partners located sixteen hundred feet of claims and set to work. They blazed a trail to bring in materials to build a dam and flume. As in most western mining districts, the first difficult task was getting enough water to wash their diggings. Johnny and his partners had to cut trees and haul logs to build cabins and rig a draining system to keep underground water out of their holes. Their work nearly brought Johnny's life as a miner to an abrupt end when a falling tree caught him, breaking his leg and almost drowning him in a mining pit. Kennedy and the others saved him in the nick of time, but Johnny caught pneumonia and lay ill for weeks. Despite protests from the others, he hired an outsider willing to work for wages to hold up his share of the partnership.

Later that spring Johnny could walk, but he lacked his former strength and needed more time to recover. Riding a horse was easy, though, so he proposed to his partners that he scout for other possible claim locations in the region. Another group of prospectors led by George Grigsby came through camp and invited Johnny to join them. Grigsby had high hopes for the Salmon River, declaring, "An Injun showed me a nugget he'd found in the Salmon. I swear it was worth at least $24."

The local Indians—the proud, independent Nez Perce—worried the intrusive prospectors. The Oro Fino mining district lay at the northern edge of their reservation, and the Nez Perce agreed to let the miners develop it only if they promised to trespass no farther. But when someone found gold at Elk City, southeast of Oro Fino, the whites rushed in without regard to their earlier promise.

The United States government was obligated by its treaty with the Indians to prevent any unsanctioned encroachments by miners. In an effort to protect Indian rights, the Army tried to restrict the miners' movements. The soldiers even pulled down some of their cabins, but their half-way measures failed to stop the flood tides of goldseekers. Understandably, the military was reluctant to use full force against white citizens responding to what many considered an irresistible opportunity.

In his column for the *Fort Benton Record,* Johnny wrote:

> A new road was opened from Walla Walla, a new ferry was established by Craig & Bell at the crossing of the Clear Water, and thousands of people began to flock in, build houses, and scatter out in all directions there in search of the yellow metal. The town of Lewiston, located between the forks of the Clear Water and Snake River, soon sprang into existence and ranches began to appear along the new road and were rebuilt as fast as the military pulled them down.[7]

# Florence

Johnny agreed to go with Grigsby and the others to look into prospects farther south on the Salmon River. On the fifth day of their trek a party of Nez Perce swooped down on them, yelling and threatening but not physically violent. "Grigsby, who was of a somewhat nervous disposition," Johnny wrote, "was several times on the point of raising his rifle to fire, but was restrained by the other men, who were far too cool-headed to risk an engagement where the chances were all against them, and there was good reason to believe that the Indians had no intention of doing us serious injury unless we commenced the battle."

The dogged prospectors pushed on, frightened but determined. They considered going back to Oro Fino to gather reinforcements and returning to fight their way through, then they encountered another party of miners. These men agreed that the Indians' dog-in-the-manger attitude was intolerable; now fifteen strong, the miners thought they could win a battle with the Nez Perce. Nonetheless, Healy and two other men hurried back to Oro Fino to ask for assistance. Twenty-five men volunteered to help, but only nine reached the mining party. These nine included some stalwart fellows, however, including Eph Bostwick, whom Healy considered one of the finest and most courageous fighting men he had ever known.

With a total of twenty-five well-mounted and well-armed men, the miners now felt equal to the menacing party of Nez Perce. Boldly they headed for the Indian camp but found it empty. Under John Dyer's leadership the men pushed on to White Bird Creek, where they wisely cooled their cockiness after finding signs that another group of Nez Perce had joined the first one. They decided to negotiate with the Indians and sent six men, including Healy, to the Nez Perce camp. The cagey whites told the surly Nez Perce that they were en route to inflict themselves on the Snake Indians—deadly enemies of the Nez Perce. But the Nez Perce knew the prospectors were lying.

Johnny recalled Chief Looking Glass's challenge: "You must either go back or fight."

"Fight it is then," cried one of the miners—but he really meant "flight," and the negotiating team galloped back to the main party. In hurried council they resolved to dash for the Salmon River and make a stand. They rode hard and hastily constructed a defensive breastwork. Time passed and the Indians did not show up. The miners took turns prospecting and standing guard.

Their search yielded some gold, but less than they could recover in the Oro Fino district. They soon ran out of provisions and had to hunt for food—and the scarcity of game made the task even more difficult. Finally they agreed to quit the area and head back to Elk City. But after three days' travel they spied another place that looked promising for gold, at least to some of the men. Johnny and a few others had become fed up with those in their party no longer driven by the desire to find gold, so the group split up. The discouraged men continued on to Elk City while Healy and the others stopped to assess the new site. After three fruitless days, hungry and depressed, they started back to Oro Fino. They traveled a day and a night on empty stomachs only to find themselves back at their starting point, confused and exhausted.

Mining history is rich with legends about chance discoveries, and the Salmon River strike followed this pattern. The great event occurred for Johnny Healy and George Grigsby when they remained in camp one day to patch their tattered clothing while the other men went hunting for game. Grigsby finished his chore, looked around and announced, "I doubt if there's a color in this whole damn country." He then grabbed a shovel, moved a fallen tree, and dug in the hole where its roots protruded. Soon Healy heard an unfamiliar glad cry: "That's good!" Looking toward his partner, Healy saw that Grigsby had just washed a pan full of dirt and examined it with a glowing face. Gold glinted among the dirt! Excitedly, Johnny began digging a six-foot hole in the soft ground, then panned the gravels with excellent results.

Shortly thereafter the hunters returned, but Johnny and George held back news of their discovery. With suppressed glee they listened as "curses loud and deep were heaped upon the country, and the unanimous belief was expressed that the basin would never be inhabited by any living creatures except, perhaps, a few miserable half starved rattle-snakes." When they could no longer contain themselves, Healy and Grigsby told their companions the good news.

Certain formalities seemed necessary: the men uttered solemn oaths of secrecy and carefully identified their claim locations. They set out for Elk City to file their claims, then continued on toward Oro Fino for more supplies. Along the way they met their friends who had started back earlier and carelessly shared their secret . Discouraged men make poor prophets, as Johnny realized much later when he wrote, "Within three months from the time Geo. Grigsby and I washed the first pan of gravel in this abused neighborhood, the basin contained a population of over five thousand souls, and within two miles of where laid the up-rooted tree, the city of Florence now stands." At the time of their journey, though, the news had not yet taken on a life of its own.

After a tough, starving trip to Oro Fino, the prospectors gathered supplies for their return trip to the Salmon River. Healy confided to Kennedy and some of the others he'd originally teamed up with about their pay dirt to the south. The discoverers wanted to avoid starting a stampede before they and their friends could get back to the new site and stake all the best ground. Miners always found it tough to slip out of a camp without rousing suspicion, so Johnny contrived a rumor that he was going to the Missouri River to salvage a wrecked steamboat. The ruse fooled all but one man—Tom Mallory—who demanded to go along.

Back at the discovery site, christened Baboon Gulch, the miners staked more claims. A contingent of 129 men stampeded in from Elk City, making for a lively time. Healy and another former dragoon named Snixter dubbed their location Dragoon Gulch. Snixter entered the ranks of legend when he recovered $8 from one pan; he bounced his head against a tree trunk to confirm that he wasn't dreaming.

When provisions ran low, Healy and several others returned to Oro Fino to replenish their goods. They traveled slowly, cutting a good path for the pack animals. But after only twenty-five miles of this grueling work they ran out of food. Fortunately, some Nez Perce appeared and greeted the miners' offers to buy food. When the supply party finally reached Oro Fino, Johnny offered his friend John Kennedy, who had gone into the packing business, an interest in his diggings at Dragoon Gulch. The prospectors' reasons for secrecy now had more to do with holding prices down than anything else. Within hours after Healy and perhaps others leaked news about the strike, the price of a horse rose from $30 to $125.

Healy and Kennedy bought $1,800 in goods on credit—or "on the jawbone," as Johnny put it—and prepared to return to the diggings. Before leaving they ran into Alonzo Leland, a reporter for the *Portland Times*, who, Johnny recalled, "was always a leading spirit in any of the mining camps in which he happened to locate." Leland convinced Healy and Kennedy to take him to the Salmon River diggings.

They faced no serious threats from Indians along the way, and the improved trail made traveling easier, although Johnny had to defend both his property and his honor from the lures of Mollie, a Nez Perce woman who fancied his mule. "She used all the artful nonsense peculiar to her sex to make me present her with the animal," Johnny wrote. "Finding me proof against her most alluring wiles, she tried the more effective, but still unsuccessful expedient of threatening to bring the whole camp of her relatives to take the mule from me by force. To avoid an encounter with the relatives of the covetous squaw we quickened our pace."

Upon reaching the diggings, Healy found the place had been surveyed in his absence and that a town site, named Florence after the daughter of the surveyor, lay platted nearby. A saloon whetted the miners' thirsts as carpenters built new homes. The news of Florence spread quickly, enticing hundreds of men and women into the large but short-lived camp.

Johnny had little praise for the town he had helped to found:

> Florence was anything but an agreeable camp, in those days, even for
> the oldest and most experienced miners, and certainly the 'pilgrims'
> could not have derived a great amount of pleasure from the peculiar
> life it afforded. There was a mail delivery at Florence, but it was costly
> and not a well conducted institution. Once a week, sometimes not more
> than once every two weeks, Wells, Fargo & Co. delivered and received
> letters to and from the camp. John Galbraith and Arthur Chapman
> were the mail carriers and they demanded the modest sum of 50cts
> each for carrying letters. Sacramento *Unions* commanded $2.50 each,
> and were probably the best read papers ever published.

But Florence had beef, Johnny recalled, thanks to

> Pony Parks, a well-known character who had the good fortune to fall
> in with a band of cattle somewhere, and sold every beef at the most
> extravagant prices. The camp had been living on scanty supplies of salt
> meats for some time previous to this, and the fresh beef was a well-
> timed luxury; but soon after the cattle had been disposed of, the trails
> closed up with the snow, and became impassable for animals and
> difficult even for foot travelers. Quite a number of men, however,
> reaped rich harvests by packing provisions and whisky upon their
> backs, from the mouth of Slate Creek, at the price of 40cts per pound.
> It was no uncommon thing for men to carry a 150 pound load in this
> manner, but after receiving pay for the same at the diggings they
> would gamble away their earnings at the faro table and then start off
> again for another load.

The winter of 1861-62 set in "with unusual violence." Stampeders
continued pouring in, sending food prices out of control. Flour went from
$40 a sack to $100, and prices for other goods increased 50 percent daily.
But the concern over inflation dimmed when someone reported that an
Indian war party was advancing on the town. At the same time, a rash
of lawlessness broke out, sparked by claim jumping and violent resistance. The squabbling turned serious at Baboon Gulch when a miner
gunned down his partner. In traditional style for a western mining camp,
the miners tried the accused at the local store; they acquitted him of
murder but ordered him to leave the diggings. "He was not slow in
making himself scarce," Johnny observed. "From this time on, lawlessness reigned supreme throughout the diggings. Claims were jumped
while the rightful owners were at dinner, and in some instances it is not
improbable that claims were taken in this manner for no other purpose
than to cause trouble and get up a fight."

The Indian scare turned out to be a hoax. Whoever started the rumor
wanted to get rid of the timid miners and redistribute their claims among
those who had the courage to stay. But the main effect, Johnny believed,
was how the threat created a stronger spirit of dependence and made the

winter less dreary than it might have been. The residents temporarily turned their attentions from digging for gold to fortifying their defenses.

*Portland Times* reporter Alonzo Leland staked several claims in the area before hurrying back to Portland to write stories about the strike. His reports set off a tide of stampeders to the goldfields, some of whom jumped his claims.

Leland did not return to Florence in 1862. Instead he remained in Portland to write a guidebook to the Snake River country, in which he expressed customary boomers' sentiments: "Some seven thousand persons have been induced to prospect and mine and trade within these districts; and the results of their energies have been the development of mines of immense richness." Prospectors would find rich deposits in all the streams flowing from the Bitterroot Mountains, Leland believed, and he deplored the Nez Perces' claim to the region, referring to the earlier treaty as "an unfortunate diplomacy which ceded back to the Nez Perce nation so much of the country. . . . But patience and skill, we doubt not, will soon devise means whereby the most valuable mineral claims will be treated for with these Indians by the general Government."[8]

After that first exciting summer and winter, Florence cooled down fast. By summer 1863 only some five hundred miners remained, and before long the ghosts took over. But the development had long-range significance because it led to the first discoveries of gold in Montana and finds in the Boise basin of Idaho. Men who were drawn to the country to seek their fortunes at Florence went on to help establish more lasting communities elsewhere in the Northwest.

An intriguing aspect of mining history is researching the names of some colorful individuals that pop up in the accounts of several different mining camps. Johnny Healy likely met Cincinnatus H. Miller at Florence, although neither man mentioned the other in their later writings, even years later after both men achieved measurable fame in the Klondike. Miller, better known as Joaquin Miller, eventually became a famous poet and an even more famous poseur; Johnny disliked haughty, insincere posturing, so he probably would not have liked Miller. During Johnny's time in Florence, Miller worked the gravels of the Salmon River and rode for the Pony Express between Florence and Walla Walla.

The Salmon River placers were rich but spotty, and only a few miners made big stakes. Johnny Healy's ground yielded three hundred ounces of gold. He might have done better if he'd stayed on longer, and probably later he wanted to kick himself for pulling out so soon. Yet, when writing his "Frontier Sketches," he managed to reflect philosophically on his decision: "The most trifling circumstance will sometimes change the whole course of a man's life and I believe the disastrous trip up the

Salmon River altered the current of my career, for had I remained at Florence I would undoubtedly have accumulated a very comfortable home stake and left the country forever to enjoy the results of my hardships and adventures." But instead he followed the wisp of rumor and drew this comparison: "Mining has many features akin to gambling and whether followed with success or misfortune it rarely gratifies the desires of its devotees, yet holds them in the strongest bonds of infatuation."

## Ascending the Salmon River

Johnny succumbed to the lure presented by "Beaver Dick" and others who arrived at Florence full of guarded talk about the discovery of a quartz ledge that assayed at $3,000 per ton. Here was a chance to make millions! Jeff Standifer and a party of men planned to voyage up the Salmon to the quartz, and when Johnny's friend, Eph Bostwick, heard about it, he talked Johnny into joining the excursion. "I concluded that it would not take more than 20 days to make the trip and return," Johnny wrote, "and as the snow around Florence had become so deep that work had to be suspended I thought that perhaps it would be as well to make the journey as to remain idling the time away in camp."[9]

The Standifer party reluctantly agreed to let Healy and Bostwick join, and on May 4, 1862, the men set out in three boats. At first Johnny enjoyed the switch from mining to boating, even though it required arduous poling against the swift current. Before long, though, the journey lost its savor. "Our struggles with the wild river began to tell upon us," Johnny wrote in his column, "and we heartily wished ourselves back again to our mining camp in the mountains." Traveling on the twisting river did not give much sense of progress. "It was nothing but cross and recross from one side of the river to the other in search of a foothold along the high and perpendicular banks. Portage after portage was made around the most dangerous rapids, many of which could more properly be termed falls, and even when the river was comparatively smooth and free from the whirlpools and rocks, the bends were so short and sudden and the current so swift that we could make little or no headway against it by the use of our poles alone."

As the men moved farther upriver, conditions grew more difficult. The party lost one of its boats as the men on the bank tried to pull it through rapids. They lost everything on board, and five men decided to hike back to Florence. The delays diminished their food supplies. Johnny figured the area held plenty of game, but the men stayed busy at the poles all day and were too exhausted to hunt when they made their evening camp.

It became clear that even harder times lay ahead when the party met two men on a crude raft coming downriver. Bill Rollins, a blacksmith from Fort Owen, and another man were heading toward Florence from a point about forty miles below Fort Lemhi. That stretch of the Salmon later dubbed "The River of No Return" lay behind them now. They had begun their journey on horseback, following a trail along the river, but they had to abandon the animals in favor of the raft when the trail became too rough. All they had to eat was a dried bearskin, which they pounded with rocks to free a few morsels. Meeting the upriver voyagers saved their lives. "Rollins begged us to return," Johnny recalled. He told the men they could not possibly reach their destination by boat. But Standifer would not listen.

Before parting company, Rollins told the determined travelers that the Stuart brothers—Granville and James—had made a strike on Gold Creek in Montana and that some others, including Fred Burr, John Powell, and Tom Adams, were living on the creek where the road to Hell Gate crossed. Since Johnny knew some of these men, he was intrigued. The Stuart brothers had spent some time at Fort Bridger and Camp Floyd (Utah) in 1858 while the Second Dragoons served there, and Johnny probably knew them from that time.

The upriver voyagers continued on to a major river fork. With great difficulty they carried their boats across a point of land to ascend the left fork, only to find it too shallow and swift for navigation. On foot they pushed on, forming into new subgroups as bitterness and privations tested their tempers. Some of the men succumbed to eating tree bark for sustenance. Standifer finally decided to turn back so he could assume his duties as sheriff at Florence. The number of travelers dropped to eight hungry men who occasionally succeeded in shooting some small game for food.

Following the turns and twists of the steep river bank was slow work for the men. Johnny wrote that on many nights, "after a long day of weary traveling, from daylight to dark, it would have been an easy matter to have fired a pistol ball into the camp we left in the morning." All but Healy and Bostwick wanted to turn back; the others wondered if traveling at such a slow pace made sense.

Their situation soon became even more perilous when Indians began stalking them. Fearing an assault, the men left their campsite after dark one night to scatter among the rocks and sleep uneasily. The next morning they encountered their pursuers on the trail. "A moment later the hills were swarming with the fiends yelling and signalling to each other," Johnny wrote. The miners took cover among some large rocks and prepared to fend off an attack. For several days Johnny had been trying to calculate how long he had to live, but the sight of the Indians, he later recalled, "seemed to put new life into us and we were now as eager to preserve our lives as if we were on a mere pleasure excursion and in the near vicinity of our homes."

The prospectors repelled several attacks over the next few days before the action quieted down. Then, on the fourth day of their siege, the men realized the Indians had disappeared. During the ordeal the miners had abandoned their equipment and made no attempt now to recover it. Survival became their main concern, so they carried little as they marched on. After traveling two days without food, Bostwick managed to kill some game for them to eat. Indian signal fires continued to startle the men, who feared another attack. But no more attacks came.

The travelers moved on into more open country that provided them better opportunities to spot marauders in time enough to devise an escape. One of the men recognized the area as near Fort Lehmi, a Mormon outpost colony deserted a couple of years earlier because of hostile Indians. "We knew the place had been abandoned," Johnny recalled in his column, "but we tried to persuade ourselves that it was again occupied, or that, at least, we should find a volunteer crop of vegetables growing on the soil that had formerly been cultivated."

For three days they staggered on toward the fort, subsisting only on wild garlic, sunflowers, and grass, barely able to make five miles a day. On June 12 they joyfully saw Fort Lehmi in the distance. In their hopeful delusions they imagined seeing smoke coming from cook fires and smelling the food they would soon be eating. When they reached the fort, however, their fantasies faded.

The place was deserted and absolutely devoid of food. The men refused to go on, so Bostwick decided to strike out on his own for Deer Lodge or Beaverhead, across the mountains in Montana, to get help from the Stuarts or other miners there. His chances of traveling so far and returning in time to save the others were farcically small, but no one had a better idea. The situation looked bleak.

Bostwick left, then returned within an hour. As luck would have it, he encountered the advance party—two mounted men—of a wagon train bound from Salt Lake City to Florence. A happy mistake had led the train to Lehmi: one of the expedition's guides believed Florence was near Lehmi; his geographical misunderstanding saved the miners' lives. The wagon train lagged thirty miles behind the advance party, so the starving men had to endure one more hungry, anxious night before they could eat. Johnny hardly slept and kept looking at his buckskin bag holding the 125 ounces of gold he mined at Florence. He had carried it close to him for weeks; now it seemed nearly worthless. Remembering how he felt that night, he later wrote, "I would gladly have given it all for its weight in flour to save myself and starving friends." The wasted men wondered if relief truly would come their way.

When the wagon train finally arrived, the men rejoiced. They tried to restrain their ravenous appetites, aware that eating too much too soon could have disastrous consequences. Despite their caution, within three days they had eaten themselves into a sicker condition than when their rescuers arrived. Wagon master Jack Mendenhall and the emigrants eventually nursed the pitiful lot back to health, and even loaned Johnny and Eph Bostwick horses so they could ride up the north fork of the Salmon and take some quartz samples. It's impossible to say whether the site they explored was the one they sought, but their samples were not rich. They gave up on finding the quartz ledge "Beaver Dick" bragged about in Florence.

Johnny believed the men owed their lives to Bostwick. His accurate shooting brought in most of the game they ate, and his courage and leadership kept their reluctant, weary feet moving along the trail. Originally from Pennsylvania, Bostwick was of that rare breed of men who could rise above adversity and inspire others to do the same.

## To New York via Fort Benton

After recovering from their near-starvation and subsequent over-eating, Healy and Bostwick left Lehmi, not to return to Florence but to look into the mining prospects at Gold Creek, Montana, where the Stuart brothers had located. The Stuarts recorded the first strike in the Deer Lodge Valley at Gold Creek in 1858, but the hostile Blackfeet made staying there too dangerous. The brothers returned in 1860 and prospected around the area before finding some productive ground in 1862. Few other prospectors worked that region; most of the men who came through moved on to the Idaho diggings. John White, one of the Idaho-bound miners, made a major strike well south of there on Grasshopper Creek in July 1862. A stampede from Gold Creek and other nearby places followed, and the town of Bannack, destined to become the first territorial capital, was founded nearby. Five hundred miners lived in Bannack during the 1862-63 winter. By the next year most of the action shifted east of Bannack to Alder Gulch, giving rise to Virginia City, and the year after that back north to Last Chance Gulch, where Helena was founded.

In 1863 Bostwick joined James Stuart and the later rich-and-famous Sam Hauser on an ill-fated expedition to the Yellowstone. The party tangled with hostile Indians and barely escaped. Wounded in five places and dying, Bostwick urged the others to get away without worrying about him. As they fled for their lives he shot himself to avoid being captured alive by the Indians. But before that fateful event, he and Johnny and the other men still had to get away from Fort Lemhi.

Healy did not stay on at Gold Creek and also missed the stampedes to Bannack and Virginia City. In the mood for a family visit in New York, he started east in August 1862 with John Kennedy and some others. They planned to outfit at Fort Benton, then voyage down the Missouri River.

The unimposing Fort Benton got its start as a fur trading post of the American Fur Company and had yet to develop into a "community." A few traders and wolf hunters lived there, and drifters came and went. But the influx of gold prospectors rejuvenated the town. As the upper terminus of steamboat navigation on the Missouri, Fort Benton's commercial importance increased; it gained prominence shortly after Healy's arrival. The major Montana gold rushes brought stampeders passing through in great numbers. As the territory's population expanded, Fort Benton became the transportation and distribution center for a huge area.

Healy, Kennedy, and company got to Fort Benton shortly before the town's much-anticipated arrival of the steamer *Shreveport*, though, with the river at its mid-August low, some residents doubted the boat could ascend beyond Cow Island or the Marias River. Since Johnny and his friends wanted transportation downriver, they decided to get a small, crude oar boat called a mackinaw and take it downriver to meet the steamer.

Indian hostility along the river always concerned travelers. Passing by the four hundred lodges of a Gros Ventres camp near the mouth of the Milk River made the men in Healy's boat uneasy, even though they considered the Gros Ventres friendly. The Indians ordered the small boat ashore, and, hoping to avoid trouble, the voyagers complied. The Indians told them the *Shreveport* was a few miles downriver. Not wishing to offend their hosts, they camped with the Gros Ventres that night and resumed their trip the next morning. As they approached the steamer great excitement broke out among the Gros Ventres, whose horses had been grazing near the river bank. "Suddenly," Johnny recalled, "without the slightest warning, a war party of strange Indians, armed with shields and spears, swooped down from the neighboring hills, captured the herd, and were out of sight almost before the Gros Ventres and white men knew what had happened."[10]

Although the combined force of the whites and Gros Ventres totaled seven hundred men, the "strange Indians" outnumbered them three to one. "We did not feel greatly alarmed for our safety," Johnny wrote. "But the hostiles continued to increase in numbers until every hill and level spot, as far as the eye could reach, [was] littered with their metallic ornaments and shown resplendent with the bright hues of their blankets and war bonnets." The Gros Ventres quickly abandoned any notion of recovering their horses.

Healy's party boarded the *Shreveport*, prepared to defend her and resolving to sell "our lives dearly as possible should a determined attack be made upon us." Captain John Labarge directed construction of a circular breastwork on the bank, which the defenders huddled behind all day before returning to the steamboat at night. They hauled the steamer out to the middle of the river as an added precaution, and Labarge kept up a head of steam to pour scalding water on any attacking parties. The Sioux did not attack but entranced their foes "with splendid feats of horsemanship and maneuvers illustrating their various methods of attack and defense," Johnny wrote, "keeping us on the alert during the night with their hideous yells and stealthy approaches towards our camp."

The event unfolding before their eyes, they later learned, was the northward migration of the Sioux. The event marked the Indians' first appearance on the upper Missouri. The whites were as awestruck as their Gros Ventres allies at the large gathering of outsiders.

Healy and Kennedy, more bored than frightened, responded to a challenge issued by an old-time French hunter and namesake of some rapids on the upper Missouri, Dauphin, who had watched the Sioux lure some Gros Ventres into harm's way by tempting them with a fine Sioux pony hobbled between their two camps as a decoy. The duped Gros Ventres dashed for the pony and were immediately driven off by a hail of arrows "that fairly darkened the air," Johnny wrote, accompanied by "a yell that would have raised the hair of a demon." The other Gros Ventres jeered at the embarrassed raiders for being tricked so easily. Dauphin urged the young Irishmen to help him take the pony just to show off. Swiftly and slyly the whites approached; Johnny cut the hobbles and the trio cleanly escaped with the pony. It was a foolish risk, Johnny acknowledged, but it had its reward: the much-humiliated Gros Ventres respected the white men for their skill and bravery.

After three days the Sioux lifted their siege and the *Shreveport* headed downriver. The rest of the trip east was less exciting but safer. Johnny took the steamboat downriver to Omaha, where he caught a stagecoach to Davenport, Iowa, then continued on to Chicago and New York by train.

Young Johnny Healy undoubtedly told this and other harrowing stories of Indian warfare with great relish when he got back among his family and friends in New York. His newspaper stories written in the 1870s show his skill as a stirring raconteur. Yet he must have balanced war stories with tales of gold, prosperity, and peaceful pursuits, because some of the New York Healys wanted to go back to Montana with him, including his uncle William, his brother Thomas, and nephews Michael and William. Perhaps with softer tales he convinced a young Irish girl, Mary Frances Wilson, to share his fortunes in Montana.[11]

The turmoil of the Civil War occupied the attention of many New Yorkers during the two winters Johnny spent there. But the ex-dragoon apparently was not tempted to reenlist for the epic struggle. Perhaps he thought western-minded Americans had war enough on their hands with the Indians. In any event, he made different plans. In September 1863 he and Mary Frances married, and by the following spring they had become parents of a baby girl.

*Marriage portrait of Mary Frances and John J. Healy in 1863.*
—Montana Historical Society

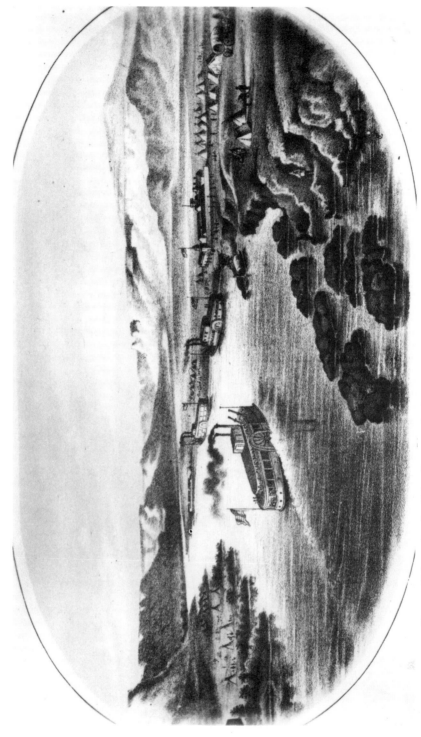

*Gustav Sohon sketch of Fort Benton, the head of steam navigation on the Missouri River, in 1862.*

—Montana Historical Society

# 3

# Fort Benton

*The world has been my school,*
*the mountains and plains, my books.*
                    —Johnny Healy

After spending the winter of 1863-64 in New York, Johnny and his bride, Mary Frances, and baby Maria made the long trip west, arriving by steamboat at Fort Benton. Several major changes around the territory had taken place in Johnny's absence. In 1863 Congress created Idaho Territory, which included today's Idaho and Montana. In 1862 the U.S. Army completed the Mullan Wagon Road—the main transportation link between Fort Benton and Walla Walla. Also in 1862 James Fisk opened a land route from Minnesota to the Montana goldfields. That year stampeders dashed to the Grasshopper Creek discovery near Bannack, and in 1863 even more people rushed to Alder Gulch and Virginia City. And regular steamboat service came to Fort Benton in 1863, increasing its prominence as the head of Missouri River navigation.

Fort Benton boomed while Johnny was in the East. It began to establish itself as the hub of trade and transportation for Montana's white population. In setting and architecture it looked as dreary as any town in the West, but it held on as Montana's commercial center until 1869-70. The completion of the Union Pacific Railroad in 1869 sharply reduced steamboat traffic, and by 1870 Helena had surpassed Fort Benton as the commercial center. Fort Benton's decline continued after other railroads reached the territory in 1880 and 1881, further reducing steamboat traffic. But at the time of Johnny's return in 1864 the town thrived. A mile-long levee protected the town's shacks from the Missouri's annual floods. One 1860s observer called the town "a dirty place, the home of cutthroats and horse thieves," but many residents would have disagreed.[12]

The town was dirty all right; there were no paved streets. Each spring the roadways turned into thick bogs that became scarcely passable by wagon. Travel got easier in summer; then dust became the main nuisance. In winter the frozen earth stayed in place. But when the weather warmed, the cycle started repeating itself. Usually the town smelled as pleasant as it looked—effluvia from mules, horses, and oxen, and piles of stinking buffalo hides filled the air with offensive odors.

The people of Fort Benton were working folk, not noble folk. Drifters formed a class of their own. They tended to speak loudly even when not cursing their oxen or each other in several tongues. Laborers of the town's main occupations—bullwackers, wolf hunters, miners, and whiskey traders—did little to encourage gracious behavior; they liked the rough prosperity of Fort Benton. Travelers usually thought little of the place and remained only long enough to get their business done.

Fort Benton started as a post of the American Fur Company. When the company dissolved, in 1864, ownership transferred to the Northwest Fur Company. It soon became a center for the free traders who took over as the larger outfits faded away. But gold mining in the Northwest really sparked Benton's rapid growth. Steamboats plying the Missouri could not ascend the river farther. Stampeders heading to Bannack, Virginia City, or Last Chance Gulch had to continue overland from Benton. All the major trails in the region, including those leading into Canada, intersected at Benton, assuring its position as a transportation hub.

Johnny Healy knew Fort Benton for about twenty-five years, when it flourished as a river transportion center—until the railroad era. The town thrived on freight and shipping operations. Several businesses maintained huge warehouses; traffic to and from these, the trails, and the riverfront kept the streets well traveled. Outfits such as Diamond R Transportation Company, Garrison and Wyatt, E.G. Maclay and Company, and Carroll and Steel operated out of Benton. By 1866, about 2,500 men, 3,000 horses, and 20,000 oxen and mules hauled goods in to and out of Fort Benton. Such solid business developments transformed the trading post from its wild and woolly character of only a few years earlier. Though still dirty and smelly, the town grew substantially as merchants and residents built to suit their needs. Skilled workers in short supply, such as carpenters, mechanics, and wheelwrights, commanded high wages until the 1880s.

Johnny had no complaints about the town's rapid growth because he always found it a haven from the perils of traveling in the hinterland. Like other frontiersmen, Johnny paid attention to the dangers that lurked beyond town. He once told Edwin Adney that more than fifty men from Fort Benton died at the hands of Indians from 1865 to 1869; the town's winter population usually numbered only about one hundred men. Surely he exaggerated, because the record lists far fewer casualties. But Johnny's high estimate illustrates the pioneers' perception of Indian violence.

Healy and most of the others at Fort Benton were boomers at heart. Boomers made the western towns. They established the commercial spirit and prevailing optimistic mood. Benton's first newspaper editor unblushingly forecast a grand destiny for his lively little town: "Who can tell of the future?" he asked. Chicago, St. Louis, and Omaha all began as "trading posts similar to Benton" before becoming "great commercial marts, the center of trade, wealth and manufacture."[13]

Western businessmen, Healy included, were necessarily boomers. They despised "knockers" who dared to doubt impending prosperity. And the boomers were right about Fort Benton—at least until the 1880s. In the 1870s the merchant princes who ruled the town through their far-reaching trade network got the stability they wanted. Even those less prosperous than the rich merchants of the class of Thomas

C. Power and Isaac Gilbert Baker contentedly put the rough old days of the 1860s behind them. The *Fort Benton Record* observed in 1878 that "those who at first were careless of their reputations, and desirous only of accumulating fortunes and leaving the country are now eager to become reputable citizens and to establish permanent homes." Now the editor could praise the town for more than its commercial prospects as culture and civility bloomed, and could describe with disdain the places where vigilantes had to keep order. "It is doubtful," the editor bragged, "whether in any town of the Territory there are now better order, a healthier morality, a greater immunity from unpleasant sights and sounds." One of the signs of a "healthier morality" was the recent establishment of the town's first resident preacher. Benton had to wait many years for a minister willing to devote himself full-time to its salvation, but frontier residents always recognized churches as significant stages of cultural progress.

The impressions of a visitor from Chicago in 1879 confirmed the locals' reasons for pride. "A person who has not visited the place since its earlier days will be astonished at the change that has been wrought there within so short a time. A wonderful change indeed! A population of uncertain character, with doubtful means of support, has changed into a well-to-do community of solid businessmen, with a legitimate trade."

Benton still prospered from trade that escaped this label of "legitimate." Many of the ox-driven wagons that trundled out of Benton— particularly those heading north—carried more whiskey than the most-thirsty white community could possibly consume. And in the 1870s much of it was consigned to Johnny Healy.

## The Army Posts

Local events compelled men like Healy more than national ones. When Healy had left Montana for New York in 1862 he encountered the huge northward movement of the Sioux. The U.S. Army advanced against the Sioux in 1863, commencing a long era of Indian wars. The Indian conflict weighed heavily on Montana's affairs for many years. Some political re-organization occurred in 1864 when Congress concluded that Idaho Territory was too large, and formed Montana Territory. Transportation improved that year, too, as the Bozeman and Bridger Trails were laid out to accommodate prospectors and other adventurers from the East to the fast-developing new territory.

The Army stationed troops at Fort Benton in 1866-67, then moved most of them to other posts. From 1869-81 they kept a small detachment in town to protect what they saw as an important center on the line of communications extending over the whole Northern Plains. Fort Ellis, established in 1867, Fort Shaw, built the same year, Fort Assiniboine to the north, built in 1879, and Forts Buford and Abraham Lincoln down river were linked by telegraph to Fort Benton, which was also the supply center for the other Army posts. But Fort Benton was never a place dominated by a military presence. The Army usually based troops near larger Indian reservations, as with Fort Shaw, located at the Sun River crossing of the Mullan Road, south of the Canadian border.

Whites in Fort Benton and elsewhere in Montana expressed ambivalent feelings toward the military. Johnny Healy typified the frontiersman, believing himself an expert on managing Indians in peace and a shrewd strategist in war. The military found it impossible to carry out its responsibilities in a manner that consistently satisfied civilian residents. The civil authority in Washington, to whom the Army command was answerable, expected the Army to carry out humane Indian policies that recognized the needs and grievances of the natives. White settlers, Healy included, maintained a simplistic view of an extremely complex problem. Healy blamed the federal government, not the Army for the problems with the natives. Fort

*Advertisement from an unidentified newspaper showing Fort Benton's place in the transportation network of the 1870s.*

# OVERLAND DISTANCES
## From FORT BENTON to

| | | | |
|---|---|---|---|
| Sun River and Fort Shaw.. | 60 | Phillipsburg................ | 285 |
| Helena.................... | 140 | Maria's Cros'g, Simmons F'y | 75 |
| Blackfoot................. | 170 | Fort Belknap.............. | 90 |
| Diamond City............. | 175 | Blackfoot Agency......... | 140 |
| Deer Lodge.............. | 195 | Fort Walsh........ } B. A. | 160 |
| Missoula................. | 2 ;0 | Cypress Mountain. } | |
| Boseman................. | 240 | Fort McLeod........ " | 225 |
| Virginia City.............. | 265 | Fort Edmondton.... " | 475 |

**Stages leave Benton for Helena Tri-Weekly.**

**"       "     Helena for all Inland Points Daily.**

Shaw was "rendered useless for the protection of white men because of the policy of those at Washington listening to the counsels of the sentimentalists and sending out as agents men who thought to control the Indians by prayer—before the Indians had learned—if they have ever done so—to respect the White Man's God," according to Johnny.[14]

Healy's sentiments, hauntingly similar to those heard often during the recent Viet Nam War, favored the Army: "The army men, who really understood the Indian and his social necessity for war and an enemy's scalp as proof of his courage and right to stand as a real man among his own people—these army men had their hands tied."

Johnny's movements in 1864-65 after returning to Fort Benton are hard to date, because he recorded several different dates for some of his major activities. He made a trip to Edmonton and also spent time mining at the goldfields of both Virginia City and Helena. He returned in 1865, none the richer for his endeavors. Mary Frances either accompanied him to the goldfields, or, more likely, remained in Benton. In fact, he may have brought his family west only when he had given up on mining and had made the Edmonton trip. He did tell of a second trip east in 1864 or 1865, going from Virginia City to Salt Lake City, then eastward to the railroad on Ben Holiday's stage line.

## The Edmonton Venture

In 1864 Johnny made a trip into western Canada. He sometimes described it as a prospecting venture, but it turned into a commercial connection. He found no gold if he was prospecting for minerals, but he found that the prairie province of Alberta looked like a place where he could make money. Thousands of buffalo roamed the grasslands and were only being hunted by Indians. Trade prospects looked good because the Hudson's Bay Company (HBC) had not been very aggressive about establishing posts on the prairies. Few whites paid attention to the border regions and Johnny Healy wondered if fortune would smile on him there.

Healy visited the trader at Fort Edmonton, all eyes and ears for what he might glean of market conditions. While his travel companions pushed on to Fort Garry, he wanted to hang around Edmonton for a while. The trader in charge, a former American Fur Company man who had joined the HBC when the American concern fell on hard times, enjoyed imparting his wisdom to the young man. He offered his visitor a meal—not much of a meal, just pemmican—but Johnny "didn't kick." In fact, the pemmican tasted especially good to him because its place on the table confirmed his growing feeling that Canada was the land of promise for a hustler who knew how to buy and sell. If the trader in a well-established post had such poor provisions to eat, Healy concluded, he had a place.[15]

Why look to eastern Canada, Healy asked the trader. He could bring anything the trader wanted from Fort Benton in less time and at less cost than could any Canadian outfit. They quickly struck a deal and Johnny started back for Fort Benton, taking a French-speaking mixed-breed along for greater security on the trail. Healy's French was as poor as his companion's English, so the men showed their cosmopolitanism by conversing in Indian sign language.

The trip had its perils. A party of unpleasant-looking Kootenays stopped the travelers and demanded tribute. The Indians' leader demanded Johnny's gun and, to add a demeaning insult, also demanded a personal service—the American must fill the Indian's canteen from a nearby waterhole. Healy's companion interpreted for the Indian as Healy's face turned a shade darker. "God damn him," he replied, "tell him to go to hell and get his own water." As the Indian knew some English and recognized his antagonists readiness to defend himself, he decided that he was not thirsty after all. But he had greater needs: Healy was riding his horse and he wanted it back. "Liar!" cried Healy.

It never paid to get too hot when you were out-numbered, Healy knew. He remembered just in time that he and the Kootenay shared a Christian heritage. Most of the Kootenays had been converted by Catholic missionaries so Johnny showed one of his prize physical blemishes: an elaborate cross that a Brooklyn dock tattoo artist had once imprinted on his forearm. The Indians were impressed by the tattoo. It evidenced a shared commitment to high living and an abhorrence of theft, and their mood lightened at once. The men were clearly brothers in Christ. Now the Indians insisted that the travelers must visit their camp and take food. Greatly relieved at a close call, Johnny and his companion consented to ride with the Indian party.

While the Indians welcomed the visitors to their camp and fed them, the man who had admired Johnny's horse continued to covet it. He proposed a favorable trade of horses to which Healy agreed, because the travelers needed fresh mounts. With the trade settled the travelers retired for the night. In the morning they were ready to leave when the Indian refused them their new horses. Allegedly, their original ones had been stolen during the night. The rascally Blackfeet had probably raided the camp quietly and made off with the horses, said the Indian with a straight face. But he offered another deal: If Johnny would give up his guns he could have the horses. By this time Johnny had taken enough. "I went to rope the horses, gun in hand."

No one stopped him, and a squaw even slipped Johnny some elk meat before they rode off.

On the trail back the travelers stopped at another Kootenay camp. The people were friendly, and hungry. It was Sunday, and, for religious reasons, they would not hunt on Sunday. Healy gave them some of his elk meat and was impressed by their piety. "A bell rang and they knelt to pray. I never felt so awkward as I didn't know it was Sunday and didn't care." Johnny, a Roman Catholic who in recent years had paid little attention to Sunday worship, was struck by the piety of the Indians.

The Indians insisted upon providing an escort for the travelers all the way to Fort Benton—150 miles away. Johnny recalled this generous offer in his journal, but the Indians would have been unlikely to offer to go through the Blackfoot country near Fort Benton, regardless of their friendliness. At any rate, the journey started pleasantly. Johnny was young and vain enough to wow the party with some feats of horsemanship along the way. His companion told the Indians how Johnny could ride at full speed and pick up a rope from the ground without slowing, and they called for a demonstration.

A more important demonstration came when the party approached within fifty miles of Benton and spotted signs of an Indian war party stalking them. Johnny's party reached a point of near panic, and he told them "I never got caught yet and am not going to be caught now." He then dashed hard for the safety of Benton without further pause on the trail. He arrived without trouble, and his companions arrived "just before me." This account makes a good story, but if, as is likely, the Kootenay escort left him before reaching Blackfoot country, it is more fiction than fact.

After arriving back in Benton from his Canada trip Johnny Healy became a trader. He bought forty barrels of flour, hired teams and carts, and brought his brother Tom in as a partner. Tom had joined Johnny at Fort Benton a short time before, and other members of the Healy clan of Brooklyn moved west within a couple of years, adding to Benton's large Irish contingent.

After assembling the supplies Johnny left Benton for longer than the one month the round-trip to Edmonton to deliver the freight would have taken. In one account of his movements he said that he went east via Salt Lake City. More likely he went to the goldfields after coming back from Edmonton, then went south to Salt Lake City, traveling east from there.

In an account given to a writer for the *Saturday Evening Post* years later, Johnny described the Edmonton venture as a disaster owing to the nastiness of the Hudson's Bay Company. He claimed that gold prospecting rather than trading was the trip's purpose, said we "built one of the strongest and biggest carts I have ever seen." They took provisions to last them their extended trip, and Johnny planned to stop in St. Louis after visiting New York to buy rolled "copper sheets to save gold on."

On reaching the HBC post Johnny's men tried to buy food and other necessities, but the HBC trader refused their money. "Trade not prospecting is what you are after," charged the HBC factor. "We don't want you here." The Americans insisted that they were innocent of any intention of competing for the Indian trade, although, under the circumstances, the factor's suspicion seemed justified. At any rate the Americans were forced to hang around the post over the winter and cut wood, for which they were paid the measly sum of two pounds of pemmican for each cord they cut. Over the long severe winter several of the men sickened due to insufficient rations. Finally, Hartley McEwen, a tough Scotsman, shot one of the HBC's steers and gave his hungry companions a big feed. The factor summoned McEwen for a dressing down but was met by a fierce defiance. "I meant to kill two cattle," McEwen growled, "because we are sick of starving and being treated badly. Gold is all we're looking for, and we have nothing to do with any scheme to start competition against you." When the factor ordered McEwen to leave the country the Scot raised his rifle. "Our boys are starving. I killed your ox for them, and by heavens, I'll kill you too." At this threat the factor backed off even though his men heavily outnumbered the Americans. Until spring, when the Americans returned to Montana, they were able to buy what they needed from the company.

When Healy heard about the incident he resolved to have his vengeance, "I vowed that the minute I got $50,000 ahead I would go up into that country and make them abandon their fort if it was the last act of my life." Four years later he moved north and tied up all the buffalo meat in the country. What he could not use or give to Indians he dumped in the river. Soon the factor who had tried to starve out Johnny's men was forced to abandon Mountain House, "a fort that had cost them $30,000." As a result of annoying Johnny the company lost out, "but I had gained the entire trade of the whole region, and I held it until I was doing a good business and had a post that cost me $15,000."

Johnny tells a good story of revenge, but one that cannot be confirmed by HBC or other records. Perhaps the HBC obstructed him, but when he made his major relocation to Alberta the HBC was outside his trading area.

Regardless of the accuracy of the colorful incidents, Johnny expressed a contempt for the HBC typical of many U.S. residents. To many, the company practiced a transplanted European despotism in the New World. Its charter gave it absolute power over people and resources, and subverted the North American style of democracy. Besides that, American critics argued that the company showed its backwardness in its inability to develop the country it ruled. As one American magazine writer put it in 1870, "The sluggish apathy and morbid caution of our venerable trans-atlantic progenitors, when contrasted with the fearless, dashing spirit of enterprise and prompt execution which characterize the achievements of our people, receives a forcible illustration in the glaring truth that they, for more than a century, having been pursuing the 'penny wise and pound foolish' policy of barring up all avenues of approach to this vast tract of fertile country; and for what purpose?"[16]

Some Canadians feared the aggressiveness of Americans who coveted the western provinces in the 1870s, but the Canadians had little reason for concern. Americans who favored expansion northwards believed their superior institutions and commercial abilities would eventually bring western Canada into the Republic without any need for direct action. Johnny never recorded his thoughts about national expansion, but his ambitions were to exploit the fur trade rather than to annex territory. His Edmonton venture appears to have laid the groundwork for even bolder moves into the Canadian prairies.

After his Alberta trip the gold excitement at Virginia City drew Johnny for a time. While there he became a vigilante, to help clean up the Plummer gang. Johnny also spent some time in Helena before returning again to Fort Benton.

The vigilante's action against the Henry Plummer gang forms one of the best-known episodes of Montana's history. Healy claimed to have been a vigilante but told no stories about it. He may have kept quiet because he had been sworn to secrecy as a vigilante or he may have had little to tell. While some men who joined the force limited their participation, Johnny rarely played a minor role when events became lively. But for the mention of Johnny by X. Beidler, one of the vigilante leaders, we might question Johnny's membership. In his account of the vigilantes Beidler describes one incident that involved Johnny.

Beidler related the aftermath of the fall 1863 trial of Henry Brent by the vigilantes. They acquitted Brent, a young man of good family, and ordered him to leave Montana. "John Stuart, James Arneaux, J. J. Healy, and I had to ride 60 miles to get home," wrote Beider. That night they encountered Brent, who warned of an Indian war party.

Soon Indians appeared, and in the battle Brent was wounded. Brent insisted that the others must leave him and seize their chance to escape, because he was too badly hurt to go with them. Stuart insisted upon defending the man, who was much bothered by the charges that he had been one of Plummer's road agents. When the men all insisted that they believed in his innocence, Brent was happy. "Then I can die easy," Brent said, and shot himself. If we can believe Beidler, the four vigilantes took time to set up a cross with an inscription: "Here died a brave young man to save others their lives."[17]

The brevity of Johnny's sojourn in the goldfields before he turned to other pursuits may explain his minor role as a vigilante. Had he been involved more, he likely would have left some record of his activities beyond this mention of Beidler's. Henry Plummer would have interested Johnny enough to warrant a mention in Johnny's journal because of Plummer's infamy, and because the two men had something in common. Plummer married his wife Electra at Sun River. Electra was the sister of James Vail, an Ohio schoolteacher sent out to manage the government farm at Sun River. A few years later Healy became involved with the government farm.

## Sun River

Johnny returned to Fort Benton from New York in 1864 a family man and cast about for opportunities to make money. A solution presented itself in an offer of employment from Gad E. Upson with the U.S. government on the Indian reservation at Sun River. The job would permit Healy to trade, and he would also draw a salary for managing the government's horse farm. Upson, the agent on the reservation, had a hard time keeping whites employed because they could usually find higher-paying jobs at Fort Benton or in any of the gold boom towns. Many of the men who took minor reservation jobs or hung around reservations were, as one Indian Bureau agent put it in 1863, often "the worse classes of our own people" who, "by means of gambling, the whiskey traffic and every species of vice and immorality," plunder the government and debauch the Indians.[18]

Blackfeet occupied the Sun River reservation under a treaty they made with the United States in 1855. The Indians agreed to keep the peace with other tribes, to hunt only on designated grounds to avoid conflict with nomadic natives, and to allow peaceful passage to whites, which included approval to build roads and military posts. In return the government agreed to give $20,000 in goods each year and provide another $15,000 for education in agricultural and mechanical pursuits. Breaches and renegotiations occurred, but the situation remained reasonably stable until the Civil War years.

The Indian Bureau expected Upson, Healy, and other government employees at Sun River to instruct Indians on the means of providing themselves with the necessities of life. According to a Bureau directive the Indians would be taught to earn "their subsistence by labor on the soil" on reserves where whites could not interfere with their pursuits.

The Sun River experiment had good land and ample water, but nature became uncooperative. In 1864 flash floods of the Sun River ravaged the farm three times, destroying crops and ruining equipment. Over the next couple of years a variety of natural disasters, including grasshopper infestations, droughts, and untimely frosts undermined all the efforts the Bureau men made. Healy was in charge of stock raising, while others directed the Indians' farming efforts.

Healy left no record of his thoughts on the experiment, and it is hard to imagine him being optimistic. Even some career members of the Indian Bureau considered the project impractical. Healy admired Upson and presumably did his best to arrest the decay the Sun River experiment was undergoing. Upson, on reporting for duty in 1864, told his superiors that the buildings were dilapidated, that only a handful of acres were under cultivation, and that previous employees had grossly neglected all work to protect the property.

Government officials were considering creating an "Indian Territory" extending from the Missouri River to the international border when stirring events interfered. In the winter of 1866 some five hundred men stampeded to Sun River. The strike amounted to virtually nothing but caused much misery to stampeders, some of whom the Indians fed. Some men liked the area well enough to stay and try their hands at ranching. With eager settlers filling up the area the government decided it was politically impossible to create a giant reserve. Agents had to turn to other means to make the Sun River farm viable.

Upson's term ended with his death in 1865. Judging from the turnover in the agency's direction, his successors found the task beyond their means. Over the next nine years, from 1865 to 1874, the experiment went through ten different periods with and without agents, including one of eighteen months without an agent. The Blackfeet came to believe that the government neglected them, and agents worried about protecting reservation property from them. As a proud race of warriors, the Blackfeet felt justified at times in taking their due from a convenient government reserve.

# Sun River Raid

Healy officially began trading in March 1869, when Governor Thomas Meagher issued a permit from the executive office at Virginia City. The permit authorized "John J. Healy of Fort Benton to trade with the Indians of the Blackfoot, Gros Ventres, and Crow tribes for the period of one year." He presumably received other permits including one for the store he opened at Sun River while still in charge of the government horse farm.[19]

Johnny's residence and store at Sun River were protected by heavy shutters over the windows and loop holes for firing on assailants. He made sure of the building's sturdiness because he had a wife and young daughters to protect, and at times trading could be a hazardous business. Since he doubled as assistant Indian agent and protector of seventy-five government horses he also felt the need for defensive measures.

An incident in 1871 showed that marauding Indians made vigilance necessary at all times. At his house, besides his family, Johnny had his brother Tom, a cook, and his interpreter Francois Vielle. Johnny had given floor space to two men passing through, Floyd Keating and Johnny's old friend from Idaho days, John Kennedy. All were asleep when Vielle came running into the house, crying that Indians had run off their horses.

Everyone grabbed for guns. Healy dashed to the corral with his Prussian needle-gun. "I had no sooner got there than down came the gate and out came the Indians on horseback. I let go and knocked one off his horse." The Indians returned gunfire, and Healy rolled behind a log and shot another raider who was on foot. Friendly Canadian Indians who had camped nearby joined the battle against the marauders, but as the engagement became more widespread Johnny had to dash for his house as the hostiles moved to surround him. "We ran back as fast as we could and just got the strong door open and shut again when there came a rattle of bullets against the house. I made my wife and little girls lie close to the floor so the bullets would not hit them." An Indian's head appeared at the window and one of Healy's visitors shot him.[20]

Just a quarter mile from his place was camped a large village of friendly Bloods down from Canada. Another clamor at the door came from a wounded Indian chief, Many Braids. Healy let him in then opened the back door to other Bloods who had fled to the house for protection. When the gunfire from outside died down Healy went outside to find other friendly Indians wounded in the attack. One young warrior announced, "I'm very poor." He had a severe leg wound. "He had lost his woman only a short time before," Healy said, "and he had a little boy. I knelt down beside him, and seeing he would die, I said to him, 'Die easy, father. I will take care of your little boy.'" The little boy, Joe Healy, became a member of the Healy family.

Johnny asked at nearby Fort Shaw for soldiers to join him in a chase after the raiders to recover the stolen horses. The officer in charge refused to help without permission from higher authority, infuriating Healy, who questioned why the government stationed troops in the country if they were unwilling to let them protect people. Johnny set off in pursuit with the two travelers who had been his overnight guests. Judging from the haircut of the raider killed in front of his house, Johnny thought the party were Crows from the Yellowstone River country. "The Crows were a bad lot," Healy believed. "They were supposed to be at peace with the white man, but they scalped and stole whenever they saw an opportunity to do so without detection. . . . We were not surprised when we found the trail of the horses leading off to the south."

As the three pursuers followed the trail it veered to the west, and Healy, examining a medicine bag and arrow dropped along the way, concluded that the raiders were Nez Perces or Flatheads rather than Crows. The Flatheads had been converted to Christianity by the Jesuits and were friendly to whites, yet the tracks made by the stolen horses led right to the Flathead reservation. Johnny asked the Indian agent who accompanied him to call on Big Canoe, the Flathead chief. The chief's lodge filled up as the men talked, and the women began handing around rifles. After trailing the raiders for two weeks Healy was in no mood to run away, so he challenged Big Canoe, telling him, "You can kill us, but we will die fighting as long as there is a breath left in our bodies." Then the Great Father will send soldiers, Johnny continued. "There won't be as much as a blade of grass to show that an Indian ever lived here. You will be wiped off the face of the earth." The daring bluff worked. Big Canoe admitted that his warriors had intended to steal horses from the Blackfeet at Sun River and had not expected whites to interfere. Big Canoe had the stolen horses brought to Healy, who dazzled everyone with his generosity by allowing each raider to keep one horse.

Indian-white relations were particularly tense in the years between 1863 and 1870, and settlers in the West raged against what they saw as the indifference of the government to their need for protection. Some federal officials accused the settlers of reacting hysterically to imagined Indian threats or of bringing danger to themselves by adopting bellicose stances. But the government response only made the whites more angry and contemptuous, as many had experienced close encounters like the raid on Sun River, and knew what is was to fear for their lives.

# Sun River Neighbors

Among Healy's Sun River neighbors was a Welshman, Robert Vaughn, who spent several years as a miner and butcher at Nelson Gulch and elsewhere in Montana's goldfields before moving to Sun River in 1869. He homesteaded in Chouteau county, with his ranch nine miles from the Sun River crossing. He was apprehensive about Indian aggression because of Blackfeet raids in 1867-69. Shortly after his move the Army retaliated against the Indians with its Piegan War massacre of two hundred inhabitants of a Marias River village in January 1870. Although many whites decried the brutal killing of innocent people, Vaughn was more concerned about the Indians' retaliation. When the Indians did not retaliate Vaughn reflected that "the battle was the best thing that ever happened in Northern Montana at that time. For several years afterwards the Indians were very shy, although some roving war parties of different tribes would cross the country and kill people and steal horses and cattle."[21]

Two years before Vaughn arrived, John Largent and Johnny's brother Joseph built cabins, giving the Sun River community its start. Largent kept a store and blacksmith shop at the river crossing, near where Johnny Healy and Al Hamilton established their trading post on the north bank of the river. In the early seventies other settlers moved into the region and started farms. Other men brought in cattle and established several ranches. Sun River enjoyed a small boom, and for some years it was the only appreciable community in Chouteau County aside from Fort Benton.

In the winter of 1872 Vaughn participated in his first buffalo hunt, describing the chase as exciting and enjoyable. He and his companions found a great herd between Sun River and Fort Benton. Vaughn said that they "could see that the lake flat was entirely covered with buffaloes. It was a sight to behold. Without exaggeration there were a quarter of million buffaloes in sight; the main herd covered eight miles by three miles, and they were so numerous that they ate every spear of grass as they went." Vaughn exaggerated, even if he disclaimed it: a quarter of million buffalos in sight is a grossly high estimate.

Vaughn and his companions charged the herd and opened fire. "And now the fun began. Tens of thousands of these ponderous beasts were running at [such] a furious pace the earth trembled, and the clicking of their hooves could be heard for miles away." Vaughn rode into the herd, moving along with its pell-mell pace, and shot two of the beasts. When his horse tired he stopped, feeling good about his baptism by fire as a buffalo hunter. He saw Indians pursuing another section of the herd in similar fashion as he rested.

Vaughn's frontier experiences were tamer than Johnny Healy's, but he made similar reflections on the Indian peril. "Though a frontier life is free and fascinating, still, like everything else, there is a dark side to it." He listed every incident he knew about of Indians slaying pioneers so his readers would "understand what it cost to come here in the early days."

Vaughn insisted that neither the Pilgrim fathers nor the California argonauts had it as hard. "Montana was a thousand miles from any ocean, a wilderness in the center of an untrodden country with savages in her every pass and valley, and so, necessarily, every man that came here among the first was in some ways a soldier." He believed author Joaquin Miller's argument that Montanans performed better than soldiers put in the field by Caesar, Bonaparte, and Grant, who "had their governments to clothe, feed, pay and pension them, but the hero of Montana stood alone."

Vaughn's sentimental effusions on Indian violence describe grieving relatives and unknown victims:

> Slain by Indians a pioneer was found,
> His home or his kindred nobody knew;
> Over his cold form bendeth
> The grasses in tears of dew.

The sentiments of Vaughn and Miller, although one-sided, clearly express the pioneer view of the Indian. Issues of justice to natives and rational government policies weighed less heavily on their minds than did sorrow for slain whites. Whites were brave heroes—warriors of the frontier who were forced to live in dread of a treacherous foe.

John Largent was another Healy neighbor. The American Fur Co. sent him from St. Louis to Fort Benton in 1862. At that time the fort was the only building at Fort Benton, and it housed some twenty-four whites, then "fully half the white population of Northern Montana." Largent became as proficient in Indian languages as he was in standing off hostiles with his Kentucky rifle, which warriors learned to respect. By the time Largent settled at Sun River, life on the upper Missouri had become tamer, but he was happy to see settlers coming in.

Both Vaughn and Largent had stories to tell of Johnny Healy, and Vaughn included many in his book, *Then and Now*. Vaughn first met

Healy in 1866 when Vaughn worked as a freighter with the Sutherlin brothers, who took the first ox-driven wagon train from Virginia City to Fort Benton. At Sun River the freighters had to make the river crossing on Healy's ferry, a small, crude craft made of whip-sawed lumber that could carry only one wagon and its yoke of oxen at a time. The ferry, which was hooked to a cable and moved by a hand-powered drum mechanism, was out of service when Vaughn's train got in. Healy had left the previous day for Fort Benton to get a replacement cable and took several days to return. He returned with thick hemp rope, and he and others used oxen to place it in position, a job that taxed everyone's nerves. Healy also brought news of an aggressive Blackfoot raiding party in the region, so Vaughn had to stand a night watch over the rest of the trail into Fort Benton.

Vaughn also told a story about Healy that Johnny never told himself because the incident embarrassed him. It concerned an attempt Healy and others at Fort Benton made to impress visiting Indians with the firepower whites had on hand. A pack train arrived with a small brass cannon lashed to the back of a mule. Someone led the mule to Front Street for a demonstration: the men would fire the cannon at a high cut-bank a half mile away across the river. Unfortunately, the animal broke free just as a man held a lighted match to the cannon. The mule leaped, spun, and twirled wonderfully as the lit fuse sputtered and glowed. "There was a perfect stampede; many [people] went over the bank into the river, others were crawling on their hands and knees, while many lay flat on the ground, broadcloth and buckskin alike. Luckily, on account of the bend in the mule's back, the shot struck the ground but a short distance from his heels."

Among the spectators noted by Vaughn was Johnny, who "had fought Indians and assisted in arresting some of the worst desperadoes in the Northwest . . . but the mule was too much for him, and he was seen going for dear life over the bank into the river." Healy's acquaintances thought it a huge joke on Johnny, particularly because some wit on the scene doubled the humor by remarking loudly that "it was the first time anyone ever saw Healy 'take water.'" Johnny was also famous for taking his whiskey—lots of it—straight.

When it came to telling stories about men under stress, Johnny liked those about Francois "Crazy" Veille, his interpreter at Sun River. Healy described Veille, a Canadian whose father was French and mother was an Indian, as a coward, especially in the face of Indian threats. After the 1869 Indian attack on the Sun River post, Healy reproached Veille for cowering in a corner rather than shooting back at the attackers. Veille insisted that he had a gun "but Mrs. Healy took it from me." Hearing this excuse, Mary Frances scoffed, "Oh get out, Veille, it wasn't a gun I took away from you. It was a broomstick."[22]

Earlier Johnny sent Veille to take two Jesuit priests to St. Peter's Mission, ten miles from the trading post. Hostile Indians had been reported in the area, making Veille particularly alert. "They had gone some miles," Johnny recalled, "when all of a sudden Veille jerked up his horse and called out, 'Injuns!' and pointed to a little cloud of dust off on the prairie and at the same time he turned his horse's head, ready to run. 'Don't fear, my son!' said one of the priests, Father Hogan. 'Our black robes and the sign of the cross will protect us. Trust in God. We will be protected.' 'All right,' answered Veille. 'You trust in God. I trust in my horse.' And with that he put spurs to his mount and tore away as fast as he could go." Veille got back safely and so, later, did the priests, who were taunted by their craven guide for relying on Providence longer than was prudent.

For a time Alexander Culbertson often visited at the Sun River post. He had been the chief figure in the fur trade of the upper Missouri for the American Fur Company before retiring in 1861 after the company sold out to independent traders. Culbertson married an Indian woman, the sister of the Blood chief Seen From Afar, and moved to the Blackfeet reservation at Sun River in 1864. Culbertson told Johnny many stories of the early days of Missouri River trading.

As manager of the government horse farm and then with Al Hamilton, as Indian trader, Healy and his family lived a comfortable life at Sun River. But listening to the stories of the great old days from Culbertson and others piqued Johnny. The pioneers had achieved their special status because of their daring—because they had been among the first to do something. He believed himself daring also, and he pondered an opportunity that could make him a fortune. Montana was filling up with people, but Johnny saw the prairie provinces of Canada more open than ever to enterprising fellows. The HBC had given his trading party a rough time in Alberta, but lately they had given up on the country. Opportunity seemed to be smiling.

# 4

# The Whoop-Up Trail

*I do not take the view that
all Injuns were bad Injuns . . .
but one or the other had to yield.*
                    —Johnny Healy

J ohnny decided it was a good time for a trader to clear out of Montana. Time was when men of initiative were respected for their strenuous efforts to build up the country through trade; now the government was going all out to destroy commerce in the territory, thought Johnny. Healy had been closely watching U.S. Marshal William F. Wheeler's law-enforcement crusade against illicit traders, considering his alternatives. One of them was obvious: earlier he had supplied a trader in Alberta and looked over the prairies of western Canada thoroughly. He could easily make a fresh start there, but he would need a chunk of money to build a trading station and haul in goods.

Wheeler started harassing Montana's whiskey traders in 1869, sending deputies down the Missouri River during the winter to observe any booze being sold to Indians and to seize the goods of offenders. At first the traders had trouble understanding Wheeler's attitude. When a deputy confronted a Hudson's Bay Company trader operating on the Flathead Reservation in September 1870, the whiskey seller protested bitterly. He had always sold freely to half-breeds and whites on the reservation and saw no reason to quit just because treaty negotiations had determined that the reservation was within American territory.[23]

The Justice Department first convicted a whiskey trader in 1871. John Davidson, the victim of the new federal vigilance, had been most unhappy when a deputy closed down the saloon he ran on the Flathead Reservation. "It was damn mean of the government," Davidson cried, "to punish a white man for selling whiskey to Indians." Davidson had been selling whiskey in Montana for fourteen years and had never been bothered. At trial his attorney argued that Davidson was an English citizen and was being improperly tried. But Davidson had once run for office in Fort Benton, negating this defense.[24]

Whiskey trading continued, but federal enforcement quickly shutdown the old open method of dealing and reduced the numbers of traders. A few traders continued to work the border region with a mobile operation. If deputies got near, they packed their wagons and crossed hurriedly into Canada.

Western Canada became particularly attractive to Healy in 1869, because that year the Hudson's Bay Company turned over its vast domain of Rupert's Land to Canada. The region extended west from the Great Lakes to the Rocky Mountains, encompassing an area of about a million square miles. No enterprising American merchant involved in the buffalo-hide trade could miss the significance of this land transfer. The HBC was retrenching. The company never had a great interest in the prairie provinces, and it was now throwing the region up for grabs.

The government in Ottawa happily acquired title but lacked immediate plans for policing or economic development.

Few whites lived in Alberta or Saskatchewan among the Piegans, the Bloods, and the Blackfeet—the main Indian groups. The métis, mixed-blood descendants of the French Canadians, who had done most of the trapping for the HBC and the Northwest Company in the early days, formed the largest non-Indian community and ran most of the trading posts on the prairies.

The American market for buffalo robes was beginning to deplete the herds in Montana and other regions of the States by 1869, but the Canadian herds had seen little commercial hunting. The HBC's policy of discouraging both white settlement and the development of bulk-freight shipping routes helped preserve the herds. The freight costs to ship robes to eastern Canada were too high to make the commerce feasible. Of course, the freight rates on goods shipped west were equally high for want of active, competitive shippers in the field—hence the opportunity for traders based in Fort Benton. While the freight costs from Fort Benton to various Canadian posts on the Whoop-Up Trail added to the price of goods, they remained far cheaper than when shipped out from eastern Canada. Authorities in Ottawa heard about the intrusion of the Americans soon after Healy made his move. They were displeased by the news but were slow to respond.

While other Americans pondered their opportunities in prairie Canada, Johnny Healy acted decisively—as was his custom. He talked his Sun River partner, A. B. Hamilton, into helping raise money for a post in Canada and securing regular provisions from a Fort Benton supplier.

Healy gave a lively description of his move from Sun River to Canada, but an unlikely motivation for it. He claimed that his outrage at local Republicans levying a $500 political contribution on him determined his move. As a Democrat he objected to helping a Republican presidential candidate. "It was too much for me. I decided to leave the country," he later explained. Johnny also claimed that gaining revenge on the HBC gave him his motivation.[25]

On his move north Healy had to avoid the soldiers of Fort Shaw, located only four miles from his place, who were patrolling the border. The soldiers knew Healy was moving north because he had made public his plans and had even secured a travel permit from the Army. They expected that Healy could cross the reservation with plenty of whiskey, which they would enjoy seizing. Gen. Alfred Sully's permit authorized Healy and Hamilton, who had to post a $10,000 bond, to travel across Montana to the border. "They are also privileged," the permit stated, "to take with them a party of from 20 to 30 men and six wagons loaded with supplies provided there is no spirituous liquors in the wagons except a small quantity which may be taken safely for medicinal purposes."[26]

Leaving his wife behind, Healy took several days moving his wagons and goods out gradually, hiding them in a coulee a couple of miles from his store. When he had everything ready he set out from his place at midday for Fort Benton, riding his favorite buffalo horse, a splendid black-maned stallion. The party rode sixty miles to Fort Benton, the nearest telegraph station, where Healy wired Hamilton to rendezvous with him east of Benton for the crossing to Canada. As Healy expected the government telegraph clerk advised Fort Shaw of the trader's plans. The reported rendezvous, of course, was a ruse. Healy and his men rode back to Sun River after dark, gathered their hidden wagons and struck due north for the border, marching right across the reservation. He outfitted the wagons with long poles that dragged behind, leaving impressions like those left by the traverses of Indians, and the Army missed him. "The cavalry were sent off up east seventy-five miles out of the way," he said, "and before they found out their mistake I was through the gap and well on my way into Canada." The story of the Irish trader's daring escapade made a big hit at Fort Benton, especially among those who resented the military. "I crossed the reservation in spite of them," Healy wrote, "as I said I would do."[27]

Healy and Hamilton and the traders who followed them had other sound reasons for moving into Alberta. Gold discoveries in Montana had upset the Indians and forced the Blackfeet to move north of the Marias River within Canada. Traders in buffalo hides depended upon Indians for hunting, so moving north was a convenience to the trade, especially after federal liquor sales restrictions cut out a medium of exchange. But the best reason for relocating became evident by the success of Healy and Hamilton during their first season of 1869. When other traders heard that the enterprising partners had made $50,000, a number of them packed up and headed north.

At the crossing of the St. Mary's and Oldman River (or Belly River, as it was called before offended Lethbridge merchants insisted upon a name change), about two hundred miles north of Fort Benton, Healy and Hamilton built their post, Fort Hamilton. Its original location, four miles south of Lethbridge, gave a start to the pleasant city that is the major population center in southern Alberta. From the modern university campus built on the river bluff, visitors have a dramatic view of the region and can gain some sense of why the Montana men chose the location.

The post quickly became famous but was always called Fort Whoop-Up rather than Fort Hamilton. The old North Trail from Montana and onward into Canada also took the name of the Whoop-Up Trail. Several stories gave conflicting accounts of the name's origin. Perhaps T. C. Power originated it when he described the traders there "whooping it up," or it may refer to "whooping" the oxen along in driving supply wagons to the north. Historian Joel Overholser believed that the name derived from the inclination of a whiskey runner, loaded with wet goods at Fort Benton, to depart at night and whoop it up for the border. Anyway, the name stuck and was closely coupled with the name of Johnny Healy—who was fast becoming a famed man in Montana.

Traversing the country between Fort Benton and Fort Whoop-Up never inspired lyrical descriptive prose from travelers. Trader Charles Schafft, who made the trip in 1874, noted the small monument marking the border about one hundred and thirty miles from Benton. "The whole road travelled over between Missoula and here was devoid of interest. A rolling prairie, cut up occasionally by collies [sic]—covered with short, dried up grass and prickly pear—no other vegetation, and not a stick of wood between the Marias and Belly Rivers." Schafft also found the country around the post uninviting. He seemed unimpressed by the striking cuts made by the rivers as they coursed between high bluffs. Schafft noted some Cottonwood trees along the river bottoms but surmised that the land was unfruitful. "No farmer would ever choose this as a country to make a homestead in," he argued.[28]

The original fort, located in an arc formed by the confluence of the two rivers, consisted of eleven log cabins surrounded by a picket fence. Fire, probably in 1871, destroyed the compound and the partners rebuilt on a grander scale. Although the $10,000 cost reported by Charles Schafft, who worked there in 1874, sounds high, some modern writers have suggested it may have cost up to $25,000. Healy told a magazine writer the new post cost $15,000. Certainly he and Hamilton spared no expense to make the post secure.

W. S. Gladstone, a Canadian who had settled at Fort Benton, was the architect and head carpenter. The post was solidly built of square logs in the form of a hollow square. It had ramparts, loopholes for defensive gunfire, and bastions at opposite corners. Three wickets were available for trading; Indians were excluded from the compound. The residents opened a heavily fortified gate only when supply wagons arrived from Fort Benton with goods, and the wagons were then sent south laden with buffalo robes. A two-inch muzzle-loading cannon was mounted on one bastion; the other housed an alarm bell, a mountain howitzer, and a water well. The main gate provided the only opening to the outside from the square. All other compound doors and windows opened on the central square.

*Indians sitting outside Fort Whoop-Up, c. 1872.* —Montana Historical Society

Healy's accounts of the Fort Whoop-Up years include little detail, but others have contributed a good deal of information. His adopted son, Joe Healy, watched the post being constructed after traveling there from Sun River. Young Joe admired the fort's design and marveled at its security. Because of the cleverness of the builder "the white man could remain within for days, while the wild, drunken Indians fought without." In his later years, Joe condemned the works of his namesake. He lived until 1936 and came to censure the enterprise in which he had once fully participated as a family member. "In this wild atmosphere Fort Whoop-Up prospered. The days of scalping were at their height, and the raids and threats of savage Indians became a horror. . . . There was no law, justice, or a demand for peace. Fort Whoop-Up was the jolly home of American desperadoes, the meeting place of Indian tribes," he explained.[29]

When Indians approached the post to do business the trader stood at a wicket with a tub full of whiskey, dispensing it by a tin cup through a small opening in the oak gate when an Indian slipped a buffalo robe through for exchange. Steele's and other accounts in which authors have been keen to show the wickedness of American traders, give an appearance that Indians wanted only booze. Contrarily, when Healy discussed the trade he never mentioned whiskey. Healy traded guns, cooking utensils, axes, ammunition, sugar, flour, tea, salt, knives, tobacco, cloth, and blankets too. Yet Healy and other traders preferred to trade whiskey because it was relatively easy to ship, commanded a high value, and they could easily dilute it. Many recipes exist for diluting whiskey. Most feature the use of red pepper or something else hot to sustain the immediate "kick" after the whiskey is diluted with water. But traders had to give value up to a point. Their diluted rotgut still had enough alcohol to ravage thousands of Indians.

If Healy ever suffered any attacks of conscience for his long-term contribution to the degradation of the Indians he never admitted it. You had to be tough and indifferent to suffering to stay in the whiskey trade when you saw its effects. It helped too if you believed that the destruction of the Indians was inevitable, necessary to the advance of white civilization. Many whites found the whiskey trade morally justified and viewed federal enforcement efforts humorously. When the *Helena Daily Gazette* reported in 1872 that Healy and Hamilton "are doing well this winter" at Fort Whoop-Up, the editor observed that "no U.S. detective or spy dare invade their quiet rendezvous; nor is whiskey ever confiscated when it gets to that 'happy hunting ground'!"[30]

Accounts differ on the value of whiskey as a trade item. The exchange for a robe depended upon its quality and varied upwards from two cups of whiskey, sometimes with a blanket thrown in. For a fine pony Indians expected four gallons of whiskey. Guns were an important trade item, and a trader expected a stack of robes the height of a rifle in exchange for one. According to Donald Graham the standard robe price at Fort Whoop-Up in 1872-73 was one half-gallon of liquor.[31]

Healy and Hamilton made money, and the men they employed also did well. Of these Donald Davis later represented Alberta in Canada's

Parliament. Davis went to Fort Whoop-Up in 1869 or 1870 and remained there several years. In a letter home he boasted of his wage of $150 monthly plus board, "which is what a man slaves for on a farm for six months."[32]

A trader could easily arrange to have an Indian girl share his bed if he desired it. None of the traders brought his wife into the strange world of an isolated post in Indian country. Healy "married" the daughter of a war chief, an arrangement that offered sexual convenience and a useful relationship with important members of his trading community. Apparently, he fathered no children by this Indian woman.[33]

Johnny never mentioned this living arrangement, and he was equally reticence to discuss matters of Indian family diplomacy. By establishing a relationship with a tribal woman he gained unique opportunities for learning Indian ways. He undoubtedly took advantage of such opportunities, but his anecdotes only reveal the crude, courageous bluffer.

## Tales of Violence

Johnny loved telling stories about his encounters with Indians, particularly if they allowed him to boast of his daring and acumen. The story of Weasel Head was one of Johnny's favorites. The incident occured after Whoop-Up country traders agreed to ban the sale of liquor. While agreement on this prohibition seems unlikely, except perhaps as a noble experiment of short duration, the traders reasons for coming to such a decision make perfect sense. Selling whiskey to the Indians was not a moral issue—"It was only wrong to lie, cheat or steal," Adney reported Johnny saying—but whiskey set Indians to fighting, and sometimes they attacked traders. At times the carnage was awful. During one winter of the early 1870s the Bloods reportedly lost seventy men in drunken quarrels. Others were killed by whites, starved, or perished in the cold while drunk. A Helena newspaper reported in spring 1872 that seven traders had been killed at Fort Whoop-Up. The HBC stopped selling whiskey in the 1860s because of these effects, but the Americans all operated under independent management, making agreement on any common policy difficult. Even capable, intelligent chiefs like Crowfoot, whose hunting grounds were near Spitzee Post on Highwood River and Lafayette French's Post at Blackfoot Crossing, avoided interfering with the whiskey commerce. So long as the Americans dealt fairly, he considered them friends; he knew he was powerless to stamp out the evil, and he sometimes got violently drunk himself.[34]

During this time of prohibition, according to Johnny's story, Weasel Head, "a big, tall, fine looking fellow," came to Fort Whoop-Up and demanded whiskey.

"No," cried Johnny righteously, "we are not selling whiskey."

Refusing to accept this unfamiliar denial, Weasel Head returned with "a big six-shooter thrust into the bosom of his shirt and he carried one of those wicked Hudson Bay daggers."

"I want whiskey!" he cried while driving his dirk into the top of the counter until it quivered.

Johnny knew this was tantamount to a declaration of war. Continuing his story, he said, "I jumped over the counter and before he had time to reach the dagger I took him by the ear and started him for the gate." As the Indian tried to reach his six-shooter Johnny maneuvered to reach the derringer he often kept in his pocket. "I just let go, stepped behind and quick as a flash I had him by the other ear with my left hand and then I could reach my pistol. The other Indians were all looking on. I had him outdoors almost before he knew what had struck him." Johnny called for Hamilton to disarm his opponent, then noticed that Weasel Head's pistol had been cocked, which indicated a murderous intent. "I was so angry that I brought my pistol down smash full in the face, and he fell like a hog."

The Indian recovered and left but returned two months later with sixty braves. Weasel advanced on the fort and signalled that he wished to shake hands. Healy's only weapon that day was a penknife, but, because he wanted to avoid indicating fear by arming himself, he approached the Indian. Big Weasel was naked except for his breechclout, but he had on his best smile and carried a rifle in his left hand as he extended his right for a handshake. "I knew the Injun character," Johnny said, "and I saw at a glance what his plan was. He intended to kill me, but was going to touch me first . . . our hands met. That Injun never knew what happened to him! As his hand touched mine I gave him a sling and a twist as quick as a cat and with all my force. He hit the ground head on, then cried for mercy."

But Johnny avoided killing customers. He instead invited all the Indians in for a drink on the house. The other Indians accepted Weasel Head's misfortunes with nonchalance, allowing them to drink and eat with gusto. After these refreshments the guests traded all the robes they brought along. Whether they received more whiskey in exchange is unclear, but Big Weasel became a good friend and insisted that Johnny be made a member of the tribe. Thus, through quick thinking and powerful arms, Johnny "was taken in as a member of the Black Elk Band of warriors. They made an Injun of me!"

Healy had the friendship of a number of prominent Blackfeet, including Calf Shirt. In a rare understatement Healy referred to Calf Shirt as a "turbulent character," a soft description for a man who helped kill twelve white woodchoppers on the Missouri River in 1865. However, the story has extenuating circumstances, which Johnny related in the *Fort Benton Record*: Another Blood chief made the mistake of bragging at Fort Benton of his "coups" over whites, and two traders killed him on the spot. When the Bloods heard about the killing, they set out for Fort Benton to investigate the incident. Along the way the band of two-hundred warriors, Calf Shirt included, encountered the woodchoppers at Ophir, a new town site, and attacked them.

James Willard Schultz said that Calf Shirt was a powerful man, brave and brutal, "greatly feared by all the tribes with whom he was at war, as well as by his own people." Calf Shirt's tendency toward violence while in a drunken rage presaged his violent end. His last dispute was at Fort Kipp where he demanded whiskey despite lacking the money to pay for it. When trader Joe Kipp refused, Calf Shirt threatened to kill him and whipped out an old powder and ball revolver. Kipp, younger, quicker, and sober, reached for a loaded revolver that he always kept under the counter and blasted point blank at the chief. Calf Shirt walked away, staggering, and Kipp shot him again as he left the room. Other traders also opened fire but the chief walked on for one hundred yards, reaching a deep excavation and falling in. When examining his body later the traders counted sixteen bullet holes, any one of which might have been fatal. Although the traders admired the chief's last show, they put him under the river ice without shedding any tears for his loss.[35]

According to Blackfoot legend, the chief's wives recovered his body and found a medicine man capable of restoring his life. After the medicine man sang special songs Calf Shirt's cramped legs unfolded. Crowfoot and other Indians were aghast and restrained the medicine man who had called for a drink of whiskey for Calf Shirt, which would certainly have brought him to his feet—mean as hell. Never mind, they advised, we prefer him dead.

Kipp told the story to James Schultz, who wrote the first account of it. Johnny knew the story and told Adney about it, referring casually to the killing by "Joseph Kipp, an excellent citizen whose mother was an Indian of fine presence and character."[36]

# Trading at Whoop-Up

A number of visitors to Alberta described the prairie scene—the Indians, the buffalo, and the American traders. One of these, young Donald Graham, went out to Alberta in 1872-73 from Winnipeg and was especially thrilled by a buffalo hunt. The buffalo hunt was a memorable experience for many young men of western Canada and the States, white and Indian. Graham traveled on a Red River cart and made his first kills near Fort Edmonton. Later he traveled south and was amazed at the number of buffalo. "I never saw cattle thicker in any pasture than the buffalo herds we encountered. There must have been ten of thousands of them. We travelled in an open space not much more than half a mile across. The buffalo opened out in front of us as we passed and closed up behind us," he explained.[37]

Graham, later involved in the infamous Cypress Hills incident, called at Fort Whoop-Up where Donald Davis entertained and advised him. Graham wanted to go on to Fort Benton, but Davis warned him not to travel alone. "The Indians met would be Bloods and Blackfeet," Davis said, "and as they might be the worse of liquor, it would be very dangerous, to say the least." Graham waited for other travelers before leaving the fort.

Graham's description of the post's facilities give a clear view of the trading transactions: "The post consisted of three rooms, general living room and cooking room, store room, and trading room. Along the front of the latter was a passage way about seven or eight feet wide; into this the Indians come to do their trading. It was connected with the trading room by a trap door which could be let down quickly in an emergency. I was told that on no condition must Indians be allowed inside."

Graham perceived a flaw in the defenses: what prevented Indians from scrambling up on the roof and breaking in? Davis laughed. They had tried that once or twice, and the defenders "lit the candles for them" to permanently discourage the practice. "Lighting the candles for them" consisted of shooting through the roof with Winchester rifles whenever you heard footsteps above, which proved effective. Six men manned the post, including a black interpreter.

Graham learned that whiskey was "the greatest trading article. . . . This consisted of ten gallons of alcohol to a forty-gallon barrel filled with water and colored with burnt sugar." If this recipe prevailed throughout the Healy/Hamilton tenure, they sold a less vile concoction of tobacco, ginger, peppers, and other unwholesome ingredients that other traders have been charged with preparing.

Graham had a good chance to observe the trading process. He noted that the Indians proceeded in an unhurried manner, usually passing a small keg and a buffalo robe through the wicket. "Into the keg a half gallon of liquor was poured, which was the value of a robe at the post. This worked out at between fifty and sixty dollars for each gallon of alcohol."

Graham witnessed no disorder in the vicinity of the post. "The Indians were not encouraged to drink around the post, rather the reverse; but liquor was the cause of many bloody forays in their own lodges." Graham observed an example of Davis' care for an Indian who was wounded by

55

another shortly after leaving the post. "His wound was dressed by Mr. Davis and a bed made for him. He was at the post for several weeks, receiving every possible attention."

Graham's observations show more effort for critical objectivity than most accounts of the era. For a time he roamed the country with a party of wolfers, the bounty hunters from Fort Benton who killed and poisoned the carcasses of buffalo and gathered the hides of wolves who died feeding on them. Wolfers got from $2.50 to $3 for each hide at Benton, but they ranked even lower on the social scale than whiskey traders. After feeling a little anxious over the threatening manner of a wolfer he was traveling with, Graham reflected on his uneasiness. "I rode on feeling as if I were in a strange country, and as a matter of fact, I was, . . . north of the Red Deer River [was] a fairly orderly country consisting of Cree Indians, half-breeds, the Hudson Bay Company and British traders; south of the Red Deer river [were] Bloods, Blackfeet, whiskey traders, wolfers and American western influence—chaos, in fact."

Howell Harris, a young American bullwacker, left some impressions of the whiskey trade. He reached Montana from St. Louis in 1863 at seventeen years of age, hoping to find gold. By 1868 he took up freighting from Fort Benton and made his first trip to Fort Whoop-Up in 1871. Before Harris reached the post he heard an Indian had shot one of the traders just outside the stockade. Harris insisted that Indians burned down the original post while he was nearby with Al Hamilton. The only person inhabiting the place had been an Indian woman who perished in the flames. In the following year Harris freighted to Fort Conrad and got into several bloody fights with Indians. After a few more years of freighting Harris took up the more peaceful pursuit of ranching in Montana, then later went into the livery business at Fort Benton with Billy Rowe.

Other American traders, keen to emulate Healy and Hamilton, built Fort Stand-off, Fort Slide-out, Fort Kipp (Robber's Roost), and Fort Conrad in the early 1870s. Charles Thomas and Joe Kipp built Fort Stand-off in 1871 at the confluence of the Waterton and Belly rivers, naming it for an encounter with lawmen. Charles D. Hard, the U.S. deputy marshal of Helena, showed particular aggression against whiskey traders. He had a posse of soldiers in hot pursuit of Joe Kipp and caught his prey at the Cut Bank River. Kipp, the son of James Kipp, a famous early Missouri trader, argued that the river bank formed the Canadian border and Hard must turn back. The deputy doubted the accuracy of the trader's geography but he was not certain and, as Kipp threatened to shoot anyone who crossed, he desisted. Kipp and his men went their way north, chortling, covering another 110 miles before founding their post and naming it for his successful bluff of Hard.

# The Spitzee Cavalry

Another famous stand-off of the Whoop-Up country involved Johnny Healy. Of the several versions of the story, the one told by Healy shows a remarkably restrained tone. All of them, however, reveal the Irishman's fighting qualities.

Healy described the traders who followed him into Whoop-Up country as "the best band of prairie men that the world produced doing legitimate business. Wolfers, scorned by Healy and anyone else, then worked their way north. The wolfers were despised by Indians and other whites for their primitive, destructive ways. Each fall they set out from Fort Benton, hunted buffalo as wolf bait, then waited for wolves to feed on the buffalo. They sprinkled the dead buffalo with deadly strychnine, the wolves died as they were feeding, and the men gathered their pelts. Even in those hard days, this practice seemed brutal. Indians lost many dogs to poison and they killed the wolfers when they could. Wolfers, who had more reason to fear Indians than did the traders, wanted traders to respect the ban on the sale of repeating rifles and ammunition to natives.

Healy and the other traders showed little consideration for the wolfers' fears so they organized the Spitzee Cavalry. According to Paul Sharp, whose lively history, *Whoop-Up Country,* is a western classic, the Spitzee Calvary's ambitions went beyond gun control. The wolfers hoped to drive the traders entirely out of the Whoop-Up country. Healy and some others in Fort Benton believed that the I.G. Baker and Conrad commercial interests were backing the wolfers as a means of forcing out traders who bought goods from T.C. Power, Baker's big rival. Healy and Hamilton were among the traders affiliated with Power.

In their initial forays the Spitzee Cavalry terrorized a number of Power's traders into signing pledges enjoining them from selling arms and ammunition to Indians. By extending their restriction beyond repeating rifles the wolfers encroached severely on the customary trade. But the traders felt forced to sign the pledges when the wolfers showed up in force, heavily armed and talking mean. News of the wolvers' movements soon reached Healy, who knew himself to be their prime target as the biggest trader and notoriously uncooperative to interference with his business.

To eliminate any misunderstanding Healy bought the stock of a trader who the wolfers "fined" $1,300 in buffalo robes after he violated his oath and sold arms to Indians. Healy dispatched this message to the wolfers: "I have this day bought the stock of Williams, and am going to sell the Indians anything they want to buy. I will have traders out on the prairie. You may meet some of them. Please don't interfere with any of them, as they are under my orders, and if you have anything to say, come to me. I am the one who is responsible."[38]

A force of eighteen well-armed members of the Spitzee Cavalry soon called at Fort Whoop-Up where Healy received them graciously. He had sent all his assistants away except for his cook so that they would not be involved in gun play. Healy ordered another employee to ride off in a hurry and round up all other available men when the Spitzee Cavalry was seen approaching the post. "If they don't find me," Johnny said cryptically, "tell them to dig under the cellar, there they will find me."

Healy intended to stand up to the threats of a gang of bounty hunters. His problem was how to confront adversaries with a superior force. He lacked the necessary manpower, but he had a powerful piece of armament, a cannon, so his firepower potential exceeded that of his opponents.

The trader prepared the big room of the fort for a confrontation. At one end of the room there was a rail surrounding a platform. Under the room was a cellar where buffalo robes were stored "and there was a little beaver slide down into it, where I could slip if I had to." Healy prepared his little howitzer, loading it with six pounds of powder and three rounds of balls. "At one end of the room I cut out a piece of the log wall and I put this back in place and I set up the cannon so as to rake the whole store, and hung a blanket over the place." He cut the barrels off a shotgun, loading it with flattened bullets, loaded a couple of revolvers and a Winchester, "and put them all on a shelf under the counter so they would be in reach of my hand, and I was ready for them. I went about in my shirt sleeves. I was feeling just as good as I ever did in my life."

Impatient to begin, Healy rode out on the prairie looking for his foes. He met a friend who warned him that the cavalry had been trying to augment its force with local men because they heard that Healy had thirty or forty men waiting for them. As a keen student of human behavior in times of crisis, Healy was cheered by the news: "They've stopped to get more men," he said. "Then I've got them beat."

The cavalry eventually rode in and Healy admitted them to the post, inviting them to a supper that had been laid on for them. After a pleasant repast Healy decided the time had come to talk business in the big room. Healy took his place behind the counter and queried the visitors' concerns.

Harry "Kamoose" Taylor, an old enemy of Healy's, explained that they had heard that Healy sold guns to Indians and they would now like to have pen and paper so that they could properly record the formal proceedings to follow. Healy had a table placed against the wall where he had hidden the cannon "so I could blow the log, shot and all, out, and blow them all to hell. I had chairs brought out and they all took their seats around the table. Then the secretary Taylor got up and read a long paper, something about selling to the Injuns contrary to the orders of their organization . . . and against the wishes of all the white men in the country . . . and what did I have to say . . . 'Guilty or not guilty?'"

In telling this story years later Healy recalled that instead of preparing a set speech, he figured that his glibness and sense of the occasion would inspire his talk. Sure enough, he found words and addressed himself directly to Taylor, saying, "guilty—and you be damned. What right have you to come down here to try me? Who are you? What are you? A renegade from justice! You! You! You're a mad dog got among a pack of decent hounds and poisoned them."

Taylor lost his tongue for a time, but one of the other men, who said he represented the Baker and Conrad company, approached in a menacing manner. Healy brought out his shotgun and made a speech, accusing the men of intent to steal goods belonging to Tom Power, "a good man you owe for your own outfits. He was good to you and gave you credit. And you are owing him and now you would turn around and repay his kindness by destroying and confiscating his goods." An Irishman among the visitors, Mike Walsh, broke the ice after Healy finished talking. "Gentleman," he said, "I move that we all go down to the river and wash some of the wool out of our eyes."

Healy won the day through his belligerence and eloquence, and the story of his daring defiance added to his reputation. In another even more dramatic version of the episode, Healy threatened to drop his lighted cigar into an open keg of gunpowder, which sent his antagonists dashing for safety.

In the jubilation of victory Healy held a grudge only against Taylor, who got his nick-name "Kamoose," or "Woman Thief," from the Indians. Johnny believed that Taylor, who "was wanted for killing a man in Washington, though afterwards acquitted," had been a good enough "prairies lawyer" to pit the wolfers on the wrong course of action. He knew all the wolfers, and some were traders, too. "There were good men among them, the best there were in Montana, but there were some hard men also among them," he explained

# Cypress Hills Massacre

The "hard men" Johnny referred to included those who instigated the Cypress Hills Massacre, one of the more infamous confrontations between whites and Indians. This bloody event of 1873 had far-reaching implications in Whoop-Up country. While Healy was always reluctant to censure whites in any conflict with Indians, he probably considered the whites' behavior in this event reprehensible.

John Evans, a leader of the Spitzee Cavalry, and other wolfers were in an aggressive mood following an incident near Fort Whoop-Up. During the spring following Healy's stand-off of the Spitzee Cavalry, Indians killed two whites near the fort. Members of the Cavalry, which had been fading fast since their embarrassment at Fort Whoop-Up, called on Healy in great excitement over the killing of the two men. Healy had heard about the killings but felt little sympathy to the victims. "I didn't know what they did but they had been indiscreet about an Injun camp, and so it was a good deal their own fault."

The Wolfers saw the matter in a more serious light. They insisted that justice, honor, and self-respect demanded that they storm the little Indian village to avenge the whites' deaths—or so they said. To achieve their lofty purpose of upholding the values of civilization they needed ammunition but lacked cash. Healy, who had sound commercial reasons for keeping Indians alive and friendly, doubted that honor was the issue with the wolfers. "You want to go over there and wipe out that village, and you won't do it," Healy said. "I won't let you have any ammunition."

When the wolfers protested, Healy made an offer. If they gave him command, he would lead them to the village to search for the murderers and help hang them if found. But this plan didn't suit the wolfers, and Healy told them why. "Then you don't want to get the murderer. You want to murder and loot the village and take their goods and their horses and run them off." The truth made the wolfers uncomfortable, except for a big Canadian, George Hammond. Hammond, who was well-armed, denounced Healy as a swelled head over the Spitzee Cavalry stand-off. Healy slapped Hammond down and booted him out the door as the other wolfers laughed. Once more Healy prevailed.

Inevitably, the wolfers over-reacted to an incident with the Indians. The Indian theft of horses from a party of wolfers camping near Fort Benton on their return from their fall hunt in Whoop-Up country triggered the terrible affair at Cypress Hills in 1873. The wolfers hiked into Benton, angry and disgusted at their loss. The Army commander at Fort Benton lacked the men to help them recover their horses, so the wolfers returned, gathered a few volunteers, and set out to find the marauders. Besides John Evans, the force of hunters, trappers, and wolfers included Thomas Hardwick (the only one with a disreputable reputation), Ed Grace, George Hammond, Axis Lebompard (a French Indian friend of Healy's who had warned him of the Spitzee Cavalry's approach), and others.

The Fort Benton men crossed the Milk River and the international boundary as they followed the Indian trail due north toward Cypress Hills. At the trading post of Abe Farwell the group halted to rest and drink. Farwell was in a foul mood. Indians in the area had been restive and drinking heavily. Just the night before an Indian party that had enjoyed Farwell's hospitality stole thirty of his horses when they left. One of the horses had belonged to George Hammond, and the Indians returned it to him on his arrival in exchange for a suitable reward. The next morning Hammond discovered that they had stolen his horse again, and he was furious. "Why they have stolen my horse again, let's go over and take theirs in return," said Hammond. Farwell tried to restrain him. As the resident trader he stood to lose if Hammond and the others stirred up trouble.[39]

Farwell managed to restrain the Benton men while he went into the nearby Indian camp to discuss matters with Chief Little Soldier. Unfortunately, Little Soldier was too far gone with drink to understand much or to calm his young warriors who were aroused by the presence of aggressive whites. From this point the sequence of incidents becomes unclear. Both sides were growing more angry, and the Benton men became anxious when the Indians sent their women and children out of the camp. Someone opened fire, and a battle followed—Farwell believed that Hammond started the shooting. The outcome was clear from the beginning because the whites were protected behind the cutbank of a shallow coulee while the Indians were in the open. Volleys of rifle fire from the whites devastated the Indian ranks, but they rallied three times to attack the whites' position from the front, then flanked it to force them to retreat to the fort. An Indian killed Ed Grace during this attack. From within the walls the whites continued to fire, pinning the Indians in the field before the fort until darkness, when they managed to slip away.

The aftermath of the battle was still more brutal, according to Farwell, whose testimony later presented a black picture of the wolfers. After the Indians withdrew, the whites invaded the Indian lodges and slaughtered everyone they found, including children and women, whom they first raped. In the morning they pulled down the lodges and made a great bonfire of the Indians' possessions.

Some of the raiders hit the trail to continue looking for their stolen horses. Some days later they showed up at Fort Whoop-Up and heard that a party of Bloods, who they thought to be the horse thieves, was camped some miles to the west. The Benton men pushed on and almost over-reached themselves. The Bloods had fifty lodges, were well-armed, and angry. With some daring the whites called on the chief to ask about their horses and were relieved to learn that the Bloods did not have them. After this encounter they hurried back to Fort Benton.

61

Most of the people in Fort Benton, after listening to the stories of the raiders, applauded them for their manliness in teaching the Indians about justice. In Canada people had a markedly different response: Intrusive Yankees had victimized the Canadian Indians, slaughtering them savagely and indiscriminately in a drunken fury without troubling to find the actual thieves. A roar of disapproval came from Ottawa and elsewhere. The Canadian government felt unable to ignore its obligations to police the West.

Canada's press described the invaders harshly as "fiends in human shape," "desperadoes," and "American scum bent on murder." Editors ignored that George Hammond, perhaps the most provocative of all the wolfers, was one of several Canadians involved.[40]

Another Canadian, Donald Graham, a well-educated man, wrote a different account of the affair from that given by Farwell. Graham's story has credibility because he had reliable accounts of the massacre from some of the participants. According to historian Hugh Dempsey, however, Graham had not traveled from Fort Whoop-Up to Cypress Hills with some wolfers as he later claimed. At any rate, Graham put the number of Indians killed at thirteen rather than the forty some Canadians claimed. More significantly, Graham argued that the Mounted Police and Rev. John McDougall, who later traveled in the area, gave reports that exaggerated the details and were dead wrong in presuming that the battle was an "unwarrantable massacre." Graham concluded that the preacher and the police would have returned the fire of the Indians if they had found themselves in the same position as the wolfers.[41]

Graham faulted both the wolfers and Indians for acting hastily, and he believed the true culprits were the whiskey traders. Montanans would have rejected Graham's view just as they did the Canadians'. Bias against the Indians—based on a deep-rooted fear of them—made it impossible for most people to reflect objectively. The wolfers were the darlings of the public's eye, heroes, and the shock troops of civilization who had given a nasty bunch of savages just what they deserved.

Canadians were thwarted in getting the kind of justice they believed was warranted by the Cypress Hills affair, but their concern signalled new policies for the West.

# 5

# The Red Coats Are Coming

*[The Mounties] fetched their men
every time.*
—*Fort Benton Record*

In spring 1875, nearly two years after the Cypress Hills battle, the Canadian government's investigation of the violence finally reached Fort Benton. The investigation was conducted by the recently established North West Mounted Police. Lt. Col. Acheson G. Irvine learned much from Alexis Lebompard, who had witnessed the fight, and at Fort Benton Charles and William Conrad, partners of I. G. Baker, cooperated fully. Another police officer, Col. James F. Macleod, also interviewed witnesses in Montana and gathered enough evidence to support indictments. The Benton merchants were not hostile to the Mounties and welcomed their efforts to transform the Alberta frontier into a law-abiding community. Security was better for business.

As a result of the police investigation Canada issued warrants for the arrest of John Evans, George Hammond, Thomas Hardwick, Trevanian Hale, John Duval, George Bell, Jeff Devereaux, Philander Vogle, John McFarland, James Hughes, James Marshall, Charles Smith, Charles Harper, and Moses Solomon. Washington officials ordered Montana Governor B. F. Potts and United States Marshals Charles D. Hard and John X. Beidler to cooperate in the extradition proceedings. Federal officers arrested some of the men at Fort Benton in June 1875, but without the assistance of County Sheriff Hale. Unlike American officials and Fort Benton merchants, ordinary folks in Montana vociferously opposed the Canadian prosecution and denounced federal officers for assisting it.

During the extradition hearings in Helena people demonstrated all over the territory. What was the West coming to, the protesters asked, if white men could no longer defend themselves against Indian attacks? They also questioned the American government's willingness to help the Hudson's Bay Company run American trade rivals out of Canada.

The extradition issue also provoked anti-British sentiments among Fort Benton's large Irish population. The Montana Irish often expressed their bias against Britain and supported the Fenians, an Irish organization that actively resisted British rule in Ireland. In Benton the Fenians were led by John J. Donnelly, a lawyer who seized on the extradition cause to decry British aggression in Canada. Donnelly went beyond talk; he earlier led abortive invasions of Canada from Vermont and Dakota Territory.

The prosecution made trader Abel Farwell its chief witness. The defense caught Farwell in several lies, including details about the decapitation of Chief Little Soldier and telling another trader soon after the battle that the Indians had started it, discounting his colorful account of the wolfers' atrocities. Neutral witnesses, like the métis men who looked on without getting involved, said the Indians started the shooting. Because the Canadians' evidence was inconclusive, the court commissioner refused to grant extradition.

The people at Fort Benton went wild when they heard the verdict, and when the freed men reached town a joyous festival commenced, with rousing speeches by Donnelly and others. John Evans soon took commercial advantage of his celebrity status to open a saloon—fittingly named "The Extradition."

The matter remained unsettled, and the police arrested Philander Vogle, George M. Bell, and James Hughes in Canada. In Winnipeg the government set the trial on charges of "wanton and atrocious slaughter of peaceable and inoffensive people." Folks in Fort Benton raised money to hire a crack defense attorney while the prosecution fretted over the lack of eyewitnesses. The best witnesses were still under indictment and would leave the States for Canada only if the prosecution granted them immunity.[42]

The long-delayed trial opened in June 1876. Abel Farwell, four métis, and four Indians served as witnesses for the government, but the prosecutor failed to secure the testimony he wanted from them. A Winnipeg priest urged the men to tell the truth, leading three of them to testify for the defense while only two testified for the government. The accused were acquitted in short order. James Wickes Taylor, the American consul in Winnipeg, reached the interesting conclusion that T. C. Power had deliberately misrepresented "what was an ordinary Indian fight, as an outrage by the whites, and by criminal prosecutions, to exclude competition from the Cypress Hills in the trade for buffalo hides." Farwell, "a liar and perjurer," according to Taylor, was Power's instrument. Whatever the truth of the matter, other evidence indicates that the two major Fort Benton traders, Power and Baker, were not shy backwoodsmen when it came to emulating the nasty tricks of some better-known eastern robber barons.

# Mounties Go West

For several years in the early 1870s government leaders in Ottawa ignored cries of alarm about lawless conditions on the prairies. Some reports gave sensational accounts of rapacious American traders terrorizing Indians and fostering disorder. Canada needed to send a large army to control its western provinces, argued some extremists. The government disliked the idea of supporting a western army and of alarming Americans with troops on the border. Americans generally resented Britain's aid of the South during the Civil War, and Fenians in the States were always warning of imperial aggression.

# WANTED IMMEDIATELY BY GOVERNMENT.

**20** Active, Healthy Young Men, for service in the Mounted Police Force in the North West Territory. They must be of good character, single, between the ages of 20 and 35 years, capable of riding. They will have to serve for a term of 3 (three) years. Their pay will be 75 cents per diem, and everything (uniform, rations, board, &c., &c.) found, and on completion of service will receive a free grant of 160 acres of land, with right of choice. For further particulars, apply without delay to Captain C. Young, Halifax Hotel. 3t pd    sept30

*Mountie-recruiting advertisement from an unidentified Ontario newspaper, c. 1873.*

Ottawa finally found an answer to this dilemma by creating the North West Mounted Police in 1873. The police force consisted of six divisions of fifty men charged with the duties of patrolling the border against smuggling, resisting any Fenian invasions, and keeping an eye on the Indians.

Organizing and training the force took a full year, and Whoop-Up traders knew that conditions would change when the Mounties reached the West. Johnny Healy figured that 1874 would be his last season and made arrangements to clear out of Canada in a timely fashion. To inform Indians about the police, Ottawa commissioned the Reverend John McDougall. He told the Blackfeet that protection from the Americans was coming from the Queen. The government would not ask them to join in any battle, but just to greet the police in a friendly way.

John McDougall despised the Whoop-Up traders for their role in demoralizing the Indians. He knew first hand the ravages of the whiskey trade. McDougall gives an interesting but suspect account of his reception at Fort Whoop-Up. He said Healy greeted him by calling out, "unbuckle and lay off your armory for the moment, Parson John." The preacher named the trader as Joseph Healy, but more likely it was

*Sam Steele as a young Mountie in Alberta where he first met Johnny Healy.*
—Glenbow Archives

Johnny rather than his brother who received the reverend. The trader and his men were "pretty well braced" with liquor, but Healy was willing to talk. He assured McDougall that the government had no reason for intervention because he and his friends always kept the rough element out of the country. "For instance, there was so-and-so," McDougall quoted Healy as saying. "He came in and was going to run things. He stands under the sod at Standoff. And there was [another rough character]. . . . He went wild, and we laid him out at Freeport. . . . These bad men could not live in this country. We simply could not allow it."[43]

McDougall described the encounter as if he gave Healy the first news of the Mounties when he read him the government's proclamation. According to the preacher, "Healy drew a long breath and gave a solemn sign of resignation." McDougall also quoted trader Donald Davis's announcement that "we will flood this country for one more year with whiskey." It is doubtful that Davis, a future member of Parliament, would have been so indiscreet.

Inhabitants of Whoop-Up country received a steady flow of reports on the westward progress of the police in their remarkable scarlet coats. From Manitoba, with flags flying and bands playing, the force set out on July 8, 1874, for an eight-hundred mile march. The men soon realized that they would find progress difficult. Carts broke down and horses went lame. The men, inexperienced in western travel, suffered considerably. And, adding heavily to their discomfort, the police knew little about the lay of the land in the western regions; their half-breed guides had not traveled west of Cypress Hills. The long march began to resemble an ignominious retreat as discarded equipment and abandoned horses littered their route. News of the inglorious march reached Fort Benton from many sources, and more than the Fenians were amused at the clumsiness of eastern Canadians in "protecting" the prairies.

By mid-August the police feared that because of their inaccurate maps and inept guides they might be caught on the open plains by early seasonal snows. Summer was devastating enough with livestock stampeding all directions during thunderstorms and dying for lack of grass. And sometimes lightening would spark deadly prairie fires. An early blizzard would certainly decimate them.

Natural vicissitudes crippled them enough, but the Mounties suffered too from exaggerated fears of the Indians and the whiskey traders. They heard rumors that Johnny Healy had gathered a large force of gunmen and Indians to defend his territory. The thought of armed resistance by a few unsoldierly Yankee rascals did not worry the police in Ottawa. But the harsh realities of travel in the western lands increasingly troubled the Mounties. That Healy bunch knew the West and knew how to defend their home ground. By frightening contrast the police realized they had demonstrated their incompetence in making even a peaceful march. As for fighting against a determined, skilled army of western men—well, could they doubt the outcome?

The Mounties stumbled into Whoop-Up country in early September as they reached the South Saskatchewan River. Their maps showed other rivers flowing into the South Saskatchewan from the west, but they could not find any. Their information indicated that Fort Whoop-Up lay at the junction of the Bow and Belly rivers, instead of its actual site at the St. Mary and Belly rivers. After one scouting party returned without finding Fort Whoop-Up, another tried and also failed. Although the Mounties were within seventy-five miles of the famed whiskey fort and a only few miles off the much-traveled Whoop-Up Trail from Fort Benton, they had hopelessly lost their bearings. Lt. Col. George Arthur French noted gloomily:

> And so we were at last at our journey's end, the Bow and Belly rivers, where there was supposed to be such luxuriant pasturage; according to most accounts, a perfect Garden of Eden, climate milder than Toronto, etc. As far as our experience goes that vicinity for at least sixty or seventy miles in every direction is little better than a desert, not a tree to be seen anywhere, ground parched and poor, and wherever there was a little swamp it was destroyed by the buffalo.[44]

Snow began to fall. Men and animals desperately needed a week's rest, but they feared pausing in the threatening weather. The police marched to the Sweetgrass Hills near the international border, looking for food caches they hoped boundary survey parties had left behind. Finding none, French had to swallow his pride and seek help in a hurry. With a small party he rode to Fort Benton, a well-marked place on his map—the origin of the notorious whiskey traders for whose suppression the police had made their long trek.

Folks in Benton welcomed French warmly; few there defended the whiskey trade. They gave French all the information he needed, including a memo from I. G. Baker describing the whiskey trade and the country. Baker explained that the whiskey traders had been in retreat for some time. With a force of fifty men, Baker said, the Mounties could easily control all of Whoop-Up country. French bought food and equipment and returned to his men to find that an American trader had already reached the camp and opened a store for the travelers. Soon, guided by Jerry Potts and Charles Conrad, who both worked for I. G. Baker, the Mounties resumed their journey. On October 9 they finally reached Fort Whoop-Up.

Donald Davis, nominally in charge of Fort Whoop-Up, was absent, as was Healy. Dave Akers and a few Indians were the only ones on hand to greet the Canadians. Akers either worked for Healy and Hamilton or was just squatting. By this time few traders were left in the country; most had gone to Benton to find a new line of business. Johnny, always reluctant to credit the Mounties with stopping his trade, received buffalo robes for the next couple of seasons.

Back in eastern Canada many stories circulated about the historic march of the Mounties. Journalists with nationalist sympathies, aware that strong heroes make good stories, described events as they might have happened. Soon a pleasing legend developed: the Mounties had "won" the West; they were the pioneers and the conquerors and all things wonderful and virtuous.

The expression of tribute about the Mounties always getting their man evolved much later in the popular conception of the officers. But on their first march they did get their man, in a sense. They got Johnny Healy, or at least by virtue of their creation, forced him to stop trading whiskey. So they became heroes despite clumsy beginnings. In time they became an efficient organization—and Johnny Healy would one day acknowledge their prowess by calling on them when he got into a tough spot.

Historians of the legendary police force have been too nationalistic to praise Johnny Healy, but the whiskey peddler from Montana contributed mightily to the organization's fame. Healy, and others like him, inspired the Canadian government to establish a western police force that brought order to two distant frontiers: the prairie provinces and the Yukon. Johnny's place in the story of the Mounties in the Yukon is considered later.

Folks at Fort Benton learned to respect the work of the Mounties in keeping order among the Indians and otherwise enforcing the law. The *Fort Benton Record* may have inspired the familiar adage, "The Mounties always get their man." Historian Paul Sharp cites this terse statement in the April 13, 1877, newspaper commending the Mounties: "They fetched their men every time." The author may have been editor W. H. Buck or another writer, conceivably even reporter John J. Healy.[45]

# 6

# Wearing Many Hats

*It was not done to talk too much
in the old days.*
—Johnny Healy

Since 1870 or 1871 Johnny Healy had exchanged his furs for trading goods with Tom Power. As he did for many other traders and trappers, Power furnished merchandise for the Indian trade on a year-round invoice and took his money when the robes were sold. Another person involved in Healy's trading was Portus Weare, a commission merchant who handled the sale of the robes, then remitted to Power what Healy owed for goods. Portus Weare later became a close associate of Healy in the Yukon trade and other Alaskan ventures.

Born in Michigan in 1842 and educated well by his banker father, Weare chose to make a career of commercial ventures in the West. He precociously established a grain and commission business in Chicago in 1862 before moving into the buffalo-robe trade. He dealt with Healy and many others until the buffalo perched on the brink of extinction. Weare moved easily to other successful ventures in cattle and grain. He and Healy remained friends during the two decades before their next business together.

Tom Power did well in trade and by the mid-1880s was one of the wealthiest and most influential men in Montana—a true "merchant prince" of the northern plains. Power, I. G. Baker, the Conrad brothers, and others who had established themselves at Fort Benton after the Civil War came to take a rather grand view of commercial prospects. These merchants figured the nation's westward-moving population would eventually settle the entire vast region of the plains extending to the Rockies, and they stood ready to assist development and reap rewards.

Meanwhile the Indians and the buffalo roamed the plains. The Indians wanted goods and could provide furs and buffalo robes. Power and Baker established far-flung transportation and trading networks from west, south, and north of Fort Benton. With steamboats already reaching Benton at the head of Missouri, these far-sighted merchant princes augmented the fleet and built warehouses and outlets for trade and transportation.

Tom Power had a modest start. In 1867 he arrived at Fort Benton with a load of goods to sell to gold stampeders. Soon his brother John joined him and the ambitious men quickly rivaled I. G. Baker in enterprise. Isaac Gilbert Baker came to Fort Benton in 1864 as a clerk for Pierre Chouteau, Jr., before establishing a partnership in fur trading with his brother George a year later. George sold his interest to the Conrad brothers—William, Charles, and John—in 1873-74.

These princes were staunch Republicans and Tom Power later became one of Montana's first U.S. senators. These men traded in whiskey as much as Healy, though they pretended otherwise. They supplied peddlers such as Healy with whiskey and illegal arms and ammunition for trade with the Indians. The arms sales became a sensitive issue during the Indian campaigns of the 1870s, but the princes denied violating the federal laws they considered restrictive.

Healy used his influence with congressional delegate Martin Maginnis to help Power counter the threat of Canadian customs on American goods shipped over the line. Power secured a permit from Canadian authorities allowing him to ship goods from England or eastern Canada in bond to the western provinces. The arrangement gave him an advantage over the Hudson's Bay Company because of cheaper transportion via the States to western Canada. Power got Healy, a Democrat, to help by lobbying Representative Maginnis for an exclusive permit that would enable Power to freeze out the Bakers. Healy told Maginnis that the permit would benefit himself as well as Power, adding, "I understand that I. G. Baker is after the same favor—but I must say that you owe him nothing. . . . Tom will call on you and explain matters fully." As it turned out, the government granted all the Fort Benton traders permits, so Power's monopoly bid failed—but not for lack of Healy's help.[46]

Power came to some kind of agreement with Baker and other major traders, and the Americans prospered by dominating the western Canadian trade. I. G. Baker provisioned the Mounties for years, and other Fort Benton firms brought settlers their favorite English-made goods. With the benefit of the bonding arrangement a large international trade developed on the Northwest frontier to enrich the merchants of Fort Benton.

Johnny was a loyal Democrat, but his business interests took priority. Although the Bakers and Conrads were Democrats, too, Johnny's ties to T. C. Power, a Republican, proved stonger. Maginnis looked after all the leading Montana merchants, including the powerful S. T. Hauser of Helena, who invested in both Power's and Baker's companies. As Paul Sharp wrote, "the Benton men had little difficulty in securing favors from the United States government," a cozy deal that "frequently went so far as to call for the shifting of army troops or the redrawing of Indian reservation boundaries to satisfy the desires of the merchant princes of the northern plains."[47]

Canadians also fell under the influence of the trade out of Fort Benton. In exchange for lucrative stock, for instance, Lt. Gov. Edgar Dewdney secured the Mounted Police provisioning contract, among others, for I. G. Baker's company. Fort Benton so dominated Canadian trade that half the money Ottawa appropriated for policing the North West Territories went to Montana traders. Baker also got the contract to supply Canada's reservation Indians with beef after 1877, spending up to half a million dollars annually to buy cattle for shipment north. Some Canadians complained to their government about so enriching the American traders, but its support of the Benton economy prevailed for years.

The already high cost of shipping from Benton to Canada threatened to rise more as the buffalo trade declined. Without robes to haul, freighters deadheaded on their return trips. Fortunately, Nicholas Sheran, an Irish immigrant to New York who took up gold prospecting after the Civil War, discovered coal near modern Lethbridge, Alberta. Sheran convinced Tom Power that hauling coal to Fort Benton made sense, even at $25 a ton freight cost. Sheran also provided coal for the police posts and other Canadian settlements before Sir Alexander T. Galt, using British capital, expanded coal mining into a major industry for southern Alberta.

## Healy's Woes

Back at Sun River after withdrawing from Fort Whoop-Up in 1874, Johnny Healy felt restive. He had plenty of money-making schemes but lacked the capital to carry them out. He made good money during his years in Canada, but his attempt to sell his trading post to the Mounties failed. His bravado in refusing to quit Canada before he was ready cost him dearly. He had to pay extra for the goods he exchanged for robes, then got caught with a large inventory of robes when the market crashed. In 1875 he sold 2,500 robes for $6 each, a dollar or so off the usual price, but he held many more that he could sell only at ruinous prices.

Healy blamed Power for the misfortunes he suffered while closing down his Canadian trade. In a letter to congressional delegate Martin Maginnis in August 1876, Healy complained that Power had "gone into the swindling business as it pays better." He believed Power was robbing him and he felt defenseless. "I am a total wreck financially and have none to blame but Power for it," Healy wrote. In all he lost $12,000 on his buffalo robes—a fortune to him.[48]

Elsewhere in his letter Johnny held Power only partially responsible for his woes, noting that a plague of grasshoppers had wiped out his farming investments; also, he acknowledged a slump in the territorial economy after many Montanans stampeded to the Black Hills goldfields. "The only thing that can save us," he told Maginnis, "is a railroad to the head of navigation and I think your Missouri River appropriation will help that matter."

Healy sued Power in 1879 over the low returns he netted for his robes, but the litigation failed to expose any fraud by Power. The merchant prince's attempt to dominate trade at Fort Benton and drive out smaller operators like Healy, who lacked capital, aroused Johnny's ire. But Power's tactics hurt Healy less than the 1876 tariff schedule, which doubled the taxes due on imported robes and pelts. Market prices on robes fell sharply during this period, leaving Johnny with an excess of robes on which he had already paid a high tariff.

Johnny hoped Maginnis would reward him for his long and loyal political support. "Times are very bad here," he wrote the delegate in 1878, "nothing doing—but all hoping," He confessed tactfully, "some of my friends have been pushing me all winter for to write you, and press myself. . . . I am satisfied that you will find an opening for me when you can." Apparently Healy hoped Maginnis could influence an Army contract for the trader, but nothing came of it.[49]

Healy and his brother Tom worked hard to develop their interests at Sun River after they pulled out of Fort Whoop-Up. In one of their first projects they built an addition to their grist mill. The *Fort Benton Record* saluted their enterprise, stating, "This year they will turn out the finest flour produced in Montana or anywhere and invite farmers of the Teton and the Highwood to bring in wheat."[50]

The Healys figured in the social as well as the commercial news from Sun River as when "numerous members of the Healy family performed the principal parts" in a musical show. "Lillie, age 7, would do credit to Jenny Lind," according to a *Fort Benton Record* reviewer.

Johnny went north with wagons to gather buffalo robes in May 1876, returning some six weeks later. The *Record* needed little detail in identifying Healy in news or social notes as he was one of the best known men in the area by this time. The reputation he developed later in the North, though, made references to his popularity interesting. "Healy is one of the most popular and genial residents and his absence is always regretted," according to the *Record*. Even given the tendency of a newspaper to speak well of a friend and advertiser (Healy advertised his flour as "Unsurpassed by any brand"), others must have recognized his geniality.

# Healy the Journalist

Johnny's various business ventures, including an attempt to develop a town site at a place at Boulder, Montana, fell on hard times. In August 1877 he moved to Fort Benton to become "the local and general agent for the *Fort Benton Record*." His job to "collect all bills due and solicit subscriptions at Benton or elsewhere" resulted in less of a comedown for the once-prosperous trader than it first might appear, since Johnny became a part owner of the paper as well as its business manager. When he traveled from Benton to Helena, the rival *Independent* graciously conceded that the *Record* "could not have a better agent."

Johnny made a major contribution to both journalism and history in 1878-79 with a series of personal reminiscences published in the *Fort Benton Record*. Initially he hesitated to write the stories, fearing people might think he was aggrandizing himself. Yet he believed that his experiences could instruct others, particularly regarding his dealings with Indians. He believed, for instance, that many people either forgot or never knew what terrors the Indians had caused in earlier days. He wrote:

> Hundreds—yes, thousands, of unfortunate victims are known to have met their doom along the current highways leading to the Pacific coast. Hundreds upon hundreds of families, of whom nothing is known but that they died miserably upon the plains, have been found and buried or left to molder and mingle with the dust; and those numbers are swelled to still greater apportions [*sic*] by a vast army of unfortunate beings of whose fate nothing has ever been learned or can ever be recorded.

By beginning his long series of newspaper reminiscences with an account of his adventures on the Oregon Trail, Healy affirmed his convictions about pioneers and their nemeses. He firmly believed in but one Indian policy: Whites must appreciate Indians for their past atrocities and their potential for doing more harm.

Healy wrote engaging stories with lively details in an interesting style, though they were sometimes slow-paced. For the most part he avoided the kind of moralizing common among many writers of the time and only occasionally intruded with his general reflections. Montanans enjoyed reading his "Frontier Sketches" in the *Fort Benton Record*. The Helena *Independent* commented, "Mr. Healy does not need to varnish his sketches for his adventures in these mountains are as full of romance as the most brilliant of imaginative writers could desire . . . and they are the records of facts."[51]

Johnny often expressed admiration for the region's earliest pioneers. As a young dragoon in Utah he eagerly studied the adventurers of Jim Bridger. And as a journalist he was among the first to call attention to the particular role played by "men of the mountains and plains" or "mountaineers"—the first traders and trappers, who, in Johnny's time, had not yet been celebrated by historians.

"My definition of a mountaineer is this:" Johnny wrote, "a man who was able to literally 'live off his rifle' in the heart of the fiercest wilderness, hundreds of miles from the habitations of civilized man, and without a single human companion." He was thinking of men like "Bridger, Fitzpatrick, the two Carsons, Vanderberg, Johnson,

Beckwourth, Mildrum and other genuine mountaineers." With "a good horse, rifle and knife," Johnny continued, a mountaineer "was the most independent and self-reliant man on earth."[52]

Healy expressed the essence of a mountaineer's skills in terms of always being wary—"to detect his enemy before the latter saw him. Herein lay the whole problem of safety from the Indian prowler. . . . These men practiced precautions [in choosing campsites and travel routes] which now seem far-fetched and almost absurd," Johnny wrote. Aside from his own keen sense of observation and his rifle, "the mountaineer's dearest possession was his horse. . . . There was not a mountaineer worth mentioning whose life was not saved scores of times by the sagacity, the swiftness or the endurance of his Indian bred horse."

The full scope of Healy's journalism is difficult to measure. Historian Paul Sharp believes that Johnny wrote regularly for the *Fort Benton Record* as early as 1875 and cites unsigned articles critical of the Mounted Police, among others. All of Montana's newspapers commented upon reports in the Canadian press that criticized Americans generally or Fort Benton traders in particular. When the Reverend John McDougall, a stern critic of the Yankees, issued a pamphlet damning their illicit dealing, the *Record* argued that it "was on behalf of the Hudson's Bay Company." A writer in the *Record*—Healy perhaps, because he identified himself as a former whiskey trader—denounced McDougall for condemning "every American in the Northwest . . . as a murderer, cut throat and whiskey trader." The preacher too readily exaggerated the faults of Americans, the writer believed, because a few of them had "followed the example of Canadians and half-breeds in trading whiskey." This and other unsigned articles published in 1875 accurately reflect Johnny's sentiments on the Canadian censure of traders, the treatment of them by police, and antagonism over the disruption of what had been a lucrative business.[53]

Although Healy had no conflicts with the police over peddling whiskey, other traders were reluctant to obey the law. The *Record* commented hotly about the prosecution of J. D. Weatherwax of Fort Benton. Police charged him with selling whiskey to Indians from a post at Pine Coulee. They conveniently arrested him near the newly built police post at Fort Macleod, where Weatherwax maintained another store. He denied involvement with the Pine Coulee trader, who fled prosecution, but the Canadians fined and jailed him anyway.

In a *Fort Benton Record* article, Healy or another writer, perhaps editor W. H. Buck, tore into the Canadians. "To the scarlet uniforms belongs the fame—we will not mention the gain—of destroying the whiskey traffic," and the police now were jailing innocent men. "We know from experience that wherever the English flag floats, might is right, but we had no idea that the person and property of American citizens would be trifled with. We surmised, however, that on our frontier, within marching distance of our troops, almost within hearing of our gas-bag . . . legislator, the Bull dogs would be properly chained and controlled."[54]

Because Healy and many of the other Fort Benton Irish were Fenians, highly charged rhetoric, such as calling the Canadian police "mounted grabbers of spoil," was proper form. But, according to Sharp, other citizens of Benton objected to the slur and got Healy fired from his editorial position. Sharp's view is difficult to substantiate, as is whether Healy was an editor or a regular contributor as early as 1875.

*Magazine sketch of a whiskey trader's trial by Mounties at Spitzee Post, c.1875.*
—Glenbow Archives

# 7

# Warpath

*Hear me, my chiefs,*
*I am tired; my heart is sick and sad.*
*From where the sun now stands*
*I will fight no more, forever.*
                    —Chief Joseph

I n spring 1875, while waiting on the Marias River for a wagon train from Whoop-Up, Johnny Healy suddenly found himself besieged by a hostile party of marauding Sioux. The Indians set fire to the I. G. Baker station where he holed up. Fortunately, the green logs repelled the flames, sparing Johnny's shelter. But the Sioux did not give up so quickly; they held him at bay in the log structure four days and nights while they considered other ways to take his life. On the fifth day Johnny ran out of water. Cautiously venturing outside, he found that the Indians had left as quietly as they had appeared. The next day a couple of his employees arrived and they all set out to find the war party, without success.

This was the year the economy turned glum for Healy. His slowness in pulling out of the trade in Canada set him back financially. By 1876 he was willing to undertake anything to make money. He even tried to interest congressional representative Martin Maginnis in funding a mercenary force against the Indians. "Nothing left for me now but to join Gibbon or some of those fighting fellows," he wrote that August, barely a month after Custer's misfortune at the Little Big Horn. "I can take 100 white men and 100 to 200 Blood Indians to fight the Sioux providing I can get any authority to do so. In fact I am open for any enterprise now that don't necessitate road agency."[55]

Although Johnny needed money, he was serious about organizing a force of irregulars to destroy the Sioux. He remembered well how they terrorized him at I.G. Baker's stage station in 1875. For years he had lived warily on the frontier. Now, as more whites moved west, the threat of Indian warfare increased.

## Frontier Tensions

For nearly a decade the Army tried to establish its presence in Montana, starting with Fort C. F. Smith in 1866, but they still found it difficult to contain the Indians and protect the new settlers flowing into the country. White pressures on the Sioux and Cheyennes crowded them into southeastern Montana, where they in turn forced the other Indians from their homelands toward the mountains and white settlements farther west. The whole territory was upset. Hysteria among the whites and incidents of Indian aggression disrupted the Army's plans for keeping peace.

From 1865 to 1867 Montana's acting governor and territorial secretary, Thomas Francis Meagher, contributed to the turmoil. An Irish native banished to Tasmania in 1849 for sedition, Meagher escaped the authorites and immigrated to New York in 1852. During the Civil War he organized an Irish brigade, got an appointment as general, and fought well in several campaigns. After the war he moved to Montana. Meagher viewed the Indian threat with strident alarm and demanded more federal troops. Such views disturbed Gen. William Tecumseh Sherman, commander of the Division of the Missouri, which included Montana. "I fear civilians in the style of T. Francis Meagher may involve the frontier in needless war," he wrote another officer in 1866.[56]

Over the winter of 1866-67 settler John Bozeman believed the Sioux under Red Cloud would invade the Gallatin Valley. Though he lacked evidence to support the claim, Bozeman warned the valley's settlers to prepare for an evacuation. In response to the threat, Meagher wired President Ulysses Grant, saying, "The most populous and prosperous portion of our Territory . . . is threatened by the Sioux. The greatest alarm reasonably prevails. . . . Danger is imminent. . . . We earnestly entreat permission from the War Department to raise a force of one thousand volunteers for menaced quarters to be paid by General Government."

After the Sioux killed John Bozeman, Meagher acted without looking for the government's approval—which it probably would have denied—and issued a call for six hundred volunteers. Under General Meagher the volunteers spent $1.1 million gearing up for a Sioux attack that never came. The idle army awaited orders from its commander when word came that Meagher had drowned in the Missouri river at Fort Benton in July 1867. Critics said he was drunk; supporters claimed he was pushed.

Indians continued sporadic raids on travelers and settlers in Montana, particularly as gold discoveries brought in hordes of prospectors. The U.S. Army designated a separate military district for Montana in 1866, with Fort Shaw the regimental headquarters. Conflicts increased in 1868 with Blackfeet attacks along the overland route from Minnesota to Montana. A raid that year on the Upper Yellowstone at Dearborn Creek and another in 1869 near Fort Benton motivated some of the town's residents to shoot down two innocent, friendly Indians in the street. Retaliatory raids by Piegans, Bloods, and Blackfeet cost the whites several lives and a thousand horses.

In 1870, after the Indians killed a well-known settler near Helena, the Army declared war on the Piegans, which culminated in the massacre of 173 friendly Piegans, including 53 women and children, by troops under Maj. Eugene M. Baker. Conflicts became less frequent for several years after that bloody episode, then increased markedly as the prospects of gold drew whites into the sacred Black Hills, enraging the Sioux under Sitting Bull. In 1874 Lt. Col. George Armstrong Custer led troops to the Black Hills to restore peace.

Two years later the Army decided to route the hostile Sioux and Cheyennes from their stronghold in eastern Montana. Gen. George

Crook led forces northward from Wyoming to rendezvous with Brig. Gen. Alfred H. Terry, who marched west from Fort Abraham Lincoln near Bismarck, North Dakota. At the same time troops from Fort Shaw, Camp Baker, and Fort Ellis in Montana moved to join Crook and Terry for the destruction of the Sioux.

In May 1876 the Montana soldiers under Col. John Gibbon joined forces with Terry's command, supported by Custer's Seventh Cavalry, on the Yellowstone. Terry ordered Custer to follow an Indian trail up the Rosebud but to avoid detection so the Army could keep its advantage of surprise. Custer, ambitious and frustrated at being passed over for Terry's command, acted impetuously when he discovered his proximity to the Indians; he believed his command could outmatch all the Sioux. On June 25, 1876, he led his troops to the charge for the last time. The Sioux under Gall and Crazy Horse counterattacked and annhilated Custer's entire force—some 260 men.

That summer folks in Fort Benton and Sun River grew anxious about the Indians. A mass meeting in Sun River spawned a proposal to create a militia dubbed the Sun River Rangers. On July 14, the *Fort Benton Record* reported a settler's prediction that "A horrible outbreak is feared at any time." Colonel Gibbon had already taken most of Montana's soldiers to eastern Montana, leaving few to protect the settlers nearer the Rockies.

Col. Nelson A. Miles and his Fifth Infantry engaged a large camp of Sioux south of the Yellowstone that fall. He conquered the main body of warriors, but Sitting Bull's braves evaded him and escaped to Canada. Miles relentlessly pursued all who participated at the Little Big Horn through the winter and spring. The Indians could not cope with such sustained pressure. Before letting up he subdued eight hundred of Crazy Horse's people and two thousand more under other leaders. Miles effectively ended the Sioux menace. Only Sitting Bull and a dejected few remained at large in Canada. Despite Miles' success, the whites in Montana remained insecure, fearing the return of Sitting Bull.

# "No Ordinary Foes"

The 1877 course of Chief Joseph and his seemingly unstoppable band of Nez Perce as they passed through Montana did not reassure the settlers, even though these Indians avoided conflict with civilians and tried to do the same with the Army during their four-month odyssey. They sought refuge in Canada after becoming convinced they would not be treated fairly on their Idaho reservation. Athough Joseph shared leadership with others, from the start of the chase whites had singled him out as the strategist.

The Army's first attempt to halt the Nez Perce occurred at Lolo canyon with soldiers from Fort Missoula. The Indians evaded the soldiers and moved up the Bitterroot valley without harming any settlers. General Oliver O. Howard, commander of the Department of the Columbia, pursued the Nez Perces all the way from Idaho but was outmatched or outmaneuvered at every turn by their speed and cunning. Colonel Gibbon brought his men southwest from Fort Shaw and surprised the Indians at Big Hole, where Joseph and his warriors quickly rebounded from the ambush and succeeded in driving off the white soldiers, inflicting 40 percent casualties.

Col. S. D. Sturgis planned to cut off the band of Nez Perce warriors, women, and children in Yellowstone country. While he waited for the Indians at the canyon of the Stinkingwater River, Joseph avoided the trap by taking another route. Sturgis pursued and eventually caught up to the crafty Nez Perces north of the Yellowstone River in Montana, but they soundly defeated the colonel's men.

As the Nez Perce moved into Montana, Healy took on scouting duties for the Army, which allowed him an outstanding opportunity to send dispatches to the *Fort Benton Record*. Johnny often rode between the Army field headquarters and Fort Benton. The Indians continued moving north until Colonel Miles intercepted them at the foot of Bear Paw Mountains in October. Exhausted from their 1,800-mile chase, Chief Joseph and his band of one hundred warriors, three hundred women and children, and two thousand horses surrendered to Miles after a final three-day siege.

The *Record* reported that George Croft and John J. Healy left Fort Benton "with dispatches for General Miles." A week later Healy, "the *Record's* enterprising representative," returned "with full particulars of the Snake Creek fight and Miles' dispatches to General Terry." Editor W. H. Buck told readers that "Healy wishes to thank Miles, Howard, Lt. Long and others for courtesies while staying with them and the facilities afforded him for obtaining complete and correct information."[57]

Healy told a story rich in detail on the battle and the surrender. He described the discovery of the Nez Perce camp by the Army's Cheyenne scouts and the movement of mounted troops to the bluffs in preparation for a charge. "There was no time for reconnoitering the enemy's position, as it was feared the Indians would try to escape, and to prevent this it was highly important that the attack should be made before they could reach the herd," Healy wrote. The troopers charged into the camp where "the Indians received them with a terrible volley and seemed disposed to fight the battle on open ground, but with the Infantry coming up they were unable to withstand the fierce onslaughts of the combined forces, and suddenly dividing into three bodies they fell back slowly and in good order, keeping up a constant and well-directed fire upon the troops." Once the Indians took positions in the brush with their fire "sweeping the bottom with volley after volley from their unerring rifles both the Cavalry and the Infantry were compelled to fall back to the bluffs, leaving sixty of their number dead and wounded on the field."

On the following morning General Miles brought up two artillery pieces to fire on the strong Indian positions. After the shells drove the warriors from their hastily dug fortifications, General Miles, reported Healy, "sent an interpreter to demand the surrender of the whole camp." The messenger shouted his demand, and "Joseph answered by asking what terms the Gen. would give him. Miles replied that he must give up his arms. The Indians then put out a white flag, and Joseph with a small party came to headquarters with about fifty stand of arms." After officers demanded all the arms, Joseph refused to surrender those still held by the living. "He said, however, that he was willing to surrender upon favorable terms, as he saw no use of fighting against such odds, but that White Bird would rather die than surrender." Eventually Joseph agreed to terms. Healy reported that "Joseph, accompanied by about twenty-five warriors, rode up to headquarters and gave up their rifles. About sixty warriors were killed and wounded."

Johnny arrived on the scene while the Indians were turning over their weapons. He said the Indian force "numbered about 350 men, women, and children. They appeared to be in excellent spirits and not the least disheartened by their defeat."

The victors were impressed by Joseph's dignity in defeat just as they had been awed by his skill in warfare. But historian Mark Brown has put Joseph in a different perspective: "Thus . . . the legend that Joseph was the great chief of this faction, the mighty leader in battle, and the clever strategist seems to have been born. Unquestionably, Joseph was a towering figure, and had he possessed the degree of authority the Joseph legend has ascribed to him this futile flight would probably have ended at Kamiah [Idaho] on the morning of July 16. Unfortunately, the governing body was a tribal council dominated by Looking Glass, White Bird, and Too-hool-hool-kote."[58]

Regardless of Brown's reservations, most historians of the conflict have followed contemporary opinion in focusing on Joseph. The soldiers and others present at the surrender clearly appreciated that they had vanquished a foe of great quality. John F. Finerty, the famed war correspondent for the *Chicago Times* noted that the government "dealt leniently with Joseph, in view of the humanity and valor he had displayed throughout the whole brilliant, but lamentable, affair. The Nez Perces, who were inclined to be friendly and Indians capable of progress, had been harshly treated, and much unnecessary misery and bloodshed was the result." Finerty also quoted Col. Nelson Miles, who "stated that the Nez Perces are the boldest men, and the best marksmen, of any Indians I have ever encountered, and Chief Joseph is a man of more sagacity and intelligence than any Indian I have ever met. He counseled against the war, and against the usual atrocities practiced by Indians."[59]

Neither Irishman, Finerty nor Healy, indicated any collaboration with each other during their brief time in the same camp. Finerty, a professional who had been with the Army since the previous year, would have had little curiosity about another civilian scout and little concern about being surpassed by a casual frontier-town journalist. But a comparison of their remarks on the affair reflects, as might be expected, less sympathy for the Indians from the frontiersman than from the Midwestern correspondent. Still, Johnny paid tribute to the Nez Perce in the conclusion of his report:

> So ended the most remarkable Indian battle on record. The Nez Perces, of course, deserve little sympathy; but they fought as bravely as any men could have fought, and conducted their warfare more like civilized people than savage Indians. During the siege they never harmed a wounded soldier, and on no occasion have they been known to take a scalp or otherwise mutilate a victim.[60]

Healy knew the *Fort Benton Record's* readers wanted to know much about Chief Joseph, so he described the leader's conduct after the surrender fully:

> Joseph was walking about among his people, talking to the wounded, and occasionally addressing the warriors by signs, but seemed quite unconcerned about his defeat. He is a fine, intelligent looking man, nearly six feet high, about thirty-five years of age, and weights probably 180 pounds. He does not speak English.

The fortifications such as rifle pits and sharpshooter stations the Indians prepared in anticipation of battle impressed Johnny. "From this it may be seen," he wrote, "that Gen. Miles had no ordinary foes to contend with. Considering that they had but few implements to work with they constructed their defenses with marvelous rapidity and in a manner that could hardly have been excelled by experienced and skilful engineers; and their marksmanship was truly wonderful, and their courage and coolness unsurpassed by the bravest troops that ever faced an enemy."

Johnny Healy's newspaper scoop on the Bear Paw Mountain battle and surrender rates him modest mention among American war correspondents. He might have been better remembered if he had reported Joseph's surrender statement of October 5, 1877, as recorded by an Army officer. Joseph's simple assessment expresses rare eloquence:

I am tired of fighting. Our chiefs are killed. Looking Glass is dead. Toohulhulsate is dead. The old men are all dead. It is the young men who say yes or no. He who led the young men is dead. It is cold and we have no blankets. The little children are freezing to death. My people, some of them, have run away to the hills and have no blankets, no food. No one knows where they are—perhaps freezing to death. I want to have time to look for my children and see how many of them I can find. Maybe I shall find them among the dead. Hear me, my chiefs. I am tired; my heart is sick and sad. From where the sun now stands I will fight no more, forever.[61]

## Sitting Bull

Healy also reported on another celebrated Indian leader, the Sioux chief Sitting Bull, who escaped the vengeance of General Miles after Custer's defeat at the Little Big Horn by crossing the border into Canada. Sitting Bull's presence posed a problem for the Canadian government: while it refused to grant the U.S. permission to pursue the Indians across the border, it also did not want the potentially threatening Sioux warriors to remain in Canada. The situation required international negotiation.

Representatives from the U.S., including Commissioner A. G. Lawrence and Gen. Alfred Terry, and Canada, led by Commissioner James F. Macleod, met with Sitting Bull at Fort Walsh in Cypress Hills. Inspector John M. Walsh of the Mounties escorted the Sioux to the meeting place. In tow, Terry brought reporters Johnny Healy, Jerome Stillson of the *New York Herald*, and Charles Dehill of the *Chicago Times*.

Terry, an imposing warrior six-feet, six-inches tall with a Vandyke beard, was an affable man whose mission was to support Commissioner A. G. Lawrence. Terry met Walsh at the border on October 15 and considered the Canadian police escort of twenty-five red-coated Mounties, in pillbox caps and carrying lances, smart-looking but inadequate for protection. Terry got Walsh's permission to haul three companies of the Second Cavalry, recent victors against Chief Joseph at the Bear Paw Mountains, along in wagons.

Two days later at Fort Walsh the meeting with Sitting Bull convened, and Terry read the president's message calling for the Sioux's surrender, assuring they would not be punished for having taken to the warpath. Sitting Bull responded eloquently, defiantly, and with deliberate insult to the Americans.

For 64 years, you have kept and treated my people bad; what have we done that caused us to depart from our country? We could go nowhere, so we have taken refuge here. . . . You think me a fool; but you are a greater fool than I am; this is a Medicine House; you come to tell us

86

stories, and we do not want to hear them; I will not say any more. I shake hands with these [Canadians]; that part of the country we came from belonged to us, now we live here.[62]

Walsh and Macleod met with the chiefs after this abrasive encounter, hoping to keep the negotiations alive. The officials warned that they considered the Indians American rather than Canadian and that they could expect protection from the American soldiers only if they cooperated peacefully. The Canadian officials could not induce the chiefs to talk further, despite their earnest pleas.

Upon the sudden break-up of the conference the newsmen raced to telegraph Sitting Bull's sensational defiance to the world.

Johnny's dash to the telegraph and his exciting newspaper scoop were significant, but his behavior before leaving Fort Walsh was bizarre. According to legend Healy offered to shoot Sitting Bull if the chief refused to surrender, until General Terry pointed out that he would be charged with murder. Dismissing the notion that the Mounties could catch him, Healy said, "Give me ten minutes start and all the Mounted Police in Canada won't catch me."

Healy created no need to escape the police but still used his riding skills. Boasting his skill as a hard rider, Johnny assured Stillson, the *Herald* reporter, that he could cover the 340 miles to the telegraph station in Helena within forty-eight hours. Terry insisted the feat was impossible, so Johnny immediately took off in a rush to prove himself.[63]

He rode all night, making one hundred miles before getting a fresh horse at Milk River, where he had the good luck to meet a freighter with horses. He made good speed on the hard, dry trail over the plain. His back pained him considerably, but he stopped only for water. At Twenty-eight Miles Spring he changed horses again. His legs stiffened and sand burning in his eyes distorted his vision.

Twenty-four hours into his ordeal Healy reached Fort Benton, where his horse, a tough little mountain-bred cayuse, collapsed. He grabbed a meal and a refreshed himself in a bath before resuming his journey to Helena on the old stage road, riding a fine thoroughbred. Fatigue caught him dozing in the saddle now and then. After sixty miles he changed horses and continued down into Prickly Pear Canyon at a rapid pace. Upon reaching a store within thirty miles of Helena he found himself too dizzy and stiff to mount a fresh horse on his own, so others helped him.

He arrived in Helena forty-three hours after leaving Fort Walsh—five hours ahead of his boastful deadline. Johnny's story appeared in the *New York Herald* only three days after the conference ended, giving the *Herald* a scoop over other papers. Healy's epic ride received recognition from his fellow Westerners and, once again, he had shown the world that he was a tough and resolute fellow.

*Sitting Bull at Fort Walsh, Alberta, in 1878.* —Public Archives of Canada

*Mountie Inspector J. M. Walsh, in 1878.* —Public Archives of Canada

Healy's discription of Sitting Bull in the *Fort Benton Record* withheld the praise he had given Chief Joseph. While in some ways Johnny esteemed Sitting Bull, he did not like him. The Custer battle bothered him, and, more significantly, Sitting Bull's aggressive, hostile manner aroused little sympathy or regard in Johnny.

Describing Sitting Bull as a "short, thick-set man, about 45 years of age, and . . . 175 pounds," Healy discounted the chief's intelligence and bravery. According to Johnny, Sitting Bull had appealed to some French Indians at Fort Walsh for protection when two Americans approached the house where he was staying. "If the conqueror of Custer was afraid of two unarmed citizens, it is safe to say," Healy argued, "his fame is not all deserved. The report that he is a fine, intelligent half-breed, classically educated, is of course false. He is a full blooded Sioux and not a very remarkable one at that."[64]

Healy accurately reported Sitting Bull's speech but seemed unmoved by the warrior's stirring words. He disliked the man and diagreed with the idea that the whites' conduct justified the Indians' violence.

War correspondent John Finerty observed Sitting Bull at a conference between the Sioux leaders and Inspector Walsh in July 1879, and gave this mixed impression:

> He had strong personal magnetism. His judgment was said to be superior to his courage, and his cunning superior to both. He had not, like Crazy Horse, the reputation of being recklessly brave, but neither was he reputed a dastard. Sitting Bull was simply prudent, and would not throw away his life, so long as he had any chance of doing injury to the Americans.[65]

Some modern historians have taken a kinder view of the Sioux chief, reporting favorably on Sitting Bull's indignation against the American Army officers and praising his greatness as a leader. One biographer in particular, Stanley Vestal, championed Sitting Bull and his place in history. He observed how the "Frontier shaped America . . . and Sitting Bull, leader of the largest Indian nation on the continent, the strongest, boldest, and most stubborn opponent of European influence, was the very heart and soul of the Frontier. When the true history of the New World is written, he will receive his chapter, For Sitting Bull was one of the Makers of America."[66]

Privately, Healy blamed Inspector Walsh for encouraging Sitting Bull's deliberate insult to General Terry. But it is unlikely Walsh would have been so petty, and Johnny's story reflects not only his distaste for the Mounties and the Sioux but his Fenian inclination to take swipes at British authority as well, even (perhaps especially) when another Irishman represented it. And Johnny's view might also reflect Army gossip on the affair. Years later he described the Mounties as "fine men," but at this time he remained a bitter, anti-British Irishman who had recently been forced out of a thriving whiskey-trade business by Walsh and other Mounties.

Sitting Bull's conduct provoked Healy, probably even more so because the leader brought a woman to the conference and allowed her to speak— an act Healy believed the Indians recognized as the ultimate insult. Supposedly it was at this point that Healy told Stillson he intended to kill the chief. According to the version relayed later in newspapers, Healy was so anxious to submit his newspaper dispatches that he left without shooting the chief.[67]

After such events Johnny may have found it hard to settle down to the more mundane concerns of Fort Benton. But he had to make a living, so soon after his return he and Judge John Tattan bought the Overland Hotel from William and Charles Rowe, and Johnny also assumed the office of county sheriff.

When the Nez Perce left their reservation and crossed the Missouri on their way to the Bear Paw Mountains, Benton citizens formed a volunteer militia in the tradition of Thomas Meagher under John J. Donnelly. The volunteers rode off to save a wagon train from an attack but found no Indians to fight. Johnny probably joined the Benton Home Guards after this affair. Donnelly led the militia as its captain with assistance from Lt. Johnny Healy and 2d Lt. John H. Evans. Like Healy and Evans, most of the Guards were former Whoop-Up country traders. As it turned out they never found occasion to fight.[68]

On returning from a trip in November 1877 to Sun River, Sheriff Healy advised the residents of Benton that sixty Sioux from Canada had joined the Nez Perce in the Bear Paw Mountains. Two weeks later he predicted trouble and deplored the Army's reluctance to take protective action. By the month's end, though, the only reportable news about Johnny in the *Fort Benton Record* included his throwing a big turkey dinner at the hotel and arresting a "colored man for carrying too many weapons." Public feasts and peacekeeping aside, Healy remained focused on the Indian scare.[69]

Most Montanans continued to feel anxious about the Indians through 1877 and into 1878. Healy feared a spring Indian war in a February 1878 letter to Martin Maginnis. Predicting the Canadian refugees would cross the border to attack American settlers and American soldiers, he said, "The Sioux are gathering near the boundary line, and when the grass grows green again the Red and the Blue will have an opportunity to test their qualities as soldiers and policemen." Healy accused the Army of gross negligence and Gen. John Gibbon of "a particular spite against this place, and never will send one man to guard the interests of the place." General Miles understood the threat, Healy argued, but Gibbon always contradicted his reports to Washington on the basis of information received from the Canadians. Healy felt annoyed that Inspector Walsh and Commissioner Macleod always denied reports that the Sioux were preparing to leave Canada and make war.[70]

It turned out both Healy and the Canadian officers were wrong. Sitting Bull returned to the States peacefully. He came to terms with the Army and settled his people quietly on a reservation.

Johnny Healy held no policy-making roles during his years on the Montana frontier, but he participated extensively in Indian affairs. Capping his years as trader and miner by serving as a correspondent at military negotiations with two of the West's best-known chiefs brought Johnny considerable pleasure. For years before then he had dealt with Indians, but on these post-battle occasions he knew that he was witnessing historic events.

# 8

# Sheriff of Chouteau County

*A spirit of fair play is
the western man's bible.*
—Johnny Healy

I f the residents of Chouteau County thought electing whiskey-trader Johnny Healy as sheriff amounted to putting the wolf in the hen house, they didn't say so. Most of the county's residents actually liked having a chance to vote for Johnny, a strong man and local hero they trusted to keep order.[71]

His election in 1878 and reelection in 1880, following his appointment in 1877, attested to his reputation as a tough, courageous veteran of Indian fights as well as to his party loyalty. Businessmen in Benton recognized Johnny as one of their own—a trader with a record of fair dealing—even if he was somewhat tougher and rowdier than most. Besides, selling whiskey did not make a man a criminal. Most of the county's sheriffs peddled whiskey at some point in their pasts. In Montana, the rough-and-ready fellow suitable for peacekeeping had likely traded with the Indians before.

Healy earned his party's nomination to office by working actively for the Democrats in the county, particularly through his service as county chairman. When he desperately needed a job in June 1877, Montana's party leaders rewarded him with an appointment as sheriff after his predecessor quit.

Historian Paul F. Sharp credits Healy's "iron-fisted authority" in transforming Fort Benton from a crude, seamy frontier town to a respectable community. "Healy's fearless, energetic, and devoted efforts captured the public imagination to establish a legend of law enforcement in the high border country," Sharp contends. He may have exaggerated a bit. Although Johnny brought excellent credentials and strong determination to his position, he hardly transformed the place single-handedly; the process had been going on for years. In 1877 Fort Benton was no longer the lawless hole it had been a decade earlier.[72]

Johnny kept order with tough talk and stern action. His reputation as a hard man aided his efforts immeasurably. Clearly he was not timid. Even while campaigning for office he would more readily threaten voters than beg them for support. A visitor in Fort Benton heard the sheriff tell citizens, "If any of you is going to steal horses during the next two years, he had better vote against me, for by God! if I catch him, whether he's voted for or against me, I'll hang him."

Whether Johnny actually made such threats is doubtful, since horse theft was not a hanging offense. But the existence of such stories signifies the public's view of his stern resolve against criminals.

Healy told his biographer, Edwin Tappan Adney, that he was offered the sheriff's job when the incumbent resigned over the escape of a prisoner. As the new sheriff he set out at once to recapture the prisoner, and succeeded. On their ride back to Benton, a distance of sixty miles, Healy assured the man that he would try to settle the pending charges and even dared to arm the prisoner when a group of unidentified Indians approached. After the Indians left, the prisoner happily surrendered his gun. At Benton, Healy managed to help the prisoner, and the court agreed to drop its charges if the man left Montana.

Another Healy story concerns a challenge to serve papers on some miners involved in a heated mine claim controversy. The mining area lay outside the county, yet the sheriff, incensed by the suggestion that he feared the miners, accepted the chore anyway. Healy chose to approach without arms: "I simply walked straight toward them, as unconcerned as if it were an ordinary matter and had no feeling of being in real danger." As the miners stood over the disputed heap of precious ore, they ordered Healy to stop, but he kept right on. When he got close enough to ask what the problem was, the miners told him their woes, then Healy convinced them that accepting a summons would resolve their problem.

Stories about Healy's fearlessness in confronting tough characters abound, but he believed firmly that he faced little danger. "This is the principle," Johnny told Adney. "No man who is sober will shoot down an unarmed man."[73]

Much of Healy's peacekeeping involved drunken men, but he did not fear them, either. "There's something about Healy," a former deputy said. "I have seen him go up to a drunken man in a saloon, push his gun aside, and tell him: 'Don't be a fool. You are drunk, go home!' Healy had a look as though he would shoot, and people respected that look. He embodied the full majesty and power of the law."

Early in his law enforcement career Healy let it be known that he went about unarmed, though he secretly kept a small derringer handy. But the appearance of being unarmed spared him many hot-headed challenges. Healy gave all his deputies this same pep talk when he pinned on their badges: "If you know you are right, fix him and hang on! The other fellow will not be so sure. You will get just the quiver of an eyelash. Then you've got him."

# Tax Collecting

Healy's exploits as county sheriff included daring improvisation in tax collecting. James Willard Schultz, who rode with the sheriff on his fiscal mission, described the incident with gusto. An interesting character, Schultz chose a singular life on the Montana frontier after leaving his upstate New York home in 1877. Voyaging up the Missouri River to Fort Benton, the young man presented a letter of introduction to trader Joseph Kipp and got a job with him. Joseph Kipp's father was James Kipp, an early fur trader with the American Fur Company; his mother was the daughter of a Mandan Indian chief. Under Joseph Kipp's tutelage Schultz traded with the Blackfeet and closely observed their culture. Eventually he married an Indian girl and lived with her people. Schultz became famous from writing about his experiences among the Indians.

Schultz's initial acclaim as a writer came with the publication of his memoir, *My Life as an Indian*, in 1907, which became a frontier literary classic. Among his other books, a compilation of sketches, *Many Strange Characters*, includes one on Sheriff Johnny Healy of Chouteau County.

Schultz included the tax-collection episode in his sketch of Johnny. According to Schultz, county officials were having a hard time making ends meet in the early 1880s. Fort Benton's once-thriving buffalo-robe trade had declined, and the small population of the large county generated insufficient tax revenues to support government services. Dim prospects for drawing their salaries induced some deep thinking by edgy officials. Healy, the brightest of the lot, got an inspiration. "He had heard of a big camp of Red River breeds over in the Judith country," Schultz said, "who were right in the midst of a big buffalo herd, and 'twas reported that they had more robes than their carts could hold."[74]

Healy presented his scheme for taxing this resource to the other officials, supporting it with cogent arguments. While the buffalo hunting party was Canadian and by the strictest interpretation of the law exempt from county taxation, perhaps, Johnny reasoned, they were "taxable to a certain extent." They used the county roads, or would if the county had any, and used buffalo and Indian trails over county lands. It seemed only fair to Healy that the travelers pay taxes for use of trails that might become roads some day requiring maintenance. And if the county could hold the travelers liable for road tax, they could also hold them accountable for the poor tax and the tax on personal property. So why not go after these rich, delinquent travelers, Healy asked? "The officers considered the question," Schultz wrote. "They thought of their back board bills, they looked at their seedy clothes, and told the sheriff that his plan was, so far as they could see, perfectly legitimate." Healy then got the officials to agree that, as the travelers were unlikely to have any money, it was proper to accept prime buffalo robes valued at $7 each for tax fees.

Johnny struck out over the trail on his big black mare, followed by his deputies and three four-horse teams and wagons. A week later they returned with the wagons piled high in buffalo robes. "Nine hundred robes there were, which sold for $6,300, of which each officer got his share." The town witnessed great rejoicing that night but after paying old bills, celebrating, and playing poker, the officials soon found their money gone.

Court business continued to be slack, except for a couple of drunken bullwhackers shooting up a saloon, and officials saw a continuing unsteady flow of revenues. Thus, when trappers came to town and reported another camp of Red River people on the Milk River, Johnny grabbed a bunch of tax receipts and headed off again, taking along his brother Tom, Jeff Talbert, and Schultz, whom he recruited at his trading station along the way. "He talked me into going with him as deputy; at five dollars a day," Schultz said, "and a share in the whack up." This time Healy did not even bother to bring wagons. "He intended to hire the breeds, or force them, to haul into my place the robes he would collect, whence he could ship them to St. Louis by steamboat in the spring," said Schultz.

Later that night the sheriff's party reached the camp of the Red River folks. They had set up a large one for wintering and each family had its own cabin made of cottonwood logs. On arrival Schultz acted as spokesman, using his "best and politest coyote French," and eventually explained the sheriff's mission. Predictably, the camp leaders exploded with protests: They were Canadians who did not plan to stay in the States and would pay nothing. Schultz looked at Healy, who "sat and listened quietly until they were out of breath, and then, with a cold look in his gray eyes and a determined set of his jaw, he said: 'Enough of this. No more words now. Whether you are foreigners or not makes no difference. You are now in the United States and the territory of Montana, getting rich off the buffalo and the other game belonging to us. Therefore, it is but just that you help us bear the expenses of our government. I know you have no money, so you will bring, each of you, two good head and tail robes to this cabin, and I will give you a receipt in full for your taxes, and no delay about it.'"

The sheriff's boldness overwhelmed resistance. The Canadians brought in their robes, trying at first to get by with inferior ones which Healy rejected with contempt. Schultz and other deputies kept busy all day writing out receipts and baling the robes in bundles of ten. At day's end they had three hundred robes, but Healy felt unhappy because many men held back.

The next morning the Canadians, reinforced by the arrival of a party of well-armed men, had a change of heart. They approached Healy's camp and demanded their robes back. Healy blustered about calling for the Army but the Canadians seized the Americans' horses and refused them any food. After the sheriff and his deputies brooded and discussed tactics through the day, Schultz stole away with a horse and rode hard to an Army detachment at Wolf Point. The commander was keen to help but insisted on authorization from headquarters at St. Paul first.

Politically, the situation was a tricky because the Canadians had camped on a reservation, involving the Department of Interior in any confrontation. Schultz could only return with as much food as he could carry. After an absence of four days he slipped into the cabin held by the sheriff under gunfire from the Canadians.

The outcome looked hopeless, so Healy took advantage of an offer made by the owner of his cabin. The Canadians planned to storm and burn the cabin so the owner agreed to bring horses for their escape while the other besiegers slept. Healy would also have to pay the agreed-upon rent for the cabin. The Americans got away safely. The Army arrived far too late to protect the tax-collecting enterprise of Sheriff Healy.

After this fiasco Healy advised county officials to find other revenue sources. Johnny decided the time had come to quit such hazardous pursuits, which also held the risk of federal prosecution.

Frank M. Eastman, the U.S. Attorney for Montana, heard all about Healy's raids and felt little sympathy. His understanding of the unsuccessful raid differed in some details from the story Schultz told, but it substantially confirms the affair. Eastman knew that Healy's commissions as sheriff, county assessor, deputy collector of customs, and special deputy U.S. marshal for the ostensible purpose of stopping Canadian half-breeds from smuggling trade goods onto the Milk River Reservation only covered up a money-making scheme. According to Eastman, the Canadians continued smuggling goods for sale on the reservation, and when Healy asked for taxes they were "satisfied that this was his only business, and soon began their interrupted sale of liquor and contraband goods."[75]

But Healy fooled them. He figured their tax contribution was separate from their illicit activities, and he arrested them. Because he lacked the means of bringing the Canadians to Fort Benton, he confiscated their trading goods as security for their appearance before the U.S. Commissioner. Eastman thought the confiscation was irregular, but because the sheriff lacked the means to move prisoners he advised the attorney general that "the necessities of the case may perhaps be considered as excusing if not justifying such a course."

If Healy had known that federal officers were tracking and second-guessing his tax expedients, he would have been doubly furious at the raid's failure. Like other frontiersmen Healy was outraged at the federal government's interference in local matters. Yet the pioneers liked to note the arrival of amenities as the frontier developed, and they took pride in their contribution to the advance. Johnny lost his elective office a few months after attracting Eastman's attention, which avoided a confrontation between federal and local lawmen over tax collection.

# Lynching

While Western mythology has glorified lynch law, sober citizens have always recognized that its use reflects poorly on their community's reputation for lawfulness. Many people find it hard to speak well of an expedient that disregards legal processes.

Montana's bloodiest resort to vigilantism occurred at Virginia City in 1864, when angry men brought an end to the depredations of the Henry Plummer gang. The community had yet to develop an efficient agency for law and order, so some fifty men banded together and signed this solemn oath: "We, the undersigned, uniting ourselves together for the laudable purpose of arresting thieves and murderers and recovering stolen property, do pledge ourselves on our sacred honors, each to all the others, and solemnly swear that we will reveal no secrets, violate no laws of right and never desert each other or our standard of justice, so help us God."[76]

With great spirit the vigilantes set to work, and over a two-month period they tried informally and hung twenty-four men. The vigilante group expanded to include perhaps 1,500 men, including Johnny Healy. The vigilantes were otherwise respected citizens and most people honored them for doing what needed to be done.

At Benton in the sixties vigilantes lynched only one white man. In 1868 William Henson moved to Benton from Helena where he had been arrested for murder, then released for insufficient evidence. He was a loud, lively man who deplored the lack of a town policeman to patrol the streets at night, and offered his services. Once in authority Henson worked hard, especially at rolling drunks. Protests of his depredations followed, but Henson denied any wrong and urged citizens to form a vigilante group to control the crime wave. Once again citizens responded to his eloquence but directed their attention to him.

The vigilantes called on Henson and told him: "We've caught the fellow who has been doing these robberies and in half an hour we're going to hang him. Have you got a rope?" Henson, eager to help hang a scapegoat for his own crimes, hurried out and spent his own money on a rope. The mob quickly slipped it over Henson's head and raised their night patrolman on high.[77]

With ineffective law-keeping agencies in the Fort Benton of the sixties, such shameful informal proceedings were understandable. A visitor in 1866 aptly described the town as a community with "neither village nor city ordinance, neither Territorial nor Federal law, no, not even moral law."

But by the mid-seventies Fort Benton was maturing and respectable residents wanted more-professional order keeping. Some even found the lynching of Indians intolerable. In 1877 the editor of the *Fort Benton*

*Record* cautioned readers to disdain lynching. "Only one half of the persons lynched are guilty of the crimes for which they suffer, and not infrequently the ends of private malice are gratified under the pretence of punishing wrong-doers," he opined. Too often citizens ignored such wrongs, the editor admonished, because "the victims were usually Indians."

Someone other than Johnny Healy was in office in April 1875 when a Fort Benton mob took two Indians accused of murder away from the sheriff and shot them dead. The *Fort Benton Record* refused to white-wash the mob's conduct, describing the nasty deed as one that filled "every God fearing citizen with horror, disgust and contempt." It was "a wretched reminder that Benton is not yet free from that barbarous class of society so common to new settlements on the western frontier."

With this commendable shift in public opinion under way the lynching of a white man in 1881 would seem unlikely. Yet it occurred, and the affair exposed some negligence in Sheriff Healy's office. Healy's old friend and partner Al Hamilton served under Johnny, and Hamilton's conduct was questionable. Healy had installed Hamilton as his deputy at Sun River when he first came to office.

Hamilton, born in New Haven in 1839, came out to Montana in 1863 and shared the ups and downs of trade with Healy at Sun River and Fort Whoop-Up. When Healy moved from Sun River to Fort Benton for newspaper work, Hamilton established a store at Choteau, a settlement between the juncture of Muddy Creek and the Teton River. In 1879 voters elected him to the territorial legislature. Hamilton liked Choteau where he lived comfortably with his Indian wife. He became a locally important individual. By 1881 he had established a new general store and had become perhaps too busy to exercise reasonable caution in protecting a prisoner.

Cowboy Brackett E. Stewart disturbed Choteau's peace when he drifted into town in June 1881. Mrs. Annie Armstrong, who was separated from her husband, had the misfortune to hire Stewart as a ranch hand. She ran a cattle ranch with the help of her foreman, Joe Morgan, and other hired hands. Stewart, a boozer, sometimes whiskey trader, and horse thief, started scheming when Annie sent her cowboys out to make the spring round-up. In their absence Stewart complained of mice and rats in the bunkhouse, and Annie allowed him to share Joe Morgan's room in the ranchhouse. On the first night, as Morgan slept Stewart slit his throat with a razor, then shot Annie Armstrong. Two little girls who lived with Annie fled for their lives. After hiding themselves under the house for a time they escaped to seek help. Henry Kennerly, a local rancher, met them, heard their grisly story, and sent for Sheriff Hamilton.

Meanwhile, Stewart found only $150 cash in Annie's trunk. He had expected more. Before moving on he splashed kerosene around and set the ranchhouse afire. Jimmie Armstrong, Annie's son, and his friend, William Ralston picked up Stewart's trail. The pursuers paused at Blackfeet camps along the way to inquire about a traveler leading a pack horse. At their third stop an Indian girl threw up the flap of a lodge to expose a man asleep in a blanket marked with an "A", an Armstrong ranch identification.

Stewart woke rudely to see two six-guns pointing at his nose. His captors took no chances, lashing him to his horse for the trip back to Choteau. Once in Hamilton's custody a preliminary hearing established that Stewart was the killer. The two girls easily identified him. The cause of justice, so far, was sailing along in good order. Choteau was too small to have an assembly of volatile saloon loungers crying out for summary justice. Anyone anxious to lynch Stewart needed a little time to organize others. Either by design or chance, Hamilton provided that time by disdaining the sensible precaution of departing for Fort Benton with his prisoner immediately after the hearing. Perhaps he was busy at the store, but why would he want to risk a night-time ride with a murderer? Hamilton must have realized that Stewart, charged with the most heinous crime in county history, deserved great care.

Vigilantes spared Hamilton a night ride. After nightfall the deputy was just seeing to the manacles on his prisoner, who was seated in a buggy and ready for the trip to Fort Benton, when the vigilantes arrived. A dozen men pointed their weapons at Hamilton and urged him not to sacrifice his life needlessly. Soon another twenty men appeared and Hamilton stood aside.

The vigilantes hung Stewart quickly though less neatly than he requested. His last words were "Boys, give me a good drop and break my neck." He failed to realize that the boys were amateur hangmen, uncommitted to turning him off gently. Because the mob had no reason to fear the timely arrival of law officers they tried to wring a confession from their prisoner. They raised him by the neck with a rope thrown over the branch of a stately cottonwood, asking each time for a confession. Stewart's only words were instructions on how his captors should break his neck. Finally, in disgust at the culprit's poor attitude, the lynchers left him hanging. Stewart twisted for a long time while he strangled. A day later men took down the body and buried it at the foot of the hanging tree. With due regard for history and record keeping they posted a sign. "Here lies buried beneath this tree the remains of Stewart, Brackett E. He gave up Christianity to become a beast. And was hung from the limb that's pointing east."[78]

When the news of the lynching reached Fort Benton it infuriated Sheriff Healy. Although he had joined the vigilantes when the country was raw and the Plummer gang posed a genuine menace, the Stewart case was different. While he avoided public displays that would embarrass Hamilton or his administration, the mockery of the law insulted him terribly. Of the many stories about his activities Healy later told to Tappan Adney and others, he excluded the Sun River lynching episode despite its dramatic interest.

County officers took action against the vigilantes. Judge John W. Tattan convened a formal inquest into Stewart's death at Fort Benton. Hamilton described his care in protecting his prisoner until he was confronted with an overpowering force. Oddly enough, he could not positively identify a single member of the lynching party.

The Benton people who attended the inquest were probably amused by the hearing and may have found Johnny Healy suppressed signs of stormy passion. But the judge in charge, John Tattan, carried the inquest off with his usual dignity and amiability.

John Tattan was an old friend of Johnny's and his partner in the ownership of the Hotel Overland. Like Johnny, Tattan was born in Cork County, Ireland, but seven years later. Because of his father's prosperity, Tattan also received a strong education before he emigrated to New York in 1865. As a trained civil engineer Tattan went west to Minnesota to practice his profession in the iron mining industry. He probably did poorly because he enlisted in the army in 1870. Assigned to Fort Benton in 1872, he took his discharge there three years later. Soon after his discharge, Tattan was elected to the office of county probate judge, a position he held until 1889, except for one two-year term. In 1877 he was admitted to the bar and went on to become county attorney, and in 1900 federal district judge, an office he held for many years.

These last two distinctions lay ahead of Tattan in 1881 when he had to protect the sheriff, who was the godfather and namesake of his son and boiling mad to do something to somebody. But the situation called for the discretion of a Tattan rather than the mad-dog courage and belligerency of a Healy, and the judge brought it off.

Historians of Chouteau County have argued that Johnny was not given his party's nomination for sheriff in 1882 because he was spending too much money enforcing the law. Several incidents explain why he lost some popularity. People were annoyed at the cost of the new jail and concerned that he was not more accessible at Fort Benton. It is also possible that some folks blamed him for Hamilton's submission to the mob and a lynching that was reminiscent of earlier lawless days.

# Horse Thieves

According to historian Paul Sharp, Johnny's execrable judgment in insulting an Indian was decisive in ending his career as sheriff. The incident reflected Johnny's crude sense of humor, perhaps at a moment of drunken whimsy. Healy had arrested Bad Bull for horse theft. After the Indian spent some time in the county jail, his day of release dawned. But Johnny wanted to send Bad Bull forth with a defacement that would help the Indian recall his misdeeds and set an example for the general community. While deputies held Bad Bull down the sheriff clipped off all his long hair, then released him to face the derision of other Indians.

The incident failed to amuse the editor of the *River Press:* "Notwithstanding his protest and piteous appeals his long black hair was soon clipped and Bad Bull, like Sampson of old, was shorn of his pride and strength. The sheriff laughed. Everybody laughed. It was brave indeed!" Public officials are wise to avoid a reputation as jokesters. "A funny man for sheriff may be a very nice thing on the outside," observed the *River Press*, "but he should not endeavor to work up his humor when in the performance of his official duties."[79]

Johnny's prank occurred in 1881 at a time when he worried less about threats from Indians than he had earlier. Others in Montana felt less relaxed. If Bad Bull or another Indian determined to avenge the insult upon some innocent settler, would the sheriff still think the incident funny? Other Montana newspapers censored the sheriff. The *Bozeman Avant Courier* denounced the hair cutting as "very thoughtless and indiscreet and deserves the severest condemnation of all peaceable and law abiding citizens."

Political foes used Healy's more legitimate zeal against wrongdoers against him. The *River Press* raised a ruckus over the sheriff's good work in capturing an escaped prisoner in another county. "It is a pity that Choteau county is made to pay such heavy bills of costs as the capture of this class of criminals involves. It is a pity, too, that when one of the parties takes the trouble to put himself out of the county, and a good ways out, that he is not allowed to remain. We are sorry that Talbert's rifle failed to kill the party, which would thus have done the county the greatest possible service by saving it all the costs, that must accrue from his capture and prosecution."

The public's disdain for Johnny's zeal in his second term probably owed a good deal to the class of criminals that engaged most of his attention. The sheriff worked with Granville Stuart and other members of the newly organized stockholders association. These ranchers were up in arms over thefts of steers and horses, but some town folks concluded that their sheriff was devoting too much time protecting the ranchers' property and too little providing for their security.

Healy's involvement with the stock association illustrates his participation in a significant transition of Montana's economy. The region had recently developed into a major cattle-raising place. The ranchers appealed to the Chouteau sheriff for protection and guidance, and Healy responded with enthusiasm.

Granville Stuart and Healy started talking about the ranchers' concerns in May 1880 when they happened to meet while visiting a friend's ranch. According to the ranchers, Indians, both from Montana and those who had moved to Canada but made raids across the border, were stealing livestock. "They defy the white men," Stuart said, "and the military pay no attention to them except to report to headquarters, and then inspect their forts and test their safety in case of an attack. Occasionally a squad of ten men and a lieutenant are sent out to 'order the Indians to return at once' at which the chief would smile, grunt, ironically admire the brass buttons on the blue coats, and pay not the least bit of attention to the order. The Indians continued on their way robbing ranges, frightening women, stealing horses and subsisting on our cattle."[80]

Stuart had impressive statistics. "Between the months of November, 1880, and April, 1881, three thousand head of cattle were wantonly butchered by Indians in Choteau and Meagher counties . . . a destruction of $60,000 worth of property by the malice of Indians."

Cattlemen were unable to survive such heavy losses so they followed the precedent set in other cattle states and formed a stockmens' association for mutual protection. The ranchers determined to stop the Indians and "whiskey peddling fiends" who encouraged the Indians' theft of horses by demanding mounts, ignoring the question of the stocks' previous ownership.

In August 1881 the stockmen of Chouteau and Meagher counties met at Fort Benton to form their organization. They chose a Fort Benton rancher to accompany Healy on "all expeditions taken in behalf of the Stock Protective Association, who was to be paid by the association." They also offered a five hundred dollar reward for the apprehension and conviction of whiskey sellers who sold their goods to Indians, and paid for a standing advertisement of the reward in the Benton newspapers. They offered one hundred dollars reward for conviction of anyone giving liquor to "half breeds upon the range." Finally, they made arrangements to hire range riders to look out for Indians, with the intention of sending Canadian Indians back. If they or the American Indians persisted in coming through the range, the stockmen declared that "they did so at their own peril, and the final issue would be raised then and there."

Sheriff Healy addressed the stockmen with a proposal of his own. If they approved, he would organize a force of fifty men, well armed, and ready to move at all times. Indian raiders were rumored to be moving toward the Judith River at the time, and Healy offered to intercept them immediately. If they refused his order to halt "the issue at once becomes made," as the *Record* reporter put it, "and the Indians will have to return or fight."[81]

The ranchers agreed with Healy's plan and formed the Stock Protective Association for Chouteau and Meagher counties. Fees assessed on the ranchers would provide money to pay posse members. Some ranchers opposed the majority and objected to Healy's bold measures. At a Sun River meeting several men protested that "the course proposed would most certainly precipitate an Indian war." The more remotely located ranchers, particularly those in the Teton valley, voiced the strongest argument for caution. Eventually the ranchers decided against employing Healy's posse but passed strongly worded resolutions against the sale of booze to Indians and against their wandering off their reservations.

Other newspaper notices indicate the sheriff's activities to which county residents probably objected. On one occasion he returned to Fort Benton after pursuing Indian horse thieves for twelve days to recover horses stolen in the Yellowstone country and elsewhere. Healy got back some horses and also arrested Bad Bull for the theft.

Granville Stuart and other stockmen felt particularly pleased with Healy's capture of Bad Bull. News of a raid on Yellowstone ranches by Canadian Indians reached Benton just after the association meeting. Healy took off north at once to look for stolen stock, taking one deputy and a local rancher along. According to Stuart, Healy found two horses on the Blackfeet Reservation, "right at the agency and directly under the eye of one agent," and captured Bad Bull there. "Bad Bull was an ugly customer," Stuart noted, "and gave his captors no little trouble by resisting arrest and by his attempts to escape. He was held hostage at Benton and sent word north to his friends and relatives that he would not be released until the stolen horses were recovered."[82]

Healy's relentless campaign impressed Indians. Two weeks after he brought Bad Bull in shackles through a watchful Piegan camp, Chiefs General and Middle Bull disturbed his slumber at an early morning hour. The Indians had traveled a good distance to Benton to deliver a stolen horse that had come into their hands. "It may be taken," the *Record* noted, "that the sight of an Indian in chains had a good effect on them." However, Healy's later cutting of Bad Bull's hair hurt his standing with both whites and Indians.[83]

Healy's popularity as sheriff diminished even more as Fort Benton residents became resentful of his concern with the stockmen. The axe fell in August 1882 when Democrats nominated James McDevitt rather than Healy for their candidate in the primary. In the election McDevitt defeated his Republican opponent. Some Democrats felt badly about Healy's rejection and proposed him as town constable, but the party also denied him that lesser police office.

During his years as sheriff Johnny remained active in other civic matters at Fort Benton. In 1881 the Montana Irishmen were upset over the Irish Land Act that the British government had recently legislated. Three Benton men, Healy, O'Connor, and Father Sheehy issued a manifesto denouncing the act as oppressive.

"Lying accounts from Ireland seek to produce misleading impressions in America," the manifesto read. "Ireland is represented as lulled by the Land Act. . . . It is false, most false. The lull in Ireland is but the preparation for the storm." Tenants will refuse to pay rents and now "stand face to face with one of the most trying situations that ever tried the manhood and patriotism of a nation."[84]

Some months later the Benton men founded the Irish Land League with Judge John W. Tattan as president and Healy as a member of the Executive Committee.

Soon after losing his job as sheriff Johnny went into business for himself as an auctioneer, advertising his "professional" services for the sale of "every description of property sold to the highest bidder." Healy indicated that he had taken on his new task "by request of a number of citizens of Benton and to fill a long felt need in this community." Unfortunately Fort Benton had less of a need for an auction house than Healy hoped, and he gave up the venture after a short time.[85]

Apparently Johnny declined to join a venture with his brother Joseph and several friends, including his former deputies Al Hamilton and Jeff Talbert, in Alberta. Copper and other mineral discoveries in Alberta in the early 1880s drew a number of stampeders from Fort Benton. Healy's former deputies purchased what they believed to be a promising silver claim at Silver City near Banff. Their claim was easy to reach, lying along the Canadian Pacific Railway grade 140 miles from Calgary. Despite their initial glowing reports to friends in Montana, the property proved to have little silver. Rumors in Canada held that the whole scheme had been a promotional fraud, aided by mine salting.[86]

At Fort Benton Healy was doing as poorly as his friends. He sold his flour mill at Sun River, the last of his Montana properties, and looked for something new. His old stamping grounds in Montana looked empty of opportunities for him and enticed him to look elsewhere.

106

# 9

# To Alaska

*I have never missed
calling the turn in Alaska.*
—Johnny Healy

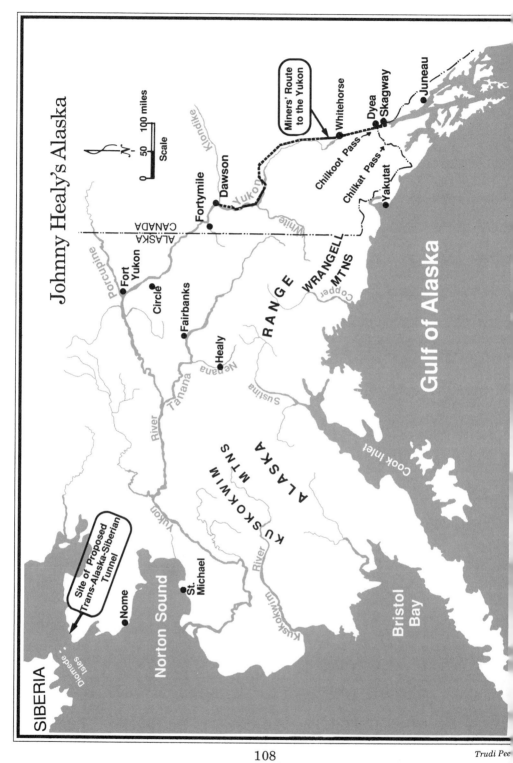

Johnny Healy's Alaska

Trudi Pee

hy Alaska? What tempted Johnny to try his fortunes in the distant north? The Healy legend contends that Montana had become too crowded for him, but the truth is more mundane. He needed to earn a living after his Fort Benton auction house failed. He had to do something else and was open to opportunities anywhere they might surface.

Montana men with an interest in gold took notice when prospectors discovered the precious metal in the Cassiar district of northern British Columbia in the 1870s, then at Sitka, and particularly when Juneau boomed in 1880. Some of Johnny's friends had gone to Alaska and he decided to try the new country himself. His wife Mary Francis died in 1883; he was restless and free to go. If he stayed in the North he could send for any of his children who might wish to join him.

A story in the *Choteau Calumet* noted Johnny's visit there from Fort Benton to say farewell to Al Hamilton and other friends. In a warm tribute the paper called for a "correct history of Montana" that would record the activities of "one of the most prominent and heroic characters of our early civilization." They described Healy as "a leading spirit in all our political contests, as the originator and promoter of many successful enterprises for advancing the welfare of the communities in which he has resided, as a fearless, uncompromising enemy to crime, and as one of the most efficient, daring yet charitable officers of the law that has ever held a responsible position in this or any other State or Territory." Montana was sending Alaska one of its most intelligent, energetic, and useful men, the writer observed. "It is no exaggeration to say that the trials, hardships and adventures of Mr. Healy's eventful life are almost unrivaled in either fact or fiction and that they alone would form a most interesting and useful literary work." Concluding, the writer predicated that Healy's Alaskan adventures and achievements would likely equal those in Montana.[87]

In November 1885 Johnny took a train to the coast, noting the many changes since he had gone out over the Oregon Trail twenty-five years earlier. From Portland he sailed to Alaska. The ship stopped briefly at the old Russian capital of Sitka, then went on to Juneau, the largest community in the territory. Bishop Charles John Seghers looked the place over with disdain shortly before Johnny landed there: "Its houses appear as if they had fallen pell-mell from the sky," Seghers said. "One house is turned towards the west, another seems to be looking for the rising sun, a third turns its back to the water and its front to the mountain, as if it were about to start on a climb along the steep slope of the bluff, —another, instead of appearing to stand on the ground, seems to be made fast and hanging from the side of the mountains. Sidewalks, twelve feet above the ground, are connected over the street by means of a bridge."[88]

Johnny liked Juneau's atmosphere. For a small place it had a notable bustle, a sense of excitement, an expectation of big things ahead when prospectors found the great mineral deposits of the interior and elsewhere in southeastern Alaska. He relished the ambience of big deals being made on street corners, saloons, or wherever men got together. He had big deals he wished to make himself. For example, he longed to buy into some of the valuable mining properties in the Silver Bow basin—but he lacked capital. At a younger age he might have provisioned himself for prospecting in the Yukon or elsewhere and started off. Juneau was the jumping-off place for prospectors usually outfitted in Juneau and took a small steamer or even an Indian canoe about one hundred miles up Lynn Canal to its head. From there they took the land passage over Chilkoot Pass to the upper Yukon River, where they began searching. Johnny decided to leave the prospecting to others, figuring he could rely upon his commercial experience to give him better money-making possibilities.

As an old journalist and a man who liked to encourage his friends in Montana, Johnny wrote the editor of the *Choteau Calumet* in January 1886. He described the huge Treadwell Mine and explained that most miners hired were "Indians and Chinamen . . . as white miners are not to be had and will only work long enough to get a prospecting stake." He also praised the climate and described the means of travel. Transport was mainly by water, Healy reported. "A man might as well be without a horse in Montana as to be without a canoe here. Everything is transported by canoes along the coast. There is only one steamship a month from Portland to this place and Sitka."[89]

One could quickly become an Alaskan expert and figure out the region's problems, particularly if, like Healy, one had frontier experience. "If this country had a territorial form of government it would soon settle up," Healy advised. "Mining, fisheries, oil manufacturing and lumber will be the industries. At present it is a hard country for one accustomed to the plain. There are no prairies, all mountains are covered with timber. . . . What prospecting has been done is along the coast; but there will be many outfits for the Yukon next season, as I understand there has been good float gold prospects found on the Stewart River, a tributary of the Yukon." He advised Montanans who had homes and businesses to remain in Montana, but, "to those who are hardy, young, and possessed with some means, wanting a new field for adventure, and possibly profit, I would say come. They can find all the excitement here they want, and when they get here the star of the empire will have changed its course from west to north."

After Johnny had been an Alaskan for one month, he wrote again to the Montana newspaper, praising the reasonable cost of food and freight rates, the climate, the industriousness of the Indians, and the situation for traveling into the interior. He understood that seventeen men were wintering in the interior and that many more prospectors would go into the country in the spring. The country seemed promising. "Capitalists seeking investments can come here with their experts and find a greater and more promising field for their money and labor than is offered in any other part of America." He suggested that young men who knew something about prospecting should come, but only if they had enough money to return if prospecting failed to pan out. "Don't come without some resources. It is too early. But the day is not far off when there will be employment for the thousands." The government had extended mining laws to Alaska so that prospectors could make valid claims, but it had yet to establish land laws for lack of surveys. This put residents at a considerable disadvantage because it was impossible to "take up or cut timber."

Johnny liked more of what he saw in Alaska than he disliked, particularly in the people. "This place has the best lot of pioneers I ever saw. They are all whole-souled, self-made, and invariably old timers from Cahoo, California, Cassiar, Nevada, Idaho or Montana. It appears to be the Montanan's country. They will capture the Yukon this summer. The field is large and cannot be prospected in twenty years." He encouraged his Montana friends to come but warned them to come by water, "and bid good-bye to broncos if you intend to remain here. Don't forget your pocket-book and come determined to stay, as the walking home is very bad should you get discouraged or broke."

Writing to Montana again in mid-March, Johnny was obviously caught up in the excitement of the rush into the interior. "About twenty men have started already," he wrote. "They are provided with sleighs and snow shoes. . . . The Indians pack from tide water to the head of the lakes, a distance of thirty-five miles, for which they have heretofore charged 10 cents per pound, but now I understand that they are charging 20 cents per pound. This may cause trouble."

News about Indian packing rates also caused him to think about his own prospects. He had yet to decide on what ventures to undertake, but one the former Sun River ferry operator considered was how a hustler from Montana might get into the Chilkoot Pass packing business.

He asked questions about the local Indians and what he heard pleased him. "The Indians are peaceable, and if let alone and not 'reserved' by the government, there will be no trouble with them, unless the gunboat now in Alaska waters is hauled off. Think of the immense country you could steal Montana and Dakota out of then have enough left, guarded by one old gunboat capable of making but six knots an hour."

The lack of crime and disorder also pleased Johnny. "Criminals are scarce here. Every man is on his good behavior. No pistols or fights, as a man who commits a crime must face the music. No dodging or hiding." And it helped that Alaska had "the best class of citizens." Men of another class "are soon given to understand what is expected of them, and that without the aid of 3-7-77 [the numerical sign posted by vigilantes in Montana to signify their hangings]. None of that needed."

Johnny made his first commercial venture with the purchase of a boat, which was remarkable for a man who had been navigating horses in the interior country for many years. He bought the little schooner *Charley* as an affordable means of jumping right into the commercial movement of miners towards the interior. Miners needed supplies, and they needed transport on Lynn Canal and to wherever else along the coast they wanted to prospect. The transport field was uncrowded, so he moved into the maritime world with high expectations of profit.

Apparently Norman A. Fuller, a Juneau founder, loaned Johnny the money he needed for his commercial ventures. Fuller had been a trader at Sitka when he grubstaked Joe Juneau and Dick Harris, who discovered gold at what became the town of Juneau. Harris, another roving Irish prospector, was unable to hold on to gains from his discoveries. He was working for wages when Healy was in Juneau and later fell on even harder times. Fuller later sold claims to John Treadwell who developed the great quartz mine named for him on Douglas Island near Juneau.

Johnny eventually repaid Fuller's loan, then during the Klondike rush hired Fuller, who had suffered reverses, to supervise mining properties that allowed him to restore his fortunes.

Operating a boat in the waters of southeastern Alaska is a difficult and hazardous undertaking. The many islands offer some protection from high seas, but storms blow fiercely at times, and the innumerable rocks and reefs off the mainland coasts and islands pose additional perils. Johnny learned to navigate the hard way and later liked to claim that he "found all the rocks in Alaska."

Another Healy legend, which he fostered, concerned his explorations of the coast for passages to the interior. He enjoyed bragging about such activity, but he arrived late on the scene to be an explorer. The U.S. Coastal Survey had charted the coastline well and the approaches to the interior were known by the time he ventured to sea. However, he did investigate much of the shoreline closely looking for mineral signs, and was pleased to discover what appeared to be a valuable marble formation in Glacier Bay.

On May 12 Johnny wrote to Montana from Chilkat, at the head of Lynn Canal. He had just completed a voyage from Juneau to Sitka to get his license as a coastal trader, thence to Chilkat or Dyea. In stormy waters he had hard going. It took twenty-five days to complete the rather short passages. "I am now fairly started as a coaster. It is a venture for want of something better." But in the Chilkat region he saw further trading opportunities. "This place may in time become an important point. I remain here. It being the key to the Yukon country, I like the location." Ever since landing at Juneau he was aware that the Dyea region provided entry to the interior, and that the local Indians were willing to pack for prospectors but considered the Chilkoot Pass their monopoly.

As Johnny sized up the situation, it would take a determined fellow to break either the Alaska Commercial Company's hold on the Yukon River route or that of the Chilkat Indians on the overland passage, perhaps someone like himself. The Alaska Commercial Company (ACC) reminded him of the Hudson's Bay Company and the American Fur Company in keeping the country to themselves. He had long fancied that he had invaded Whoop-Up country in daring defiance of the Hudson's Bay Company, so the notion of overthrowing the ACC on the Yukon must have crossed his mind. His present meager finances prevented him from seriously considering putting steamboats on the Yukon himself, but he could conceive of getting into the upper Yukon trade. "It is impossible to go in by May from the mouth of the Yukon River, as the trading company only run their boats from San Francisco, and it is doubtful they would carry any freight or passengers," he noted.

He figured the ACC would have plenty of trade and transportation competition from Portland or elsewhere on the Pacific Coast if a major gold strike occurred in 1886. "At present the only practicable relief is for some enterprising party to construct a pack-trail through the Chilcat [Chilkoot] Pass, place pack-animals upon it, and set the Indians at defiance." Johnny had yet to resolve himself to be that "enterprising party," but he hoped someone would take on the task in the present season. "The interior would then settle up rapidly, as the country thirty miles back from tide-water is British ground and being covered by British law, a man knows exactly what to do."

That Healy, faced with the uncertainty of American law in Alaska, now praised British law showed his pragmatism. In Montana and in Whoop-Up country he took advantage of lax law enforcement. Now he wanted the security of established law. His comments on laws affecting natives and regional development were interesting, given his frontier experience. "At present Alaska is simply held as a piece of property . . . for the benefit of a few individuals who appear to have gotten control of the country. . . . It is not even regarded as Indian country, and it is doubtful whether the natives are Indians or American citizens." The government denied the natives any rights and seemed unwilling to open up the

Healy and Wilson's store at Dyea, established in 1886 (shown here in 1898).
—University of Alaska Fairbanks Archives

country for settlement and commerce with the natives. "Why prohibit the importation of arms and liquor when no tribal relations among the Indians are recognized. It looks to the few white people who are here as if the government were keeping Alaska for private speculation, probably to sell again."

Soon after weighing all the prospects at Dyea, Healy teamed up with Edgar Wilson, an Ohio native and Civil War veteran, to establish a trading post. Johnny chose a strategic location—one of the most strategic points in Alaska, the place that about ten years later was the point of entry for an estimated 22,000 gold stampeders. He and Wilson built a store in the spring of 1886 at the head of Lynn Canal near one of several Indian villages in the vicinity. The place was variously called Taiya for the river there, Chilkat, as in Healy's first letter from the place, Portage, or Healy, until it became famous as Dyea during the gold rush.

Wilson ran the store during the spring and summer months when charter business for *Charley* was brisk, but Johnny was often there delivering passengers and stock from Juneau. The store did a good business, particularly in the summer, and the partners also earned a commission by arranging packing by Indians over the Chilkoot Pass.

Johnny found himself too busy to write letters to Montana newspapers, but editors kept readers informed of his affairs with reports from other travelers. In September 1886 the *River News* editor opined that "friends of J. J. Healy will be pleased to learn that the famous rustler is once more on the highroad to fortune." A Captain McCafferty reported that Healy "is prospering in a decided way and has a golden opportunity to mend his broken fortunes." He had a good trade with the Indians, "whose language he has mastered with surprising rapidity and over whom he wields a wonderful influence."

Others preceded Wilson and Healy as traders among the Lynn Canal Chilkats and Chilkoot branches of the Tlingit Indians. Resident white traders were first tolerated in 1879 when George Dickenson and his Indian wife located there. Previously the Chilkats traveled to Sitka or other stations for trading. In 1880 the Chilkats also welcomed Presbyterian missionaries who founded a mission and school at what became Haines and drew Indians from other villages, particularly from Chilkoot. Aurel Krause, a distinguished ethnographer who visited in 1881-82, stayed with Dickenson. Dickenson's wife, Anna, a Tsimshian Indian educated at an English mission school, became a missionary. While George ran the store at Chilkoot, she taught at the Presbyterian mission school. Krause learned a good deal about Tlingits from Anna, who spoke their language fluently, but nothing from George, who regarded everything Indian with contempt.

As a long-time Indian trader Healy felt little contempt for his customers, but he intended to have business matters his own way. He wanted to avoid conflict and to make money. He had a complex attitude toward the native culture, but he tended to be paternal. He had less interest in native cultures than a scholar such as Krause and less zeal for Indian salvation than that expressed by missionaries, but he liked learning the native ways. Essentially he was a pragmatist. The only good Indians, he might have said, are those who are good customers and don't cause trouble.

Johnny had less to fear from the Tlingits of Alaska than he had the Blackfeet of Montana. Although the Tlingits made war on the Russians and other Indians on occasion, they were much less combative than the mounted warriors of the lower Northwest. The upper Lynn Canal Indian population of about one thousand in the 1880s was gathered principally in four villages, Klukwan, Kutkwutlu, Yondestuk, and Chilkoot. Among the smaller ones was Diyei (later Dyea). The Chilkats' domination of the trade between the coast and the interior made them prosperous. Chilkats provided European trade goods to Indians of the upper Yukon, packing their wares in over the Chilkoot Pass, which they came to regard as their private highway. The Chilkats reacted to the Hudson's Bay Company establishing Fort Yukon in 1847 and Fort Selkirk in 1848 with anger at the interference in their trade. In 1852 Indians traveled to the upper Yukon and burned down Fort Selkirk, but subsequently calmed down. At the time of Krause's visit the Indians looked with favor on the increasing traffic of white men over the pass because they made good money as packers, but the harmony was inconsistent.

## Message to McQuesten

Healy's life had been marked by fortuitous timing, including his participation in the Idaho gold stampede and in Montana and Alberta trade opportunities. In Alaska, too, he profited from good timing, locating a store on the main route to the interior shortly before the first major gold discovery in the Yukon. For a decade prospectors had searched for gold along the tributaries of the great river. Pioneers among the Yukon miners included several men who doubled as traders, notably LeRoy Napoleon "Jack" McQuesten, Arthur Harper, and Alfred Mayo, all loosely affiliated with the Alaska Commercial Company. In 1874 McQuesten established a trading post called Fort Reliance about six miles downstream from the mouth of the Klondike River, and his presence encouraged prospectors to investigate other nearby Yukon tributaries, including the Fortymile, the Sixtymile, and the Seventymile rivers.

116

The Alaska Commercial Company commanded most of the Alaskan trade after the U.S. acquired the territory from Russia. Though interested primarily in harvesting fur seals from Pribilof Island, the San Francisco-based company also sent its own traders to replace the Russians at posts along the lower and middle Yukon and provided a small steamboat to carry freight on the river. The ACC had more interest in furs than in gold, but the sympathies of men in the field like Jack McQuesten determined that reliable prospectors could always get grubstakes. Eventually, in 1886, prospectors began reporting strikes.

Johnny Healy played a part in bringing the dramatic gold discovery story to the outside. Early in 1886 miners had found some gold on the Stewart River and McQuesten established a store there to serve the miners. But Howard Franklin, Frank Buteau, and others moved on downriver to the Fortymile where they found much better prospects. Over the years prospectors had found small quantities of fine flour gold in various places, but the Fortymile discovery looked like the start of a bigger strike when the men found sizeable nuggets. McQuesten had already left Alaska for San Francisco when the Fortymile (named for its distance from Fort Reliance) strike occurred. Encouraged by the Stewart River activity, he urged the ACC to send more supplies and food to the Yukon in 1887. He advised that more miners would move north, and the ACC had to order provisions months ahead for them to be available by the time Yukon River navigation closed down for the winter.

Arthur Harper saw the urgency of getting a message to McQuesten about the Fortymile as soon as possible. Now the need for a big increase in trade goods was certain. Harper hired Tom Williams and an Indian lad called Bob to carry a letter for McQuesten and other mail to the coast. It was December 1 when the two messengers started up the Yukon for the headwaters and the Chilkoot Pass. With the help of three dogs and a sled, they were probably making the first attempt at winter travel over the route.

Conditions varied over the trail as the men moved along. They mushed on top of the river's frozen surface unless conditions forced them to follow a trail along its bank. On December 11 Williams noted they had "traveled all day through heavy pack ice, making only about 10 miles. If the ice continues in our road, we will have a long, weary trip." Three days later their sled broke through the weak ice covering the river, after which they lost several hours making repairs. December was too warm for the river surface to freeze firmly. On December 17, while moving ahead of the sled to test the icy surface, Bob fell through and got soaked.[90]

By mid-January they reached Lake Lindeman at the river's headwaters and encountered fierce snow storms that confined them in camp. Most of their food was gone as they finally trudged up the Chilkoot Pass.

They left behind their sled and one dog too weak to follow. A blizzard caught them near the summit, forcing them to halt again. They waited five days for a break in the weather with nothing but a little flour to eat. Williams suffered frost bite and came down with pneumonia. Bob tried to carry Williams down to Dyea on his back, but after several days and only twelve miles progress he was near exhaustion. Some Chilkats found the travelers and carried Williams and Bob down to the Healy and Wilson store.

Johnny was away, but Edgar Wilson listened intently as the dying Williams explained his mission. He refused to give the location of the gold strike but assured Wilson that the information was in letters he had cached back near the summit. Williams then died. Wilson sent some Indians out to look for the letter cache but another snowstorm made their search impossible. A couple of days later Johnny arrived from Juneau. He had a larger schooner now, the *Yukon*, which he had recently purchased. He also had ten passengers, miners who were veterans of the interior and willing to undertake a winter trip. As the miners went out to look for the cache, Johnny took Bob to Juneau for medical treatment, particularly for his badly frozen toes.

In Juneau, Healy's news stirred everyone. For years folks had waited to hear about a big strike in the interior. Now, apparently, it had happened, but where and how big remained unclear. Rumors flew and most were exaggerated. A newspaper reported that the mail, when found, would "disclose what all have been looking for—the biggest 'find' of the Northwest. Everybody who knows anything about the country says it is there, and that time is bound to show it up."

Frank Dinsmore, Billy McPhee, and others formed a fund-raising committee to finance a search for the letter cache. Dinsmore, a Yukon veteran, had a smattering of Indian language that enabled him to get some cache location information from Bob. At a town meeting the men raised $125 and gave it to Johnny Healy. Johnny left for Dyea (a.k.a. Chilkat, Portage, or Healy). The *Yukon* lost her rudder along the way, making the trip a tough one. Johnny arrived to learn that Wilson's second search party had also failed to find the cache. Johnny went out with the benefit of directions gathered from Bob and found the letters. He took the letters to Juneau and the mail recipients passed along the jubilant news: Fortymile miners had found nuggets as well as the usual flour gold.

Juneau men rewarded Bob as the bearer of glad tidings. They sent him back to Dyea with Johnny a few dollars richer and in possession of a Yukon sled valued at $8. The men left Healy unrewarded for his part in the affair. Town gossips even complained about Johnny's role. "People are asking what became of the money Tom Williams was carrying," said a Juneau newspaper. "We feel that John Healy should explain the matter to the satisfaction of the public."

Healy seethed at the imputation of dishonesty. But, characteristically, he refused explanations. When he received a letter from Jack McQuesten, which finally reached Juneau in May, he released it to the press. McQuesten acknowledged the reasonableness of Healy's charges for services performed and approved his use of some of Williams' money.

# Capt. William Moore of Skagway

Capt. William Moore always had his eyes open for commercial opportunity. A veteran Canadian mariner, he had navigated a boat on the Stikine River during the Cassiar gold rush and had a long involvement in coastal trade. In 1887 he went over the Chilkoot Pass to look over the Fortymile country, then signed on with William Ogilvie, who arrived at Dyea that summer to survey the region for Canada. Like Healy, Moore believed that eventually the interior would boom. He appreciated that Healy and Wilson were in a pretty good position to make a fortune when a major rush occurred because of their location near the foot of Chilkoot Pass.

But Moore searched for a better route. In investigating Skagway Pass (later named White Pass), which roughly paralleled the Chilkoot, he became convinced that it was a more favorable route—longer but with a less precipitous ascent. With the construction of a proper trail pack animals could make it over Skagway Pass while the steep final stage to the Chilkoot summit would always bar pack animals.

A local man, Skookum Jim, accompanied Moore on the Skagway Pass investigation. Jim and George Carmack were later celebrated as the discoverers of the Klondike riches. Carmack, another local man, was poorly regarded by the settlers of the area, partially because he had married an Indian woman. Sometimes Healy hired him to help out on odd jobs. Later, as the discoverer of the Klondike, Carmack's fame soared and less-fortunate men spoke better of him.

With Canadian surveyor Ogilvie in the field, Moore figured he had a chance to interest the government in helping him develop the Skagway Pass. He told Ogilvie that the future lay with the Skagway Pass, but the Canadian surveyor felt less sure. Ogilvie looked over the ground, however, reported his observations to the government, and renamed it White Pass after Canada's minister of the interior.

Meanwhile Captain Moore and his son Bernard got to work. They claimed a homestead at Skagway, a few miles from Healy's place, and built a log cabin. Skagway was the logical jumping-off place for crossing White Pass.

Capt. William Moore, founder of Skagway. —University of Alaska Fairbanks Archives

The Moore settlement meant two bright men with years of frontier experience, Moore and Healy, had located in the same area. Each man was gambling on his judgment in selecting a particular location. Who would win, if either did? In 1887 Healy had the edge. In the great stampede of 1897-98 most of the traffic flowed over the Chilkoot Pass, but Healy had long since moved to the interior when the boom hit. Eventually Billy Moore's forecast of the preferred route to the interior proved right. He noted in 1887 that deep water off Skagway made docking there possible, and the shallow Dyea waters would prevent it. Most of the gold rush ships docked at the Moore wharf in Skagway in 1897-98. His judgment about the White Pass was finally confirmed when the railroad builders chose it for their route. After 1899, travelers abandoned the Chilkoot to ride in comfort on the White Pass and Yukon Railway.

## Indian Troubles

Traders located at Indian villages occupied a delicate position. It behooved them to possess diplomatic skills and to understand native sensitivities. After several Chilkoots were killed in a fierce dispute among upper Lynn Canal tribes in 1881, a U.S. Navy officer tried to restore peace. Master G. C. Hanus learned that hootch distilled from molasses had set the Indians on their drunken, violent course. At the time George Dickenson had the only store in the area and the Indians had purchased the molasses elsewhere for their hootch. When the trouble broke out Dickenson shipped what molasses he had in stock to Juneau just to make sure it stayed out of the hands of hootch makers. Dickenson, noted Hanus, "is a man easily scared, and I found him and his Indian wife thoroughly frightened."[91]

From his first days in Dyea Johnny took a firm line with the local Indians. In Montana and Alberta he learned that a trader's survival depended upon having the respect of the natives. They must respect his fairness and his vigorous determination to defend himself and his property in any conflict. In the buffalo trade he had the advantage of providing goods Indians desired without threatening their livelihood. But at Dyea his ambitions extended beyond trading and provoked violence.

In the summer of 1886 the traffic of prospectors moving into the interior over the Chilkoot Pass accelerated and caused trouble. Despite the efforts of naval officers on several earlier occasions to convince Indians that they had to allow everyone free passage, the Chilkats still cherished their monopoly on the pass. A couple of hot-tempered prospectors who wanted to hire packers provoked them and brought the free-passage issue to a head. Jack Wade and John Burke had agreed to pay the Chilkats $10 per hundred pound pack, but the Indians decided that they wanted $13. The miners refused to pay more and the Indians refused to pack. After two days of stalemate the Indians called on the miners, seemingly prepared to work at the lower price. With the miners were the Yukon's first Catholic priests bound for the interior to begin missionary work. The priests were led by Archbishop Charles John Seghers, who died some months later at the hands of Frank Fuller, one of his travel companions.

As the Indians and the travelers discussed packing, the Indians shifted back to their $13 demand and reneged on another offer of free packing from Haines to Healy's place they had made to the priests earlier. Seghers remonstrated with Klanot, the second chief who governed packing arrangements. Klanot showed off a large, ribboned document, given him earlier by the U.S. *Pinta*'s commander, testifying that he was a "good Indian." When the archbishop threatened to tell naval officers that the chief told lies the Indian chucked him lightly under his nose.

At this Healy and the miners went for their guns. Healy warned the miners to avoid any Indian attempts to surround them and provided arms to the whites who lacked their own. There were 108 natives and 11 white men; except for three rifles, the Indians had only knives. For a couple of tense hours the whites waited in Healy's store while the Indians held a council. Finally, they offered to pack for $12 and the miners accepted their price. The archbishop had to borrow money from Healy to pay for packing. Until this dangerous encounter Healy and the priests had been having a good time visiting and sharing stories of their mutual friends in Montana. Shortly after the incident Alaska Governor A. P. Swineford called at Haines and, with Deputy Marshal Healy's help, arrested Klanot. The governor wanted Klanot prosecuted for extorting money from the archbishop. At Juneau the U.S. commissioner swiftly released the Indian for lack of an arrest warrant. Sitka's newspaper, *The Alaskan*, applauded the governor for acting quickly to make the Indians "behave properly," arguing that "Gov. Swineford's action was expedient and therefore right. . . . The protection of whites from Indian aggression is far more important than any sentimental reverence of the red man's peculiar privileges."[92]

Later in the season miner Henry Davis, who was returning to the Yukon after a provision buying trip in Juneau, also had trouble with the Chilkats. The Chilkats were angry because Indians from the village of Hoonah offered their packing services to prospectors going into the interior. When Davis landed his winter supplies the situation was explosive as Chilkats and Hoonahs milled on the beach threatening each other. Healy had already sent to Juneau for help. The might of the U.S. government in Alaska was primarily represented by a small naval warship—actually an armed tugboat—rather grandly named *Pinta*. Shortly thereafter the *Pinta* arrived, and naval officers met with the Indian chiefs and Healy in a two-hour conference. The meeting settled the matter, with the Chilkat packers agreeing to carry Davis's provisions to the summit for $12.50 per hundred pounds.

In summer 1887 the Canadian government sent a survey party under William Ogilvie to map the routes to the interior from Lynn Canal. This clearly signalled that the government took the interior gold discoveries seriously and expected the country to show further development.

The Chilkats, however, remained uncooperative, and the following year Ogilvie depended upon Healy's negotiations to gain the use of packers. Johnny handled the situation with a lack of regard for the local Indians. Ogilvie wanted to hire some Stick or Tagish Indians from the interior who had come to Dyea to trade at Healy's store and were willing to pack for $9 per hundred. But he wanted assurances from the U.S. Navy that the packers would be protected. Assurances were not forthcoming, so Johnny offered to hire the Sticks himself. Ogilvie feared that the Sticks of Canada would have to fight the American Chilkats and did not want to risk an international incident. Healy then successfully proposed another plan, arranging to pay the Chilkats $10 for packing to the summit and the Sticks to carry from there to Lake Lindeman.

Lt. Comdr. J. S. Newell believed that hootch drinking created much of the Indian belligerence and asked Governor Swineford to ban the sale of molasses and other hootch makings. Swineford replied, "I regret being compelled to say that the law places no restriction upon the sale of sugar and molasses to the natives, and that I am powerless in the premises. All I can do, at the most, is to refer a request to the Juneau traders that they desist from making such sales, and leave them to heed the request or not, as they may see fit."[93]

Newell reported on the packer situation after undertaking a peace-making mission in April and May 1887. He took the *Pinta* to the head of the inlet and "impressed upon the Indians that this vessel was there as much in their interests as in the interests of the white people; that they [the Indians] could make their own bargains and work or not work, and that they could not interfere with or prevent the whites or others passing through the country. . . . This seemed to be understood by them."[94]

Newell saw the conflict as one between the Chilkats and the Sticks over packing rights rather than between whites and Indians. Although an occasional miner complained over the Indians' packing charges, the greater disturbance was with the Indians over Healy's evident intent to establish a toll road on the pass. "The Indians . . . consider this trail the property of their tribe . . . and look upon its becoming a highway as an infringement for which they are entitled to compensation." They were worried about Healy's work on the trail. Healy wanted to make the trail suitable for pack animals and bragged to Newell about the toll road he had controlled in Montana, probably in reference to his bridge over the Sun River. Newell could see discord ahead: "Already the Indians regard the work done with suspicion, and Klanot has requested Captain Healy, so the latter informs me, to withdraw his men, which request was refused." Newell's understanding of events was confused because of "the jealousies existing between the traders . . . especially so where in their intercourse with the Indians the son of one trader [Dickenson] acts as the interpreter for the Indians in their talks with the other trader [Healy]."

A month later, Lt. Alexander McCracken reported fully on the dispute. He noted Klanot's ascendancy over the old chief, Donawauk— "all seem to be afraid of him," and the Sticks fear that they would not be allowed to pack once the navy men left the area. George Carmack, who packed for Healy along with his Indian brother-in-law, was one of McCracken's chief informants. Klanot was angry at Healy but McCracken believed that the recently appointed Indian police could keep order and that Klanot would honor his promise to allow Indians and whites passage without interference.[95]

Klanot told the navy men his fears:

> Mr. Haley [Healy] wishes to take away our road or trail to the Yukon, which my tribe does not like, as we made it long ago, and it has always been in my tribe. We fixed the road good, so that the miners would not get hurt, and Mr. Haley is putting sticks or logs on it, so he can get pay for people going in over our trail, and we do not want to see that. When the miners come here I talk kindly to them, but some of them begin to swear, and then they say that I began the quarrel. I always treat the miners kindly, and when they do their own packing I tell them they had better let the Indians do their packing, so the miners will not hurt themselves on the trail, and some of the miners tell me it is not my business, which hurts my feelings. When the miners treat me right I will and do treat them as my children.

While whites who traveled the pass never confirmed Klanot's complaint that Johnny was sabotaging the trail, the chief had other grievances: "My tribe borrowed lots of money from Haley and were going to make money by packing to repay Mr. Haley." The chief claimed that Wilson had tried to kill him after taking some packing customers away from him. Klanot argued that he would allow other Indian or white packers but objected "to Haley . . . claiming our trails and monopolizing the packing." Klanot had another grievance with Healy: "We used to get all the furs from the Stick Indians, but they now trade with Mr. Haley, which ought to satisfy him without taking our trail."

124

Over the winter the tension between Healy and the Chilkats intensified. When the 1888 travel season opened Healy did not try to charge tolls on the trail—if it had ever been his intention—but he contracted with Stick Indians to pack for miners under his management. Klanot precipitated a tense encounter when he threatened the Stick Indians. Healy felt justified giving work to the Sticks. He appreciated their trade at his store: "We gave the business to the men who in return bought our blankets, while the second chief would take all his money and go off on a spree to Sitka and spend it there." What Healy failed to mention is that by trading directly with the Sticks he cut out the Chilkat middlemen and got furs for a better price. Because Klanot also felt bitter about Healy's part in his arrest earlier, the trader's employment of Sticks particularly annoyed him.[96]

Violence finally erupted when Klanot and other Chilkat packers attacked the Sticks' leader, Big Tom. The fight started right in front of Healy's store where the Chilkats menaced the Sticks and Healy. Klanot advanced on the trader menacingly and Healy knocked him down. Big Tom then jumped Klanot. As the men grappled Klanot shot Big Tom with a revolver, but the tough Stick wrestled the gun away and, with the gun empty, smashed in his enemy's skull. Another Stick buried a knife in Klanot's back. By this time Healy had his gun, and he and Wilson tried to stop the fight. They failed and the Chilkats went after Big Tom and the Stick who had killed their chief. A Chilkat later killed Big Tom in the hut where he had taken refuge.

The fight alarmed all the whites in the area, and for a time Healy was besieged in his store. The whites of "Chilkoot Portage" dispatched an urgent message to Juneau asking for a posse of armed men. "We are not a lot of women to be easily frightened," the message said, "but can take care of ourselves as long as ammunition holds out but something must be done for the safety of white residents." By the time the posse arrived from Juneau the situation had settled down, but for a time Johnny must have felt as threatened as he often had earlier in the Blackfeet country. The Tlingits of Alaska, despite the incidents related here, were usually friendly and peaceable. Over the long period of Russian and American activity in the eighteenth and nineteenth centuries only a few incidents of violence against whites occurred.[97]

While Healy involved himself in the conflict with the Indians around Dyea, others precipitated the confrontation. The Indians resented whites' use of the trail before Johnny arrived. The events typified the problems throughout the nation as whites moved into Indian country. Whether someone more intelligent, more tolerant, and more persuasive would have performed better in his shoes is moot. Klanot overstated his partially inaccurate charges. Healy had ambitions and a lack of respect for the Chilkats' concerns, but also showed some benevolence in his pursuit of his goals. He aggressively but usually scrupulously asserted his commercial interests.

## The Deputy Marshal

In the spring of 1888 Johnny's life took a decisive turn. In Juneau he married Isabella M. (Belle) Boyd, whose husband, George Finley, had recently died in a Montana insane asylum—or so Belle said. Apparently she had voyaged to Juneau at Johnny's suggestion. Belle fibbed about George Finley—he survived until 1898—making her marriage to Johnny bigamous.

Belle settled in at Dyea and provided a more pleasant household for Johnny. She got along well with the Indians and other whites in the little community, which helped Johnny, too. Belle also enabled her husband to establish another trading post a few miles from Dyea at another Indian village, because she could mind the store when he was absent. The family expanded further in 1890, when Johnny's son, Thomas Constantine Healy, joined them.

Johnny sometimes involved himself with the Indians in an official capacity as well as a commercial one. He took a commission as a deputy U.S. marshal to add to his prestige among the Indians, but policing sometimes pitted him against them. One incident in 1888 involved the truculent Chilkat chief, George Shotridge, and an Indian named Koo-too-wat. Shotridge helped Koo-too-wat resist an arrest by Deputy Marshal William McLernon. Since the Indian had been charged with maiming another Indian by cutting off his ear, Koo-too-wat considered it good fun to threaten "to eat" the deputy unless he left the village. Another deputy, Max Endelman, visited later and with Healy's assistance made the arrest.[98]

In 1889 Johnny hoped to travel to Montana, but had to postpone the trip. Writing to Al Hamilton at Choteau, he explained, "I know I can make a winning by sticking to it. It is hard and slow, but I hate to give it up." Shipwrecks had set him back. Johnny continued, "have been stranded twice and lost everything two or three times, but started in again. . . . This is going to be a good country, but will develop slowly until capital comes in." He also had some promising "placer claims to the westward which will pay me as soon as I can get water on." Some two hundred miners were wintering in the interior and "the Yukon is undoubtedly the most extensive gold field on the continent." Healy gave Hamilton news of some other Alaskans, including Jeff Talbert, once Sheriff Healy's deputy at Fort Benton; Ed Flint, ill with stomach cancer; and George "Tuck" Lambert, a Fortymile discoverer, who "has gone to the Bering Sea after quartz." Healy was losing patience with the slow pace of Alaska's development, but he maintained his cautious manner of boosting the country. "I must say it is the roughest country I ever saw for a poor man. None but the strongest men should come here, and then they should be provided with some means . . . only capitalists capable and willing to endure great physical hardships can hope to prosper. . . . The country is liable to remain undeveloped for some years to come."[99]

Johnny served as deputy collector of customs as well as deputy marshal. Neither job provided a salary, although he could collect expenses and a few dollars in fees. As custom collector the ex-whiskey trader had to prevent traffic in liquor among the Indians—a tough job. In March 1891 he complained to U.S. Marshal Orville Porter about whites who were selling smuggled booze or hootch makings—sugar, molasses, and lemon extract—to Chilkats and Chilkoots. Healy had reformed his character concerning liquor and Indians. More exposed to the consequences of booze-induced violence at Dyea than he had ever been at Fort Whoop-Up, he wanted no part of it.

That winter violence had erupted at Chilkat, a village two miles from Haines Mission, after a drunken spree. When one drunken Indian fatally knifed another the local whites clamored for the blood of the assailant. The Indians, too, demanded vengence. Johnny feared the consequences of their unrest more than he worried about the actions of the whites, who practiced a more selective lust for justice. Acting quickly with the help of trader George Dickenson, Healy met with the Indians and agreed to turn the slayer over to them, letting "them settle it in their own way." He made no apology to the marshal for his handling of the dispute. "There was no other way possible . . . no one to testify against the guilty," and it would have been "a folly" to try to take the slayer to Juneau.[100]

On other occasions Johnny arrested Indians and sent them off to Sitka for trial without any trouble. Once, when natives protested his arrest of an Indian who killed his wife, he bluffed them into agreement by using a little guile. He impressed them with his letterpress, using the unfamiliar machine in the presence of Indians who then warned the others that powerful magic was working to achieve the deputy's will. He loved to get his way by bluffing but he recognized when, as after the knifing, his games would fail.

The whites spoiling for vengeance after the Indian killing blamed Johnny for making an unreasonable assessment of the situation. They were furious at Healy because he denied them a lynching while still resorting to an informal solution. He warned the marshal that he had gained "the enmity of the rough element of the place"—a bunch of noisy, hard-drinking whites who would now protest to Juneau. "There is a brotherly feeling among this class throughout the country," Johnny told Porter, and they had threatened Johnny's removal, alleging that they wanted "an efficient" officer to replace him. "It may take more than one officer if the whiskey peddlers can find as profitable a field as last summer," said Johnny. Some of these fellows "kept their hand in" over the winter by robbing another trader's store. Johnny easily identified the culprits, but had "no show to arrest or examine" suspects as the whites united to protect each other.

Even with his impotence in the robbery incident Healy's presence discomforted the other whites who took the trouble to petition for his removal. Johnny believed they were motivated less by civic zeal than by whiskey trading, and most of them lacked any other reason for being in the region. The petitioners charged that Healy sold whiskey at Dyea "for the last three years . . . and this hampers discharge of his duties."[101]

Porter believed his deputy was blameless of selling whiskey and considered him more reliable than his accusers. Healy's foes had sordid reputations. One of them, Jack Wade, was charged with murder a few years later after a drunken shooting affray. And judging from the memoirs of Healy's neighbor, Bernard Moore, Johnny was a law-abiding citizen. Bernard was only twenty years old when he and his father built a cabin at Skagway. Later they took out citizenship papers in Juneau to assure their right to a homestead. Young Bernard found Belle and Johnny Healy the most pleasant of his neighbors. Belle, the only white woman in the region, was kind and motherly to Bernard and Johnny was something of a hero.

Healy had yet to adopt the sour, taciturn air that characterizes descriptions of him from the nineties. Still the Irish raconteur, he eagerly filled Bernard's ears with "tales of hairbreadth escapes and adventures which he had experienced years before in Montana, Fort Benton, and on the Missouri River."[102]

At the Healy's, Bernard found more domesticity than existed at his place. He loved to watch Johnny carefully grind coffee beans before making a pot of brew, telling Bernard that this was the only way to assure freshness. Mrs. Healy put out a fine spread of food, including her own jellies and jams, for all visitors. Bernard thought her "a fine woman, a loyal wife and helpmate to John Healy," and the good friend of many prospectors. "She spoke the Tlingit language well, as also did her husband, and knew every native within miles around."

Bernard and most of the residents of the area were amused by an incident that involved missing rum, even though Johnny found little humor in it. Healy and U.S. Commissioner Theodore Pointdexter seized a barrel of rum from smuggler Billy Leak as he landed it from a fishing boat. Pointdexter, who operated a store at the Pyramid Harbor (Chilkat

Inlet) salmon cannery, placed the rum in his store for safekeeping. News of the seizure spread widely, and one enterprising man crawled under Pointdexter's store, drilled through the floor and into the barrel, inserted a pipe, and neatly removed all the rum. For 25 cents a drink customers at the local saloon enjoyed the rum. Bernard learned later that the thief was Jack Olson who boasted of making $1,200 from the rum.

Healy never determined the culprit but may have suspected Olson, with whom he had crossed swords over other matters. Bad blood between the two men led to a fight shortly after the theft. Johnny's prowess left Bernard, a bystander at the battle, amazed. Olson, who had been drinking, went into Healy's store and got into an argument with Johnny. Olson abused Healy and made a movement toward his hip pocket for a gun. "In an instant," Bernard noted, "Healy had put one hand on the counter and leaped clean over it, and was on top of Jack in a flash." The men struggled over the gun until Johnny wrestled it away and smashed Olson's head with it. "They were both mighty good men in a fight, and fearless too," Bernard said. "But Johnny Healy was quick as lightning and would as soon fight as eat any time, despite his age, which I should judge was at that time in the neighborhood of fifty years."

If Bernard or anyone else doubted Healy's honesty as a trader they never mentioned it. Bernard, who married the daughter of Indian chief George Shotridge, criticized Juneau shopkeepers who customarily cheated Indians. Those who complained about Healy usually mentioned his "hardness" or "arrogance" rather than his dishonesty. One unhappy Healy client, mining engineer Isaac B. Hammond, rapped him for an unpleasant voyage in the schooner *Yukon*. A prospector who claimed he had discovered a valuable mine duped the engineer as a means of getting free boat passage. Hammond chartered Healy's boat and was chagrined when the prospector got where he wanted to go and disappeared. After storms and engine trouble in "that noted sheet-iron water-coffin, the ancient steamer *Yukon*, a boat which always threatened to conduct her passengers to the bottom," Hammond had gained nothing. Then, to compound his discomfort, "the ironclad skipper, Captain Healy," explained that he had carried Hammond for the two hundred miles agreed upon and now demanded more money. They were only five miles from Juneau yet the captain wanted $100 to complete the voyage—$25 more than the charter contract for the original voyage. "I saw that there was no use in arguing the point with our headstrong commander."[103]

Healy miraculously survived the perils of his small-boat navigation with meager training and experience as a sailor. Among his other achievements he carried the pioneer miners of Lituya Bay to their diggings on several voyages. Lituya Bay, now part of Glacier Bay National Park, was a graveyard for mariners because of its treacherous entry. But hazards lurked everywhere he sailed, and, as he freely admitted, he had been shipwrecked several times. After 1891 he retained the title of "captain," but contentedly left the bridge to others.

Johnny's praise of the character of Alaskans he met during his first months in the country switched to grumbling in a letter Johnny wrote to U.S. Marshal Porter after a few years at Dyea as deputy marshal. "I have been many years in official harness and have had some experience with criminals, but I must say that this part of Alaska can furnish more petty, trifling criminals, and shady men than any other portion of the U.S.—taking the population into consideration."[104]

Writing to the marshal five months later he expressed his disenchantment with the government's manner of doing business. Despite his complaints he had yet to receive money to build a jail. And when a newly appointed U.S. commissioner arrived without the necessary forms to issue an arrest warrant Healy wanted, Johnny was distressed. Soon, he told the marshal, the place "would assume its old-time lawlessness as it is almost useless to attempt law enforcement." Weary of struggling "against the combination here," Johnny asked Porter to accept his resignation. "Thank you for the confidence shown in me. I hope in a short time you'll know more about me which will strengthen that confidence and our relationship will continue to be friendly."

That summer Healy also wrote Lyman Knapp, governor of Alaska, advising him on the necessity of "restoring confidence" with the Indians before serious trouble developed. He omitted details of his expertise in Indian matters, contenting himself to a modest reference to general experience: "I have always been a pioneer."[105]

Governor Knapp, apparently impressed with Healy's judgment and good intentions, commissioned him to conduct a special investigation of local Indian affairs. Johnny reported in October 1891, providing a terse summary. "The resident native population of Chilkat and Chilkoot number about eight hundred . . . confined to a narrow strip of country extending from Point Sherman on Lynn Canal to the boundary line, about ten miles north of Klaw-Kwan," the report reads. "They are dependent for support on the salmon." Since losing their interior trade to whites who established themselves on the Pelly River, the natives had depended upon selling salmon to canneries that had located in their region over the previous four years. "The action of the cannery men this year alarms them, and they are commencing to realize that it will be but a short time before their means of support is taken from them. They object to fishermen entering their river with nets, as they stop the run of salmon."[106]

Healy recommended that the governor recognize the Indians' demands. They wanted a reservation established that included the Chilkat

Flats. Such a reserve would keep cannery fishermen from netting the migrating salmon as they entered the river to spawn. Indians fished on the river and their comparatively modest catch did not threaten the spawning cycle. "I am in a position to know their feelings on the subject," Johnny wrote, "and while I know them to be kindly disposed, if let alone, I believe that should they be forced to protect their food supply by force of arms; it will be an expensive and unfortunate war for southeastern Alaska, as it may mean a war with the entire Klinkit [Tlingit] Nation."

Johnny also addressed the liquor problem. "They are very quarrelsome when drunk, and all their sprees end with some cutting scrape. The Indian policemen are unable to cope with the evil. Sometimes the entire settlement is in a drunken uproar, and if this state of affairs be permitted much longer the able-bodied men and women will soon be killed off." The Indians asked Johnny, as deputy marshal, to forbid the sale of lemon extract and other foods used for hootch, "but I am unable to accomplish anything but arrest where some crime has been committed in my presence, as these people will not lodge a complaint against one of themselves, knowing that by so doing they lose all chance of getting paid for injury done them. There should be some means here of enforcing law and order."

Enforcing law and order remained a problem after Healy quit as deputy marshal. During the summer of 1892 four saloons operated at Chilkat, where the few white customers could hardly have supported one. Indians could buy whiskey despite its illegality, and a terrible outburst of violence marred that year's Fourth of July festivities. The trouble started in the Silas Gibson saloon near the Healy and Wilson store when a drunken Indian fell against Jack Wade, whose negotiations for packers in 1886 had occasioned controversy. Wade, who was drunk himself, knocked the Indian down. Another Indian fell through the window of the saloon, angering the proprietor Gibson, who fired his pistol at the culprit. Meanwhile, Indians jumped on Wade, who shot and killed one of them while he lay on the ground. The Indians fled, but the dead man's wife appealed to the warrior instincts of Tom, a native leader. According to a Department of Justice investigator the widow called for "an eye for an eye," according to custom. "Tom," she reportedly said, "'you profess to be a brave man; avenge the death of my husband.' Tom sallied forth with his gun and shot the first white man he met, which happened to be Frank Marx. . . . Neither Marx nor Tom had been engaged in the drunken row of the night previous."[107]

Jack Dalton, the deputy marshal who replaced Healy, arrested twelve whites and Indians. Eventually Tom was convicted of murder while Jack Wade was acquitted of manslaughter.

Johnny's motivation in resigning from office in fall 1891 went beyond reacting to affairs in Dyea: he had new commercial plans. He had pondered the future of Alaska long enough. He looked beyond his role as a petty trader and a scarcely paid deputy marshal to far greater possibilities. He was ambitious—and confident. The boom would certainly come, and he wanted to position himself to take the fullest advantage of it. He thought to follow the example of William Moore and prepare to capitalize on his key location at Dyea, but that plan had limited possibilities. Other merchants would flock in to compete for the trade that he had cultivated, and he was powerless to keep them out. But he had another, bigger, plan. He would jump in big with an entire trading and transportation network, challenging the ACC's dominance on the Yukon. It would require huge amounts of capital, but he knew where to look for it.

# 10

# Empire of the North

*I prefer riding high
to joining the hard mushers.*
                    —Johnny Healy

When Johnny left Dyea for the Outside in late 1891, he knew what he wanted and had some idea who would provide it. En route he stopped at Helena to visit old friends and swap stories—and perhaps to sound out some local men on his northern schemes. In the six years since he had left Montana he had changed a good deal. Johnny even found himself something of a celebrity as a survivor of the old days. One friend, Hugh McQuaid, urged Julian Ralph, a *Harper's* writer, to interview "a very remarkable man, who used to be a terror to road agents and Injuns . . . a man from another world."[108]

To Ralph, Healy looked ordinary enough. He appeared to be in his mid-fifties, "very spare and hard of flesh, with brown hair and moustache and a grizzled goatee." In his correct business suit he looked nothing like a man from "another world," and declined to talk about earlier times. "He was willing to tell me all about the people and resources of Alaska" because the selling of Alaska was much on his mind.

Tom Power's greeting showed his appreciation of his friend's persistence in tackling life on a new frontier. "Johnny," called Power, now a U.S. senator, "you don't mean to say you are still at it, with your hand on your gun and the border life around you?" It probably took Healy only a short time to convince Power that his motivation was soundly commercial rather than adventurous. Healy likely gave the merchant prince of Fort Benton an opportunity to invest in his Alaskan scheme, but, if Johnny did, Power declined. Later communications between the two indicate that Power probably offered to help out in Washington where he could. Johnny may have later induced Power to provide capital; that Johnny named a Yukon River steamboat after him suggests he did.

Eventually Power and Healy got to reminiscing, giving Ralph a chance to hear Montana adventure stories—but only after McQuaid placed him where Johnny could not see him. While Edwin Adney, describing this event, stresses Healy's modesty around journalists, the visiting Alaskan more likely lacked the time or interest in the old days just then.

Healy's Fort Benton visit in December gives us an idea of what he had given up and what he had gained in Alaska. His pioneer achievements gained him popularity and the appreciation of Montanans. Alaska's scant population makes it difficult to gauge his standing among Alaskans at that time, but when the Yukon population soared a few years later, many viewed him disparagingly. In Montana, however, he remained a favorite son. Most of Montana's newspapers heralded his return. The *Helena Herald* reporter acknowledged that more recent residents might know little, if anything, about Healy. "But . . . the old-timers will recall scenes and incidents of the early history of Montana in which he was a prominent actor." Healy's adventures in Alaska, the reporter noted, are "as interesting as the tales of Rider Haggard or Henry M. Stanley." Healy has been a trader, miner, trapper, and now plans "one of the greatest salmon canneries on the Pacific Coast." The reporter told of Johnny's election as second chief of an Indian tribe, of immense copper deposits in the interior, and of Johnny bringing with him "the finest collection of furs ever seen in this country." Reports of Healy's greeting of his children after seven years absence betrayed some confusion. "He congratulated his unmarried daughter on her choice of her husband and got gloriously mixed up in his bearings due to his long absence." Even so, "The reception of Mr. Healy by the old timers was in the nature of an ovation."[109]

Another newspaper expressed even more exuberance in welcoming the much-admired pioneer to Helena. "If there be an old timer or resident of six years in Montana who has never heard of Johnnie [sic] Healy let him stand up and be counted in the realms of unspeakable ignorance. If you had seen the old boys gather about him yesterday afternoon you would have known that he was a man of some reputation, a good fellow, or both." Healy came to Montana "years and years ago, and he has enjoyed or suffered more interesting experiences than any known Montanan. If these could be rightly told a volume or so of charming reminiscences would be the result. Mr. Healy is too modest to tell all in detail, but his friends know a good part of his history. . . . Fifty-two years weigh lightly on his face and form. His hair is yet dark, though his moustache and long goatee are streaked with gray. His body is lithe and slim and as straight as ever. . . . He was quite as glad to see old friends as they to find him and grew animated and reminiscent as old times were recalled."[110]

The newspapers emphasized in Healy's Montana adventures their sense of significant past events. The *River Press* published a story of Johnny's claim to have first seen Sitting Bull at Fort Lincoln in the 1860s when the Indian was a so-called blanket Indian, a loafer around the store. Johnny also claimed that when Sitting Bull was kicked off the military post he organized an army and was cunning enough to make himself its leader. "Then came the terrible Custer massacre, in which Sitting Bull played no active part, but for which he secured a newspaper reputation as the greatest of Indian statesman." Later, the newspaper reported, Healy witnessed Chief Joseph's surrender and the famed meeting of army officers with Sitting Bull in Canada. "Mr. Healy has thus seen two great pictures in the fast disappearing history of American Indian life. He has been in fights with bands and individuals when only his desperate courage saved him." On the less heroic side the paper reported that Johnny was keenly interested in the coming Chicago

World's Fair, and "is gathering a large collection of Alaska curiosities for that exposition."

The Montana homecoming gratified Johnny, although he felt anxious to get on to Chicago to present his proposals to businessmen there. When he reached Chicago he made his first call on an old business connection from his buffalo-robe-trading days, Portus B. Weare. Weare had purchased most of the buffalo robes gathered in Montana and the adjacent regions of Canada during the 1870s and 1880s. When the buffalo trade died Weare moved into meat packing with stockyards in Chicago and Nebraska. Weare knew little about Alaska, but Johnny, eloquently persuasive, soon convinced him that the territory was about to boom and that a well-funded commercial company could make huge profits.

Existing portraits that show a stout-figured, comfortable-looking man, belie Weare's adventurous nature. A timid, conventional businessman would not invest in Alaska. The North was terra incognita to investors, save for those canny men in San Francisco who nurtured the Alaska Commercial Company. Weare trusted Johnny Healy's conviction that the ACC lacked the means or the will to run a rival company off the Yukon River.

The ACC, originally the Hutchinson, Kohl Co., emerged from the pack of traders who flocked to Alaska after its purchase in 1867 to dominate northern commerce. The ACC assured its trade dominance by securing an exclusive lease on the fur-seal rich Pribilof Islands. Other traders compete for the fur trade of the Yukon River and elsewhere, but the ACC held a huge margin in fur-seal profits. With the entry of LeRoy "Jack" McQuesten, Alfred Mayo, and Arthur Harper in 1874-75, the ACC had the services of capable men who kept the fur flowing from the Yukon country and also made money supplying miners.

A review of the ACC's apparent reluctance to expand its trading network despite the heavy influx of prospectors convinced Weare of the soundness of Healy's judgment. The ACC had only three cranky, low-powered little steamers on the Yukon River, the *Yukon*, the *St. Michael*, and the *New Racket*, until the Fortymile strike in 1886. They then added a larger vessel, the *Arctic*, at one hundred and forty tons, which sunk in its first season. Healy planned a boat for his company's first trading season that had a greater capacity at two hundred tons than the entire ACC fleet—a boat that was the beginning of a fleet that would dominate the river. He argued that the pioneer company, deeply committed to its traditional fur trade, was ignoring opportunities for more business. He told Weare of the ACC's laggardly response to the request McQuesten made for more goods after Stewart River mining developed. The company woke up some when the dramatic message about Fortymile gold reached San Francisco, but it still remained tentative about opportuni-

*John J. Healy in 1893, a year after the founding of the NAT&T.*
— Montana Historical Society

ties that seemed obvious to Healy. Weare, convinced by Healy's presentation, offered $50,000 to capitalize the company.

Healy and Weare agreed that their new company would put steamboats on the Yukon River and open stores without delay. Weare promised he could work fast to provide cash by summer 1892. Weare also obtained a relatively small investment from John Cudahy of the great Chicago packing interests, then a much larger one as well as money from several other Chicago men. Articles of Incorporation filed March 30, 1892, showed Weare's subscription at $19,700 (shares were $100 each); Healy's at $16,700; William J. Fyffe at $10,000; and C. A. Weare, John L. Fyffe, John Cudahy, and Oswald F. Wolfe at $1,000 each. Weare and Healy controlled the majority of the interest in the company, holding 370 of the 500 shares issued. When they later increased the capital stock, Cudahy's subscription became more substantial, and Cudahy family members became involved in company management—a move that proved unfortunate for Johnny. After the initial stock expansion Healy and Weare may still have held one-third each, but as capital needs accelerated their shares grew proportionally smaller, as did their ability to control policies. Besides cash, Healy also contributed the plan of organization and his experience, taking on the task of directing field operations for the North American Transportation and Trading Company (NAT&T), as they named their new company.

## The First Season

The men made preparations in a remarkably short time considering the scope of the new company's enterprise. In June, Johnny and Portus Weare left Chicago by train for Seattle. In early July 1892 they voyaged from Seattle on a chartered steamer, *Alice Blanchard*. Other NAT&T personnel aboard included Charles Hamilton, bookkeeper; Capt. John C. Barr, a Missouri steamboat skipper who would take the company's first riverboat up the Yukon; other river boat crewmen; a blacksmith and sixteen carpenters to build the boat; Weare's son William; and Johnny's wife and her maid. Also present was Wilbur F. Cornell, a correspondent for the *Oregonian* of Portland and the *San Francisco Examiner*.

Captain Barr documented the momentous beginning of the trading company. Without duties aboard the *Alice Blanchard*, he was free to write lively letters about the voyage to a friend in St. Paul. The ship, with her heavy load of trade goods and construction materials, was a slow sailer, giving the passengers plenty of time to talk. In the ward room Johnny's stories of buffalo and Indians seemed tame compared with the sea yarns of ship officers, commented Barr. Being familiar with all the Montana stories, he found the sea stories novel. The mariners told of terrible storms, shipwrecks, whaling ventures, and the recent excitement over pelagic sealing that brought about a confrontation between Americans and British over hunting regulations. Healy and Weare understood why the U.S. opposed pelagic hunting. Such sea hunting included the killing of pregnant cows and interfered with the orderly, controlled harvest of fur seals on the beaches of the Pribilof Islands. Even though the prohibition of sea hunting would benefit the ACC, their trading rival on the Yukon River, they opposed it as patriotic Americans and conservationists. Perhaps the former buffalo-hide traders had learned something from their role in exterminating the buffalo; at any rate, they warned fellow passengers that the fur seal, too, would disappear unless the American position prevailed.[111]

In time the slow ship reached Dutch Harbor for a refueling stop that provided its passengers a chance for socializing with other mariners. The ships in port included *Glory of the Seas*, one of the last and grandest of the famed clipper ships, several whaling ships, and one of the ships of the U.S. Revenue Cutter Service (forerunner of the U.S. Coast Guard) on Bering Sea patrol. Revenue Cutter Service officers and the whaling masters told good stories, helping the waiting time pass agreeably.

From Dutch Harbor the voyage continued to St. Michael on August 2. St. Michael, originally a base of the Russian American Company and later a station for the ACC, was located on an island in Norton Sound, near the wide-spreading delta of the Yukon River. Ocean ships could get only as close to the Yukon delta as St. Michael Island, beyond which the water became too shallow. On the island were about twenty buildings, providing housing for natives and a handful of whites, and a Russian Orthodox Church.

The "very cold reception" given them when they called on the ACC trader to discuss the best place to land their cargo and construct a river steamboat shocked the naive traders. The ACC management felt threatened by the competition of the first substantial rival it had ever encountered in the Yukon trade. With Chicago meat-packing money and direction by a well-known veteran trader with Alaskan experience, they took the NAT&T seriously. While the traders did not "expect to be greeted with open arms," they were startled when the ACC denied them use of the island's newly fenced waterfront. The ACC installed the fence to keep the NAT&T out, but it failed in its purpose. Johnny found what he considered a better landing place and boat construction site near the ACC post. They quickly started work on a station to be called Fort Get There (renamed "Healy" in 1897), and unloaded the *Alice Blanchard*.

Once unloaded, the *Alice Blanchard* steamed south to Seattle with Weare aboard. He took charge of directing the Chicago and Seattle offices of the company.

*The steamboat* Portus B. Weare *taking on wood and Indian visitors on the Yukon River, 1895.* —Presbyterian Historical Society

Healy acknowledged Weare's importance to the company when he named the company's first steamer *Portus B. Weare.* While Healy was nominally in charge, Barr supervised the boat construction, and he launched the boat on September 15. The construction period was tense for Healy because much depended upon completing the *Portus B. Weare* before winter closed the river.

Barr disliked what he saw of Alaska and Alaskans during these hectic weeks. "I think I will come home after my year's contact is up," he wrote a friend, "because this is a country for the rich." He felt homesick and weary of St. Michael, a wind-swept, dismal spot that few travelers have described with any warmth. His only joy was gathering a few gift items for friends, including an oosik, the club-like bone of the male walrus's penis—an ever popular collector's trophy.

Regular transportation service from Pacific Coast ports to St. Michael was unavailable, so Johnny solicited government help through the efforts of Senator Tom Power of Montana. The U.S. Treasury ordered Capt. Michael Healy (no relation to Johnny) of the revenue cutter *Bear* to call at St. Michael on its voyage south to pick up the carpenters who built the *Portus B. Weare*. Johnny and Mike had discussed the matter in Seattle but needed official approval. Johnny considered Mike a man worth cultivating in the company's interest. The captain was friendly enough but close to the ACC managers, and Johnny wanted to woo him with favors. "His present ambition," Johnny wrote Power, "is to be sent to Paris to attend the Seal Arbitration. I told him I would write you on his behalf. I feel certain that it will be of great benefit to us if he learns that we have influence to secure him the appointment he desires."[112]

Johnny had more than a mercenary interest in Mike Healy. He considered the captain "the best posted man on the seal question in the service of the government as well as in Arctic and Bering Sea explorations." Mike Healy, who took ships of the Revenue Cutter Service into the Bering Sea and Arctic for many seasons, was a talented and personable mariner who, unfortunately, was an alcoholic. On a couple of occasions he nearly ruined his career until his excesses finally unhinged him some years later.

While building the boat, Barr was finding some of the first white Alaskans he encountered as ugly as the island. A Koyukuk miner who owned a twenty-ton schooner offered to show Barr the best channel route through the maze of the Yukon delta. Because he would soon have to pilot *Portus B. Weare,* Barr gladly accepted the opportunity. Barr learned that boat owners usually hired Indians to pilot boats on the river. The miner's style of command over his two Indian crewmen, demonstrated as he poured whiskey for himself and his guest in the wheelhouse, shocked Barr. Barr was accustomed to rough language on the Missouri River, but the Alaskan's introductory orders to his pilot and engineer set standards new to Barr. "Damn you," the miner told the pilot, "if you ground this boat or hit a rock I'll throw you overboard." Turning to the engineer his threat was "damn you, if you let the water get below that string on the gage I'll put a bullet in you." As Barr gaped the miner poured more drinks: "I guess we will have time to take a drink before anything serious happens," he said.[113]

Off they went. The miner drank steadily except when napping or eating, always remembering to say grace before meals—"a good, sound, orthodox profanity," as Barr noted. But the engineer refused to eat, claiming illness; then when the miner was busy at the table he forced open the trunk holding whiskey and got drunk. The miner thrashed the Indian and put him ashore as Barr marveled at the gentleness of Yukon natives. "Bless me if that had happened among the Sioux."

The ACC manager played dirty tricks in opposition to their construction project. Healy had a hard time hiring natives because "the ACC by bribes and threats did all in its power to keep them from working for us." When the NAT&T men offered natives wages in silver coin they refused it because the ACC trader had convinced them that silver was valueless. The men found signs of sabotage by unknown persons more alarming. When the boat's engine misfired during a trail run, Barr found gunny sacks stuffed in the exhaust and nails in the pumps.

The *P. B. Weare* was ready for the Yukon River on September 24. With relief the traders started off, then a grounding on a sand bar at the river's mouth delayed them for two days. Barr had hired an Indian pilot but the ACC had seen to it that the experienced men were not available. Of course, sandbar groundings were commonplace and only caused consternation when the season was advanced. But as the boat moved upriver, the men had ample sign that winter was near. Snow fell October 1, and three days later ice began forming in the river.

On October 5 the traders reached the village of Nulato, site of a trading station of Gregor Hakara, better known as Kokrine, a Finn who operated independently of the ACC. Nulato also had a Catholic mission, one of those the Jesuits had founded after Archbishop Seghers visit to the Yukon River. The Jesuits had sent nuns in 1888 to teach school at Nulato and Holy Cross on the Yukon. Nulato was 650 miles from St. Michael and the traders' destination at Fortymile lay another 1,300 miles ahead. Nonetheless, the voyage was over for the season. Ice prevented further progress. Johnny was bitterly disappointed to stop so far down river because it delayed the possibility of earnings for months.

For the other stranded voyagers the quiet winter life afforded few diversions. By hunting bear, rabbit, grouse, pheasant, and caribou to supplement their stock of groceries, they ate well, but it was gloomy without mail or work. Both Healy and Barr brought ample libraries along, giving them plenty to read, including Pepys, Burns, Emerson, Lamb, Chaucer, Byron, and Elliot. But, for all his experiences with the vicissitudes of frontier travel, Healy felt restive and depressed. Had he lost his grand opportunity to steal the march on the ACC? Had his grand commercial scheme failed ignominiously at the very start? Aggravated to be imprisoned by ice, he could do nothing.

The success of Charles Hamilton, the company bookkeeper, in reaching the Outside with dispatches from Healy provided the most cheering event of the winter. Information from Healy enabled the other company directors to prepare well for the 1893 season.

Hamilton, young and vigorous even if inexperienced in northern travel, left the boat in late November with the Rev. Jules Prevost and a couple of Indian guides. Prevost, an Episcopalian, was traveling upriver from Anvik, a village where his denomination had started a mission in 1887. Instead of following the Yukon all the way to Fortymile, they ascended the Tanana River some three hundred and fifty miles to celebrate Christmas at Nenana, an Indian village, then pushed on to the Tanana headwaters, crossed over to the North Fork of the Fortymile, then went down river to reach the camp on the Yukon by January 14. Almost two hundred miners resided at Fortymile and would have been good customers for goods aboard the *P. B. Weare*, especially, Hamilton thought, for sweet stuff like sugar and molasses, much in demand for the several liquor stills there. The camp's two saloons had closed for the season for want of bottled goods. Jack McQuesten, although affiliated with the ACC, greeted Hamilton amiably. McQuesten saw a bright future for the country; he had taken in more gold in 1892 than in any earlier season.

Prevost stayed at Fortymile, but Hamilton continued on with John Reed, a six-year veteran of the country. The men pushed upriver to the headwaters, thence over Chilkoot Pass to Dyea. Hamilton felt relieved when they got through safely, because he knew all about the tragic trip of Tom Williams and Indian Bob in 1886. At Dyea he stopped with Edgar Wilson, still Johnny's partner although the store was not part of the NAT&T network, before making it to Juneau and eventually to Chicago.

Folks in Juneau were impressed with Hamilton's travels, believed to be the first winter crossing to the coast from the interior since Williams and Bob had made their ill-fated and much shorter journey from Fortymile in 1886. A Juneau newspaper described the twenty-two-year-old Hamilton, "who was every inch a gentleman," as extremely modest over his 1,500-mile journey on snowshoes. The newspaper willingly publicized Hamilton's accusations against the ACC's conduct and sabotage at St. Michael, because Juneau people resented the near monopoly of the ACC on the Yukon, and the town's merchants believed that miners would be better off outfitting in Juneau.[114]

One of the letters Healy entrusted to Charles Hamilton was addressed to Al Hamilton, his friend in Montana. It showed little discouragement at the steamboat's delay. "I think I have struck another Whoop-Up country," Healy told his old Fort Whoop-Up partner, "though much quieter and safer, but a healthy and good country to live in." He expressed confidence that "I have got into an unexplored gold field. There is years of work ahead, and when all other fields of exploration are exhausted the miner and prospector will turn to this, the great forgotten and misrepresented country."

As always in letters to the Outside, he referred to the government's neglect in providing mail, surveys, and developmental help, which delayed settlement of the territory. "I am contented now, but will be more so when we can read news of the world along the entire length of this river once a month. Think of a river one-third larger than the Mississippi and nothing known about it. We are here to develop and will in time make known its richness."[115]

## The Second Season

With the ardently awaited break-up of the river ice in April 1893, Healy moved upriver to Fortymile. He chose a site just across the river from McQuesten's store and named it Fort Cudahy. He contracted with a local carpenter, Tom O'Brien, to build a store. O'Brien was willing to take a $1,000 note from Johnny, who pretended that he lacked cash because the key to the safe had been mislaid. Fortymile miners laughed at this story. They had sometimes been short of cash themselves and recognized Healy's dilemma. But they liked Healy no better for being strapped for cash. Healy's years of trading at Dyea and ferrying many of the men on their passage of Lynn Canal from Juneau to the Chilkoot, had made him few friends. He struck prospectors as a pushy old fellow, a know-it-all. The trader presumed to challenge the rich and well-established pioneer company yet lacked enough money to hire a carpenter. This apparent folly gave the miners plenty to hoot at, but they could find a greater cause for derision in the trader's choice of his first store at Fortymile. Miners thought that Healy showed a lot of gall in starting a direct rivalry with the best-loved man in Alaska, Jack McQuesten. Men appreciated having other traders in the field and disliked the ACC, but they felt intensely loyal to Jack, who often enough had provided their grubstakes.

Many miners, including Frank Buteau, believed that the ACC only increased food shipments for Stewart River in 1886 because McQuesten had threatened to form an independent post. "They shipped the food and one could easily see from the brands and quality . . . that they did not want any miners in the Yukon River Valley. The bacon was in slabs three feet long, all of which was yellow . . . the flour was moldy, the rice was lumpy, the fruit was green, and in the beans were plenty of rocks and gravel." This diet, Buteau argued, made scurvy inevitable.[116]

The ACC's interests were well looked after in Washington. In 1889 the company steamer *Arctic*, loaded with provisions, sank on the Yukon. Later the company got the steamboat back into service, but the accident forced Fortymile miners to abandon their camp and retreat down river to St. Michael for want of food. There the company fed twenty-five to forty miners on credit. Come spring, the miners refused to settle their accounts, charging that the company's negligence had compelled their exodus. On the ACC's appeal to the government it received $4,000 compensation for feeding "destitute" men. "Quite a profit," considered Buteau.

Buteau was probably glad to see Healy's outfit come to the Yukon. "If you could see the food we had to eat from 1886 to 1893," he said in later years, "you would laugh, but if you found yourself a thousand miles from civilization, without roads, as we were, it might bring tears to your eyes."

Johnny knew some miners resented him, but he lost no sleep over it. He made a bad start because of the delayed voyage and temporary cash shortage but his company had the means to make the ACC anxious—as soon became clear. As for the antagonism of miners, well, he figured that most men would buy where they could do best, and he meant to undersell the ACC. Johnny had been trading for quite a while and discounted the loyalty of customers to any cause but their pocketbooks. Besides, the country was filling up with men who knew nothing of Jack McQuesten or the ACC.

Johnny would have been well advised to look to his unpopularity and try to make a few friends. His style of doing business and the demeanor he developed in Montana fit poorly in interior Alaska. Individuals in the small white community had, of necessity, formed the habit of looking after one another. McQuesten, of course, had been grateful to every new prospector who ventured into the interior and treated them accordingly. Healy represented a new commercial era, one that miners welcomed in some respects but deplored in others. And, somewhat unfairly, they directed their scorn at Healy.

Johnny's air of certainty, even of arrogance, masked his serious worries over other aspects of his business—and perhaps deep insecurities. Trading and transportation on as large a scale as he conceived for the Yukon, was new to him, and he had never been so much at the mercy of the climate, with the short navigation season. But he opened up with high hopes and survived his first actual trading season. He fostered considerable growth over the next couple of years, so that by 1895 he could make clear his intentions and muster up a confident air. The area boasted of a newspaper, the *Yukon Press*, where he placed a large advertisement to announce his ambitions:

STAND FROM UNDER!

PRICES ARE FALLING,

WE HAVE COME TO STAY.[117]

The ad promised that "we will buy goods on commission, freight the same to all points on the Yukon, buy gold dust and furs, furnish estimates on mining machinery, supply traders and ship their collection of furs to the best houses in America and England. We will have gold dust run into bars and have the assay value stamped on same. We will buy gold bars and transact a general banking business at Ft. Cudahy, N.W.T. and Circle City, Alaska. Our principal distributing posts are Fort Get There, St. Michael's Island, Alaska; Fort Cudahy, N.W.T.; Fort Morton, Kotzebue Sound; and Circle City, Yukon River, Alaska. Our branch posts are Ft. Selkirk, Stewart River, N.W.T.; Miller Creek, Ft. Weare, Ft. Healy, Ft. Hamilton, Anvik and Minuke, Alaska. The distributing posts will be in charge of competent men who will note carefully the wants of the trade. All business conducted on strictly cash basis."

The ad concluded with reference to Healy's expertise. "Our stock of goods for the season 1895 has been selected with great care by their manager, who has devoted many years studying the wants of miners and mountaineers."

The *Yukon Press*, a pioneer weekly founded in 1894 by the Rev. Jules Prevost at Fort Adams (Tanana), was usually printed with the help of prospector and independent trader Gordon Bettles. The newspaper's very existence signified the development of the Yukon since the Fortymile strike.

Gordon Bettles, who worked without compensation on the paper, was the kind of trader who was popular in Alaska. Bettles arrived in 1886 at age twenty-six after a varied career as a typesetter, a miner in Colorado, Idaho, and Montana, and a short stint as a Montana cowboy. He worked briefly at the Treadwell Mine of Juneau-Douglas, then crossed the Chilkoot Pass to go into the Fortymile in 1888. He prospected, then kept several stores on the Yukon and in the Koyukuk country. Like Jack McQuesten, he gave liberal credit to prospectors, and he clearly identified closely with the men he provisioned. Bettles was always good companion for the mining men, quick of wit, and ready with a story. The inscription he blazed on a tree atop Wolverine Mountain near Rampart expressed his exuberance on an early prospecting venture. "I claim all the land I can see from here," the inscription read. He found little gold and made little money as a trader, but he could claim many friends.[118]

As the NAT&T advertisement made clear, Healy defied the pleasant informality of the old days by insisting on a "strictly cash basis." This cold manner of trading annoyed the miners accustomed to the easy credit policies of McQuesten and other traders. Easy credit amounted to grubstaking. It offered a great help to miners, and it acknowledged that they were appreciated as daring pioneers. But with an unpleasant jolt, Healy introduced modern, cutthroat commerce on the Yukon. If you want low prices, don't look for credit. It made good sense to Healy who figured that the miners would first protest, then buy the cheapest. He was right to some extent, but he wrongly assumed that the miners would not bear a lasting grudge. As the pace quickened on the Yukon and new men poured in, the old-timers always had time to knock Johnny Healy,

146

and the recent arrivals promptly joined in with their own complaints.

Healy's detractors predicted that his company would fail and ardently wished for it. Writing from Fortymile in July 1893, John Twan reported that "the new company is in a bad fix." Twan thought Healy was the problem. "No one here seems to like Healy. He gets little trade because the miners are down on him, and even the whites and Indians he had on the steamer all left him except for the captain and engineer." Twan thought that if the company failed to send another manager, "it will go up the flume." But Twan's report also noted that food prices at Fortymile were "not bad." Flour cost $7.50 a hundred pounds, while beans and bacon went at 18¢ and 40¢ a pound, respectively, despite the high freight rates from St. Michael—$150 per ton. A month later Sydney Wilson reached Juneau from Fortymile to report that both McQuesten and Healy's stores were doing well and that food was "remarkably cheap."[119]

Life on the Yukon was strongly tied to river steamboats like *Portus B. Weare*. The boat, similar in design to those used on the Missouri River, was a stern-wheeler, three decks high, with two smokestacks behind the wheelhouse. The bow and stern were flat platforms designed to be on a level with the bank when moored. The enclosed first deck held freight and steerage passengers. The second deck had a few private cabins and a large dormitory area. Around its walls were bunks and in its center sat a wood burning stove for heating and cooking. The top deck held the wheel house and captain's quarters.

On a typical voyage the *Portus B. Weare* would navigate the eighty miles of open sea from its dock at St. Michael Island, then move cautiously into the Yukon delta. At this point the salt water had to be pumped from the steam engine and boilers and replaced by fresh water. Then the monotonous river voyage commenced, especially slowly along the shallow lower river. Stops at native villages and missions, and more frequently for wood, provided diversions. In the early days wood cutters had yet to established yards along the river, so crew members had to cut their own wood along the way. Boats burned plenty of wood. When the current was especially swift, the *P. B. Weare* needed a cord and a half to two cords per hour. The boat made slow progress, with eighty miles a day about the average. The eighteen hundred miles to Fortymile took about nineteen days. Coming down went much faster, taking around ten days. First-class fares were $65 to Circle, about half of the fare for ocean transport from San Francisco to St. Michael. For freight, NAT&T charged 53¢ per ton per running hour during the boom years.

# Call for the Mounties

Life in river towns such as Fortymile was often flavored by the contrasting, and often conflicting, personalities of the town's residents.

The Anglican bishop at Fortymile, William Bompas, had little in common with Johnny, but they reached an agreement on an important matter that had far-reaching effects on later Yukon development. Bompas believed that the town of Fortymile was within Canada even if much of the mining district lay on the American side of the border. And Bompas hated the miners' debauchery of the natives with the help of whiskey.

Johnny also disliked the abuses of liquor, and had other reasons for annoyance with Fortymile's lack of law and order. Alaska's court system had been established nearly a decade earlier in 1885 at Sitka, but the government had yet to assign a deputy marshal or judge anywhere in the interior. For any criminal or civil dispute residents convened a miners meeting to settle it. This traditional mining-camp means of keeping order sometimes worked well. Miners could direct a thief to get out of the region, and intervene to settle violent disputes, but it was subject to abuse. As an unpopular trader, Johnny feared rough handling by the meeting. He got a taste of it when he and Belle locked out her maid who had been spending too much time on the town at night. The maid appealed to the miners for back wages and money to get back to the States. Pleased to hear the girl's complaints, the miners meeting ordered that Johnny pay her a year's wages and provide her transportation to the Outside.

Johnny immediately reacted with anger. He remembered how the Canadian government had formed the North West Mounted Police to deal with Yankee whiskey traders on the Whoop-Up trail. He had distanced himself from Fenians and from knocking the Canadian police and other British institutions. What Fortymile needed, concluded the trader who had long since quit the illicit whiskey trade, was proper Canadian law enforcement supported by his old friends the Mounties. Healy wrote to one friend, Mounted Police Officer Sam Steele, and explained the situation. He also directed his bookkeeper, Charles Hamilton, to write to the appropriate officials in Ottawa. Bishop Bompas wrote to the Canadian authorities at the same time. The NAT&T's letter stressed the money Canada was losing in uncollected customs and the mistreatment of Indians by miners. These issues were both mentioned several times in a Privy Council Resolution of 1894 calling for action.

Action swiftly followed. The government ordered the Mounties to establish a base at Fortymile. In the summer of 1894 the police arrived and started building their station at Fort Cudahy. Whether by accident or because Healy provided the site, the Mountie post stood close to Healy's store. Healy was pleased to have the police in the country, in contrast to his attitude at Alberta twenty years earlier. On both occasions, though, he had much to do with the assignment and the activities of the Mounties.

Healy's miner neighbors were less happy about the police. Most Yukon miners were Americans and felt comfortable with the absence of authority. Now they were subject to foreign rule; they would have to face Canadian taxes and restrictions. They vehemently blamed Healy for bringing in the police and disliked him more than ever.

The arrival of the police must have improved the social life of the camp because the new residents included several wives of officers. Residents or visitors reported little of the social life at Fortymile in the mid-1890s, but a much traveled Englishman recorded some gossip. Talbot Clifton, a wealthy eccentric, reached Fortymile in 1895 via the Chilkoot Pass, seeking relief from boredom. A spoiled lad, he had inherited a great family estate at age sixteen, then squandered his income while fooling his way through Eton and Cambridge. Financial advisors, alarmed at his mounting debts, sent him abroad to "rough it" until estate income caught up with his debts. The precocious young rake was roughing it in a Palace Hotel suite in San Francisco, unable to make ends meet on his $5,000 monthly allowance, when someone sparked an interest in him about Yukon prospecting. Suddenly his usual pursuits—gambling, polo, collecting art, making music on his solid gold flute, and roistering with many loving American gals who helped spend his money—seemed fatiguing. Impetuously, he sailed for Alaska to find gold.[120]

Talbot reached the crude mining community of Fortymile and found little to his liking. He remained nine days, waiting for the steamboat heading down river, staying in a log shack with three miners and an Indian woman. To pass the time he visited the Mounties at Fort Cudahy and got busy putting out a local newspaper with some other men. "We are working hard at it," he wrote a friend. "We are all disappointed because we cannot find any scandal. Twenty-five copies are to be issued at five dollars each. It is not too dear as the papers will all be written by hand."[121]

According to Talbot, another Englishman, Bob Miley, was a town hero of sorts for a short while. Miley had arrived in 1894 with only $15 to his name. Within four days he paid $500 for a year's outfit. Whether he found gold or won it gambling is not clear. He soon bought a saloon and won another man's mine at the faro wheel. His hired miners washed out $10,000 and he opened a new, more glamorous saloon. Talbot and virtually everyone else in town attended a big dance celebrating the saloon opening. He danced with an Indian girl, whose body "moved as a bird's throat moves in song." Some folks lacked a sense of social democracy, Talbot observed. One woman, "full of sudden pomp and wealth, debarred Indians from her private dance given a few days later. That she should be so eclectic aroused comment," wrote Talbot.

Belle Healy also figured in Talbot's gossip. She had called on the wife of Captain Constantine of the Mounted Police, then left in a huff when the wife of the ACC storekeeper appeared. Folks laughed, yet condemned the slight as "an absurd phase of rudeness."

Meanwhile, people remained angry at Johnny Healy. The steamboat *Portus B. Weare* arrived with miners but without stores. The ACC's *Arctic* was supposed to arrive with supplies but was seriously overdue. Someone said that it had collided with the *P. B. Weare* downriver. Suspicion of foul play for commercial gain fixed on Healy. "Soon indeed, just as had been expected, prices in the store surged up," Talbot reported. "The tongues that scandalized the store-owner grew sharper. One day Healy had no butter; the next day it was salable, at a price. Healy had no medicines but, the need sharpening and the price rising, an odd bottle could be found. Healy was an affliction-monger." While Talbot alone gives this particular story of price gouging, others made similar charges often enough to suggest that Johnny took advantage of real or pretended shortages.

Harry DeWindt visited the mining camps a year after Talbot. An odd character, this egotistical and adventurous Englishman yearned for public acclaim as an explorer, although he was too late to gain the triumphs of a Richard Burton or Henry Stanley. DeWindt may have met Healy at Fortymile or Circle in 1896, when the travel writer's ambition had been to reach his home in Paris from New York via the Bering Strait. DeWindt's book detailing his journey became a best seller despite his failure to achieve his goal because it appeared at the peak of the Klondike gold excitement. The visitor derided both mining camps and sneered at the tongue-in-cheek pretensions of Circle folks who called it the "Paris of Alaska." He "failed to trace the slightest resemblance to the beautiful French city," but he found more "gaiety, or life, of a tawdry, disreputable description than at Forty Mile, for every tenth house was either a gambling or a drinking saloon, or a den of even worse description." He ignored Jack McQuesten's corrugated iron shed, a fire-proof warehouse that all miners admired. And Circle's dance hall entertainment offended him as well. "I attended one of these entertainments. . . . The orchestra consisted of a violin and guitar—almost drowned by a noisy crowd at the bar, where a wrangle took place, on an average, every five minutes." Obviously, the debonair Englishman identified little with the mud-stained men who paid a dollar to dance with a hostess and thought it well worth the price.[122]

DeWindt gave a highly exaggerated account of crossing the Chilkoot. He likened the attainment of the summit to a passage over a towering peak of the Alps. DeWindt failed to get back to Europe via Bering Strait but managed to bridge the gap going the other way from Paris to New York a few years later. His trip publicized a trans-Alaska-Siberian railroad promotional scheme that later became an obsession of Healy's.

Johnny found the field management of the expanding company was an exacting and sometimes exasperating responsibility. In 1894 the company built a new store at Fort Get There (St. Michael). That season the *P. B. Weare* carried stores up to Fort Cudahy in good order. After a good trading season, Healy felt justified in going Outside over the 1894-95 winter. In Chicago he urged the Weares and Cudahys to fund a further expansion of the company. The stampede to the Birch Creek diggings and the founding of Circle prompted the company to establish a store there in 1895, and they also expanded the St. Michael post that season.

Late in 1893 rumors reached Fortymile of a major gold discovery on Birch Creek, some 240 miles down river. When the ACC's *Arctic* reached Fortymile on its first 1894 voyage, the discovery was confirmed. Fortymile miners were also told that a base for the new diggings had been established on the Yukon—the town of Circle, which soon boomed. With this news, the rush to the new diggings from Fortymile was on. The first contingent voyaged down river on the *Arctic*. By 1895 Circle's population far surpassed that of Fortymile. Healy kept his store at Fort Cudahy open but made arrangements for a new store while wintering Outside over 1894-95 and got the company going in the new town in summer 1895. He and Belle built a large log home there as the population soared to over five hundred.

Belle Healy no sooner got established in Circle then she had to go out to San Francisco for eye treatment. Johnny also soon learned of the death of his old Dyea partner, Edgar Wilson, in mid-May. He had to make arrangements for Dyea when he got back to Alaska, he put Sam Heron, his son-in-law, in charge.

As Circle boomed, businesses and amenities developed. The Birch Creek mines were sixty-five to eighty miles from Circle so freighting became a big business. Jack McQuesten brought in books to help establish a library. Showmen arrived from Juneau and Outside to provide regular entertainment and the *Yukon Press* moved to Circle from Fort Adams. Virtually all the buildings were log cabins, but McQuesten's ACC store boasted a storehouse made of corrugated iron.

Over the winter of 1894-95 the Yukon had one thousand residents, but hundreds more came in with the opening of navigation in 1895. By the end of the season Birch Creek's gold production totalled $150,000. The flow of stampeders picked up again in 1896 and Circle's population reached seven hundred, Circle's peak year and one during which residents could either enjoy the variety show at the Tivoli Music Hall or see George T. Snow's dramas at the Grand Opera House. Later in the summer, Harry Ash showed up with another variety act, including the lovely Drummond sisters.

In the new, larger camp Healy faced less resentment than he had earlier at Fortymile. Clearly, he was "here to stay," and the majority of miners were recent arrivals to the interior. The *Yukon Press* commended him for creating interest among Outside people about the Yukon and using "his influence with the government to bring better conditions to our neglected region." The newspaper sternly denied a rumor that Joe Goldsmith, "in charge of land transportation for the NAT&T," smuggled whiskey into the country.[123]

But these favorable mentions were deceptive. Johnny made few efforts to improve his popularity and the seeds of resentment among the pioneer miners were deeply implanted. When the public needed a scapegoat to satisfy its anger at conditions, the tough, aggressive Irishman became an easy target.

The year 1896 was a watershed for Alaska and the Yukon. As the country developed, the NAT&T directors reviewed company management. The absence of company records makes judging the efficiency of Healy's management of operations difficult, but other directors felt dissatisfied. In 1896 they sent out Ely Weare, the son of Portus B. Weare (who was appointed company president that year), to oversee management. That year the company launched a new steamboat, *John J. Healy*, the largest boat on the river at 241 tons, and Johnny probably felt good when he looked at his oil portrait displayed aboard. Company capital increased to $450,000 and new officers included Michael Cudahy, Ernest Hamilton, and Charles Hutchinson.

The more sedate businessmen of Chicago must have wondered at reports of brawling among NAT&T company men on the Yukon in the fall of 1896. How odd that major stockholder and general manager John J. Healy would fight a steamboat skipper in a saloon. William Johns, who disliked Johnny, let the event fit with Johnny's disposition. "He was a strong character and extremely vindictive," Johns believed. "He told me he never felt right unless he had a fight on his hands—he usually had more than one—and he never forgot and never forgave."[124]

Johns claimed to have witnessed the fight at Circle between Johnny and Capt. E. D. Dixon of the *Portus B. Weare*. According to Johns the fight occurred because Healy, "jealous of Dixon's authority sought to discredit him," accusing him of stealing ship's stores for presents to Lottie Burns, a former dance hall girl. Mrs. Healy cheered on the fight until the men were separated. Healy fired Dixon, whom the ACC later hired. Meanwhile, Dixon appealed to the miners meeting for damages because he had a three-year contract with the NAT&T. According to Johns, the miners ruled in Dixon's favor.

A Juneau newspaper's account of the fight and aftermath seems more reliable than Johns' story. This version holds that Lottie's birthday was coming and she wished to make the other Circle girls envious. She asked the love-stricken Dixon to deposit $500 with the barkeeper to be handed over to her on the gala day in the presence of others helping her celebrate. It would be a great lark, and she would return the money later. The caper worked like a charm, then Lottie got confused about the arrangement. A gift was a gift, she told the unhappy skipper, who appealed for a miners meeting to settle the matter. Because the miners blamed Dixon's infatuation with Lottie for his inability to get the *P. B. Weare* to Circle before navigation closed, they ruled for Lottie.[125]

Dixon's failure to reach Circle enraged Healy, who suspended him pending action by the company's board of directors. Dixon, who continued to draw his salary and board at Circle, presented his case to the miners meeting. Healy demanded a jury trial. The miners refused his request, so he ignored the proceedings. Miners liked Healy even less than Dixon and awarded Dixon $4,000, then decided a couple of days later to hear the case again with a jury. Jurors arrived at damages of $2,800 and charged Healy $400 for the costs of the trial. According to Ely Gage, a NAT&T officer who probably served as the newspaper story's source, Healy was ready to pay but neither Dixon nor the court ever demanded payment. If this account was accurate, Johnny was treated shabbily by the miners meeting.

Inconsistencies exist in both versions of the story. Johnny probably would have refused to pay both the judgment and the $400 fee, if he had actually been asked.

Jim Bender told a third account of the event. Bender had an interesting relationship with Johnny: he had served as a deputy under Sheriff Healy at Fort Benton and served on the jury at the miners meeting trial involving Healy and Dixon. Bender said nothing about Lottie but recalled a struggle for authority between Dixon and Healy that led to brawling. "We had lots of fun over it. . . . Healy was lucky to get out of it. He wasn't going to have no kangaroo trial—that is, a miners meeting trial."[126]

The tawdry side of commercial affairs on the Yukon shed light beyond what they show of Healy's character. Johnny's confrontation with the miners meeting shows an especially intriguing part of the Yukon society. While some sourdoughs praised the miners meetings as pristine, effective means of swift justice and order keeping, others feared them as a form of mob rule and wanted an established system of justice. Johnny urged Weare to try to get a deputy marshal assigned to the Yukon. Weare succeeded, but it took a couple of years before Frank Canton, who doubled as an employee of the NAT&T, assumed his duties as deputy at Circle.

Healy, like the miners at Circle, enjoyed the wealth of the Birch Creek diggings but always had the sense that the big bonanza was yet to be discovered. When it was found, Alaska would explode with activity. The NAT&T would reap fortunes, as would the Montana veteran who some folks had written off as over the hill.

But when the first news of the Klondike strike reached Fortymile in August 1896 and Circle some weeks later, Johnny suffered a shock. He could hardly believe that George Carmack, a man with a reputation for laziness, had been one of the discoverers—the same George Carmack who had lived at Dyea at times, helped Healy on odd jobs, and done some Chilkoot Pass packing, grateful to earn a couple of bucks. But Johnny had little time for idle reflections of whether a court would rule that his sometimes support of Carmack amounted to a grubstake. He was swept up in a frenzy of preparation for the coming stampede that occupied him fully for the next two years. However, he made time for the pleasure of hearing Weare and others say, "Johnny, you were right. By God, you were right!" These sweet words were ones a man could hardly hear often enough.

# 11

# Glorious Dawson

*In Dawson days I always had
what was wanted—for a price.*
—Johnny Healy

Over the fall and winter of 1896 Dawson grew rapidly. By June 1897 some four thousand people lived in about five hundred buildings at a place that had been uninhabited a year before, and the great flood of stampeders from Outside was still on the trail. From its founding Dawson had a more orderly development than was usual on the frontier because Canadian officials came on the scene early. Thanks to their presence at Fort Cudahy, a few miles down the Yukon, the Mounties established a post before navigation closed in 1896 and assumed control of police and court matters. William Ogilvie, the Canadian boundary surveyor, had been at Fort Cudahy and also moved to Dawson. Joe Ladue had already built a store and lumberyard and laid out a town site, so Ogilvie made an official survey of the place, then surveyed the areas where miners were working feverishly.

As the winter progressed the world began to hear stirring reports from the Klondike. Gold-struck prospectors wrote of wonderful finds in private letters, many of which were published in newspapers and commanded a wide audience. The lucky men who arrived early were awed by the richness of the region. "Don't pay any attention to what anyone says but come at your earliest opportunity," wrote Casey Moran to his friend George Rice in March 1897. "My God! it is appalling to hear the truth but nevertheless the world has never produced its equal before." And Burt Shuler, writing to a friend in early June, assured him that "I have seen gold dust until it looks almost as cheap as sawdust." While Shuler conceded that the journey to the Klondike "is not entirely one continued round of pleasure," prospects were marvelous. Even prospectors who missed out on the rich claims could make $15 a day digging for others. These princely wages were beyond the ken of American workers.[127]

Healy knew most of the men who made the first strikes at Dawson. Billy Leak, the bootlegger whose smuggled rum was seized by Deputy Marshal Healy at Dyea then siphoned away by another hustler, was among the fortunate. Leak bought a claim on Bonanza Creek that according to Shuler "is supposed to be worth a million."

Another miner reported that "men who worked for bits last year are now talking and showing thousands, and the air is full of millions." He told his brother in San Francisco that Dawson raged with gold excitement. Stories of huge gains "are substantiated by ocular demonstration . . . some of the stories are so fabulous that I am afraid to report them, for fear of being suspected of the infections."[128]

From San Francisco and Seattle the news spread urgently after crowds watched happy miners disembark with well-filled pokes. The *Excelsior*, owned by the ACC, and the *Portland* carried the first Klondike

*Klondike stampeders moving up Chilkoot Pass in 1898.*
—Anchorage Historical and Fine Arts Museum

gold south. Newspapers told readers that "millions upon millions of virgin gold await the fortunate miner who has the hardihood and courage to penetrate into the unknown depth of the Yukon district." References to "courage" and "unknown depth" typified gold-rush reporting and reflect the high adventure of northern prospecting.

Healy understood the significance of the Dawson strike in August 1896, but it was far too late to establish a new store before winter. He busied himself making plans and sending orders to Seattle and Chicago for materials needed for expansion. He also bought some of the Fortymile district claims that men were abandoning in their hurry to get in on the Klondike. William Johns accused Healy of chiseling him out of a fortune in his vague account of an incident. In Johnny's absence Johns had helped Belle Healy travel from Fortymile to Circle when she changed domiciles and felt Johnny owed him more gratitude. Johns, at various times a lawyer, rancher, and newsman, often gave whining accounts of his northern experiences. He hit the mark, however, when contrasting the popular regard of Healy and McQuesten. Johns claimed Johnny bad-mouthed McQuesten often while his rival "never said a word against Healy."[129]

William Johns reported well on the interior as it was in 1896 before the great stampede began. As he crossed the Chilkoot into the interior, the region's uniqueness struck him. "The utter solitude, the complete isolation, the all pervading silence, broken only by the roar of unknown rapids ahead, their warning note of danger adding to the feeling of isolation and the unknown," he commented. "Other than the bear and her cubs and a solitary muskrat swimming the river, not a living thing has been seen since leaving Lake Marsh, except the sand martins, nesting high up in the face of the perpendicular sand bluffs into which they bore holes for their nests."

This sense of isolation vanished with the Klondike gold rush. The pace of life quickened dramatically, especially in Dawson and environs. While the Dawson known best to legend dates from its second year of existence in 1897-98, it was a lively place over its first year of existence, too. Building kept everyone busy who was not engaged in mining, and plenty of construction went on. The town had few amenities the first winter, but despite the sudden boom enough food was available. Most stampeders then brought stores for the winter with them, so no one went hungry. Nevertheless, residents celebrated the arrival of the first steamboat from down river in July, because they had nearly exhausted their supplies of food and their liquor reserves had long since run out.

As the summer of 1897 progressed more stampeders came in from various Yukon camps, and, as the season advanced, even greater numbers of outsiders flocked in. By the close of navigation Dawson had four to five thousand people, and one year later would grow to its peak of thirty thousand residents. Healy was one of the best-known men in town, and new arrivals gained their introduction to him in reading such descriptive guidebooks to the country as *Gold-Fields of the Klondike and the Wonders of Alaska* by Ernest Ingersoll. Ingersoll predicted that Healy, "known to northern territory as 'King of the Klondike,'" would reap a large fortune "after years of wandering and search." Ingersoll recounts some of Healy's past adventures with admiration and exaggeration by making Healy a member of one of William Walker's filibustering expeditions to Mexico. He described Healy as "a genial, whole-souled sort of a man, companionable and agreeable in all ways. His manners are quiet and gentle, and, though he likes to talk of his doings on the plains, he never does so in a boasting way."[130]

# News from the North

Early on Dawson contributed mightily to legends of high life, adventure, and romance. Stories of all kinds abounded as the Klondike became famous. People loved to hear tales about prodigal spenders such as Swiftwater Bill Gates, whose wooing, marriages, and divorces from a succession of show girls were as spectacular as his success at finding gold. Most people worked hard for a living, and expected to work hard if they went to the Klondike, but found hearing about prodigious spending by newly made millionaires especially stimulating.

The depression-ridden decade of the nineties, a long period of high unemployment and general hard times, gave the unprecedented opportunity to make a fortune with a small investment in the Klondike its special lure. Social critics who viewed the gold hysteria with alarm and disdain ignored what the event meant to discouraged and frustrated people. The North was a wonder; it offered a golden chance to those daring to risk an adventure. Thousands cried out for more information on the marvelous place, then set about preparing for a momentous journey.

With this raging interest sweeping the world, anyone from Dawson who arrived Outside was acknowledged as an expert and consulted by acquaintances and a news-hungry press. Most of these Klondikers enjoyed their celebrity and some liked to exaggerate. Speculation over how much gold awaited varied widely. Edgar Mizner, the Yukon manager for the Alaska Commercial Company, considered a leading authority by virtue of his position, was asked to write an appraisal for a San Francisco newspaper. Mizner insisted that the Klondike held unlimited wealth, calculating freely that the goldfield extended three hundred miles and he expected $5 million to come out of it in 1897. Some estimated $10 million, "but I have noticed a local inclination to brag," Mizner said, "and I want to be entirely within the facts in any information I send out from this camp of marvels." Dawson reminded him of Tombstone, Arizona, and the California camps Bret Harte celebrated in his stories, but he thought it showed better qualities. The Klondike had boisterousness, gambling, and dance halls by the score, but fair mining laws and the presence of the Mounties prevented much of the fighting over claims that erupted in earlier camps.[131]

Klondikers were interviewed in Seattle, San Francisco, and hometown papers wherever they showed up. The public accepted whatever they reported with respectful attention. James D. Clements, one of the discoverers on Eldorado Creek, wowed New York newspaper reporters with his stories and a glimpse of the bracelet of gold nuggets his wife wore. He told about the construction of a freight tramway on the Chilkoot

Pass and of his joy in stuffing his three caribou skin sacks with $30,000 in gold. Oh yes, he said, a prospector could still find plenty more gold in the Klondike, but he suffered to get his, make no mistake about it. He showed reporters the family Christmas tree loaded with nuggets for ornaments. He denied a love of ostentation, insisting that the display was a response to the vision he had one lonely Christmas while he was eating cold caribou with his fingers. The lonely, suffering prospector made a vow: if he survived and struck it rich, he would present a tree decorated in gold to his family.

Clarence Berry, another Klondike king, avoided being labeled a "colorful" character, and when interviewed by the *Chronicle* gave sober and realistic advice. Let bachelors take their chances in 1898, he said, but "I would not advise any married man to go to the Klondike in anticipation of being able to earn money to send back to his family." Stories of families selling their homes in order to get a Klondike grubstake dismayed Berry. He also felt overwhelmed by all the attention he received. Eager people even interrupted his meals in restaurants to ask his advice. People "who pretend to know me" accost me on the street, he complained.

When pioneer trader Jack McQuesten visited New York in November 1897 newsmen eagerly sought him out. Like Clarence Berry he gave sound advice to would-be stampeders and dispelled some myths of the North's severity. He made light of the hardships women stampeders would face. Earlier it had been different, he said. On his first venture in the 1870s he went for months without speaking to a soul. A man then had few "companions in misery, and if he fell by the wayside, he stayed there, with no helping hand to give him aid." Now the country was fuller and friendlier. Any capable woman could do well at dressmaking, laundering, mining, or other work. And if she wished to marry "there are whole armies of nice fellows with fine claims who are looking for wives, and unless a woman is unspeakable she seldom leaves Alaska unmarried." But he advised assertive women who demanded their rights to stay away. He also disliked the new bloomers that some women were wearing and was pleased that the Mounties had banned their appearance in Dawson.[132]

# The Stampeders

Getting to the Klondike was a matter of serious logistical inquiry. Transportation companies in Seattle, San Francisco and other Pacific Coast ports readied every vessel available, and many that were unseaworthy. Ship owners sent their vessels to the Pacific from the Atlantic, expecting to make quick profits.

All the stampeders had to look to their outfitting. They could find plenty of advice on what they would need and plenty of merchants willing to sell it. The merchants advised travelers to take everything they might need with them so that they would not be at the mercy of the northern trading companies. A typical miner started north with one thousand pounds of food, soap, candles, cooking equipment, mining gear, clothes, and a sleeping bag. Flour, bacon, beans, and sugar headed the food list, but travelers had a variety of other foods available to them. Because the food processing and packing industry had developed earlier in the century, shoppers could choose among canned, evaporated, concentrated, desiccated, compressed, liquefied, crystallized, and granulated products.

The stampeders included the obscure and the famous, the wealthy and the impoverished, the well prepared and the woefully prepared. Men fleeing from the law or their families took off for the North, as did men anxious to make a living for their families. Women went too, some with their husbands, some alone, and some in well-organized parties.

Opportunists and quacks responded vigorously to the Yukon market possibilities. The Sanders Electric Co. urged men to wear an electric belt that charged the wearer with electric energy. "It requires two kinds of capital to make this venture. The man who goes through must have strength and nerve as well as money. Weak men will lose out, but belt wearers will prevail," read the ad.[133]

Many men and women wanted to go north to get rich in ways other than mining. Why dig for gold when they could take a cargo of onions north and make a fortune? Everyone had "sure thing" ideas. The notion of taking goods north to sell at retail came easily to merchants, but many others became enthralled with the idea after reading about shortages and high prices. They were aware of established companies, including the ACC and NAT&T, but reasoned that new businesses could also thrive. Of the hundreds who got to their destination with goods to sell, those who guessed the needs well and arrived in timely fashion made money. But many others lost their investments to shipwreck, delayed transport, and market glut.

Reaching the goldfields was the most taxing part of the adventure for many stampeders. To men and women planning their journeys in Seattle, Chicago, or Montreal the routes appeared well defined. Guidebooks and newspapers gave details of costs and travel times. The shortest route to Dawson went over the Chilkoot Pass out of Dyea or the White Pass out of Skagway. Another possibility existed with Jack Dalton's trail out of Pyramid Harbor. Voyaging to St. Michael, thence up the Yukon by river steamboat, appeared to many as the safest and least arduous of the available routes. Other routes had patriotic appeal, as with the "All Canadian" overland routes via Edmonton, or the Ashcroft Trail and the Stikine River—all of which were longer and more difficult than the better-established routes.

Most of the stampeders took the Chilkoot Pass from Dyea, where Healy's store was still prominent. The store stayed small instead of expanding to outfit stampeders who needed a whole season's supplies, but it did a good business.

Whether travelers passed through Skagway or elsewhere, they later told stories about Soapy Smith, the clever con man from Colorado who they believed had established a gang near Skagway to fleece travelers while professing to be a civic leader. His greatest success came from corrupting the deputy marshal, thus freeing himself from any conflict with the law. This situation prompted a group of vigilantes to organize and led to a shoot-out between Soapy and Frank Reid which caused the death of both in July 1898.

Aside from the bizarre exploits told of Soapy Smith, the development of Skagway and Dyea followed the frontier pattern. The neighboring communities competed for recognition as the best jumping-off point to the interior. Dyea held the edge until the White Pass Railway was completed in 1899, then Dyea died while Skagway continued to prosper.

It is interesting to speculate on what Healy might have achieved if he had remained on the scene at Dyea rather than becoming involved with the far-flung NAT&T. After Edgar Wilson died in 1897, Healy retained Juneau attorney J. P. Malony to administer his estate. Though he kept an office in Dyea, Malony did not team up with Healy on any enterprises. Healy tried but failed to establish the name Wilson's Pass for Dyea prior to 1897.

William Moore remained at Skagway and his wharf earned some profit. But he had no control over selection of the town site when the great wave of stampeders hit. Healy tried to claim the Dyea town site as the place boomed in 1897-98, but the land office would not allow it. Stampeders had treated Moore's priority with ill respect and forced a reduction in the size of his homestead claim; if Healy had been in Moore's shoes, he might have shot a few of the men who dared to trifle with his property and would then have faced serious consequences that might have ended his northern adventure.

# Gossip

Gossip on the Yukon continued to hold that other stockholders of the NAT&T were unhappy with Healy's management. Miner William Johns believed that the manager's unpopularity with miners, "which bothered him not at all," caused great consternation in Chicago. If Portus Weare and the Cudahys heard many stories such as those Johns told, they might well have been alarmed. Johns claimed that Healy even mistreated his customers. He had overheard Healy screaming to one man, "Get out, I don't want your money, get out." Healy probably acted rudely with provocation, but Johns was pleased to report anything adverse to Healy's reputation and was delighted to hear that "one of the Weare brothers had been sent out to supervise matters and act as a brake on Healy."[134]

William Johns also criticized the Alaska Commercial Company, particularly for its "paystreak" bacon—so called for "its fine yellow color." The bacon's age and fattiness caused scurvy, Johns believed. "It might have lain in St. Michael for two or three years and in loading the Yukon River steamers they had a habit of piling it up behind the boilers—the last place it should have been put." Many miners neglected to parboil the bacon to rid it of salt and saltpeter before frying it.

Price gouging by both trading companies angered Johns. The previous occupant of his Fortymile cabin left a journal recording the price of goods. Prices rose fast from 1893, "as much as fifty percent as the richness of the Birch Creek diggings were realized and the two companies in San Francisco and Chicago and their greed for greater profits led them to put on all they thought the miners would stand for. Their policy culminating when the fabulous riches of the Klondike were exploited."

In spring 1897 the NAT&T directors shuffled management personnel around. Johnny retained his title as general manager, but the directors named Ely Weare, son of Portus Weare, president and sent him out to the Yukon. Ely confided to Nora Crane, who voyaged from Seattle on the steamer *Cleveland* with the company party, that he had been directed to oversee Healy's work because of a "perfect state of chaos from poor management." Unfortunately, Ely lacked the capacity to improve the situation. He was an inept drunkard, and the company removed him from office some months later.[135]

# Social Life at Circle

Nora Crane's sojourn at Circle has provided us with a lively chronicle of the Yukon traders' circle. Her husband, John Crane, was the NAT&T store manager and also acted as the U.S. commissioner, an appointment Portus Weare attained for him from the Department of Justice. Weare also succeeded in getting Frank Canton, a tough law enforcer from Wyoming, an appointment as deputy marshal at Circle, but Canton reached his post a year later, in 1898.

On the voyage from Seattle, Nora, a pleasant young woman who had been only married one year, especially enjoyed the company of "Hell Roaring" Mike Healy. Capt. Mike Healy of the Revenue Cutter Service, earlier courted by Johnny because of his ability to help the company by providing transport on the Revenue Cutter *Bear*, had been removed from his command in 1896 for his drunken conduct on his 1895 cruise. According to the Treasury Department he had placed his ship "in a perilous position while in an intoxicated condition" and had otherwise exhibited "drunkenness to the scandal of the Service." In time he bounced back because of his good record and considerable influence in Washington. When Nora met him he was traveling north on his own looking for business opportunities. Despite his disgrace Mike was a cheerful man, and he enjoyed flattering and entertaining the young woman on her first trip north. Mike Healy voyaged up the Yukon with the NAT&T party and stayed with the Cranes before returning down river and continuing his excursion.[136]

Life at Circle held much that Nora disliked. She fell ill during her first days there and felt uncomfortable: "It means a good deal to get sick here with no doctor within five hundred miles and no good when you find him." Circle's population had dropped to twenty-five since the January day when Arthur Walden had mushed in to confirm the rumors about the Klondike riches. The town had "300 log houses put down every which way on the bank of the Yukon River without regard to streets," Nora wrote her mother. "Some of them are quite nice but lonesome now. There is a layer of about a foot of tin cans over the whole place and then for diversion those measly dogs." Nora commented favorably on huckleberries, fresh moose meat, fresh lettuce "and salmon—lovely big fish steaks, nicer fish than we ever got at home. Everything else is canned, and the very best at that."[137]

The Cranes shared a comfortable enough company house with the Healys—an eight-room log structure rich with carpets, lace curtains, and good-quality furnishings. Nora said little about her housemates. To Nora, Johnny Healy was "the boss," and in letters home she was generally discreet. She cared little for Johnny, perhaps because he paid little attention to her. She vilified Capt. John Barr, upon whose river steamer her brother labored, and dismissed Capt. Joe Mariner, another steamboat skipper, as a drunkard.

Nora was delighted when the Healys moved on to Dawson, because she was freed from having to share a house with them. She considered Belle Healy a drunken "Bowery tough," but made no reference to Johnny's drinking. When Johnny later promoted her husband to station manager at St. Michael, she expressed her pleasure with the general manager's judgment, but felt less pleased when the company later refused Crane the job he wanted at Nome.

Nora's virtual silence on Healy contrasts with her joy in the gallantry of Mike Healy and other male visitors. Her reaction to these other men indicated her openness to their friendship, but she wrote nary a word on anything Johnny ever said to her. If Johnny, as it seems, was unwilling to say a kind or encouraging word to a young, vulnerable newcomer whose husband was an important employee, he must have hardened during his Alaskan years. Even a busy man has time for amenities among those with whom he shares space. Johnny's coldness and distance in dealing with underlings and customers seems manifest. And those who did business with him resented his distant manner. Before long this resentment played a part in undermining the powerful trader.

As Nora settled in to life in Circle she came to better enjoy her life there. Society improved after she made friends with Capt. Patrick Ray of the U.S. Army and Sam Dunham of the U.S. Department of Labor. At Christmas, Circle's cultured folks opened up one of the abandoned "opera houses" for a musical evening and later gave a party to forty town children, mostly Indian. Her health improved, and she came to enjoy the particular character of the North, such as the winter sun. "It was the most glorious, gorgeous yellow I ever saw in my life, but not strong enough to cast a shadow." At night she saw "millions of stars . . . the performance of the sun, moon, and stars are a never ending source of delight and wonder."

# The NAT&T at Dawson

On June 8, 1897, Johnny landed at Dawson from the steamboat *Portus B. Weare*, which had wintered at Circle. In the turmoil of establishing himself at Dawson, Healy still failed to improve upon his popularity. He moved fast and spared no time for social events. If miners had liked him better, they might have praised his prescience in anticipating the great strike. Had he shown a pleasant and generous side, they might have regarded him as a founding father, a prophet deserving of honor. But apparently he was cold and grim. Miners sharply criticized NAT&T business methods. Neither of the two major Yukon trading companies worried about supplying Circle and Fortymile in their rush to get supplies to the new boom town farther upriver, and Healy received most of the abuse for neglecting the few old customers who had not stampeded to Dawson.

Once he had landed on the Klondike beach Healy started construction of a store as soon as he found carpenters. In July he moved the company's sawmill from Fort Cudahy to Dawson. By summer's end carpenters had completed a large sawn-log store, three corrugated-iron warehouses, and a residence. According to Sam Dunham, who reported on Yukon conditions for the U.S. Department of Labor (and later wrote a couple of books of Klondike poetry), Healy spent $150,000—a staggering amount for the day and one that must have caused anguish for shareholders in Chicago. The brisk trade added to the positive side of the ledger, though, despite the competition from the ACC, Joe Ladue, and several other storekeepers.

Nora Crane came up to visit Dawson on the new steamboat, *John J. Healy*, and saw "a wilderness of tents, bogs over your rubber tops and log houses, saloons and dance houses until you can't rest." The nonstop spending by miners impressed her. One gambling place boasted of earning $12,000 a night, but "this company store is about as good"—with sales ranging from $3,000 to $13,000 daily, averaging $8,000. Prices were high—too high, she thought, "but that is not my business."

Of the town's men Nora had little good to say. "Some of these miners are perfect animals. . . . I think men as a whole are as near P. B. Armor's chief product [hogs] as they get. If you don't believe it just live around a few hundred who have been away from civilization and women for awhile," she wrote her mother. Among the hustling crowd she observed some signs of gentility. "This place is full of nice people; ex-ministers to Austria; would-be actors; ministers' sons; and disowned bankers' relations; to say nothing of the nobodies who are nice, working side by side, hustling logs, running saw mills, and digging in the mines. From the most disreputable, worst dressed one in the pot you can hear English that would sound well in Chauncey Depew's mouth—such are the fortunes of a mining town."

# Jack London

The stampeders of 1897-98 were a mixed bag. Among them was Jack London, who later turned his experiences in the Klondike into stories of northern adventure. London's literary accomplishments include a treatment of Johnny Healy. Some years after returning to the Outside he made Johnny Healy a character in one of his novels. London landed at Dyea in the summer of 1897 and noted the prominent place of the Healy and Wilson store as he hustled to get ready for the Chilkoot Pass crossing. The husky, vibrant twenty-one year old probably felt less anxious than many other immigrants because he had plenty of other adventures behind him as seal poacher, hobo, oyster bed raider, jute mill hand, and cannery worker.

Aboard ship from San Francisco, he'd formed a party with a few other young men eager to pool their resources and their labor for the work

*Jack London, author of* Daughter of the Snows.
—University of Alaska Fairbanks Archives

ahead. When they reached Dyea they knew just what to do. They decided that their strong backs and weak wallets meant no hired packers for them.

Near the foot of the Chilkoot Pass trail on August 8, London wrote a brief note home. Exhausted from paddling one hundred miles from Juneau, he had no energy for fine writing: "I am laying on the grass in sight of a score of glaciers, yet the slightest exertion of writing causes me to sweat prodigiously."[138]

When London's year-long adventure in the Klondike was over, he wrote that he brought nothing back from Alaska "but my scurvy." Actually he brought back $4.50 in gold, which he sold to an Oakland merchant. He also brought home a notebook packed full of character sketches and insights about life in the North.

As the writer and his companions packed up the trail, London began to feel good about his physical prowess. Back and forth, his group covered twenty-four miles a day, relaying their 150-pound loads, until at last they reached the summit and beyond to Lake Lindeman. This tough work took a couple of memorable weeks. In his first novel, *Daughter of the Snows*, London described vividly the long line of straining backpackers marching toward the summit:

> Time rolled back, and locomotion and transportation were once again in the most primitive stages. Men who had never carried more than pencils in all their lives had now become bearers of burdens. They no longer walked upright under the sun but stooped the body forward and bowed the head to the earth. Every back had become a pack-saddle, and the strap galls were beginning to form. They staggered beneath unwonted effort, and legs became drunken with weariness and titubated in diverse directions till the sunlight darkened and bearer and burden fell by the way.

Along the way to the goldfields, London rejoiced in participating in an event that offered so many opportunities to view the behavior of men and women under stress. He noted the courage and fellowship and less admirable examples of cowardice and greed. It all served as grist for his mill. Some of his observations showed his good humor. He could even praise the cunning of the fierce mosquitoes that were such a burden to all Northerners. "Badly bitten under netting—couldn't vouch for it but John watched them and said they rushed the netting in a body, one gang holding up the edge while a second gang crawled under. Charley swore that he has seen several of the larger ones pull the mesh apart and let a small one through. I have seen them with their proboscis bent and twisted after an assault on a sheet iron stove."

London and his friends floated downriver to Dawson without undue incident. They looked the famed town over, then acquired a mining claim on the Stewart River, sixty miles south of town. The writer and a small community of miners settled in for the winter's digging after building a log cabin. Even if London rarely got to Dawson to take a few convivial drinks at the saloons, he heard the same gossip and concerns. Everyone talked about leading personalities such as the superb gold-finder and relentless lover, Swiftwater Bill Gates, and such famed visitors as Joaquin Miller, the poet and veteran frontiersman whom London consulted in Oakland before he sailed north. Since everyone had his mind on grub, the leading storekeepers—Johnny Healy, J. E. Hansen, and Edgar Mizner—were also familiar, much-talked-about characters.

*Snow slide on Chilkoot Pass, April 3, 1898.* —National Archives

London decided one Yukon winter was enough. In the summer of 1898, he voyaged down the Yukon through interior Alaska for St. Michael and sea passage home. Like most returning Klondikers, he lacked the fortune he had come north to get so he worked as a fireman aboard ship to get home.

London sold his first northern stories in 1899 and became a wild success. His plots had various origins. A news clipping reporting on the death of an enterprising vendor from Sausalito at Rampart on the Yukon provided the basis for one story. John Snell had started upriver from St. Michael with 1,500 dozen eggs after hearing about the high prices eggs had commanded in Dawson. Unfortunately, low water on the river halted his steamboat at Rampart—far from his goal. The winter closed Yukon navigation. Snell was stuck with his eggs, and they spoiled. He brooded for a time, then affixed a note to his cabin door saying "Gone Out." Several days later, a friend forced open the cabin to see Snell "suspended by a wire rope from the rafter of the cabin, cold in death." The

*Heavy Klondike-bound traffic in a canyon on Chilkoot Pass, 1898.*
—National Archives

story London told of the tragedy, "One Thousand Dozen," captured the terrible tension beneath commercial daring.

London depicts another daring man of commerce, John J. Healy, in his novel, *Daughter of the Snows*, published in 1900. London portrays Jacob Welse as a captain of industry and reigning capitalist who dominates the northern trade. Although "a child of democracy, he bent all men to his absolutism. . . . Single handed he had carved out his dominion till he gripped the domain of a dozen Roman provinces. At his ukase the population ebbed and flowed over a hundred thousand miles of territory, and cities sprang up or disappeared at his bidding."[139]

This highly charged portrait of an all-powerful tycoon purposefully misrepresents Healy. For the novelist, the real Healy provided a starting point, a foundation for one of the characters he created as vehicles of his social Darwinism theories. What he learned about Healy while living in the North and from Edwin Tappan Adney's *The Klondike Stampede of 1897-1898* served his creative purposes. Healy, like the fictional Welse,

*Main street of Dyea, Alaska, in 1898.* —Special Collections, University of Washington Library

had been active on other frontiers. "The trapper father had come of the sturdy Welsh stock which trickled into early Ohio out of the jostling East, and the mother was a nomadic daughter of the Irish emigrant settlers of Ontario. From both sides came the Wanderlust of the blood, the fever to be moving, to be pushing to the edge of things." In describing Welse's youth on the Red River of the North in Indian country, London relied to some extent on what he had heard about Johnny's earlier career. "A town," he wrote, "was a cluster of deer-skin lodges; a trading post a seat of civilization."

London's heroine was Welse's daughter, a capable and beautiful young woman. One of Healy's daughters was in Dawson during London's time, also a beautiful young woman. But the author relied upon his imagination to concoct the romantic incidents of Frona Welse's life. The novel fails to meet the standards set by London's other books and was unpopular with readers.

## At Home in Dawson

E. Hazard Wells, one of the many journalists on hand to keep the outside world informed on the colorful gold town, got a better opportunity to know Johnny at Dawson. Wells had reason to consider himself a northern veteran. He had been a member of an 1890 exploration expedition headed by E. J. Glave, who had African exploration experience. Glave, on the advice of knowledgeable government officials, hired Alaskan Jack Dalton as guide. The party landed at Pyramid Harbor, then crossed the pass into the interior to observe the country and the Indians before returning to the coast. As a result of this trip and others, Dalton, who succeeded Healy as deputy marshal at Dyea in 1892, began working on a trail to the interior from Pyramid Harbor easy enough for pack animals, as the Chilkoot Pass was not. By the time Wells met Dalton again, at Dawson in 1897, the Alaskan was a famous man whose Dalton Trail, a toll road, was being used by a comparatively few stampeders willing to pay for travel privileges.

Healy ignored Joaquin Miller, a veteran of the Florence, Idaho, gold rush who was also in Dawson as a journalist, but he did invite Wells to his home. In addition to Belle, Healy had family members with him in Dawson, including his son, Thomas Constantine, usually referred to as "T. C.," and a family man himself. He had joined his father at Dyea in 1890 and later returned Outside to marry Sarah Watson. Sarah gave birth to a daughter at Circle in 1896, a winsome babe who charmed Wells on his visits to the Healys. Sadly, Regina Mary, known as "Tot" died a couple of years later, as did T. C.

Wells, like other Dawson men, figured that Johnny was a millionaire. "The Healy family," he reported, "has skillfully contrived to purchase either whole or part interests in nearly thirty mining claims here, the value of which is as yet impossible to compute. It is safe to say, however, that the properties will reach several millions in the aggregate. . . . The Healys are shrewd buyers, especially the Captain, who has been an Indian and frontier trader all of his life."[140]

Had Johnny been interested in setting the record straight he could have made it known that he purchased his claims for the NAT&T rather than as personal investments. If he acquired any claims on his behalf, they were of little value, and he was less successful in buying rich claims for the company than others imagined.

The Healys lived a relatively simple lifestyle in Dawson. They had a modest five-room house, "carpeted and comfortable, but plainly furnished." Johnny's youngest daughter, Alfreda, only nineteen in 1897, also lived there. An acknowledged beauty, she was also rich, according to Wells. "She owns a valuable Bonanza mining claim about nine miles up the gulch, on which she proposes to locate herself in company with one of her relatives. She will reside in a cabin, the same as other miners, and will superintend work on her claim. In this she will copy the example of her mother, who is a capable business woman, and who operates a number of mining claims, independent of any direction of her husband." Wells was unaware that Belle was Johnny's second wife and not Alfreda's mother. The journalist was beguiled by young Alfreda, "who is by all odds the prettiest girl in the Yukon," and knew the value of her physical and financial assets. She told Wells that she would go east in a few years "under the guise of a poor girl. If the right man comes along then and wants me real bad, probably I will take him, knowing that it is not my money he is after."

Johnny's oldest daughter, Maria, and her husband, Orin Jackson, were also members of the household. The gathering of his extended family at Dawson probably gave Johnny a source of satisfaction. Poorly situated during his first decade in Alaska, he discouraged Fort Benton people from relocating, and the region held little appeal for them until the Klondike discovery. Satisfying, too, was knowing that back in Montana he was famous and respected for his daring and enterprise and also widely acclaimed as a self-made millionaire sitting atop the world at storied Dawson.

# Dawson Characters

Dawson sometimes seemed to draw the most interesting and colorful people in the world. Johnny knew many of them from other places and encountered others for the first time in his store or on the streets. Besides the fun-loving Mizner brothers were characters such as Swiftwater Bill Gates and Jack Smith. Sportsmen, including Tex Rickard and Jack Kearns, were there, as were theater men, including Alexander Pantages and Sid Grauman. Well-known women residents included Belinda Mulroney (Carbonneau), who established hotels at the mines and in town then later went into mining and banking in Alaska, and Mrs. George Black, who later became the Yukon governor.

The best reporting on Yukon life was done by young men and women, usually in letters sent home. Marshall Bond, a wealthy college man, had rushed to Dawson from San Francisco for the adventure and because his father made his fortune in mining. He found little gold but certainly helped his friend Jack London by introducing him to his dog, Buck. Buck, a strong, good-looking beast, had lived a sedate city life yet inspired London to make him the hero of his most popular novel, *Call of the Wild.*

Bond reflected lightheartedly on his mining work over the 1897-98 winter in letters home. Several times he and others dashed from Dawson to some distant place where a new gold discovery had been rumored. Bond described the rough living on one such excursion. "Twenty of us cooked, loaned each other plates and cups without even washing them, prepared dog food, and occupied every available foot of the cabin that night. The dogs slept or fought, as the spirit moved. Crackling oaths coupled with the Savior's name interlarded the exchange of ideas and sentiments." [141]

Food was short on the trail, and Bond resolved to make up for scarcity when he reached Dawson again. "Henceforth I live to eat. Much reflection convinces me it's the highest aim of man. Those who dedicate their lives to ambition and think to inscribe their names in the book of fame in letters of gold by making a million are but building in sand and have developed but a low degree of consciousness. I would build pyramids of porterhouse, obelisks of oysters, and punctuate the meter of my poetry with pie."

In Bond's letters we glimpse a recurring theme of the gold rush— youthful aspirations highlighted by adaptability, easy humor, and a great zeal for a shared, comradely experience. Years afterwards Bond still found pleasure in recalling his friends and "the occasional meetings of genial spirits just down from the creeks, after a freezing walk of from fifteen to thirty miles, as they ran into one another at the bar seeking a drink of Scotch. After a few drinks they would burst into song."

Bond and London spent most of their time with other young men and in saloons where high livers of all ages gathered. A more youthful Johnny Healy, freer of corporate entanglements, might have revelled with these

*Miners working the El Dorado Mine near Dawson in 1898.*
—University of Alaska Fairbanks Archives

spirited young men and had fun. But the Dawson glitter held little appeal for him. He worked hard, went to bed early, and worried about business. And the grim-visaged, aloof Healy had few friends or supporters in Dawson.

Bond made one unflattering mention of the major trading companies. He commented that "there is in Dawson no newspaper, no bank, no such thing as an insurance office, no shops except those of the two trading companies, where the clerks are to be bowed down to. They are most insolent in their manner of charging 3,000 percent profit for a candle. One in Dawson must consider that he is being done a great favor to be allowed to purchase anything, and it is a curious sight to see Alec McDonald, worth several millions, endeavoring to be very polite to a puny clerk from whom he wishes to buy a few pounds of nails for one of his hundred cabins."

Two frontiersmen whose careers vaguely paralleled Healy's were prominent showman and traders in town, Arizona Charlie Meadows and Jack Crawford. Crawford was an Irishman too, born in 1847. He enlisted in the Union Army for Civil War service and was wounded in action. About 1870 he went west. He served as an army scout in 1876, during the battle of Slim Buttes he served under Gen. George Crook against the Sioux under Sitting Bull. After that battle Crawford made a daring, celebrated horse ride to the nearest telegraph station bearing the news of the battle much as Healy had after the defeat of Chief Joseph. Crawford's poetry initially attracted the public and press, and he became renowned as the poet-scout of the frontier. After becoming a showman with Buffalo Bill Cody in 1876-77, he branched into acting, lecturing, and writing poems and plays. On stage he liked to play frontier-hero roles. He won fame but not the wealth he sought as ardently. Over the years he had done some prospecting for gold so was easily drawn north to the Klondike. He lived in Dawson from 1898 to 1900 and was involved in mining and in a store called the Wigwam.

Once more wealth eluded Crawford, but he was much liked by folks in Dawson. "Probably nobody in the Klondike region has a wider personal acquaintance and fewer enemies than Captain Jack," reported the *Dawson News* when Crawford prepared to leave. "He has traveled the country over, riding fast and riding slow, and whatever the weather or other conditions nobody ever met him without receiving a hearty greeting. . . . The Captain hasn't got rich in keeping with his deserts in this country, but nobody may say he has not a rich heart and infinite good temper."[142]

Johnny never mentioned Crawford or Meadows to Adney, probably viewing them as dubious examples of heroic frontiersmen—primarily showmen who built stage careers on the exaggeration of short-lived western adventures.

Arizona Charlie Meadows built the Palace Grand Theater in Dawson. He had also been with Buffalo Bill's show after serving as an Indian scout for the Army during the Geronimo campaign. Meadows amazed people with his skills as a roper and bronco rider, and he showed much imagination as an impresario. One of his notable promotions was a buffalo fight at Cripple Creek, Colorado, that ran afoul of American laws against such sports. Among the concessionaires on that occasion was "Soapy" Randolph Smith, of later Skagway fame, then known as "the Denver Bunco Kid." Meadows brought a large outfit to the Klondike in '97 but lost all of it in an avalanche along the trail. At Dawson he starred in his own productions, playing an "Injun-killing" scout who rescued the innocent maiden just in time, and made daring jumps with his horse into a water tank on stage.

The community tolerated individuals whom they considered "characters," regardless of their behavior. Swiftwater Bill Gates, for example, seemed to provide everyone with fun. He retained the status of a millionaire playboy, a man with the Midas touch who was fully entitled to throw money at showgirls, marry them, discard them, and find others. Gates was an entrepreneur as well as a miner, so he, too, milked money from the populace. Yet the descriptions of his antics after he went into show business only enhanced his legend as a fabulous prince of the goldfields who was free to indulge in expensive whims.

Gates joined forces with Jack Smith after Smith opened the Monte Carlo, the first variety theater in town. Men could drink, gamble, and dance with bar girls at Smith's and other pleasure resorts, recovering from hard labor in the mines or elsewhere. They could watch the rich men at their sport and speculate on who might strike it next. Characters like Alexander Pantages, a bartender, attracted little attention. Then another nobody, he before long founded the Orpheum vaudeville circuit and became the king of the nation's show business.

Gates helped finance the new, luxurious, permanent Monte Carlo. Then before freeze-up in 1897 Bill dashed for San Francisco to gather showgirls and whiskey. While enjoying the Bay City's watering places Bill regaled newsmen with marvelous stories about himself and Dawson. Anyone who doubted the wonders of the new camp could call on Bill at the Palace Hotel, drink his drinks, and perhaps pick up a nugget or two. Gates was a superb showman, armed with natural enthusiasm, a sense of daring, and a mighty appetite for the good life. A swell dresser, he wore a Prince Albert coat, studded shirt, and the silk hat that set off his beard so well.

Gates assembled his entourage and started back for Dawson. He also organized a transportation company and in Seattle he used the lovely dance hall girls to attract attention to his business. When he got back to Dawson people were delighted to see him despite knowing that he was a liar, poseur, and an eager litigant willing to go to court before paying just debts. People laughed at him, and other theatrical men produced comic bits of his life on the Dawson stage, but he remained a popular man.

Hazard Wells and other observers thought Healy had it good, but Johnny's throne atop the world was an uneasy one. Despite his long anticipation of the boom, distance and the furious pace of events constrained his ability to direct the activities of his company. No one could effectively manage an enterprise as huge and far-flung as the NAT&T operation had become by 1897. His Chicago backers were unhappy, and he had become no more popular with the public by moving to Dawson. Now the grumbling of a few angry miners echoed among a much larger population. Dawson still lacked a newspaper to pick up the anti-Healy sentiment, but it was only a matter of time.

Johnny felt frustrated, especially because he was right—about everything. When the system broke down, hindering business, it was always someone else's fault. His family often heard about the treachery, laziness, and incompetence of others, and sympathized. But outside his home he received no sympathy, and few were willing to defend his conduct. On the streets and on the creeks he was wrong—about everything.

# 12

# Fears and Failures
# in Dawson

*There was never*
*a man in any country*
*as lied about as I was.*
—Johnny Healy

In the summer of 1897 Outside newspapers included Johnny Healy among the Klondike heroes. The *Chicago Tribune* gave readers a glowing story about the "old-time Indian fighter . . . who broke the Klondike trail." Perhaps with help from NAT&T headquarters the reporter claimed that Captain Healy "brought on the present Klondike excitement." The writer recalled "that it was Healy who found Chief Joseph and induced him to surrender to General Terry when he was making his celebrated detour through Montana after the Battle of Big Horn at a time when the army people were unable to corral him." Such distortions must have amused folks who knew Healy's role at Joseph's surrender and those who knew that the Battle of the Little Big Horn involved Sitting Bull rather than Chief Joseph. [143]

The writer concocted another bit of spice concerning Healy and Sitting Bull. "The government had spent millions of dollars in futile effort to subdue Sitting Bull," wrote the *Tribune* man. "Healy made an offer to deliver him alive at Washington for $50,000, and every commanding officer who knew him said he could do it."

*Store and warehouse of the NAT&T at Dawson in 1899.*
—University of Alaska Fairbanks Archives

Unfortunately, Johnny's course was becoming much rougher than the *Tribune*'s tribute suggests. Fast-moving events in the booming gold town now threatened to label him the pariah rather the hero of the Klondike gold rush.

## Starvation Panic

Edwin Tappan Adney reached Dawson in October 1897, just in time to observe a general panic over the food situation. As early as July Outside newspapers voiced the possibility of a famine over the 1897-98 winter. "How About Grub?" one editor asked. "Miners Cannot Eat Gold." Other papers picked up on the whimsical appeal in imagining men with pockets full of gold threatened by starvation. Reporting from St. Michael to the *Chicago Tribune* in August, Sarah Beazley predicted disaster. She praised the efforts of the NAT&T to get goods upriver and noted the concern of company officers that no blame fall on them. "They have repeatedly warned people to wait until next spring before going in." Beazley, who probably favored the company because of its Chicago base, even professed to have heard much praise on "the generalship and management of Captain J. J. Healy" and expected that "he will not desert these poor miners."[144]

Early in August, Portus Weare of the NAT&T had wired the U.S. Interior secretary thanking him for warning the public about the possibilities of starvation and urging the appointment of the company's manager at St. Michael, L. B. Shepard, as U.S. commissioner. Weare assured the secretary that "we are making gigantic efforts to get food into the country." By Weare's reasoning starvation could be avoided if the public heeded the warnings and the traffic coming into the country slowed down. "If more go than can be taken care of they can go down river as late as September 20 and out on our steamers and sailing vessels."[145]

Editors of the *San Francisco Chronicle*, perhaps fearful that a disaster in Dawson would leave them open to charges of reckless encouragement of stampeders, assumed that the worst would happen. "The *Chronicle* wants no better attestation than its files that it told them not to go." The editors insisted that they misled no one and had carefully warned prospective stampeders about the consequences of "the blackness of the long arctic night and the freeze of the long arctic winter" for those lacking food.[146]

Miners who left Dawson for the Outside in August included many who feared starvation. Stampeders heading upriver aboard the new NAT&T steamboat *Charles H. Hamilton* were taunted by a load of returning Klondikers aboard the *John J. Healy*. "What are you going to eat when you get there?" called the *Healy* passengers. Journalist William A. Ryan and others aboard the *Hamilton* felt apprehensive. They had already heard that the *Portus B. Weare* on its previous trip to Dawson had landed far more liquor than food. Ryan condemned the avarice of the NAT&T, "but the criticism applies with equal force to each company. Avarice is the marked characteristic of both companies at St. Michael . . . it is nothing less than a crime for these transportation companies to scatter advertisements . . . broadcast and bring so many people into the country."

When the steamboat *John J. Healy* reached Dawson in July, Healy responded violently to the callousness of other company men. He dashed aboard, gruffly greeted President Ely Weare, and demanded an account of the cargo. Anxious men lined the river banks—they, too, were keen to know how much food was aboard. In disgust and anger Healy listened while Weare, proud of his business acumen, explained that the cargo was almost all high mark-up whiskey and equipment. Orin Jackson, Healy's assistant, voiced little surprise at what occurred next. "Healy lunged at Weare in a blind fury, grasped him by the throat, and shook him like a rat, demanding to know why his orders . . . had been disobeyed." Luckily

*Clerks at work in the NAT&T store in Dawson, c. 1900.* —University of Alberta

for Weare, Jackson pulled Healy off and protected Weare until Johnny cooled down. Weare blamed Charles Hamilton, then in charge at St. Michael, for countermanding Healy's orders. Walter Curtin, who worked for Pat Galvin, another Montana man, also witnessed the wild dock scene. Curtin appreciated that Healy had only nominal control over shipments. "The miners blamed Captain John J. Healy personally, as he was on the ground and the only one in authority whom they knew," Curtin said, "but he was not responsible, as he had given direct orders to load all of his company boats with food and clothing, and his disgust and rage when he learned that this had not been done was worse than that of the miners themselves."[147]

Diverse opinions from many sources, a general lack of knowledge about northern conditions, and the slow movement of news out of the interior complicated the famine issue. A cool appraisal of the shipments en route from the major companies would determine that provisions would be short over the winter, yet the distinction between short supplies and certain famine was blurred. To complicate matters, no one knew how many travelers were underway to the Klondike or how many would come later.

Criticisms of Healy and the NAT&T from August 1897 were more common than praise. Rumor had it that the company's policy of hiring cheap labor for boat crews resulted in the sandbar grounding of the *P. B. Weare*, further reducing prospective food supplies in Dawson. Residents condemned both major companies for bringing in whiskey rather than food. Stampeders at St. Michael, advised by NAT&T company agents in Chicago to buy their food and supplies when they got to the Yukon, leveled other charges against the company.

Healy's refusal to fill orders placed in the spring or early summer of 1897 for fall delivery became an even more inflammatory issue among veteran miners in Dawson. In what they considered an outrageous breach of contract for goods for which they had already paid, Healy cut their orders and returned an appropriate portion of their money. Arthur Celene was one of many miners treated in this fashion. He had ordered $900 in food and received one sack of flour "and a few other things, in proportion." He figured Healy should have given his paid-up order priority over the needs of newcomers to the country who had neglected to provide for themselves. The irate miners objected to having to supplement their stores by over-the-counter purchases because prices were rising fast. "Everything eatable," Celene said, "was selling at figures from $1 up per pound. Flour was $1.50 to $2.00 per pound. Fresh meat was about the same price."[148]

It is difficult to determine the extent of price gouging in the various stores. Thomas Magee, who left Dawson shortly after the stores virtually ran out of food, reported that prices remained stable as the situation became critical because they had already been pegged high in anticipation of shortages. Yet Sam Dunham, the official observer on the labor and economic situation for the American government, considered food prices expensive but fair. He found prices for clothes and other dry goods high but food prices equivalent to those he noted in 1877 when Tombstone and Tucson, Arizona, were booming.[149]

By October 15 Healy was openly "distressed" by the outlook for food. He had anticipated several more boats and a smaller number of stampeders would reach Dawson in late fall—the NAT&T books showed seven hundred unfilled orders. With most of his stores depleted it appeared that a quarter of the Klondike residents still needed winter supplies.

# Holding Up the Steamers

Miners downriver from Dawson were unwilling to face the scarcity when food was within reach. In September, men at Circle forcibly took stores from ACC and NAT&T steamers en route to Dawson. Most of the 180 men involved had recently arrived from Dawson, heeding the word of authorities that food would be available downriver. Reaching Circle they found that food was short and felt justified in demanding food from the last steamers carrying food upriver to Dawson. When Ely Weare, aboard the *P. B. Weare*, refused their demand, they pushed crewmen aside and took what they needed. Shortly after the miners stormed the steamer *Weare*, they boarded the ACC's steamer *Bella* for the same purpose. *Bella*'s skipper, Capt. E. D. Dixon, who had once worked for Healy and had brawled with him, was furious but impotent. Lt. Patrick H. Ray, a passenger aboard, lectured the miners on the law and the dignity of property but also failed to stop them.

In consideration of Dawson residents, the miners took only a portion of the food cargos and paid for what they landed. The Yukon had only two Army officers, Lieutenant Ray and Lt. Wilds Richardson, to maintain the federal government's authority. Ray was furious and, in reporting to his superiors, called for "a military government with power to hunt to the death the lawless element."[150]

While Healy did not urge a "hunt to the death," he was upset about the lawlessness and advised Washington "in behalf of American miners . . . to send us the strong arm of the military for protection" along the entire Alaskan Yukon. "The mining industries," he warned, "will be seriously crippled, if not entirely paralyzed, by reason of it not being safe to run steamers and land supplies at any of the mining camps along the river. The great rush of the people to the Yukon makes it probable that armed raiders will hold up the steamers and loot the stores of their supplies, consequently the merchants and the transportation companies will be obliged to confine their business to the Canadian side of the Yukon Valley, as the Northwest Mounted Police offer protection to life and property." Johnny worded his appeal to make the maximum effect in Washington. What American official could ignore the invidious comparison to the Canadian peacekeeping force?

Healy sent his message to Washington in December 1897, commissioning E. Hazard Wells for the long journey. He advanced $1,000 to Wells but expected the government to reimburse him. Wells was one of the alarmists. On October 12 he noted that miners would dig from thirty to fifty tons of gold within the next six months but "a multitude of wretched persons, stranded without provisions, will probably sicken and starve. Bread riots are almost a certainty and blood will be shed. . . . The men who are in possession of six or eight months' supply of provisions will fight to prevent spoliation by the famished hoard. . . . Twice already has the ready Winchester cracked on the streets of Dawson and bullets have pursued fleeing bread thieves. . . . Panic reigns."[151]

Famine reports caused considerable anxiety among relatives and friends of stampeders. A San Francisco newspaper reported in November that "there are over 1,000 people in Dawson City without provisions. An equal number, including women and children, are living in tents, and today a heavy snow is falling." The October 15 story indicated that people lacking enough supplies were still arriving. "Caches are being robbed daily. One man was detected in the act and shot through the leg. He is not a natural thief, but was driven to desperation by hunger." William J. Jones, the Dawson reporter, described the hold-up of the steamboats at Circle and demanded government help. "The people of the United States and Canada ought to send a relief expedition, headed by hearty Alaskan frontiersmen like Jack Dalton, with food for the destitute, so as to reach here by February."[152]

# Whom to Blame?

In Dawson, Edwin Adney viewed the situation in a calmer light. He watched Healy in mid-September take charge of distribution of food from the *P. B. Weare*, setting up a platform right on Front Street where all could observe the proceedings. Healy refused to give more than a two-week supply to anyone, arguing that more boats would be coming in. Then Capt. J. E. Hansen of the Alaska Commercial Company arrived from Fort Yukon on a poling boat with the news that low water would probably prevent the arrival of any other boats that season. Hansen contributed mightily to the panic, running up and down the street, urging men to flee for their lives before it was too late. The Mountie officers accepted Hansen's appraisal and arranged free transportation in October for those willing to go downriver. By then they could not make it to St. Michael and Outside transport, so they would have to winter over in other Yukon towns where ample supplies were said to be on hand.

Healy protested this plan. He knew that the Yukon settlements had little food, and an influx of men from Dawson would prove disastrous. And he was right, as evidenced by the lack of steamer traffic. The majority disregarded his opinion, though, and, ironically, when the panic passed, some people believed that he had objected to the exodus because he feared losing customers. Healy also argued that Dawson had enough food on hand to feed everyone through the winter.

Healy tried to strike a deal with Hansen so that the traders could meet most of the demand. He had plenty of bacon, sugar, and other foods, except flour. According to Adney, Healy offered to trade for flour and proposed that both companies fill outstanding orders for eight months rather than twelve. Reducing orders by one third would allow the camp to hold out until June, when more food would be available. But Hansen refused to trade. "I must fill my orders," he insisted.[153]

To Adney, Healy's proposal seemed the most rational course. For want of cooperation Healy had to conserve supplies by rationing them regardless of prior orders. Adney thought Hansen ridiculous for honoring his orders even while panicking the miners to clear out before freeze-up.

Dawson residents misunderstood and misrepresented Healy's position, Adney noted. Hansen remained popular despite his hysteria and being dead wrong on the available food supplies downriver. Dawson newspapers, particularly the *Klondike Nugget*, later vilified Healy for his handling of the crisis.

# And Still They Came

As winter closed in on the Yukon everyone saw that the stampede to come in the spring and summer of 1898 would make that of 1897 look like a trickle. Tens of thousands of people were ready to head north. Preparing for this huge influx of customers was a demanding task for ACC and NAT&T men but pleasurable, too, because the new season promised great profits.

The Canadian government, fearful that the Americans would take over the Klondike, prepared a military force to support the Mounties by the summer of 1898. Because of cries of corruption and other complaints from miners, the government also dispatched a new gold commissioner, Maj. John M. Walsh, giving him virtually dictatorial authority. Johnny knew the former Mountie well. Walsh had been stationed in Whoop-Up country and had directed the meetings between Sitting Bull and American officials. Healy's *Fort Benton Record* had treated him severely for his alleged criticisms of American soldiers and whiskey traders. Walsh was caught by the river freeze-up en route to Dawson and finally reached his headquarters in spring. But he significantly reformed the supply problem by requiring that all stampeders over the Chilkoot Pass carry at least one ton of provisions with them.

Meanwhile, the United States government responded to the threat of famine, although with little success. Several people, including Sheldon Jackson, the missionary who had introduced Siberian reindeer into Alaska for the use of the Eskimos, concluded that reindeer could be driven to Dawson for food. To achieve this, Jackson was sent to Norway and Sweden in December 1897 to buy reindeer, which reached New York by ship in February. Besides the 538 head of reindeer, the expedition included 113 drivers with 418 sleds, 411 sets of harness, and plenty of reindeer moss for forage. The animals survived a transcontinental train voyage to arrive on March 7 at Seattle where they were housed at the zoo until the authorities could arrange transportation. Meanwhile, word came from Dawson that they had averted famine.

But the reindeer show went on. The expedition reached Haines by ship in May. From this port at the head of Lynn Canal, the drivers started them over the Dalton Trail. Once they reached the Yukon the expedition would head downriver to Circle, since Dawson no longer needed the food. For nine months the drivers pushed the animals along, wondering why officials had assumed that reindeer would eat the moss found along the way when they had exhausted their imported forage. The reindeer did not like the local moss and all grew wretchedly thin. Many died of starvation or were carried off by wolves. The pitiful remnant of the herd eventually reached Dawson with 114 surviving animals.

# Commercial Expansion

To prepare for the crush of new arrivals, Healy's company prepared to expand its facilities at St. Michael, building a large hotel in the summer of 1897. Portus Weare told Chicago newsmen that he hoped to have the hotel completed by January 1898 with two hundred first-class and two hundred second-class rooms. It would dwarf every other hotel then standing in Alaska, with its four-wing, two-story structure connected by one-story galleries enclosing a hollow square. Construction would be "the biggest job of the kind ever attempted in the world," said Weare. Charles Barber, "well known in Chicago as joint owner of the House of David" was to manage the hotel. Barber believed that guests, most of whom would be waiting for riverboats or ocean ships, would have little interest in gambling or resort-style amenities, but they would pay a steep rate, $4-$8, for rooms. Barber would offer none of the elegance of the House of David. He would not greet them in a swallow-tailed coat or kid gloves, nor expect them to be splendidly attired either. So long as they paid their bills and behaved themselves within reasonable bounds, he foresaw no trouble.[154]

Weare changed the name of the company's St. Michael station from Fort Get There to Healy. The place had boomed. Prior to 1897 only three or four ships called at the old Russian post during a season. In 1897, 36 ocean-going ships and 15 river boats entered the port; in 1898 they expected 118 ocean ships—24 from foreign ports—and 113 river boats. The site also has heavy construction activity because many of the river steamers were shipped in a knocked-down condition and assembled there—as was the hotel.

St. Michael had always been an important port to both major companies, serving as their transportation and supply center. Weare felt pleased when his post manager, L. B. Shepard, was appointed U.S. commissioner at his request. Shepard's dispatches to the company's Chicago office gave the Outside an important source of information on the latest conditions during the Bering Sea navigation season. He fully agreed with Healy that Dawson would not face starvation. As the steamer *Portland* left St. Michael for San Francisco on August 16 it carried Shepard's assurances "that all danger of starvation among the miners is over."

Shepard had urged the NAT&T to construct the hotel because he predicted that the freeze-up would catch many miners leaving the country along the Yukon, and would trudge down to St. Michael over the 1897-98 winter for its comforts. "Most . . . will be well supplied with dust and eager to spend it," advised Shepard.

Shepard and Healy often advised the company and the American government to take a long view of the gold rush. They predicted that the rush, presently confined to the Yukon Territory, would in time spread when prospectors found similar great goldfields in Alaska. NAT&T officers in Chicago used some imagination to improve their Yukon situation. In October 1897 they presented the government with a bold scheme, citing "a deplorable deficiency in the exercise of judicial authority." They asked the government to create a separate Yukon region from Alaska, a political division to be called Lincoln. Since the Secretary of Treasury Lyman Gage's son, Eli Gage, worked for the NAT&T, they expected the secretary to favor the appointment of Eli as the governor of the new territory. Weare wanted his friend, U.S. Senator Thomas Carter, to introduce this bill but the scheme failed.[155]

Regardless of such far-reaching schemes, the ACC and the NAT&T, despite their experience and established locations, lacked the capacity to meet the sudden influx in 1897 and the far greater one a year later. To supply the hordes coming in other entrepreneurs had to leap into the field, and they were eager to do so. The old traders could not respond fast enough to the change. The new realities demanded men of a different temperament.

ACC's managers handled the crush of new arrivals and the food shortage with the same mixed results as Healy. Captain Hansen of the ACC, who spent more time weighing out flour than pondering larger commercial questions, floundered as the population boomed. People in Dawson laughed at hearing that he was conned by an attractive young woman. She came to him with a babe in arms, distracted and sad; her husband was broke and the cupboard was bare. She begged for food. Hansen behaved like a gentleman, saying "Certainly, Madame. Your pretty baby must not starve, nor shall it starve as long as there is a pound of grub for its mother in this store." Within three weeks—as the story goes—eight mothers with babes called on the gallant captain, and he began to wonder about the birth rate. One of his assistants eventually located the one well-used baby who had made all the trips to the ACC in the arms of different "mothers."[156]

Hansen had other problems, too. His drinking caused the company to later fire him. When he found himself, years later, reduced to a seaman on a ship, he jumped overboard to his death.

The disgrace of the ACC's Yukon manager, Edgar Mizner, pushed Hansen into the lead role at Dawson. Mizner, known widely as "the Pope" for his lordly, arrogant ways, was a reckless gambler. He was the brother of two geniuses, the madcap bon vivant wit and writer, Wilson Mizner, and Addison Mizner, the architect who designed many of the millionaires' palaces during the Florida boom of the 1920s. Both Addison and Wilson rushed to Dawson. The architect soon left, but Wilson found the northern air congenial and the opportunities for fleecing the unwary abundant. In Nome he became a celebrated prince of the demimonde, a hard drinker, gambler, con man, raconteur, and scamp. He later went south and found wealth for a time by marrying the millionaire widow of Jake Yerkes, "the traction king," then went to Hollywood to write movie scripts.

Over the 1897-98 winter Edgar Mizner drank and gambled more than usual, perhaps because he was sad about losing his lover, show girl Grace Drummond, to miner Charley Anderson. Anderson, known as "The Lucky Swede" got rich after buying a claim while drunk as unknowing friends sought to unload a poor investment. Charley loved Grace and Grace loved money. She agreed to marry him in exchange for $50,000. He was delighted to pay, to take her on a world tour, to build her a turreted castle mansion in San Francisco, and to pay her many bills until his money was gone. Then she was gone. Charley went back to Alaska to prospect but never regained his wealth.

One night Edgar started playing roulette. As the wheel spun on he found himself out of control and losing steadily. The news spread throughout the town and miners, who disliked Mizner as much as Healy, flocked in to watch the debacle. When the wheel finally stopped Edgar had lost $20,000. The next day Edgar used ACC credit to pay his I.O.U.s, and two months later his employers in San Francisco heard about it. Shocked at Edgar's "poor example to our other men and our customers," they sacked him. Edgar had actually been on borrowed time since the ACC he had made him Yukon manager in 1896, when he swiftly infuriated old customers accustomed to the genial ways of Jack McQuesten. The company sent him to Dawson in 1897, allowing him to retain his title of river manager, but restricting his authority to Dawson affairs.

# Newspaper Attacks

When navigation opened in spring 1898, Dawson miners waited expectantly for the throngs of gold rushers they knew to be underway. Stores had been ample enough over the winter and spring to prevent any hardship, but the earlier panic left men sore at the two trading companies. Some old-timers, who chose to forget that Healy had stood fast against exaggerated predictions, recalled a pattern going back a decade of cries of scarcity echoed each fall. Traders blamed shortages and resulting high prices on the failure of the last boat to get upriver through the ice or on sandbar groundings. The *Klondike News* described the situation: the miners were the prey of companies who "could get more money for a few provisions at famine prices than they could for ten times the amount at regulation store prices."[157]

Traders were devious, alleged the *News*. To avoid the opprobrium associated with openly raising prices the traders customarily pointed out their empty shelves to customers, then lead them to the stores of supplies kept for their employees. The trader would agree to sell some of his supply surplus for "fancy prices" so that miners would have their necessities. The *News* conceded that Captain Hansen of the ACC refrained from playing this trick over the winter, "however, this does not exempt them altogether from censure for the suffering, anxiety and damage they caused in years gone by."

Healy, according to the *News*, robbed the miners whose guaranteed orders he refused to fill, claiming that price rises were necessary to cover the cost of hauling goods from Fortymile by dog team. Healy made money but "scared 1,000 chechakos from the country" and indirectly stimulated the formation of new trading companies eager to sell at the prevailing high prices. But Healy's exploitation misfired, the *News* claimed, because he bought the outfits of fleeing miners. When the Canadian government insisted that stampeders bring in a year's provisions, Healy was stuck with a warehouse of goods. "So the company with millions of dollars invested, have enough supplies to feed every man in the Klondike, and not enough patronage to keep a one-lunged clerk busy."

The *News* writer bitterly continued his article. "Now, Capt.? you can go lock yourself up in your little glass office and no one will bother you this season. The ladies won't come frightened with famine and listen to your off color antediluvian stories for the privilege of paying you two pieces for musty canned goods, while the miners will see that neither themselves nor your friends go near your pawn shop."

This vicious attack on Healy appeared in the first issue of Dawson's first newspaper, which had wide circulation. By June another newspaper, the *Klondike Nugget*, took up the attack on Healy and persisted in it. Its editor interviewed Portus Weare when he visited, demanding to know whether the company would remove its Yukon manager. Weare indignantly replied, "No sir. No changes whatever will be made. The affairs of the company are being satisfactorily conducted, and a change of management has never for one moment been considered."[158]

In July the *Nugget* posed a series of questions to Healy, asking him "is it true that last winter it was impossible for the average citizen here to get goods at your store, and yet the women of the town were never denied any article in your warehouses?" By "women of the town," the paper meant whores, whom they suggested had found a special place in the heart of the crusty old merchant. "Is it true," the paper asked further, "that last fall you had orders on your books for goods and the gold . . . in your safe, yet those orders were filled only in a limited percentage while the newcomers and the gentle sex—especially the latter—had no trouble getting winter stock? Is it true that the confidence of miners and their rights as pioneers of the country had been so abused by your company, that but for the presence of the police here last year, personal violence would have been done you?"

Other queries in the *Nugget* concerned excessive charges for tobacco, refusing steamboat passengers the right "to dicker" with Indians for souvenirs, and requiring miners to cut wood before selling them food, then reneging on the promise to sell.

*Nugget* readers saw another slam at Healy on July 20 in a story describing miners cheated by a mine owner. "The owner, a certain Mr. Healy, well known from one end of the gulch to the other," paid off miners with gold valued at $17 an ounce. "The gold was probably worth that money," the story went on, "yet when the men reappeared at Healy's store a few hours later to purchase supplies, not a cent more than $16 would be allowed them. The latter price is that which gold is used uniformly in this section, either in payment of wages or for merchandise."

Johnny, showing his typical disregard for the corporate art of public relations, declined to answer the paper's impertinent and scurrilous charges. But the *Nugget* continued its assault, unconcerned by its failure to get a rise out of him. In August it offered a story headed "Grab and Rule Even If It Ruins." Some passengers on the steamer *Weare* bought tickets to St. Michael for $100 although $150 was the established rate. Competition from the ACC's new boat, *Susie,* had prompted the NAT&T to reduce its rate. The newspaper resented this because some of the *Weare*'s passengers had paid the full price, and because the editor was desperate to condemn Healy. While the papers usually applauded competition and lower fares, the *Nugget* contrasted the high-minded refusal of the ACC to reduce fares and condemned Healy's unfair competition. The paper was later pleased to report on a Healy dispute with steamboat seamen over wages and a lawsuit over a mining claim. Healy should have lost the suit because of his sharp practices, according to the *Nugget.*

Into September the *Nugget* pounded away at Healy, making the price of potatoes the issue of a contrived comic dialogue between "Messrs. Sourdough" and "Chee Charko." The villain was Healy, whose price gouging at Circle before Dawson's founding was described. Another story in the same issue censured Healy for creating "havoc by reducing prices" on drinks at his cafe. The paper accused Healy of disrupting normal commerce by using inappropriate means to regain his company's lost trade. Earlier, the paper opined, the company held a monopoly, advertising Outside that it commanded all the boats and all the wood on the Yukon. Now with plenty of competition, Healy was being removed. "His successor is on the way."

On September 24 the paper headed a gleeful piece, "Farewell Healy." The NAT&T was recalling its manager and the *Nugget* wished readers to observe the lesson in his "departure" from Dawson. "He was a shrewd enough man in many ways and built up a business for the company in which he was interested that was gratifying to the shareholders." But, while Healy took advantage of the lack of competition in the country to build his trade he failed to learn from later "diminishing sales that he was overstepping the bounds of public toleration." Now, when his company should be at its peak, the paper said, the other directors were removing him because trade was bad. The company finally realized the import of its manager's unpopularity "by the immense stack of goods piled up on the sidewalks as high as the house for want of room in the crowded warehouses."

Healy, said the *Nugget*, "had the consolation of leaving here a wealthy man, many of his mining speculations having proved successful. There were no departing cheers for the captain, but it is doubtful that a man of his caliber cared for that as long as his sack was heavy."

Johnny's persecution by the Dawson press is tough to analyze. Papers freely castigated businessmen, without requirements of fairness or accuracy. If any people in Dawson disagreed or were shocked by the treatment, they failed to speak up.

In assuming Healy's removal, the *Nugget* indulged in wishful thinking. The manager was leaving only temporarily. He may have been in trouble with other company directors, but his journey outside combined vacation and business. And it provided a welcome respite for the hard-pressed businessman who had not been out of the North for several years. He stopped at Helena with Belle and one of his daughters, and received the usual accolades from the press. The *Helena Herald* noted that he had increased his fame and fortune in the North, yet appeared "as rugged as of old when everybody in the northern part of the territory of Montana knew him as sheriff of Choteau county." Healy quickly put right a reporter, who had heard rumors that Healy had lost his optimism about the North. Johnny said that "there is no place on the whole globe of which he has heard where a man can do as well in as short a time as in that country providing he goes there to work and not sit down and wait for someone to come along and buy his claim." But, cautioned Captain Healy, "the man must work and rustle and be possessed of good business judgment." Healy told newsmen that he had been avoiding interviews on his current trip. He had business to do in Chicago and "was in no sense here for the purpose of booming the country."[159]

Even though Johnny's intent was business, not booming the north country, he wanted to straighten the public out on the Dawson starvation controversy of the previous year. He pointed out that the matter resolved itself as he predicted, without any danger of famine. "Prices of all kinds rose to an exorbitant figure on account of speculation on the part of outsiders who purchased grub from the stores and advanced the price. For a while some very high prices prevailed." Seattle and other rival Puget Sound cites had raised the famine alarm, hoping to get contracts with the government for relief expeditions. Johnny also criticized Seattle interests for booming the North too much: "The country will get along well enough on its merits without anything of that kind."

Apparently Healy had plenty to do Outside over the winter and spring of 1898-99, because he delayed his return to Dawson until July. His reappearance confounded those who had happily assumed that he was washed up. He told reporters nothing about his activities Outside, but indicated that he had changes in mind for the company. To the *Nugget* reporter interviewing him he seemed energetic and optimistic and delighted to be back in the healthy North. Apparently the *Nugget's* vendetta against Healy was over: the reporter raised no questions about the matters that stirred the paper earlier.[160]

The company needed reforming, and Johnny set out to do it. A friend of former U.S. Deputy Marshal Frank Canton of Circle reported some of Johnny's actions and included some Healy gossip in a December 1899 letter to Canton. Canton, appointed deputy marshal at Weare's request, was removed by Justice Department officials when they discovered he had been fired as a deputy in Oklahoma for falsifying expenses. Canton's friend, H. Sanderson, had stampeded to Nome, then, finding nothing, returned to Dawson to mine and work at the NAT&T store. "Captain Healy fired that *Healy* steamboat captain and the manager at St. Michael for neglect of duty." Healy's removal of manager L. B. Shepard led to the transfer of John Crane, Nora's husband, to St. Michael from Circle. Sanderson also claimed that the company had cornered the market on oats and hay even though prices on both had dropped. River navigation closed early in 1899, leaving some company vessels stranded.[161]

# The Fall

As Johnny kept busy trying to improve company profits, the end was near. Apparently he failed to turn the business around fast enough for the Chicago directors, and they fired him. Perhaps they had made the decision to remove him before he returned to Chicago to argue his case, where he won only a temporary reprieve. In any event, the few months of late 1899 and early 1900 were his last hurrah in command as Yukon field manager. His partners dumped the principal founder and stockholder of their company without shedding tears. In March 1900 Healy announced his retirement as manager, saying he would concentrate on the company's mining interests. At the the time of Johnny's announcement a new manager had been on the job for two months while Healy supervised a force of one hundred miners.

A reporter probed for more information on this change, and Johnny replied firmly but gently, "I am in the same position, my boy, as a soldier, and obey the call to duty, no matter in what direction it takes me." This statement must have raised a smile among readers who knew Johnny's temper and could imagine the scenes in Chicago when he protested his deposition.[162]

The mining assignment may have provided a smoke screen to cover a graceful exit, but it appears that Healy effectively left the company in July 1899 or soon thereafter. While reserved with the press, he felt bitter about his removal.

Despite this painful firing, Johnny was unwilling to give up on himself or on Alaska. He had some surefire schemes for making money and was now free to pursue them. The company had always resisted his best ideas, telling him he was expanding too far and too fast. Now, required to make a fresh start, he could pursue some projects on his own. He would have a more difficult time getting private investors than he had lining up support within the NAT&T, but he would be freer of interference.

Whether the NAT&T would have prospered by following Johnny's urging is moot. Many of the regions where he called for expansion produced few minerals and lacked other economic prospects. But he believed that overly conservative polices resulted in the company's gradual fading against ACC competition. The company was unwilling to take the big chance that he was always ready to dare. Later he wrote a friend that "the NAT&T should own the Copper River, Tanana, Kuskokwim, and Mulchatna." Earlier he had urged the other directors earlier to seize the opportunity in all of those fields, but they resisted. "No," they said, "you're getting too much."[163]

# Appraisals

Hearsay is all that exists to back accusations of corruption made by Dawson newspapers in 1898-99 and by individual miners in Alaska. Those made by the *Nugget* owe more to a personal vendetta by the editor against Healy than any evidence of misconduct. If a merchant raises prices in a time of scarcity, he may justly be vilified, but that does not mean he was dishonest.

Johnny's ineffectiveness as a merchant prince is more easily proven. He may have been in over his head trying to direct a large company, but his vision and drive made the enterprise possible. And the failure of the company reflects nothing on his integrity.

Johnny's reputation was damaged by the way the NAT&T treated him. In contrast, one of his old acquaintances from Alberta suffered a terrible and more damning disgrace in Dawson, yet it was hushed up. John Walsh, the former Mountie officer involved in the Sitting Bull negotiations, was fired from his lofty post as commissioner of the Yukon. Apologists for Walsh point out that he and other officials faced difficult conditions. While Sam Steele and his Mounties effectively kept order in the turbulent boom town, the civil administration was chaotic. The Mounties had to take charge of all services, including that of the mail. Running the post office was a demanding job for which the police lacked the training. A steamboat might bring in as many as five thousand letters and, as restless miners waited impatiently in long lines, the Mounties sorted and handed out the mail piece by piece. One could wait in line for three days, creating a brisk market for people willing to hold a place in the queue.

According to the American missionary Hall Young, the Mounties also conducted a brisk market for those wishing preference in the mail line. Young, one of the rare dissenters among those who showered praise on the Mounties of Dawson, forthrightly stated that "right here I am going to act the part of an iconoclast and do some smashing of the idols which American Anglophiles and Canadian enthusiasts have set up. I am not wanting in respect for that heroic body of men called the Northwest Mounted Police, and the Canadian officers, but after a full experience on the frontiers of Canada and Alaska, I have not witnessed in the United States and Alaska anything in the way of graft that compared with the insolence, rank dishonesty and disrespect for the rights of men which I observed among the officials of the Yukon Province of Canada, and even in the mounted police."[164]

Young went on to describe how the mail clerks dallied over the distribution of letters until men figured out that an ounce of gold would give them instant consideration. Hall had no gold but found a $5 bill that did the trick for him.

Dawson first got a regular newspaper in the spring of 1898, so it lacked a public forum for complaining about the government or business interests when it was most needed. Once the *Klondike Nugget*, under American editors, and other papers began publishing, they carried many protests against the government, which reflected the anger of American miners at the Canadian officials and mining regulations. In September 1897 the government imposed a 10 percent royalty, which outraged the Americans. Since most Klondike miners were aliens bent on getting their money out of the country the imposition of a stiff royalty reasonably assured Canada some benefit. Americans, who forgot that aliens could not even own claims in Alaska, considered themselves victims of onerous exploitation. Canadian miners disliked it equally, especially because the royalty increased to 20 percent on mines producing more than $500 a week. Miners commonly cheated in reporting production.

Walsh assumed his duties late, because the 1897-98 freeze-up held him on the upper Yukon over the winter. He immediately came under pressure from the miners, particularly because they believed that Thomas Fawcett, the gold commissioner, and other officials were corrupt. Walsh was fifty-four years old and portraits show an imposing stiff-backed military officer, stern looking, vigorous, broad shouldered, square jawed, athletic, and handsome, with iron-gray hair and a short beard. Walsh had retired from the military fifteen years earlier and had worked as a coal dealer in Winnipeg before his appointment as commissioner.

In Canada Walsh's reputation had been inflated. While Healy remembered him as a provocateur who incited Sitting Bull to defy the American officials who traveled to Alberta to discuss surrender terms for the Sioux, Canadians considered him a hero. Canadian historian Pierre Berton glorifies Walsh's actions by claiming that "this was the same commanding figure who, a quarter of century before, immaculate in white Stetson and polished boots, had been the first uniformed man to ride into the armed camp of Sitting Bull and his warriors, from whose saddle horns the scalps of Custer's men still joggled." Without questioning Walsh's courage, Sitting Bull, in flight from American troops and seeking the good will of Canadians, was anxious to display his peaceful intent in Canada and unwilling to appear provocative.[165]

Walsh's role in Dawson required little courage but a great deal of integrity. He had little time to make his fortune in Dawson, although it appears that he had schemed to do so. After two months on the job, William Ogilvie, the surveyor of the Yukon mountain passes and goldfields, replaced him. Ogilvie had been presiding over a Royal Commission investigating charges of government graft brought by the *Nugget*. Testimony included that of Louis Carbeno, Walsh's cook, who said that he only got his job after agreeing to give three-quarters interest on any mining claims he located to either Walsh or his brother Philip. Since Walsh had been in position to have inside knowledge of the Dominion Creek claims, Carbeno's revelations were damning. Officials closed Dominion Creek, a rich area staked haphazardly in 1897, to further staking in November until they made a survey. They permitted staking again in July 1898, allowing those to whom they had issued permits in Dawson to race the forty miles to the creek. Carbeno and others went to the creek three days before the opening. Walsh had approved of Carbeno's anticipatory tactic and apparently made arrangements for his staking permit. Carbeno managed to stake a valuable claim and turn it over to Philip Walsh, who, according to Carbeno, had orchestrated the whole deal.

Except for the more complex grab of Nome mines by conspirators led by Alexander McKenzie and Judge Alfred Noyes, this scam was the most blatant fraud of the gold-rush era. Ogilvie and authorities in Ottawa were convinced that James Walsh and his brother were crooks. Either the evidence received by the commission seemed insufficient or the government wished to avoid further embarrassment, because they declined to prosecute the men.

Gold Commissioner Thomas Fawcett was also removed and the *Nugget* headed the gleeful story on his leaving as it would later that of Healy's: "GOODBY FAWCETT." Both Fawcett and Walsh were disgraced but Walsh had further to fall in popular esteem. Walsh was actually fortunate in that the Yukon scandal did not make much of a stir in other parts of Canada. He was able to resume a normal life and continued to be remembered more for being a brave Indian fighter than a dubious government official. The public raised no objections when the government put his name on lofty Mount Walsh of the St. Elias Mountains.

# 13

# Making a Comeback

*An outdoor life*
*is what I long for,*
*wild country where*
*man is strange.*
    —Johnny Healy

Johnny Healy wasted no time after leaving the NAT&T before investigating other business and mining ventures. His first venture after leaving Dawson was at Yakutat on the southeastern coast. Aside from a flurry of excitement in the mid-1880s, when miners sifted some of the beach sands for gold, Yakutat had been a quiet place. An Indian village near the huge Malaspina Glacier, it provided a jumping off place for mountaineers climbing lofty Mount St. Elias or other peaks in the chain. Healy had seen little of the region since the eighties when he carried prospectors there on his schooner, but must have determined then that it had great economic potential.

In late 1900 he and others organized the Yakutat Fishing Company, then found backers and reorganized as the Central Alaskan Exploration Company. Healy retained John Cooper and others to develop a Copper River fishery and to prospect mining claims. The hopeful entrepreneur described his intentions to Gov. John Brady of Alaska who had provided W. I. Warner of Yakutat, Johnny's partner, with information about commercial prospects in the region. "I do not hesitate to tell you," Healy wrote in his usual boomer's style, "that I have great hopes of making a very strong company of this. The capital stock will be $1 million and we have commenced to operate already. "I go East in a few days for the purpose of procuring a charter." Because the venture included a railroad of "twenty miles or more," Healy wanted help from the governor.[166]

But the new enterprise stagnated because his new partners failed to come up with the necessary funding. When it became obvious that his partners' enthusiasm had faded, Healy paid $15,000 to his original backers and abandoned the enterprise. After a year's work and an investment of $15,000, a considerable capital sum, he had nothing to show. Disappointed at the outcome of his first new venture in an decade, he still had faith in his luck and his genius. He saw successes ahead. If petty, purse-pinching men failed to follow his star they would be the losers.

Even before this setback Johnny had developed a more grandiose scheme: building a long-distance railroad from the coast to Alaska's interior. He had a weakness for railroad promotion as did many entrepreneurs who had watched the construction of the great transcontinental railroads and dreamed of duplicating the prosperity of Edward Harriman, James Hill, and other railroad moguls. Healy spent the winter of 1900-1901 in London trying to raise capital for a railroad from Valdez to the interior. The Valdez newspaper reported that Healy planned to push his railroad on to Siberia via Port Clarence and the Bering Strait, but the editor gave the proposal little credence.

People in Valdez had committed themselves heavily to another railroad project that seemed more practical and more likely to be built. When Johnny's scheme was first publicized, Michael Heney, a famed northern railroad builder, was in Valdez preparing to make a railroad survey. Heney had supervised the construction of the White Pass and Yukon Route Railway over the White Pass from Skagway in 1898-99. Alaskans admired Heney tremendously for his successes and his personal qualities—generosity, exuberance, and conviviality. "The arrival of Mr. Heney and his party," as the Valdez News reported, "caused considerable excitement in Valdez and visions of railroads floated before everyone's eyes."[167]

Alaskans had been pushing for a railroad from Valdez to the Yukon ever since the Klondike gold rush. The government built the Valdez Trail to the Yukon in 1899-1900, but folks wanted a railroad. The residents argued that the White Pass and Yukon Route Railway came far from meeting the needs for the territory's development. They demanded a railroad within the territory, a more expansive network that would open up many remote regions to mining and other economic development.

Heney and Healy were among several promoters interested in a railroad to the interior, including the owners of the copper deposits in the Copper River Valley. As rich as the copper ore was, they needed a railroad to haul it to the coast to make the deposits worth their while to mine. The conflicting claims among the discoverers were under litigation until 1903, but strong rumors about James Hill or others building a Copper River railroad had been floating around since 1901.

Healy made his move early in 1903 when he showed up in Seattle to announce the construction of the Valdes, Copper River & Yukon Railway. (Valdez was still sometimes spelled Valdes at this time.) He named J. P. McDonald as contractor and S. E. Adair and F. C. Helm of New York as his backers. He planned to move fast: by fall the line would reach Copper Center and within two and a half years they would complete it to Dawson via Eagle. The line would compete strongly with the White Pass & Yukon Route, which only extended from Skagway to Whitehorse and depended on freight boats or sleds for service to the Yukon. Healy had yet to consider the potential of the copper mines.

To the Seattle press, Johnny declared his firm determination: "There is no longer any doubt. . . . Every opposition has not been met by the promoters. However, all the money has been raised." Because a cargo of rails shipped in on the freighter *California* just arrived at the Seattle dock, people there believed that Healy's project had some substance. He would have to wait until spring to begin construction, but Healy planned a winter survey and would begin hiring the 5,000-man building crew he would need. Healy planned to pay wages of $3 per day. "I have the contract for feeding and clothing all these men, and I know what I am talking about when I say that the road will be built."[168]

On the long-term prospects of the line Healy indulged in the sweeping hyperbole that characterized railroad promoters: "The building of the road through the territory . . . will mean the settlement of one million persons in that part of Alaska." The new settlers would farm for the most part, "for there are millions of acres in Alaska on which tall grass is growing that awaits agricultural development."

Expensive railroad schemes needed grand forecasts, and the men Healy was wooing in Seattle often had difficulty swallowing them. He offered other questionable statistics to prove his sincerity: "The company has already spent more than $250,000 in the perfection of its plans. Much of this has been used in buying lands, surveying and in material. However, that is but a drop in the bucket to what will be spent before it is through."

Healy's interest in the railroad started many years before, but he had been unable to convince the NAT&T of the railroad's potential. "Four years ago I begged some Chicago capitalists to build this road. . . . I urged the building of the White Pass road as early as 1892, but they thought I was wrong. Now they see that I was not. The Copper River country alone will support one million people when it has a railroad. There are millions of acres of meadow land there awaiting settlement," he told the Seattle newspapers.

Johnny discussed his plans with President Teddy Roosevelt, "who was surprised when I told him of the vast stretch of agricultural lands there were in the Copper River country." In Washington, Healy also encouraged the congressmen he knew to pass a bill to expand homestead acreage from 160 to 320 acres. More land would encourage settlement, and a railroad would substantially reduce costs. He calculated that of the $25 now paid for a sack of flour on the Copper River, $24 of it was for freight. "I know what I am talking about, for I have spent $50,000 exploiting the Copper River country," he commented.

Railroad promoters, Johnny included, always had a fight on their hands and often felt paranoid about their competitors. "We have had our characters attacked," Johnny said, "and rivals have told lies about the country to discourage potential investors . . . however, we have come out all right. . . . Valdes will be booming."

If newspapers quoted Healy correctly, he had a free and easy way with figures. It is unlikely that he or his company spent $50,000, or $250,000, or any substantial sum on the railroad scheme. The company had yet to survey the route or undertake any heavy expenditures. Johnny also grossly exaggerated when he claimed that all the capital had been raised.

In Seattle, Healy decided not to mention the trans-Siberian extension of the line as he had previously to potential investors. He had apparently decided that he would find it easier to get capital for a less expensive railroad line. He still had faith in his favorite scheme, but he would now approach the matter more cautiously, in easily digestible stages. But even the mileage he envisioned from the coast to the Yukon was tough for financiers to digest. The project required many millions. When it came time to dig for cash, potential backers wanted to see more of Healy's one million settlers on the ground rather than in his vision. How, they asked, could you make a railroad pay with as little freight and as scanty a population as you have in Alaska? Healy insisted that a flood of settlers would follow railroad construction, but his potential backers felt less sure.

Prospectors in the Tanana valley made exciting gold discoveries in 1902-1903. Healy was ebulliently optimistic about the growth that would occur along this great southern tributary of the Yukon. For several years most of the mining excitement focused on the Seward Peninsula and Nome. Now, he told investors, attention will shift back to the Yukon. Events proved him correct. Fairbanks became the leading town of Alaska and was accessible from any rail entrepôt established on the Yukon. When Fairbanks started to boom the government shifted the interior terminal of its wagon road from Eagle to Fairbanks in recognition of the new town's place as the population center of the Yukon valley.

Indirectly, Healy played a role in the founding of Fairbanks. In 1898 or 1899 he advised E. T. Barnette, who worked for him in Dawson as a mine supervisor but wished to become a trader, to locate at Tanana Crossing (later renamed Tanacross), an army telegraph station on the Tanana near Tok. Healy assured Barnette that his railroad would eventually reach Tanana Crossing and a store there would do well. Barnette tried to heed this advice, but his little steamboat, *Lavelle Young*, was unable to reach the crossing because of low water. Barnette dropped down river, entered the Chena River, and set up shop at what became the town of Chena. Barnette was running his store when Felix Pedro announced a major gold strike, and Barnette soon moved a couple of miles to found Fairbanks.

Barnette did well by following Healy's advice even though the rail plan fizzled. As the Tanana valley boomed, Barnette made a fortune and also suffered some disasters. When he failed to share gains with his backer, James H. Causten of Seattle, Causten sued him in a Seattle court. He lost, and eventually paid Causten off. The long period of litigation brought out some sensational stories, including Captain Barnette's criminal record. In 1887-88 he served time in the Oregon Penitentiary for swindling. This exposure of the town's leading man and founder amused folks in Fairbanks, but it should have made them more wary. In 1907 Barnette's bank ran into difficulties and eventually depositors lost their money. The banker was prosecuted but narrowly avoided a criminal conviction. He left Alaska with a rich purse.

Captain Healy was far more honest than Captain Barnette. He was also more honest than rival Valdez railroad promoter Henry D. Reynolds, whose dreams turned to dust a few years later. Within a couple of weeks of Healy's first announcements in Seattle that his company was about to begin construction, he admitted that backers could expect delays. To those in the know the grand enterprise was obviously still in the pipe dream stage. He summoned the press to his quarters at the Butler Hotel, decrying those who desired Alaska's riches but withheld assistance: "It is all wrong, this idea that the businessmen of Seattle have no responsibilities where the future of Alaska is concerned." Seattle would lose its dominant position in the Alaskan trade, he warned darkly. "Seattle is not the only place on the coast that can handle the business of the north." He had hopes for Bellingham, Tacoma, or San Francisco—and made hurried visits to these places seeking money. But no one was interested.[169]

Raising railroad construction capital was tough. Healy claimed that he tried to promote a White Pass railroad in the early 1890s, a road finally built during the gold rush and became a success. "Ten years ago I tried to secure capital to build the White Pass road, but people laughed: they said I was a dreamer," Johnny complained. He insisted that people ignored the potential of Alaska. "I am a believer in Alaska, and expect before I die to cast a vote for a presidential candidate in the state of Alaska, or in one of the three or four great states which that enormous territory will make."[170]

## Domestic Woes

From 1901 to 1903 Johnny had more than railroads on his mind. He and Belle fell out in November 1901, and she filed for a divorce in Chicago. The substance but not the merits of their charges is fully documented by Cook County [Chicago] court records.

In recognition of Healy's fame, some newspapers featured the divorce story. The *Helena Independent* poked fun at Johnny over Belle's accusations, headlining its irreverent story "Captain John J. Healy as a Lothario." Healy's romantic enterprises, the story went on, are "no less extensive than his Alaskan holdings which are reported to have made him a millionaire." According to his wife, Healy had "entangled himself with actresses, adventurous women and attractive daughters of a rich mother in a fashion that would make a less venturesome lover's head swim."

The domestic trouble started in 1901 while the couple visited Europe. According to Belle, "he constantly neglected her to visit women in questionable places." During the following winter in Los Angeles he became involved with Mrs. Emily Craig of New York and her daughter Molly. Belle claimed that Johnny "has become infatuated with Miss Craig and she has heard that he has expressed his intention to marry the young woman as soon as he could secure a divorce."[171]

Johnny denied all the accusations and accused Belle of blackmail. She had retained a man named L. O. Wilcoxon, "who pretended to act as a detective," and tried to bribe several of the ladies said to be friendly to Healy to "testify to improper relations."

Belle wanted money. She claimed that she had advanced Johnny $11,000 when he was trying to finance his Yakutat venture, and he had not repaid her. Johnny insisted that he had.

Johnny's cross suit held a damaging charge. He had stopped living with Belle in 1901 when he learned that she had married him fraudulently in 1888. She had claimed that her husband had died in a Montana insane asylum, but he lived on for years, finally dying in 1898.

The Cook County court granted the Healys a divorce in May 1903. Because the couple reached a private settlement, the court in a separate proceeding dismissed Bell's claims to property and income. No records show what Belle gained as a settlement, but she probably received a good share of his liquid assets. From this point in his life Johnny lacked the means to invest much in his several business endeavors.

By coincidence, Portus Weare, Healy's old partner, took some heavy blows during the same period. The Chicago Board of Trade suspended Portus and his brother Charles for two years from March 1903. After a long hearing, board officers found both men guilty of "dishonest handling of a commission deal."

Weare, a member of the Board of Trade since 1862 and a long-time pillar of the establishment, must have been badly hurt by the suspension. Weare's separation from the NAT&T had come around the time of Healy's removal, but he had other commercial interests. Before helping found the northern concern he had managed the Chicago Railway Terminal Elevator Co., which controlled eight of the largest grain elevators in Chicago with a capacity exceeding ten million bushels. He also controlled sixty-five grain elevators in Iowa, Nebraska, and Illinois, and the Weare Land and Livestock Co., which at one time had fifty thousand head of cattle on ranches in northern Wyoming and eastern Montana. Weare also founded Morton Park, a near suburb of Chicago.[172]

## Other Reverses

Healy managed to hang on to his NAT&T stock, but, except as an asset he pledged a couple of times when he organized new companies, it gave him little return. Business stagnated on the Yukon after Johnny left the company. Dawson declined rapidly from 1899. Several trading and transportation companies consolidated because of the limited commerce. The Seattle-Yukon Transportation Company, founded by W. D. Woods, merged with the ACC in 1901. With four steamboats on the river and other holdings the Seattle-Yukon Transportation Company grossed $1 million at its peak in 1898 under Woods. Founder W. D. Woods was the mayor of Seattle when news of the Klondike discovery reached him while he was visiting San Francisco. He acted swiftly, wired his resignation to Seattle and set about organizing his trading company without a backward glance at affairs on Puget Sound.

The merger reestablished the hegemony of the pioneer ACC, now known as the Northern Commercial Company (NCC). Nordstrom of Seattle has now taken over stores in Fairbanks and Anchorage, except for the equipment outlet in Fairbanks. A native corporation has purchased stores in smaller communities and adopted the old name, Alaska Commercial Company.

Although the NAT&T management refused to join the merger in 1901, its days were numbered. For several years more the company handled about a third of the Yukon traffic, but lost $400,000 in 1903. The Fairbanks boom of 1904-1905 provided marginal profits, as the company cut costs by closing stores at Rampart, Fort Yukon, and Fortymile, and leased its vessels to independent captains. In 1905 the company was sold to a group of Fairbanks businessmen who kept the NAT&T name until 1912. That year the company closed its Dawson store, sold its steamboats, and gave up the ghost.

# Personal Losses

Johnny faced difficult times. His personal and financial woes had mounted ever since he left the NAT&T and Dawson. He suffered a more personal grief when his only son died in 1901. Thomas Constantine (T. C.) Healy died at age twenty-seven in Seattle. For two years he suffered from tuberculosis, but had nevertheless carried on working. His businesses included the Regina Club, a popular Dawson bar he had named after his infant daughter, and some mining interests. He suffered a hemorrhage while visiting Juneau and was brought down to Seattle. After three weeks at the Rainier-Grand Hotel he had another hemorrhage and died. Johnny, Belle, and T. C.'s sister Maria were all there. Five-year-old Regina Mary had just reached Seattle from Dawson when her father died. Her mother had sent her down because she was ill, and she, too, died a short time later.

Sadly, Johnny buried his son and granddaughter in a family plot he purchased at the Lakeview Cemetery in Seattle. At the same time he moved the remains of Mary Frances, his first wife and mother of all of his children, from Montana to Seattle's Lakeview Cemetery. Johnny tried to relieve his sorrow at the untimely death of his youthful descendants by working hard, hoping to avoid depression. Unfortunately, the cause of his sorrow made the point of working questionable. Johnny wondered what a man should strive for if not to leave something for his children and grandchildren. But he considered himself an old fighter; he would soldier on and give his last bit of energy to the ideal he had pursued for a long time.

# 14

# The Trans-Alaska-Siberian Railway

*All my knowledge . . .
and not . . . able to buy a packhorse.*
—Johnny Healy

C an you hear the whistle blowing, that ghostly howl of the most marvelous continent-binding railroad yet conceived? Here was a road to compel awe and wonder. Only men of great daring and confidence could throw themselves into the championship of such a magnificent scheme.

Though the expanse of each continent is great, the gap between North America and Asia is minute. Cape Prince of Wales, Alaska, and Cape Dezhneva, Siberia, lie only forty-four miles apart—about the length of the canal that links the Atlantic and Pacific oceans at the Isthmus of Panama. But even this short distance in the Bering Strait is broken by two islands, Big Diomede and Little Diomede, between which runs the boundary line separating Russia from the United States. On a clear day one can easily see across the two miles separating Russian Big Diomede and American Little Diomede.

Yet, connecting the continents was complex, politically and logistically. For Healy it involved persuading a czar and his ministers to overcome their paranoia of foreign intrusions. And it involved constructing a railroad across a region so climatically severe that it discouraged most economic development. But Healy and his partner, Loicq de Lobel, were intrigued by the challenges.

Both Johnny and Loicq de Lobel claimed credit as the Trans-Alaska-Siberian Railway's first promoter. The idea—simply as an idea—had been around for decades when the Frenchman and the American decided to join forces to transform the dream into reality.

William Gilpin predicted in 1849 that one day a railroad would link North America and Asia. In 1861, well before any of the transcontinental

*Drawing made from the 1906 sketch of the Bering Strait tunnel, entitled, "The Wedding of Asia and America."*

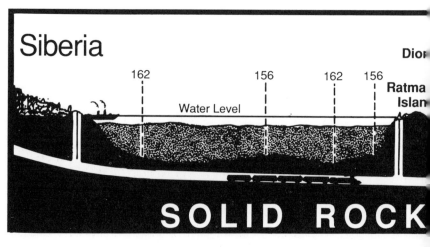

Siberia

162      156      162   156

Water Level

SOLID ROCK

railroads were built, Gilpin talked about his idea while serving as Colorado's first territorial governor. As a Colorado booster he liked the notion of making Denver the hub of a transportation network extending north into Alaska and Siberia and south into Mexico. In 1890 he amplified his views in a booklet entitled *The Cosmopolitan Railway Compacting and Fusing Together All the World's Continents.* "The more I investigated," he wrote, "the more practical the plan appeared." He noted that the Russians were constructing a Siberian railroad while "several systems in America are drawing nearer and nearer toward the narrow strait which separates the oldest continent." Gilpin grandly stated that as another "link in the great chain of progress," the railroad would help unite all the world's people in peace and prosperity.[173]

Others also believed in the destiny of a railroad linking Siberia and Alaska. The groundwork laid by the Western Union Telegraph Expedition during 1865-67 looked promising. Backers of a telegraph line stretching from western Canada across Alaska and the Bering Strait to Siberia and other countries farther west relaxed their support only after another line under the Atlantic Ocean finally connected them with Europe, rendering the Siberian route unnecessary.

But prior to that, Congress considered the northern route as one of potential value. John Wesley Powell, director of the U.S. Geological Survey, recommended to a congressional committee in 1866 that a commercial route to Asia might depart the United States from the Northern Pacific Railroad in Montana, head north through Alberta to the headwaters of the Peace River, then on to the headwaters of the Yukon, and finally jogging over to Grantley Harbor on the Bering Strait.

*Engineers said the tunnel project was impossible because of the great depth of the water.*

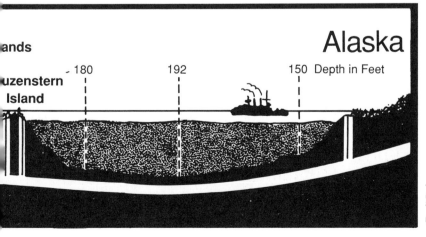

# Gold and the Railroad

The great gold discoveries on the Seward Peninsula in 1899 stimulated an interest in Siberia among American mining men. They reckoned that the opposite shores of the Bering Strait might yield similar mineral riches. Soon Alaskan prospectors started searching in Siberia. Boosters of Nome believed in Siberian prospects and responded warmly to rumors that American promoters were planning an Alaskan-Siberian railroad. In August 1901 the *Nome Nugget* featured a front-page story heralding the latest scheme: "James Hill is interested." Other railroad promoters often dropped the names of Hill, the celebrated builder of the Great Northern Railroad. "A dispatch from St. Paul says it is no myth," claimed the *Nugget*.[174]

In October newspapers offered another story about a trans-Siberian project. J. J. Frey and others incorporated the Trans-Alaska Company of Denver in Washington State and authorized the issuance of $50 million in stock. A railroad would ferry passengers across Bering Strait in the summer, but Frey and his partners failed to mention any means of transport during the eight inclement months when the ferry could not run.

Editor J. F. A. Strong of the *Nome Nugget* championed the proposed railroad. "For the last twenty years," he explained, "all Russian military maps of railroads and projected railroads have shown a projected road extending to the Bering straits." Russia needed such a road to conquer China. The railroad would carry American manufactured products directly to the front. "Alaska should be made the needed storehouse, from which Russia could draw as required all the supplies needed to carry on its aggressive policy," stated Strong. A few days later he assured his readers that the railroad would be built: "Let him scoff who will."

Strong cared little who built the railroad, but he knew Johnny Healy, whose name figured prominently in all newspaper discussions of the railroad from 1904. The editor joked about Healy's promotions, but he believed in him: "Captain Healy had always been an optimist and was probably born one so is not to blame. His optimism is of such a cheerful encouraging kind that some people might call it by another name." Strong insisted that Healy, a "pathfinder of the Alaska wilds," always succeeded to back his projects "with his own money as well as other people's." Strong pointed out that Healy's knowledge of the North "was not gained from the deck of an excursion steamer," but came from "brushing up with the country itself." When Healy talked about railroads he knew what he was talking about, said Strong. "He is a wise seer who dips into the near as well as the remote future and sees visions of what is to be."[175]

Healy involved James Hamilton Lewis of Seattle in his railroad plans. Lewis, a celebrated criminal lawyer who later became a U.S. senator, was interviewed by a Seattle newspaper in June 1901. He revealed few details of the great project but conceded that "the undertaking is an enormous one, and will require millions of capital to successfully execute it." Lewis solicited support from Puget Sound residents by pointing out that "it will be a great thing for Seattle, as it means making this city the eastern terminus of one of the most gigantic transportation schemes ever undertaken."[176]

# Harry DeWindt

The press offered a diversity of comments on the railroad project. Much of it in 1902-1903 focused on Harry DeWindt's journey. DeWindt, an English travel writer, set out from Paris for New York to establish the feasibility of such a rail route. His trip gave him adventures, a book, and plenty of publicity. DeWindt claimed a railroad syndicate booked his journey, and he may have been commissioned by de Lobel, but such out-of-the-way travels, followed by a book, provided his livelihood. His journey shed little light on the feasibility of a railroad, but he gained some publicity for the venture. Healy was happy to tell newsmen that DeWindt's journey across Siberia "demonstrated the feasibility of the route."[177]

DeWindt thought that a bridge across the Bering Strait was a ridiculous idea: "They might as well talk of a line to the planet Mars, for the mightiest bridge ever built would not stand the break-up of the ice here for a week." A tunnel seemed more feasible, and he agreed with Russian engineers who claimed that the Diomede Islands would provide places for ventilation shafts. Tunnels were expensive, but he felt that this one would cost no more than the subway tunnels then under construction in New York.

Although he refused to recommend the Healy-de Lobel plan, he conceded that a railroad would be built. "It has passed the stage of a dream," he told a journalist in 1902, "and will operate within a dozen years. "The road will be a single track one for freight, with sidings, and will enable a train to pull out of Paris, and three weeks later enter New York City." DeWindt traveled in nine days from Paris to Irkutsk on the Trans-Siberian Railroad, covering 4,000 miles, then made it to East Cape by sleigh. In all he traveled 11,263 miles from Paris to the strait, crossed over on a U.S. Revenue Cutter Service cutter to Nome, and eventually reached New York, having traveled a total of 18,494 miles.[178]

After DeWindt lectured in New York, President Theodore Roosevelt, who never missed the opportunity of talking to interesting travelers, invited him to lunch at the White House. The Englishman was ill-prepared for Teddy's "searching cross-examination" on technical matters such as fuel costs, numbers of bridges, and the depth of the Bering Strait. Roosevelt, who knew all about travel liars and fraudulent promoters, asked his visitor, with a "faint twinkle in his eye," if he had actually traveled the entire distance. By this time DeWindt realized that Teddy regarded him and the railroad scheme too seriously, regarding it "as a huge joke—the scheme . . . of 'Crooks' or 'Cranks.'" Whatever Roosevelt thought about the rail plan, he treated DeWindt graciously. "Before I left the White House, my host gravely instructed me to reserve him a first-class compartment (and, if possible, a seat in the dining-car) on the first train out from New York for France."[179]

Healy and everyone else connected with the railroad plans were ignorant of the designs an engineer had already developed for a bridge over the Bering Strait. Healy would have avidly publicized Joseph B. Strauss's design had he known about the young engineer's senior thesis. Strauss, inspired by John Roebling's beautiful bridge across the Ohio River at Cincinnati (which served as a model for Roebling's Brooklyn Bridge), designed a Bering Strait bridge for his senior thesis at the University of Cincinnati. He got his degree even though one critic called his plan "an impossible and preposterous scheme." Forty years later Strauss got his chance to create another wonderful bridge, the Golden Gate Bridge over the San Francisco Bay.[180]

*Harper's Weekly*, one of several magazines and newspapers to report on Healy's plans, joked about the Irishman's way of making it all sound so easy, quoting Shakespeare's character Puck in *Midsummer-Night's Dream*: "I'll put a girdle round about the earth in forty minutes." But the *Harper's* writer thought that Shakespeare's forecast had merit: "The poet and the explorer are the true pioneers of progress."[181]

French engineer Loicq de Lobel was Healy's major associate. Apparently they first met when de Lobel, accompanied by his family, visited the Klondike and Alaska as a tourist in 1898. The Frenchman liked to tell newsmen later that he had spent a couple of years surveying the Alaska route, but with his wife and daughters on his tour he probably spent little time surveying. De Lobel may have surveyed areas of Siberia, but the only documented surveying expedition is one that Healy led into the White River country from Dawson in winter 1906.

# Wooing the Czar

Neither the priority of ideas nor the existence of surveys mattered, however, in getting the project going. What mattered was getting the railroad concession from the Czar and securing financing for construction. De Lobel concentrated his efforts on working with the Russians and spent most of 1904-1905 in St. Petersburg. Healy had assured his partner that he would line up American capital, but solid commitments proved hard to come by. Healy finally came to depend upon de Lobel's assurances that he could find capital to help develop the Seward Peninsula properties Healy had pledged to the company. But money still eluded them.

In February 1902 the promoters told the *New York Tribune* that they planned to start railroad construction in spring 1902. The newspaper treated these forecasts of an early start as overly optimistic: "This information regarding the proposed round-the-world road should be a boon for the women who 'expect to go abroad next summer,'" the reporter joked. "They will have a valid excuse for postponing the trip. Chicago people may welcome the road with open arms. They may even try to capture the American terminal. No longer will they have to go to Europe by way of New York." But the reporter considered the railroad possible in the future. Recently completed work on Russia's Trans-Siberian Railroad had made it possible for travelers to go from Paris to Shanghai in twenty days. The Trans-Alaska-Siberia Railroad would be only slightly more difficult to build. "One may laugh at the 'windy' Paris engineer and the energetic Alaskan pioneer, but it is well to do so with a mental reservation that some day one may be glad to join with them in laughing at obstacles overcome," concluded the reporter.[182]

President Roosevelt was only one of many critics of the railroad plan. For others the staggeringly immense project seemed a chimera, and perhaps a fraud. It would cost from $50 to $200 million to tunnel the strait and build four thousand miles of railroad. Many doubted the feasibility of the line, despite de Lobel's ebullient forecast. "It would be," the engineer said, "the greatest railroading feat that ever was. No more seasickness, no more dangers of wrecked liners, a fast trip in palace cars with every convenience . . . a revolution in transportation that would shift the world's commercial axis from the Suez Canal to the Bering Strait." The magazine *Scientific American* called the tunnel plan an "absurd and impossible proposal." The *New York Times* considered the project feasible in fifty years, "but for the moment it is about as practical as a plan to colonize the dark side of the moon." A later *Times* story said, "Nearly everybody has laughed at the fantastic project of connecting New York with Paris by rail. Only Frenchmen and Russians treat the matter seriously." In so reporting, the newspaper forgot one American, Johnny Healy.[183]

The railroad venture put a considerable strain on Healy over several years, particularly because de Lobel was careless about communicating to Johnny on the progress of his negotiations. Since the two men rarely got together, most communications were by mail, when de Lobel could bring himself to write. Healy's fears of rivals put further stress on him.

213

A number of Alaskan promoters either wanted to take over the project or thwart it in favor of their own developments on the Seward Peninsula. He felt aggravated that no one with money would either invest or take on some management duties. For a time he counted on W. N. Amory, a New York businessman; then Amory, for reasons unknown, turned on him. Healy also came to consider J. Hamilton Lewis a traitor to the cause. Healy brought Edwin T. Adney, his would-be biographer, into his projects. Adney had some connections in New York and Washington but little money or experience in such matters. Yet Healy came to depend upon him for lack of other honest, committed associates.

De Lobel invariably assured the press that building the railroad presented only one difficult engineering problem, the Bering Strait crossing. He considered ferries and a bridge before resolving upon a tunnel that would connect the two Diomede Islands to either shore. "Including the approaches," de Lobel calculated, "the tunnel will be about thirty-eight miles in length, and this, with the thirty-eight hundred miles of railroad which we propose constructing in Siberia and the twelve hundred we intend building in Alaska, will go to make up our Trans Alaska Railroad. We will connect in Siberia with the 'Trans Siberian,' while our Alaskan road will pass through Council City, Nulato, and Fairbanks, connecting at a point about one hundred miles south of Dawson City with the Grand Trunk Pacific, which is planning an extension to that point."[184]

De Lobel believed that money would flow in once the Czar granted a concession. The construction would require about $250 million, but, he argued, investors would be well compensated.[185]

## Victory Seems Near

Healy's involvement in the railroad, particularly in 1905-1906, shows how much he banked on the project's success. By this point in his life he cared little about making money—but wanted vindication. He had taken hard raps from his NAT&T partners and had failed at everything since leaving Dawson. He remembered his hard times in Montana after leaving Whoop-Up country, when others had counted him out, yet he had astounded them by rebounding in Alaska. He wanted to repeat his performance. And, he decided, who could ever doubt his genius again when he ranked with the greatest railroad builders of history.

The October 1905 mining boom in Alaska's Tanana valley excited Healy. He wanted to plunge into some Alaskan enterprise, but was committed to the railroad plan. De Lobel was off to St. Petersburg to negotiate for a railroad concession and seemed confident, as always. But Healy thought that the Russo-Japanese War made getting the concession unlikely. "I am chaffing at the delay and the want of capital," he told

Adney. "I must find men who are looking westward and north-ward. . . . Think of me with all my knowledge of the country and its business, and not . . . able to buy a packhorse."[186]

A month later de Lobel wired great news: he had arranged a conference with an important minister. For some time, Healy heard nothing more from his partner, but news stories from Russia predicted a revolution. He wondered what would come next. "Our chances have been dwindling for a while—but now I am more hopeful," he told Adney. "I hope the horizon will clear now. . . . We want that ukase made public about as bad as anything I know. It means good food, fine raiment and a contented state of mind, which is of the greatest importance."

As more weeks passed without news from de Lobel, Healy grew angry with him. "His silence is inexcusable. I have lost confidence in him," he told Adney. Healy was now forced to concentrate on a trading venture to the Kuskokwim region because he needed money for assessment work on his Seward Peninsula tin claims. Unless he started work on them he could lose his properties there. He had given de Lobel his NAT&T stock in hope of raising money on it. "If de Lobel had made an effort and sent me some money on that stock I could have kept out of this business. I would not have tied myself so that I could not leave."

On March 2 Healy received the news he had long awaited. De Lobel wrote from St. Petersburg on February 10 with details on his successful negotiations:

1. The Russian government has decided to constitute a commission for the discussion of the "contract's regulations."
2. The government has authorized the survey in Siberia, letting our railway start from Kansk, instead of Irkutsk.
3. The czar has just signed a ukase, which approves the government's decisions and he has instituted a special commission for the contract's regulations, having ordered that the report of the commission's decisions should be addressed to himself . . . the czar considers the execution of our railway a very urgent thing.
4. The government has given to me all the official documents in due form, in order to enable our engineers to make the necessary survey from Kansk all along to Bering, as well as the special passports, which authorizes them to claim the support of the authorities, civil and military.
5. The czar has fixed a maximum . . . eighteen months for the set commission. . . . Our associates . . . consider that we have won a great victory in having obtained all that was desired at such a moment, when the government is wholly occupied by purely political and social situations.[187]

Despite this apparent victory Healy still felt more anger with his partner than relief or jubilation. As usual de Lobel had ignored all of

Johnny's queries and had failed to send money when Johnny desperately needed it. Healy responded coldly, saying, "I had about given up hearing from you, as all of my letters have remained unanswered. . . . I am very glad to receive this letter, as it informs me that your health is good and that your efforts have been crowned with success. It is unfortunate in a way, that you have not been able to aid me financially in the development of our tin and townsite proposition on the Seward Peninsula. The want of means to prosecute that work has made it necessary for me to organize a commercial company for the Kuskokwim River, to enable me to get to work again. Our tin and other interests at port Clarence and Seward Peninsula have been turned over to Messrs. Amory and Adney."[188]

Healy was still plagued by fears of his rivals. The March 1906 meeting between David Jarvis of the Alaska syndicate that controlled the Kennecott copper deposits and John Rosene of Seattle alarmed Johnny. As the syndicate's Alaskan manager, Jarvis had tremendous financial resources. Jarvis, formerly a U.S. Revenue Cutter Service and Custom Service officer, became a national hero after leading a reindeer relief expedition to rescue stranded whaling men at Point Barrow. President Theodore Roosevelt had wanted to make him Alaska's governor, but Jarvis chose power and wealth by accepting employment with the syndicate. It turned out to be a bad choice. When Jarvis was indicted for corrupt business practices in 1911 he committed suicide.

John Rosene had similar interests to Healy. In 1902 he organized the Northeastern Siberian Company and sent miners to Siberia. He also opened a trading post in Siberia and promoted an Alaskan railroad from the coast to the upper Yukon River. The Alaska syndicate was interested in acquiring the shipping company Rosene had developed between Seattle and Alaska. Healy warned Adney that "it means a combination to control the transportation and the copper of Alaska. You will have an opportunity of writing a bigger loot story than Rex Beach ever dreamed of."[189]

Healy's reference to Rex Beach concerned that writer's exposure of the corruption of the federal judiciary at Nome in 1900 by Alexander McKenzie of North Dakota with the help of U.S. senators, including Thomas Carter of Montana. While Healy had never expressed approval for the nearly successful efforts of the "spoilers" of Nome to grab all the valuable gold mines, he was friendly to Carter and McKenzie and depended upon their support in Congress. Healy accurately saw the syndicate's plan to control transportation and much of Alaska's mining, although it was 1911 before they were able to purchase Rosene's shipping interests. Rosene tried to remain with the syndicate, but they squeezed him badly before forcing him out. Johnny predicted that Rosene would suffer this fate at the hands of the syndicate.

Healy was concerned about the power of the syndicate in Congress. He had directed Adney to apply for a federal subsidy for the Alaska portion of his railroad. He would have had difficulty getting a subsidy under any circumstances, but it became virtually impossible when the syndicate and Rosene announced that they wanted to help in building their railroads. The syndicate was rich and within a few years constructed the Copper River & Northwestern Railway from Cordova on the coast to the Kennecott copper mines. And by refusing to ask for a subsidy the syndicate made it virtually impossible for others to ask for one.

# Healy's Winter Survey

Some time passed before Healy cooled down over de Lobel's neglect to provide funding. He busied himself with a new project for trading and prospecting on the Kuskokwim River. He wanted to go north in May 1905, but he lacked money enough. He had relied upon his old friend Portus Weare, who had let him down. Deathly weary of urban life and the vagaries of his business deals, he felt vastly relieved when he was able to go north in December 1906. Despite the lateness of the season he went to Dawson and organized a survey party for the White River region. Dawson newsmen happily reported on a transportation development that could do much to revive the declining gold town. "By next summer dirt may be flying," Johnny told a reporter. He doubted the American government would be as generous as he expected the Czar to be, but he hoped for some help. As for trade prospects, "build the railroad first," Johnny said, "the trade will follow." Journalists were impressed by the former NAT&T manager, "although white haired and snowy bearded, still a nimble man, who had enjoyed the sleigh ride from Whitehorse to Dawson."[190]

But Johnny faced something more arduous than a sleigh ride. He left Dawson on January 10, 1907, and stayed in the field until April. Doing field work during the winter months was almost unprecedented in the North. That Johnny undertook it shows the level of exasperation he had with his various affairs.

Starting their work, the party followed the White River to Ladue Creek during what had become a hard winter. One member wrote that "in 32 days the warmest day was 64 below. We were warm and snug . . . lived mostly on moose and didn't lose a man or a dog." Healy suffered from a bad case of erysipelas, a skin ailment, which he treated by bathing his face in condensed milk.[191]

From camp at Ladue Creek, Healy sent a long letter in the form of a diary to de Lobel and others concerning the progress of the survey. He was obviously pleased to be doing field work once again. Healy understood that significant copper prospects had been discovered in the White

River region and saw a possible freight opportunity for a railroad. Later investigations determined that the copper prospects were poor.

Johnny's commitment to the survey expedition allowed him to actively prosecute an old dream of finding wealth where other capitalists had been too timid to venture. Although he gave no hint of it in his letter, the expedition must have been hard on him physically. He only reported the bright side: "We have located a town site at Ladue. It is 33 miles to Ladue from the mouth of the White River and about 30 miles from the town site to the boundary and the country looks good and promises great wealth. The most phenomenal copper find in the world's history is in the canyon of the White River. . . . I am surprised to see this opportunity sleeping for the six years I have been away. I have known of the existence of the mineral but found it useless to attempt getting capital to develop."[192]

He put up all the money he had to get to Dawson and arrange the expedition, and he hoped for a response to his cables to de Lobel for more money. "I am full of hope and more sanguine than at any period of my life. The greatest mineral field on earth is for us to take. We are in the field and we should get enough of it to enrich 10,000 men. I feel like remaining here on the White River, but know I cannot. I intend leaving some men here to locate ground for us and will arrange so that we will get our share of the country. If we could commence work on this road next summer, we could dispose of town lots enough to do considerable work. . . . This is the year of opportunity."

# Disappointment

Soon after his return to the States the blow fell. The Czar smashed dreams for the great Trans-Alaska-Siberian Railway in 1907. The Czar apparently decided that allowing Americans and other foreigners special opportunities in Siberia was a poor idea. He would grant no concessions.

Johnny took the decision hard. His continuing string of disappointments made it hard for him to bounce back. And the White River expedition, his last field effort, probably shortened his life.

It's worth noting, though, that the notion of joining the continents through either a bridge or tunnel was revived during World War II. The notion encouraged construction of the Alaska Highway in 1942 with plans for it eventually to reach Nome. The onset of the Cold War dimmed all such possibilities; however, the dissolution of the Soviet Union has spurred plans for Alaskan-Siberian developments and resusitated the National Park Service's call to build an "international peace park." And, as might be expected, drums have again started beating for the great railroad that Healy envisioned.

Johnny Healy may never be vindicated on his most grandiose commercial project, but the idea of bridging the Bering Strait is not met today with derision and jokes.

# 15

# Last Chances

*Dozens here*
*would steal our eyes.*
　　　　—Johnny Healy

I take pleasure in telling you that my prospects are beyond all expectations," Johnny Healy told Edwin Tappen Adney in October 1905. The old promoter was not trying to deceive himself or Adney; prospects looked promising. He held good tin-mining properties on the Seward Peninsula and was considering a Kuskokwim trading venture. Meanwhile, he was still excited by the possibilities of the Trans-Alaska-Siberian Railway.[193]

The tin deposits in particular encouraged a man who had been unsuccessful at prospecting for a long time. "I am done prospecting, as I have all I want. It only rests with the money finders. My men have made new locations as well as eleven miles of placer tin, water rights and tunnel sites. I have enough in sight to keep a good sized bank account busy next summer." As always with Johnny, preserving pride was as important as making money. "Remember this. I have never missed calling the turn in Alaska. Some of the N.Y. gentlemen may want to investigate me again. I am still dealing in good goods. . . . I am restless and want to get back among honest money again."

A few days later Healy affirmed his hopes and specified his particular needs: "I expect you to help me this winter. I want 2 or 3 large steamers and money enough to load them. I have the most legitimate proposition ever presented to any body of capitalists. All I want is a hearing and my ideas protected. I have given away all my ideas and now I want to get some benefit." Excited over the growth of Fairbanks, he expected twenty thousand people to stampede to Alaska in 1906. If he could get into the transportation field, he expected to make a fortune. "I am chaffing at the delay over the want of capital. . . . I don't know whether I will be able to finance any of my deals. I must find men who are looking westward and northward."

Gold prospectors made the original Seward Peninsula tin discoveries in 1899 on Buck Creek. Prospectors later located other deposits on Potato Mountain, where Buck Creek originated; Lost River; Cape Prince of Wales Mountain and elsewhere. Healy made locations at Cape Prince of Wales and Ears Mountain both in 1900 and on another trip in 1904. He felt sure that Ears Mountain would prove rich. It rose 2,300 feet ten miles from Shishmaref Inlet, "a shallow body of water fifteen or twenty miles in extent, which will permit navigating steam launches with barges, which can convey the ore to the ocean, where it can be transferred to larger vessels."

Because of the favorable location Johnny saw no insurmountable problems to the development of the tin district. "The Arctic River heads in Ears Mountain and is navigable for small boats to within seven miles of the mines. Should this district develop into a large mineral district, a railroad can be built to Port Clarence fifty miles south, where 10,000 ton ships can enter and lay at wharf."

Healy drew Adney into both his Seward Peninsula and Kuskokwim projects, relying upon him to seek other investors and to work with another partner, W. N. Amory of New York, once a Chouteau County deputy under Healy. Capitalists had little interest in tin in 1905-1906 because they were "copper crazy" as the great Kennecott copper development moved along in high gear. The U.S. Geological Survey's investigation of tin prospects also caused Healy problems. "They have advertised their ignorance," Healy argued, "I am very sorry as they were the means of keeping capital out of the country." He tried to maintain a charitable view of both A. J. Collier and Alfred H. Brooks, the two government geologists who reported adversely on tin prospects. "I fully understand how little we know about tin ore. We are ignorant of its treatment at times and cannot tell it when found. I believe in giving the country a chance. The trouble has been the experts were afraid to express a favorable opinion, as all other finds in America proved worthless."

The visionary promoter could easily imagine a happy future state of affairs when construction of the Trans-Alaska-Siberian Railway was underway and "when 50,000 people are mining on Seward Peninsula." All those miners made a long-distance railroad essential in case of disaster, like a fire in a big mining town like Nome. Johnny could call upon past experiences to feed his optimism: "The tin mines in Alaska will support as many people as Butte, Montana. It looks that way to me. I saw Butte 42 years ago, and it did not look any better than Ears Mt. does now." Johnny believed that eventually five thousand men would work mining tin. "I believe that Nature placed enough in sight to excite men so he can accomplish great things."

Alfred Brooks, the head of the U.S. Geological Survey in Alaska and a well-respected scientist by the mining community, upset Healy by discrediting the tin prospects. Brooks's theories concerning tin formations differed from his. "I am no admirer of Brooks," Healy complained. "He appears to make his reports from the mass of information furnished by his assistants and supplements it all by introducing some of his own pessimistic themes. The development of the Tanana and the Kuskokwim will confound them. I pay little attention to their opinion."

Old prospectors knew better about mining. "What is needed is a man," concluded Healy. Whenever Johnny ran into theoretical resistance to his schemes he reaffirmed his faith in hard work by strong men. "An expert is useless. What is needed is powder, steel, and having some good men to use them. . . . No use in sending experts to look at surface indications. The money they waste will do the work. An expert follows the prospectors and miners."

## The Timidity of Capital

Healy considered American capitalists similarly timid and praised the English when he thought he might interest them. "It takes the English to mine tin. They know a good thing when they see it. . . . I am sorry that New Yorkers are becoming even worse, as they want the good things of the earth placed in their hands. In less than 12 months, you will see the American tin dealers ruing their lack of enterprise. Good miners don't always have to go begging."

Although Johnny had once represented the mining interests of a major company, he had since rejoined the lesser ranks. Now he reflected the suspicion independent miners had of large mining corporations, particularly the Guggenheims, who were developing Kennecott. Corporations wanted "a cinch" and tried to squeeze out rivals by pretending that good properties lacked promise. "I represent the hard working prospector, who devotes his life in pursuit of something which will keep him in food and clothing. His chances can not be thrown away."

Seeing in himself a little of the grizzled veteran, he bragged to Adney, "I am old enough to form an opinion of good goods, no matter if they are minerals. I am a rock man as well as a gum boot miner and a bean peddler. Age and the mountains is to blame for the little knowledge I possess. The world has been my school, the mountains and the plains my books. The study of man and his methods my guide as to right and wrong."

Time proved out the USGS's pessimism regarding the value of tin deposits on the Seward Peninsula. Claims held by Healy and others eventually produced only modest quantities of tin."

As investors failed to share Healy's vision of tin riches he had to rely upon de Lobel, his railroad partner. De Lobel had assured Healy of his ability to raise money for their Seward Peninsula interests, which included the townsite for the Bering Strait railroad terminal, but he failed to find a cent. Another partner, miner Joe Vint, tried to carry on the required assessment work and oversee the survey for a railroad from the claims to tidewater. Vint believed in Healy and was loyal to him. His reports of rival railroad schemes on the peninsula fueled the promoter's anxieties and were passed on to Adney and others. Eventually Vint had to give up for lack of money, and the promoters lost their claims for want of assessment work.

# The Kuskokwim

When Healy's hopes for the great railroad and his tin mines grew dim he put all his energy into a Kuskokwim River trading venture. Both Adney and Portus Weare joined with him on this project. Adney, a comparatively young man, welcomed the chance to return to Alaska. He lacked money to invest but was eager to work for the company in the field. Weare's willingness to go along on the initial voyage may have come because his suspension from the Chicago Board of Trade in 1903 destroyed all his Midwest interests.

Johnny's interest in the Kuskokwim began in autumn 1905 when the news of mineral discoveries there reached Seattle. He shared the news and his plans with Adney. Adney's interest in him and his willingness to join his ventures cheered Healy. He agreed to have a photographic portrait made for Adney's use in published promotional literature. He made a trolley car trip to Leschi Park on Lake Washington where Asahel Curtis had a photography studio. He knew Curtis as one of the several professional photographers who had joined the Klondike stampeders to record the event. He took little care with his dress: "I have no outing clothes, in fact not many of any kind, but I rather like the ones I have until I can find better." When he once again commanded a bank account he would buy clothes "for either mountain or parlor."[194]

The men developed a modest trading plan. In 1905-1906 it appeared that the Kuskokwim would boom with discoveries of gold and cinnabar. Cinnabar, or mercury, had been discovered on the Kuskokwim as early as the 1880s, but commercial production started only in 1906 when some one hundred flasks were obtained. With good prospects of gold and other minerals Johnny predicted that a well-run trading post would make good money, and that careful mining investments would bring in even more money. Healy encouraged Weare to begin preparations while he went off to raise money. Healy had a room at the Northern Hotel in Seattle for his residence and an office in the Pioneer Building for the Trans-Alaska-Siberian Railroad, Alaska Investments, and as a base for all his interests. With Weare's blessing he began negotiations to purchase a river boat, the *Nunivak*. Johnny contributed the last of his money to the new venture to get it started.

Meanwhile, good news poured in from Alaska "like a tidal wave." Equally good reports came from all sections. "I have crawled out of my shell of inactivity and am looking for a million more to go into business again. I only want some young, active and adventurous spirit, who has money, to join me. He could double an investor's money in one year." Johnny insisted that he had estimated the return modestly. In the past, he had once helped investors gain 350 percent in one year. "We will make medicine when we meet. I feel that my time has come to go to work again."

"The next great rush will be to the Kuskokwim River," he told Adney. "It is the best river of them all. There is fish, fur, mineral and timber in abundance." Winters were comparatively mild, and the river was navigable for eight hundred miles. He knew of coal and cinnabar deposits and others had discovered gold. Prospectors only lacked provisions. "The time is ripe now to make more money merchandising. . . . I do want to start a few new posts [towns] again. I never felt better or more determined."

Until this point in their relationship Johnny and Adney's discussions had always centered on Adney's biographical research. Now commerce and present adventures became more important. "All I want is some live man with me," Healy told Adney. "I want you with me. It will do you good to see the country grow. The opening of a new country is the work of men. We blaze the trail and lead the way to new fields." Adney responded enthusiastically. Looking for excitement, he felt delighted that Healy, a canny frontier veteran, had singled him out.

Moving with his old speed Healy launched his new enterprise. For some time he had felt poorly and had worried about a general health break down. But with the Kuskokwim promise of work in the field, he revived. "I made 1st payment on the boat today," he told Adney in January 1906, "and I feel 20 years younger."

In acquiring the steamer *Nunivak*, Healy had made a good bargain and gained a vessel famous from the Yukon gold rush. In 1899 the U.S. Revenue Cutter Service sent the vessel from San Francisco to patrol the Yukon River. Under Lt. J. C. Cantwell the crew wintered over near Rampart, then resumed its patrol in 1900. Cantwell collected customs, provided some emergency services, and did some policing before the ship returned south in the fall of 1900. When Healy looked at the ship it had been idle for several years and was available for a low price.

Healy planned to build another boat and barge over the winter. He figured that he could haul two hundred passengers with one thousand tons of freight north per trip. His potential passengers included Dr. Frederick Cook of New York, the explorer and mountain climber who wished to take packhorses north for the first stages of a Mount McKinley climb in 1906. Cook eventually made other arrangements and later falsely claimed the first ascent of the mountain.

# Flames of Optimism

As Johnny kept Adney informed of his preparations by letter his ebullience was striking. People were starting to come to him again for advice and help as in days past. "Things are certainly looking different. Nothing like a little sunshine to bring the butterflies around," boasted the old frontiersman. "We will not let anything of value slip again. I have been over many rapids and will endeavor to avoid them in the future." He felt confident of his knowledge of minerals and of men. He also felt certain that they could make money without becoming corrupt. "There are more good things on earth than the pursuit of money. Love and affection and the loyalty you give and true friends are more than money. Money makes it easy to entertain and serve those we love."[195]

A week later he reported joyfully that "It looks as if I am to lead again." Weare had wired him to go ahead and open an office and install himself as president of the Alaska Central Company. He was out of the "bone yard for good." Some people still had faith in his business ability. "I am going to win big and strong." The hot and cold Seattle press now praised him. "Glad hands are plenty now, and it would not surprise me to see money thrown at me, as of old." Later he walked over to the King Street depot and met Weare's train. Weare was certain that he had found investors who would provide all their immediate capital needs and would seek others for expansion purposes. "I am going to be very patient and humble in a measure," Johnny told Adney. "I will not surrender my self-respect and have hopes of 'hooking up' in clean and proper lines."

Johnny wanted to sail north by May 25. He was having the *Nunivak* refitted to his specifications and would have it ready to head north by the first of May. Adney wanted to go on the *Nunivak* and tried to get *Collier's* magazine to contract for an article as they had done in 1900 when he reported on the Nome stampede. "I anticipate a fine time wintering on the Kuskokwim," Adney wrote, although he regretted the absence from his family.

Healy's Kuskokwim plans fell behind schedule in April. He prepared to travel to New York and still felt good about the future. "I have not one dollar of my own. I am as hopeful as ever." But in May gloom engulfed him. He was disgusted with his old friend Weare, who had let him down when he needed help badly. "I will hang on until the last riffle is reached. I hate to wind up in the mud-box . . . no goods yet and no prospect of any for some time." His reports soon became worse yet. "I lost $12,000 of reservations because I could not keep our sailing date."

*Nunivak* finally departed in late May. Healy hoped to follow in June but needed $50,000 in goods. He went to Chicago where the Central Alaska Company had an office maintained by Weare and got disturbing news from Adney. W.N. Amory, a leading spirit in the Seward Peninsula interests, was now acting against their interests. Healy responded angrily: "I feel that all my learning amounts to naught and to be candid I feel like a quitter now."

He hustled around Chicago from investor to investor, unsure what would come next. Some days he determined to head for the Seward Peninsula if the Kuskokwim plans failed. The quibbling of the money men annoyed him. "I feel tempted at times to tell them all to go to hell and I will go back to the mountains among honest people," he stated. Now he believed that Weare had tried hard to raise money, but Weare's people resisted his desire to go into business again.

## Treachery

Weare and others later tried to buy Johnny out of the Central Alaska Company, convincing him that his old friend had been treacherous all along. Indignant at Weare's offer, Healy complained that Weare "expected me to walk out without any compensation for 6 months and to pay all my own expenses. . . . He is not making any effort to keep me out of the poor house." Weare's defection saddened him. "After 35 years or more I must tell others to beware of the man."

Weare's apparent treachery hurt Healy deeply. He refused to give battle. "I can play the game in war—but never among men who pass as friends. Financial war may recognize such tactics. I don't belong to that class and I never want a partner who resorts to such methods." He considered himself above such chicanery. "The earth and the rocks are my study, I can look to them for a living for they are honest." His negotiations for financial backing for his several Alaskan projects ended in failure, and he felt lost. "I have no money and no prospects. I am in debt for room and board. It looks like a black Friday for me." He blamed Weare for his woes. "His glowing promises dictated my course. Here and now he has reduced me to begging. He hopes to profit by my distress."

He felt that he had acquitted himself honorably, though. His last, best financial hope, a man named Black, had asked him to make agreements without reference to his board of directors. He refused indignantly, stating, "I have no use for any man who insists on my doing that which I don't consider right. I prefer being poor all my life." Slick dealings upset him. "People will not understand me. I have been lied about so much that they won't believe when I tell them that I am not that kind."

He believed that Weare and Black had combined to force him to accept their terms of virtual takeover of the Central Alaska Company in exchange for Black's backing. Perhaps his old age had prevented him from discerning Weare's tactics despite signs that the man had turned false. "When a man's wife and son denounces him, it is time for others to leave him alone. [A reference to some news about Weare's domestic problems.] I have been a fool sticking to him in face of all. . . . I realize now that I don't improve by age." He had put everything he had into the Kuskokwim project, including $20,000 in NAT&T stock and $18,750 in personal notes. He had also pledged $150,000 of London and Alaska Tin stock—his interest in the Seward Peninsula mines. Weare's offer was $600 for Healy's six months of work, and he demanded the right to hold on to the securities Healy had pledged.

If every one of his ventures fell through, Johnny wanted to go back to prospecting, "my old love." Maybe he would go south rather than north because he would need less, only "a horse or two." A few days later he threw in the towel. "I feel that I am a complete failure in getting money. I intend quitting promoting. A man has to be an accomplished liar if he wants to remain in the business."

For weeks he had stayed at the Great Northern Hotel, and he now lacked the money to pay his bill. As always, Weare promised to meet Healy's settlement demands then failed to come through. Chicago was undergoing one of its periodic crime-commission investigations, and Healy saw the event as another indication that Chicago was a "wicked city," a place where drift nets are floating "in every current" to trap the unwary. "I hope that something will turn up this week as I am very tired of it all."

He hired an attorney to pursue the settlement with Weare and left Chicago for Seattle. On the first of November he lost all of his Seward Peninsula holdings and all the hopes he had tied up with the Alaska and Siberia Development Company. He wondered what he had left to hope for.

226

# 16

# The Historian

*I don't want to be called
a storyteller.*
            —Johnny Healy

J ohnny Healy's forceful and direct letters reveal his nature. Whether discussing business or reminiscing about earlier days, he cared about his place in history. He sometimes exaggerated his role in western events, but, on the whole, his assessments prove more modest and accurate than those of many old-timers who accomplished much less.

He felt strongly about history and believed that some men had been denied the recognition they deserved. Historians had yet to pay attention to some of the figures Johnny admired most, including mountain man Jim Bridger. Historians focused strongly on western history as the century advanced, but in 1904-1906, when he discussed this with Adney, the West seemed to be the preserve only of dime novelists.

The fictional West appalled him. "I have a horror of the Dime Novel style of literature. The West has been slandered and ridiculed by writers of the long-haired kind." Other pioneers have shared this sentiment. In the 1930s and 1940s Andrew Garcia wrote about his early adventures in Montana but declined to publish anything or even to offer much help to a potential biographer, fearing dime novelists would seize upon his story and pervert it.[196]

Thus, Healy encouraged Adney to write the truth. "You have the opportunity of collecting data," he told his biographer, "which should make you famous for preserving the names of the pioneers of the Rocky Mountain states. It is a life work and I know of no field more interesting to western readers. The west is growing. We all want to give credit to where it belongs." Johnny found it unjust to neglect heroic pioneers. "A spirit of fair play is the western man's bible. Tenderfeet are getting away with the glory when we know that they would never blaze a trail if a painted buck was at the other end."

He made sound suggestions to Adney and named good contacts, including P. H. Ray and James W. Schultz. Healy knew Ray when he and Lt. Wilds Richardson were the only American soldiers on the Yukon and earlier in Montana when Ray impressed frontiersmen with his ability to understand Indian sign language. Schultz had just written a story about his life among the Indians for *Field and Stream*, and was becoming better known as a writer. "When I left that country he was a young New Yorker, full of Indian manner and by this time he should be an authority of Indian lore," Johnny observed.

Of the Indians, Johnny also expressed positive opinions. "I admire the Blood Indians. I fought them for years and when they became my friends I could trust them absolutely. The Piegans produced some very brave men, notably, Little Dog, White Calf, Running Crane, Old Skunk, Three Robes, Little Plume, Chief Mountain, Cut Hand, Bad Boy, Black Weasel, and many more men. I consider the Piegans the bravest of the Blackfoot

Native." About some other tribes, including the Flatheads, who raided his post at Sun River and "who always boasted that they did not make war on the whites," Johnny expressed no kind feelings.

Johnny insisted that his whiskey peddling and his share in the destruction of the buffalo and the Indian civilization had been necessary—a matter of survival. It was them or us, he argued. He had contempt for the do-gooders who tried to inject a more humanitarian Indian policy. He believed that they had a poor understanding of the Indians, and he knew damn well that they had no sympathy for the anxieties of settlers.

Sometimes he viewed history with cynicism, reflecting, in part, his bitterness over his ousting by the Cudahys and his failures to secure capital for several ventures. Others had failed to appreciate him, just as history neglected to honor the true pioneers except in false novels. He warned his biographer that "cold facts are considered romance now-a-days and the real acts of life are received with a grain of salt." On another occasion he feared that Adney would have to rely upon his imagination rather than facts to please his readers. "Facts don't draw, as you have learned," he stated. Few readers were interested in hearing about the true West. "You may tell Alaska stories and stories of Indian life and your readers will credit you as being a good pipe fiend. So on the whole it may pay you to devote your time to dreams instead of facts."

Johnny's remedy was for each state to hire a historian to collect historical data. He distrusted historical societies that seemed to honor only the favorites of those in power. The Montana Historical Society may have irked him—a Republican political foe headed the society for a long stretch.

When discussing Adney's use of his name on the title page of his book Johnny stated emphatically, "I don't wish to have it said 'as told by me.' I don't object to the use of my name but I don't like the idea of being wrote up as a story teller. I am not doing this only as a friendly turn to you, and incidentally to preserve from oblivion some of the early history of the west. . . . My own life is well known in the West."

Adney disobeyed Johnny. When he typed the title page of his unpublished manuscript in 1937 it read "HEALY: Incidents of Indian-fighting and Fur Trader Days in Montana, the Canadian Northwest, and Alaska, related by the late Captain John J. Healy." Adney might have tried to interest book editors, but he never completed the manuscript.

Healy felt proud of some of his work, as with his organization of Sun River rangers to fight Indians, but he did not want "to figure as a hero." Montana had produced "many able men, some of the very best in the saddle. I only feel proud in knowing that I lived with them, fought with them and occasionally consoled with them. . . . They helped to settle the

Indian question. They hastened the extermination of the buffalo that destroyed their commissary and they had to quit fighting."

Presumably, Adney grasped Healy's point. Johnny would hate to have his friends consider him a blowhard and braggart, but enjoyed praise and recognition. He sensibly understood that modesty served both truth and good taste. Thus he claimed to "dread" getting too much credit and admit that he was "one of many" and that "alone I would not be in it. It is a poor captain who will want all the credit. I was fortunate, very fortunate, in having good men. I learned from good men and am learning yet."

## Opinions of Other Pioneers

When Adney sent particular articles or books to Johnny, he quickly responded with opinions of their authors if he knew them. He appreciated Granville Stuart's memoirs but disliked those of Robert Vaughn. "Vaughn is a man who cannot write intelligently as much as I have put on this page. A good fellow and a good man—but unfortunately for himself the schoolmaster was not home in his country."

Johnny liked reading Bill Hamilton's memoirs. "I liked Bill and he is all he claims for himself. The story of his life is good but incorrect in many aspects. He fits characters in places which did not figure at the dates given. I knew Bill very well and admire the man."

Johnny also knew and appreciated the writing of Thomas Dimsdale, a school teacher who chronicled events of the Montana vigilantes. "Dimsdale was the first man to write anything about Montana." In discussing Dimsdale, Johnny mentioned his own connection with the *Montana Post*, the territory's first newspaper, which is curious because Johnny left no record of having anything to do with the *Post*—yet it seems unlikely that he would invent a connection of such slight significance.

Of the pioneers Healy knew only by their legends, he had high regard for Alexander Harvey, the ruthless Indian executioner and trader with the American Fur Company "Harvey was the most fearless man in the country . . . and I can tell you some things he has not credit for." Johnny never clarified the statement further, but Harvey received full credit for a mindless slaughter of peaceful Indians upon whom traders depended. He was removed from command of a trading post for his brutality and subsequently avenged himself on the comrades who had reported on his conduct. Perhaps Healy admired qualities in Harvey other than ruthlessness; Johnny behaved differently. He could easily imagine the perils faced by the first trappers. "I consider the very early trappers the bravest men the world produced. They were so few in numbers and they were working for the spirit and the excitement." Harvey's bravery, which was never questioned, may be the quality that Healy admired.

In only a few brief statements did Johnny summarize his career and give his view on the times in which he lived. He clearly felt better about his frontier adventures before going to Alaska than he did afterwards. In a way this seems incongruous because he was "king of the mountain" in the North, and he had achieved his singular, powerful status through a remarkable and intelligent campaign. Yet, he still hurt from being rejected by the Cudahys, and he found it hard to enjoy what he had attained. He eloquently expressed this mood to Adney:

> You have seen me at my worst and at the same time at my best. Many a good man was forced to eat Yukon dirt. The Yukon tried men. We were strangers in a foreign land and all gold crazy. Every man for himself and a dread of starvation hanging over all.... My Yukon experience was about the hardest of all. The treachery of my associates makes me weep for the perfidy of man.

# The Last Insult

Johnny returned south from his survey expedition in the White River country a sick man—and a poor one. He moved from Seattle to San Francisco. His daughter Maria, who had once stayed with him at Dawson, lived there. She was divorced from Orin Jackson, who had worked for Healy at Dawson, and married Frank Goudy.

We know virtually nothing of Johnny's last months in San Francisco. While staying with Maria and Frank at 640 Eddy Street he had to be taken to the St. Winifred Hospital. Whether members of his family considered his condition less than critical, or perhaps for some other reason, none was in attendance on September 15, 1908, when he died of cirrhosis of the liver. He had lived 68 years and 8 months.

A few newspaper obituaries recorded his passage. One recalled him as an western empire builder, noting that three of his four daughters "hurried to the city and were present at the funeral." Another newspaper reported that his family placed his body in a vault at Holy Cross Cemetery to await shipment to Seattle for burial and that he left a "large estate" to his daughters.[197]

But Johnny had no large estate. Judging from his impoverished condition when he made his last assault on Chicago's financiers in 1906, the Goudys probably helped him out. Whatever his circumstances at death, the disposition of his remains caused some scandal in Alaska and among California's sourdoughs. Since he owned a family plot in Seattle's Lakeview Cemetery, where other family members lay, it made sense to arrange his burial there. Yet, for some reason, a year passed before he was buried. A Cordova newspaper said that a collection was taken from Alaskan sourdoughs to cover the cost because "surviving relatives refuse to assume expenses."[198]

A day earlier the same paper recalled that "he made many enemies among the sourdoughs who are now being asked to contribute." The paper summarized Healy's career, tracing his downfall from millionaire to pauper and his removal from NAT&T management by the Cudahys. Weare had sided with Healy, so he also "was crowded to the wall." The editors moralized freely, writing, "arrogant and despotic in disposition, Healy found himself without friends when a turn in tide came to his affairs."

The Fort Benton *River Press* printed a favorable obit on the old pioneer, adding five years to his age. A lengthy story summarized his career but, oddly, concentrated on his Alaskan years despite his prominence in Montana history. Perhaps the *River Press* lacked biographical files to draw from, relying instead upon obits from West Coast newspapers that featured Healy's Alaskan career. "For nearly ten years there was no man better known in Alaska," the *Press* said. "In frontier days of Montana he had been a sheriff, . . . was an Indian fighter and soldier, as well as a keen business man. . . . He had no fear of hardships and privations of early Alaska," and in 1906, "although past the biblical three score and ten years, he headed a party of men who in the dead of winter traveled on foot from Dawson via Fairbanks to the coast." A shorter notice in another Montana paper recalled that "forty years ago Captain Healy was one of the foremost citizens of the then wild and wooly territory of Montana. . . . Captain Healy's name will live forever in connection with the history of the west."[199]

A favorable view of Johnny's life appeared in the *Outing* magazine some months before his death. The writer praised Healy's vision of the Trans-Alaska-Siberian Railroad and other matters, concluding, "Captain Healy has lived to see more startling dreams than this come true. A pioneer who has beheld great states built out of a wilderness wherein he fought savages in his youth, is entitled to hold big conception of the future greatness of the underdeveloped countries which he has helped to wrest from the frontier."[200]

## Conclusion

Biographers usually end with some praise, or an ironic twist, depending upon their sympathies. When we look at our pioneers, a note of constraint or caution is often in good order. We should avoid jumping to judgments when the record is incomplete—and the record is always incomplete.

Johnny Healy strikes me as an extraordinary man, brave, tough, honest, and farseeing. As a miner and trader he played major roles on diverse frontiers. I find his actions in these roles particularly interesting because the ironic twists of his career encourage our reflections on the man and his times.

Thinking about Johnny Healy and his nostalgia over savory roasted buffalo ribs has stimulated other thoughts about his whiskey, his friends and enemies, his defense of his attitudes, and his view of history. He has made me more aware of those long-dead folks we sometimes respect too little, the ancestors whom we glad-hand on patriotic occasions, then deride when winds of guilt or popular passions shift our views of the past.

So often, we act as if we really understand our history. In fact, like Johnny Healy, it is hard to handle.

# End Notes

Abbreviations used in the notes for the various collections are as follows:

ASA: Alaska State Archives, Juneau

ASL: Alaska State Library, Juneau

FRC: Federal Records Center, National Archives, Seattle

MHS: Montana Historical Society, Helena

NA: National Archives, Washington, D. C.

SC: Stefansson Collection, Baker Library, Dartmouth College

UAF: University of Alaska Fairbanks Archives

UW: University of Washington Archives

1. Beaumont's quote is from Nicholas Mansard, *The Irish Question, 1840-1821* (Toronto: University of Toronto Press, 1975), 43.

2. Donoughmore Parish Register, December 1817. Copy received from John F. O'Connell, an Irish historian of the Healy family.

3. Healy gave both dates to interviewers. In the Crissey interview [Forrest Crissey, "Bucking the Hudson Bay Company," *Saturday Evening Post* (June 1903), 12] Johnny said he joined the Army in 1857; others have given the date as 1858. If the latter date is correct, then the circumstances were different. Recruits sent to Utah in 1858 reinforced those who arrived the previous year. Healy never provided enough details about his military experience to corroborate one date or the other.

4. Colonel Johnston's comment and the soldiers' poem that follows are from Norman F. Furniss, *The Mormon War* (New Haven: Yale University Press, 1960), 101.

5. John J. Healy, "Frontier Sketches," *Fort Benton Record*, 9 April 1878.

6. John Linton Struble, "Johnny Healy Strikes it Rich," *Idaho Yesterdays* (Fall 1957), 23, 24, 27, for this and the two following quotes. This article reprints Healy's "Frontier Sketches" on his Idaho adventures.

7. Healy, "Frontier Sketches," *Fort Benton Record*; this and other quotes throughout this chapter, many of which are not specifically noted, were published between 12 April and 29 July 1878.

8. Alonzo Leland, "The Salmon River Mines," *Idaho Yesterdays* (Fall 1971), 31.

9. Healy, "An Adventure in the Idaho Mines," *Frontier and Midland* (Winter 1937-38), 110.

10. This quote and those in the following paragraphs related to this story are from Healy, "The First Sioux Invasion," *Fort Benton Record*, 30 August 1878.

11. Some sources identify Mary Frances' maiden name as Barsfield; for more information, see Healy family biographical data on file at the Montana Historical Society in Helena.

12. K. Ross Toole, *Montana: An Uncommon Land* (Norman: University of Oklahoma Press, 1959), 154.

13. Paul F. Sharp, *Whoop-Up Country* (Norman: University of Oklahoma Press, 1978), 157-58, 160, for this and following quotes describing Fort Benton.

14. Adney biography, Adney papers, SC, 17, for this and the following quote.

15. Forrest Crissey, "Bucking the Hudson Bay Company," *Saturday Evening Post* (June 1903), 15, 16, 17, for this and following quotes concerning the HBC.

16. James G. Snell, "The Frontier Sweeps Northward: American Perceptions of the British American Prairie West at the Point of Canadian Expansion (c. 1870)," *Western Historical Quarterly* (October 1980), 381-400; Snell is the source of the magazine quotation (p. 388) and of my comment on American intentions.

17. Helen F. Sanders and William H. Bertsche, Jr. , *X. Beidler, Vigilante* (Norman: University of Oklahoma Press, 1955), 95, 96.

18. Sharp, *Whoop-up Country*, 144, 143, for this and the following quote.

19. Trade permit, 1 March 1866, Healy papers, MHS.

20. Eugene Lee Silliman, *We Seized Our Rifles* (Missoula: Mountain Press Publishing Co. , 1982), 105, 107, 108-9, 110, for this and following quotes on the attack. Johnny's brother, whom I refer to as Joseph throughout the text to avoid confusion with the adopted Indian boy, was two years younger than Johnny, while his brother Thomas was eight years younger. Hugh Dempsey says that Joseph married a Blood woman, and their daughter, Enimaki, married John Healy, the son of Joe Healy, the Indian. At the wedding "the minister had a great deal of difficulty in understanding how two Indians, supposedly sired by Joe Healy, could get married. " As Dempsey's wife is the granddaughter of Joe, he knows the family history well. (Dempsey to author, 20 October 1989. )

21. Robert Vaughn, *Then and Now; or, Thirty-six Years in the Rockies* (Minneapolis: Tribune Printing Co. , 1900), 65-66, 124, 89, 98, 88, 101, 126, 194, for this and following quotes.

22. Adney biography, 44, 47, for this and the following quote.

23. Wheeler to Attorney General, 19 August 1871, NA, RG 60, Letters Received.

24. *U. S. v. John Davidson*, court record, Montana District Court, no. 16, RG 21, FRC, Seattle.

25. Adney biography, 58.

26. Joel Overholser, *Fort Benton: World's Innermost Port* (Fort Benton: Self-published, 1987), 347.

27. Adney biography, 59.

28. Hugh Dempsey, "A Letter from Fort Whoop-Up," *Alberta Historical Review* (Autumn 1956), 27.

29. Gerald L. Berry, *Whoop-Up Trail* (Edmonton: Applied Art Products, Ltd. , 1953), 48.

30. Hugh Dempsey, "A Letter from Fort Whoop-Up," 28.

31. Hugh Dempsey, "Donald Graham's Narrative of 1872-73," *Alberta Historical Review* (Winter 1956), 17.

32. Hugh Dempsey, "A Letter From Fort Whoop-Up," *Montana, the Magazine of Western History* (Summer 1985), 67.

33. Conversation with Hugh Dempsey, 10 August 1989.

34. Adney biography, 90, 91-92, 95, 96, for this and following quotes.

35. Hugh Dempsey, "The Amazing Death of Calf Shirt," *Montana, the Magazine of Western History* (January 1953), 65-66, 67, 71.

36. Adney biogaphy, 55.

37. Dempsey, "Donald Graham's Narrative," 16, 17, 19, for this and following quotes.

38. Adney biography, 74, 75, 76, 78, 79-81, 82, for this and following quotes.

39. Sharp, *Whoop-Up Country*, 62.

40. Hugh Dempsey, "Cypress Hills Massacre," *Montana, the Magazine of Western History* (Autumn 1953), 1.

41. Dempsey, "Cypress Hills Massacre," 2. Hugh Dempsey believes that Graham was correct but probably did not witness the massacre. (Dempsey to author, 20 October 1989. )

42. Paul Sharp, *Whoop-Up Country* (Norman: University of Oklahoma, 1955), 73, 75, for this and the following quote.

43. John McDougall, *On Western Trails in the Early Seventies* (Toronto: William Briggs, 1911), 189, 191.

44. Sharp, *Whoop-Up Country*, 85.

45. Sharp, *Whoop-Up Country*, 106.

46. Healy to Maginnis, 16 February 1875, Power Collection, MHS.

47. Sharp, *Whoop-Up Country*, 221.

48. Healy to Maginnis, 4 August 1876.

49. Healy to Maginnis, 4 February 1878.

50. *Fort Benton Record*, 25 September 1875; 1 January, 23 June 1876; 3 August 1877; 15 February 1878, for this and following quotes.

51. *Helena Independent*, 27 February 1878.

52. This quotation reflects views expressed in the *Fort Benton Record* but was actually published later. See Healy, "Men of the Mountains and Plains," *Great Falls Tribune*, 25 November 1900, reprinted in Silliman, *We Seized Our Rifles*, 112-13, 114-15.

53. *Fort Benton Record*, 15 May 1875.

54. Sharp, *Whoop-Up Country*, 94.

55. Healy to Maginnis, 4 August 1876, Power Collection, MHS.

56. K. Ross Toole, *Montana: An Uncommon Land* (Norman: University of Oklahoma Press, 1959), 103, for this and the following quote.

57. *Fort Benton Record*, 5, 26 October 1877.

58. Mark H. Brown, *The Flight of the Nez Perce* (New York: G. P. Putnam's Sons, 1967), 401.

59. John F. Finerty, *War-Path and Bivouac* (Norman: University of Oklahoma Press, 1961) 234-35.

60. *Fort Benton Record*, 26 October 1877.

61. John Kinsey Howard, *Montana Margins* (New Haven: Yale University Press, 1946), 48.

62. Grant McEwan, *Sitting Bull: The Years in Canada* (Edmonton: Hurtig Publishers, 1973), 129.

63. McEwan, *Sitting Bull: The Years in Canada*, 133

64. *Fort Benton Record*, 26 October 1877.

65. Finerty, *War-Path and Bivouac*, 284.

66. Stanley Vestal, *Sitting Bull* (Norman: University of Oklahoma Press, 1967) 315.

67. (Sitka) *Alaskana*, 6 April 1895.

68. Sharp, *Whoop-Up Country*, 154-55.

69. *Fort Benton Record*, 10, 23, and 30 November 1877.

70. Healy to Maginnis, 4 February 1878.

71. The village and the county were both spelled Choteau at the time; the town is still spelled this way, but I have used the modern spelling—Chouteau—for the county throughout for consistency.

72. Sharp, *Whoop-Up Country*, 114-15, 116.

73. Adney biography, 103, 105 for this and following quotes.

74. James Willard Schultz, *Many Strange Characters* (Norman: University of Oklahoma, 1982), 50, 51, 52, 53-54.

75. Eastman to Attorney General, 26 June 1882, NA, RG 60, Letters Received.

76. Robert Ege, "Montana's Mob Hanging," *Real West* (September 1971), 19.

77. Sharp, *Whoop-Up Country*, 111, 113, 110-111.

78. Ege, "Montana's Mob Hanging," 20, 22.

79. Sharp, *Whoop-Up Country*, 118, 119.

80. Granville Stuart, *Forty Years on the Frontier* (Glendale: Arthur H. Clark, 1957), 154, 156-57.

81. *Fort Benton Record*, 18 August, 8 September, 3 November 1881.

82. Stuart, *Forty Years*, 161.

83. *Fort Benton Record.* , 17 November 1881.

84. *Fort Benton Record*, 15 December 1881.

85. *Fort Benton Record*, ads from 21 December 1881.

86. *Fort Benton Record,* 31 August 1882. Hugh Dempsey to author, 20 October 1989, regarding the Joe Healy mine promotion in Canada.

87. *Choteau Calumet*, 13 December 1885.

88. Gerald G. Steckler, S. J. , *John Seghers* (Fairfield, Wash. : Ye Galleon, 1986), 213.

89. *Choteau Calumet*, 5, 17, and 27 February; 2 April; 24 May; 9 September 1886.

90. Robert DeArmond, "Gold on the Fortymile," *Alaska Journal* (Spring 1973), 116, 120 for this and following quotes.

91. Hanus to Commander Henry Glass, 1 July 1881, Alaska Boundary Tribunal, *The Case of the United States Before the Tribunal* (Washington, D. C. : GPO, 1903), 380.

92. *The Alaskan*, 14 August 1886.

93. Swineford to Newell, 1 June 1887, Alaska Boundary Tribunal, 388.

94. Newell to Secretary of Navy, 18 May 1887, Alaska Boundary Tribunal, 385, 386.

95. McCracken to Newell, 11 June 1887, Alaska Boundary Tribunal, 393, 394, 395.

96. Adney biography, 117, 117-20.

97. F. R. Sullivan et al. to U. S. marshal, 6 June 1888, NA, RG 60, Letters Received.

98. *U. S. v. George Shotridge*, court record, case 213, RG 21, FRC, Seattle; *U. S. v. Kootoo-wat*, court record, case 224, RG 21, FRC, Seattle.

99. *Choteau Calumet*, 15 February, 16 March 1889.

100. Healy to Porter, 24 March 1891, ASA, RG 505, Letterbook.

101. Petition to Marshal Porter, 28 March 1891, ASA, RG 505, Letters Received.

102. J. Bernard Moore, *Skagway in Days Primeval* (New York: Vantage, 1964), 135, 141, 150.

103. I. B. Hammond, *Reminiscences of Frontier Life* (Portland: Self-published, 1904), 82-3.

104. Healy to Porter, 24 March, 10 August 1891, ASA, RG 505, Letterbook.

105. Healy to Knapp, 9 July 1891, Correspondence of the Governors of Alaska, RG 348, ASA.

106. Healy to Knapp, 23 October 1891, Alaska Boundary Tribunal, 458, 459.

107. A. H. Dougall to Attorney General, 25 July 1892, Alaska Boundary Tribunal, 412.

108. Adney biography, 9, 11, 12.

109. *Rising Sun*, 6 January 1892, from the *Helena Herald*, 28 December 1891.

110. *River Press*, 6 January 1892, quoting the *Helena Independent*.

111. William Barr, "Voyage of the Alice Blanchard," William Barr Collection, UW, 13, 36, 48, 55.

112. Healy to Power, Power Collection, MHS, 7 May 1892.

113. Barr, "Voyage", 63.

114. The river is usually spelled Fortymile while the town is spelled Forty Mile, but I am using the form Fortymile for both throughout this book.

115. The letter, written 24 November 1892, was published in the *Teton Times*, 8 April 1893.

116. Herbert L. Heller, *Sourdough Sagas* (Cleveland: World, 1967), 107, 188.

117. L. D. Kitchener, *Flag over the North* (Seattle: Superior, n. d. ), 153.

118. Terrence Cole, "Gordon Bettles," unpublished article, author's files.

119. *Juneau City Mining Record*, 14 September, 5 October 1893.

120. Marshall Bond, Jr. , *Gold Hunter: The Adventures of Marshall Bond* (Albuquerque: University of New Mexico Press, 1969), 48.

121. Violet Clifton, *Book of Talbot* (New York: Harcourt, Brace & Co. , 1933), 25, 26.

122. Harry DeWindt, *Through the Gold-Fields of Alaska* (London: Harper, 1898), 161.

123. *Yukon Press*, 1 June 1895.

124. William Johns, "Early Yukon," unpublished manuscript, Johns Collection, UW, 150.

125. *Alaska Mining Record*, 17 February 1897.

126. Heller, *Sourdough Sagas*, 90.

127. *Alaska Mining Record*, 7 July 1897.

128. *San Francisco Chronicle*, 15 July 1897.

129. Johns, "Early Yukon," 150, 76.

130. Ernest Ingersoll, *Gold-Fields of the Klondike and the Wonders of Alaska* (New York: Wilson, 1897), 12.

131. *San Francisco Chronicle*, 3 August, 21 August 1897.

132. *New York Journal*, 1 December 1898.

133. *San Francisco Chronicle*, 5 September 1897.

134. Johns, "Early Yukon," 150, 93, 94.

135. Nora Crane to mother, 26 June 1897, Crane-Kepler papers, ASL.

136. Gary C. Stein, "A Desperate and Dangerous Man," *Alaska Journal* (Spring 1985), 40.

137. Crane to mother, 24 July, 25 August, 25 December, 10 August, 24 August 1897.

138. Franklin Walker, *Jack London and the Klondike* (San Marino, Calif. : Huntington Library, 1966), 174-75, 213, 58, 175.

139. Jack London, *Daughter of the Snows* (Philadelphia: J. B. Lippincott Co. , 1902), 55, 56.

140. E. Hazard Wells, *Magnificence and Misery* (New York: Doubleday, 1984), 134-35, 136.

141. Bond, *Gold Hunter*, 48, 50, 42.

142. Paul T. Nolan, "Captain Jack Crawford," *Alaska Review* (September 1964), 43.

143. *Chicago Tribune*, 29 November 1897, for this and the following quote.

144. *Chicago Tribune*, 11 September 1897; *San Francisco Chronicle*, 11 September, 21 October 1897.

145. Weare to secretary, 11 August 1897, microfilm, Interior papers, RG 48, ASA.

146. *San Francisco Chronicle*, 10 September, 11 September 1897.

147. Walter R. Curtin, *Yukon Voyage* (Caldwell, Idaho: Caxton Press, 1938), 295-96.

148. *Alaska Mining Record*, 24 November 1897.

149. *San Francisco Chronicle*, 20 November 1897; *Seattle Times*, 1 December 1897.

150. Senate Report no 1023, *Compilations of Narratives of Exploration in Alaska*, 56 Cong. , 1st sess. , 1900, 542-43 and 540-41.

151. Wells, *Magnificence and Misery*, 86-87.

152. *San Francisco Chronicle*, 29 November 1897.

153. Edwin Tappan Adney, *The Klondike Stampede of 1897-98* (Fairfield, Wash. : Ye Galleon Press, 1968), 188.

154. *Chicago Tribune*, 5 September 1897.

155. *San Francisco Chronicle*, 14 October 1897.

156. Kitchener, *Flag Over the North*, 218, 220.

157. *Klondike News*, 1 April 1898.

158. *Klondike Nugget*, 23 June, 5 July, 13 August, 20 August, 21 August, 7 September, 24 September 1898.

159. *Helena Herald*, 3 November 1898.

160. *Klondike Nugget*, 1 July 1899.

161. Sanderson to Canton, 22 December 1899, Canton Collection, University of Oklahoma.

162. *Klondike Nugget*, 1 March 1900.

163. Healy to Adney, 27 November 1905, SC.

164. Hall Young, *Hall Young of Alaska* (New York: Fleming H. Revell, 1927), 363.

165. Pierre Berton, *Klondike Fever* (New York: Alfred Knopf, 1974), 330.

166. Healy to Brady, 11 February 1901, Governors Papers, ASA.

167. *Valdez News*, 22 June 1901.

168. *Seattle Post-Intelligencer*, 4 January 1903.

169. *Klondike Nugget,* 19 January 1903.

170. *Seattle Post-Intelligencer*, 2 April 1902.

171. *Helena Independent*, 24 March 1903.

172. *Chicago Tribune*, 11 March 1903.

173. Vilhjalmur Sefansson, *Northwest to Fortune* (New York: Ovell, Sloan and Pearce, 1958), 298.

174. *Nome Nugget*, 30 August, 18 October 1901; 19 February, 22 February 1902.

175. Healy to de Lobel, 2 March 1906, 6 September 1905, SC.

176. *Valdez News*, 22 June 1901.

177. Unidentified clipping, c. 1902, Healy Collection, MHS.

178. Harry DeWindt, *From Paris to New York By Land* (New York: F. Warne & Co. , 1904), 209; and DeWindt, "Paris to New York By Car," *The Independent,* 30 October 1902, 2592.

179. Harry DeWindt, *My Note-Book at Home and Abroad* (New York: E. P. Dutton, 1923), 92-93.

180. Terrence Cole, "The Bering Strait Bridge," *Alaska History* (Fall 1990), 6.

181. *Harper's Weekly* (29 March 1902), 404.

182. *New York Tribune*, 23 February 1902.

183. Cole, "Bering Strait Bridge," 10.

184. *New York Tribune*, 23 February 1902.

185. Undated clipping, 1905-06, Railroad file, UAF.

186. Healy to Adney, 26 October, 13 November, 28 December 1905; 24 February 1906. SC.

187. De Lobel to Healy, 10 February 1906, SC.

188. Healy to de Lobel, 2 March 1906, SC.

189. Healy to Adney, 23 March 1906, SC.

190. *Dawson Daily News*, 25 December 1906.

191. Walter R. Hamilton, *Yukon Story* (Vancouver: Mitchell, 1967), 247.

192. Healy to friends, undated letter from White River, MHS.

193. Healy to Adney, 14, 18, 26 October; 5, 19, 24 December 1905; 2 March, 29 January, 6 February 1906, SC.

194. Healy to Adney, 3, 27 November 1905; 29 January 1906, SC.

195. Healy to Adney, 29 January; 6, 10, 14 February; 9, 12 May; 30 April; 4, 6, 23 June; 19, 26 July; 3, 8 August 1906, SC.

196. Healy to Adney, 1 November; 11 October; 25 August; 15, 18 October; 1, 2, 17 November 1905, SC.

197. Unidentified clipping, Healy Collection, MHS.

198. *North Star*, 15, 16 May 1910.

199. *River Press*, 23 September 1908; unidentified Montana newspaper clipping, 23 September 1908, Healy Collection, MHS.

200. "John J. Healy," *Outing* (December 1907), 349.

# Bibliography

## Primary Sources

The most significant primary sources include the Edwin Tappan Adney Papers, which contain the Healy-Adney correspondence and Adney's incomplete draft of a Healy biography from the Stefansson Collection of the Baker Library, Dartmouth College.

National Archive records used include Alaska District Court Records, RG 21, Federal Record Center, Seattle and Department of Justice Records, RG 60, National Archives, Washington, D.C.

Alaska Territorial Papers, 1869-1911, RG 48 and Correspondence of the Governors of Alaska, RG 348, are at the Alaska State Archives, Juneau.

The Montana Historical Society holds several useful collections, including the Healy Family Biographical File; Healy Vertical File; Martin Maginnis Collection; T. C. Power Collection; and the Catherine C. Young Collection. Recently the MHS acquired materials gathered by Virginia Burlingame on Healy.

For Klonkike history I consulted appropriate collections at the Alaska State Library, Juneau; University of Washington Archives and the University of Alaska Fairbanks Archives.

## Newspapers

The files of the *Fort Benton Record* have been particularly valuable as have been clippings from other early Montana newspapers in the Healy Vertical File of the Montana Historical Society; also useful have been early issues of Alaska's newspapers, particularly the *Alaskan* of Sitka; the interior's pioneer paper, the *Yukon Press*; and the *Mining Record* published in Juneau. In addition I have looked at the files of a number of newspapers for the Klondike gold rush era, including the *Seattle Post-Intelligencer*, the *New York Journal*, the *Chicago Tribune*, the *Klondike Nugget* of Dawson, and the *San Francisco Chronicle*.

# Books and Articles

Adams, Alexander B. *Sitting Bull: An Epic of the Plains*. New York: G.P. Putnam's Sons, 1973.

Adney, Edwin Tappan. *Klondike Stampede of 1897-98*. Fairfield, Wash.: Ye Galleon Press, 1968.

Alaska Boundary Tribunal. *The Case of the United States Before the Tribunal*. Washington, D.C.: GPO, 1903.

Apostol, Jane. "Charles W. Watts: An Oregonian in the Klondike," *Oregon Historical Quarterly* (Spring 1986): 5-20.

Archibald, Margaret. *Grubstake to Grocery: Supplying the Klondike*. Ottawa: Parks Canada, 1983.

Bankson, Russell A. *The Klondike Nugget*. Caldwell, Idaho: Caxton Press, 1935.

Beach, Rex. *The Spoilers*. New York: Harper, 1906.

Berton, Pierre. *The Klondike Fever*. New York: Alfred A. Knopf, 1974.

Beal, Merrill D. *"I Will Fight No More Forever": Chief Joseph and the Nez Perces Wars*. Seattle: University of Washington, 1963.

Berry, Gerald. L. *Whoop-Up Trail*. Edmonton: Applied Art Products, Ltd., 1953.

Beidler, J. X.—see Sanders.

Boller, Henry. *Among the Indians*. Chicago: Lakeside Press, 1957.

Bond, Marshall, Jr. *Gold Hunter: The Adventures of Marshall Bond*. Albuquerque: University of New Mexico Press, 1969.

Brooks, Alfred H. *Blazing Alaska's Trails*. College: University of Alaska Press, 1953.

Brown, Mark H. *The Flight of the Nez Perce*. New York: G. P. Putnam's Sons, 1967.

Burlingame, Virginia. "John J. Healy's Alaskan Adventure." *Alaska Journal* (Autumn 1978): 310-19.

Caldwell, Francis E. *Land of Ocean Mists*. Edmonds, Wash.: Alaska Northwest Publishing Co., 1986.

Callaway, Lew L. *Montana's Righteous Hangmen*. Norman: University of Oklahoma, 1982.

Canton, Frank. *Frontier Trails*. Norman: University of Oklahoma Press, 1966.

Cantwell, J. C. *Report of the Operations of the U.S. Revenue Steamer Nunivak on the Yukon River Station, Alaska, 1899-1901*. Washington, D.C.: GPO, 1902.

"Captain Healy: A Modern Pioneer." *Outing* (December 1907): 347-49.

Clifton, Violet. *The Book of Talbot*. New York: Harcourt, Brace and Company, 1933.

Coates, Ken S. and William R. Morrison. *Land of the Midnight Sun: A History of the Yukon*. Edmonton: Hurtig Publishers, 1988.

Cobb, Edward H. *Placer Deposits of Alaska*. U.S. Geological Survey Bulletin no. 1374. Washington, D.C.: GPO, 1973.

Cole, Terrence. "The Bering Strait Bridge," *Alaska History* (Fall 1990): 1-15.

———. *E. T. Barnette*. Edmonds, Wash.: Alaska Northwest Publishing Co., 1977.

Chase, Will. H. *Reminiscences of Captain Billie Moore*. Kansas City, Mo.: Burton Publishing Co., 1947.

Curtin, Walter R. *Yukon Voyage*. Caldwell, Idaho: Caxton Press, 1938.

DeArmond, Robert. "Gold on the Fortymile." *Alaska Journal* (Spring 1973): 114-21.

Dempsey, Hugh. "The Amazing Death of Calf Shirt." *Montana, The Magazine of Western History* (January 1953): 65-73.

———. *Crowfoot: Chief of the Blackfeet*. Norman: University of Oklahoma, 1972.

———. "Cypress Hills Massacre." *Montana, The Magazine of Western History* (Autumn 1953): 1-9.

———. "Donald Graham's Narrative of 1872-73." *Alberta Historical Review* (Winter 1956): 10-19.

———. "Howell Harris and the Whiskey Trade." *Montana, The Magazine of Western History* (Spring 1953): 1-8.

———. "A Letter from Fort Whoop-Up." *Alberta Historical Review* (Autumn 1956): 27-8.

DeWindt, Harry. *From Paris to New York By Land*. New York: F. Warne & Co., 1904.

———. *My Notebooks At Home and Abroad*. New York: E. P. Dutton, 1923.

244

————. *Through the Gold-Fields of Alaska.* London: Harper, 1898.

Dimsdale, Thomas J. *Vigilantes of Montana.* Norman: University of Oklahoma, 1953.

Dunham, Samuel C. "The Alaskan Goldfields and the Opportunities They Offer for Capital and Labor." U.S. Department of Labor Bulletin no. 206, Washington, D.C.: GPO, 1898.

————. "The Yukon and Nome Gold Regions." U.S. Department of Labor Bulletin no. 29. Washington, D.C.: GPO, 1900.

Ege, Robert. "Johnny Healy—Fort Benton's Town Tamer." *Real West* (August 1972): 31-34, 68-69.

————. "Montana's Mob Hanging." *Real West* (September 1971): 19-22.

"Fabulous Florence." *Idaho Yesterdays* (Summer 1962): 22-31.

Finerty, John F. *War-Path and Bivouac.* Norman: University of Oklahoma Press, 1967.

Furniss, Norman F. *Mormon Conflict.* New Haven: Yale University Press, 1960.

Garcia, Andrew. *Tough Trip Through Paradise 1878-79.* Edited by Bennett H. Stein. Sausalito, Calif.: Comstock, 1967.

Greene, Jerome A. *Slim Buttes, 1876.* Norman: University of Oklahoma, 1982.

Hamilton, David M. *The Tools of My Trade: The Annotated Books in Jack London's Library.* Seattle: University of Washington Press, 1986.

Hamilton, Walter R. *Yukon Story.* Vancouver, B.C.: Mitchell, 1967.

Hamilton, William H. *My Sixty Years on the Plains.* Norman: University of Oklahoma, 1960.

Hamlin, C. F. *Old Times on the Yukon.* Los Angeles: Wetzel, 1928.

Hammond, I. B. *Reminiscences of Frontier Life.* Portland: self-published, 1904.

Healy, John J. "Frontier Sketches." *Fort Benton Record,* 1877-78.

Heller, Herbert L. *Sourdough Sagas.* Cleveland: World, 1967.

Hill, Alexander Staveley. *From Home to Home: Autumn Wanderings in the North-West in the Years 1881, 1882, 1883, 1884.* New York: Argonaut, 1966.

Horwood, Harold and Edward Butts. *Pirates & Outlaws of Canada 1610-1932.* Toronto: Doubleday Canada, 1984.

245

Howard, John Kinsey. *Montana Margins*. New Haven: Yale University Press, 1946.

Hunt, William R. *Arctic Passage: The Turbulant History of the Land and the People of the Bering Sea, 1679-1975*. New York: Charles Scribner's Sons, 1975.

————. *Distant Justice: Policing the Alaska Frontier*. Norman: University of Oklahoma Press, 1987.

————. *North of 53: The Wild Days of the Alaskan-Yukon Mining Frontier, 1870-1914*. New York: Macmillan Publishing Co., 1974.

————. *To Stand at the Pole: The Dr. Cook-Admiral Peary Controversy*. New York: Stein and Day, 1982.

Ingersoll, Ernest. *Gold-Fields of the Klondike and the Wonders of Alaska*. New York: Wilson, 1897.

Jackson, Donald. *Custer's Gold*. New Haven: Yale University Press, 1966.

Josephy, Alvin M., Jr. *Nez Perce Indians and the Opening of the Northwest*. New Haven: Yale University Press, 1968.

Kitchener, L. D. *Flag Over the North*. Seattle: Superior Publishing Co., n.d.

Krause, Aurel. *Tlingit Indians*. Seattle: University of Washington Press, 1976.

Lavender, David. *The Rockies*. New York: Harper & Row, 1968.

Lesson, M. A. *History of Montana*. Chicago: Warner, Belles & Co., 1885.

Leland, Alonzo. "The Salmon River Mines." *Idaho Yesterdays* (Fall 1972): 31-32.

London, Jack. *Daughter of the Snows*. Philadelphia: J. B. Lippincott Co., 1902.

Malone, Michael P. and Richard Roeder. *Montana: A History of Two Centuries*. Seattle: University of Washington, 1976.

Manssergh, Nicolas. *The Irish Question, 1840-1921*. Toronto: University of Toronto Press, 1975.

Marberry, M. M. *Splendid Poseur*. New York: Crowell, 1953.

Martensen, Ella L. *Black Sand and Gold*. Portland: Metropolitan, 1967.

Martin, G. C. "The Alaska Mining Industry in 1917." *Mineral Resources of Alaska*. U.S. Geological Survey Bulletin no. 712. Washington, D.C.: GPO, 1918.

Mather, R. E. and F. E. Boswell. *Hanging the Sheriff: A Biography of Henry Plummer.* Salt Lake City: University of Utah Press, 1987.

———. "Henry Plummer in Idaho." *Frontier Times* (Summer 1985): 26-31.

McDougall, John. *On Western Trails in the Early Seventies.* Toronto: William Briggs, 1911.

McEwan, Grant. *Sitting Bull: The Years in Canada.* Edmonton: Hurtig Publishers, 1973.

McHugh, Tom. *Time of the Buffalo.* New York: Alfred A. Knopf, 1972.

McLemore, Clyde, ed. "An Adventure in the Idaho Mines," by John J. Healy. *Frontier and Midland* (Winter 1937-38): 109-116.

Miller, Joaquin. *An Illustrated History of the State of Montana.* Helena, 1894.

Moore, J. Bernard. *Skagway in Days Primeval.* New York: Vantage, 1964.

Morrison, William R. *Showing the Flag: The Mounted Police and Canadian Sovereignty in the North, 1894-1925.* Vancouver: University of British Columbia Press, 1985.

Naske, Claus M. and Herman Slotnick. *Alaska: A History of the 49th State.* Norman: University of Oklahoma, 1987.

Overholser, Joel. *Fort Benton: World's Innermost Port.* Fort Benton, Mont.: self-published, 1987.

Paul, Rodman Wilson. *Mining Frontiers of the Far West 1848-1880.* Albuquerque: University of New Mexico Press, 1974.

*Progressive Men of Montana.* Chicago: Bowen, c. 1901.

Sackett, Russell. *Chilkat Tlingits: A General Overview.* Fairbanks: Cooperative Parks Study Unit, University of Alaska, 1979.

Sanders, Helen F. and William H. Bertsche, Jr. *X. Biedler: Vigilante.* Norman: University of Oklahoma Press, 1965.

Saum, Lewis O. "Astonishing the Natives." *Montana, The Magazine of Western History* (Summer 1988): 2-13.

Schultz, James Willard. *Floating on the Missouri.* Norman: University of Oklahoma, 1979.

———. *Many Strange Characters.* Norman: University of Oklahoma, 1982.

———. *My Life As An Indian.* Boston: Houghton, Mifflin Co., 1907.

Sharp, Paul F. *Whoop-Up Country.* Norman: University of Oklahoma, 1955.

Silliman, Eugene Lee. *We Seized Our Rifles.* Missoula: Mountain Press Publishing Co., 1982.

Snell, John G. "The Frontier Sweeps Northward: American Perceptions of the British American Prairie West at the Point of Canadian Expansion (c. 1870)." *Western Historical Quarterly* (October 1989): 381-400.

Steckler, Gerald G., S.J. *John Seghers: Priest and Bishop in the Pacific Northwest 1839-86.* Fairfield, Wash.: Ye Galleon Press, 1986.

Stefansson, Vilhjalmur. *Northwest to Fortune.* New York: Duell, Sloan and Pearce, 1958.

Stegner, Wallace. *The Gathering of Zion: The Story of the Mormon Trail.* New York: McGraw-Hill Book Co., 1968.

Stein, Gary C. "A Desperate and Dangerous Man." *Alaska Journal* (Spring 1985): 39-45.

Struble, John Linton. "Johnny Healy Strikes It Rich." *Idaho Yesterdays* (Fall 1957): 22-28.

Stuart, Granville. *Forty Years on the Frontier.* Glendale, Calif.: Arthur H. Clark Co., 1957.

Steele, S. B. *Forty Years in Canada.* London: Jenkins Press, 1915.

Toole, K. Ross. *Montana: An Uncommon Land.* Norman: University of Oklahoma, 1959.

U. S. Congress. Senate. *Compilation of Narratives of Explorations in Alaska.* 56th Cong., 1st sess., no. 1023, Washington, D.C.: GPO, 1900.

U.S. Department of the Interior. *Annual Report of the Governors of Alaska 1890-1935.*

Vaughn, Robert. *Then and Now; or, Thirty-Six Years in the Rockies.* Minneapolis: Tribune Printing Co., 1900.

Vestal, Stanley. *Sitting Bull.* Norman: University of Oklahoma, 1967.

Walker, Franklin. *Jack London and the Klondike.* San Marino, Calif.: Huntington Library, 1966.

Webb, Melody. *The Last Frontier.* Albuquerque: University of New Mexico Press, 1985.

Wells, E. Hazard. *Magnificence and Misery: A Firsthand Account of the 1897 Klondike Gold Rush.* New York: Doubleday & Co., 1984.